Wayward

A Novel

Steven Paul Wilson

Double-D Ranch Books

Double-D Ranch Books — Austin, TX

Printed in the United States of America

Cover Photo Provided by Joris Visser on Unsplash

Cover Design by Cari Stanhope

ISBN: 13: 978-0-9859434-4-8

Acknowledgments

I'd like to thank the newest members of our small team: Editor and Graphic designer, Cari Stanhope; IT and Web Administrator, Jim F. Zwiener; and General Assistant, Heather Greeson. I'd also like to thank and acknowledge past contributors Brad Kelly, Maria Kennedy, Peter Hughes and Jini Smith. And, finally, I'd like to thank my family for their encouragement and continued support, making all things possible.

In Memory

In memory of my late father, Paul L. Wilson, the world's greatest dad and late stepfather Terence Grieder, the world's greatest stepfather. Thanks to both for being in my life.

Chapter One

It's funny the things that can trigger old memories. Nothing takes me back faster than the right song. Especially a song from an era of my long-lost youth. An era when it seemed anything was possible when optimism ruled and consequences never weighed. Today, I go back in time often, as music more than ever plays an integral role in my life—something that helps me fill the void of the endless monotonous days and nights.

You see, for those who don't know me, my name is Steven Paul and I'm currently an inmate in the Texas Department of Criminal Justice, a place that can truly be defined as hell, and a place that, unless my new legal team sorts it out, will remain my home.

Lately, I've been listening to a lot of Houston's classic rock station FM 93.7, "The Arrow," and when the weather conditions are just right, the station fades out and for a brief time Austin's very own KLBJ's FM 93.7's "Rock" comes through loud and clear.

Today is such a day. Austin is my hometown and the several songs and commercials that aired have sparked a desire in me to reminisce and to share, at least in part, one particular summer, the summer of '76. A summer that presented many options and dispositive choices for me. A summer when I believed I was six feet tall and bulletproof. Looking back now, it was a summer when I mostly took the wrong fork in the road, the path of least resistance, the road to instant gratification. Most people are guilty of taking these paths some of the time—I just take them more often.

If nothing else, the summer of '76 was a hell of an adventure for me and perhaps my antics, my deeds—some of which may even be construed as noble at the time—may provoke a smile, possibly even a laugh or two.

With nothing but time on my hands these days, sometimes I wonder whether my actions that summer were the beginning of a long, downward spiral, one that lead to my ultimate demise. Who knows? Stick around and decide for yourself. This is how I remember it...

Chapter Two

"So, what do you think?" the breathless Sandra asks.

"You did a fine job doctoring," I say about her removal of the field dressing: gauze and good old U.S. duct tape that patched up the entrance and exit wounds of a lucky shot. I say this even though I know that's not what she's asking.

She sighs deeply. "Not that, silly. I mean me. Did I make you feel better?"

I study her and it's hard not to study her, seeing how her hard body currently straddles me, her perfectly shaped 36Bs staring me in the eye. I'd just turned 17. "What was the question again?"

She laughs as she plucks one of my few chest hairs. "Now I know you're fucking with me."

I smile. "That I was, girl. I cannot lie, you felt wonderful."

And wonderful she did. At my age, all sex is wonderful and although I was heartbroken only a short time ago, I do now feel surprisingly better.

I met Sandra a few days before in a club in Rio de Janeiro, where the crew and I had traveled to find and rescue a damsel in distress. You see, that is what I do, that is who I am. For how long could this have possibly been my career? Well, all of about five days. You must start somewhere and so far, I haven't seen any drawbacks to my new career, supposing one was to overlook the bullet wound. And it does seem to have its rewards. Case in point: the lovely Sandra straddling me.

No, it wasn't Sandra we rescued. My current sexual liaison would be unethical if that were the case, now wouldn't it? I'd also like to believe I'd be above such temptation.

The point is, I was enamored with Sandra from the second I met her. She's a brown-eyed beauty packaged in the firm body of a woman who worked long shifts on her feet in a hopping nightclub. And, at that time, her short-shorts and pushup bra didn't hurt my feelings much either.

"Hey Steven, you still miss her, don't you? I can understand that. She seemed very nice."

"Who?"

"You know who I'm talking about, silly," she says as she plucks another offending chest hair.

Hmm, I better think about my answers from here on out, seeing how by my calculations I'm down to only ten more misunderstandings. "Ah, Candy you mean. Yeah, I kinda miss her. Her letter said she'd be back someday and this is her house, of course."

"Well, we did talk about you, and she more-or-less implied that she wouldn't be too upset if I looked after you for a while." She giggles. "So, here I am. I mean, here I am in bed with you and all."

"Well, I sure don't want to be the one to rock the boat then, do I?" I say with a smile.

"You're not going to think bad of me, are you? I mean, I like you. You're pretty funny at times." She says it without a pluck, but she does color some.

"Nah, I'll just have to live with the fact that I'm easy," I say.

In truth, I really do miss Candy and I was surprised to find her missing when we returned from our rescue mission. I don't fault her any, though. Candy has been through a lot recently. She lost the last of her family with the death of her grandmother and grandfather. Her estranged husband, a wannabe high roller and piss-poor gambler, ran through most of her inheritance, then managed to fuck a couple of mid-level Vegas mobsters out of half a million, plus German bearer bonds, which of course sent them hunting for him, ultimately ending in abduction, torture and the murder of her friend Kelly, her dog sitter and University of Texas freshman. Deep, yeah, I know.

"I can see why you would miss her," Sandra says. "She's nice and she's beautiful on top of that." She twirls a finger through the meager patch of chest hair. "She never really said how you guys met."

"It's a long story, but in a nutshell, the crew and I, excluding Felix, were right outside in Reed Park when we spotted Candy's dog, Bonnie. Of course, we didn't know whose dog it was at the time but the poor thing looked thin and hungry.

"Anyway, when I approached Bonnie, she fled through the partially open side gate and disappeared into the house through the open sliding glass door. It was then I noticed how unkempt the yard was, which is highly unusual for this exclusive part of town, so I took it upon myself to investigate. I found the house ransacked and in disarray. Among the debris in the kitchen, I found a can of Alpo and a dog bowl. I ended up luring her out of the house and feeding her.

"The next day, since I love animals, I went back for her. Two days later, Jim, James, Andy and I were involved in a shootout—"

"Wow, a shootout! That's wild. Here in Tarrytown?"

"Yep, right here in Tarrytown. Anyway, one of the investigating officers, a black detective named Williams, spotted Bonnie's tags, knew who the dog belonged to and informed Candy where she could find her dog. The rest, they say, is history."

"Candy and you sure hooked up fast, didn't you?"

"Yeah, I guess we were the answer to each other's needs at the time. Plus, I used my charm and plied her with lots of beer."

Sandra laughs. "Now, the second part I can definitely see. I like your friends, too. All of you guys are so different." She laughs once more. "You sure are rough on poor Andy at times."

Still lying down, I manage a shrug. "Only building character. Can't knock his entertainment value, now can you?"

"No, I suppose not. Still seems mean at times."

"We love him in our own special way, but push comes to shove, we all have each other's back. Being homophobic among other things makes him an easy target."

"That boy sure can eat, can't he? I have never seen anyone eat so much and stay so thin. In the couple days I've been here, I haven't seen any blacks or Mexicans in the neighborhood, so it makes me wonder how you and Felix became such good friends."

"I met him thanks to Congress, the Supreme Court and desegregation. It affected our high school in my freshman year. I started buying joints from him that year and we soon became friends. We mostly shoot the shit, but sometimes we squeeze in a round or two of golf. Neither of us is worth a shit, but that makes it even more fun."

"I like the area around here," she says. "The mansions on Scenic Drive, the park next door. And this house is in a perfect location. So, if this is Candy's house, where do you live?"

"A few blocks over. All of us live within blocks of each other, except for Felix, that is."

"Candy told me you were only 17. Your parents don't worry about you?"

"I'm sure they do. They hedged their bet with a double- indemnity life insurance policy."

She laughs. "I doubt that. You're kidding, right? I can never tell when you are bullshitting me."

"I'm kidding, of course." I think.

"Does it hurt to get shot?"

"Inquisitive, aren't we? Not at first and it even took a few seconds to start bleeding. What really fucking hurt was when Felix cauterized the wounds. Now that fucking hurt." At the recollection, a shudder runs through me. I hope to never go through that again.

"Okay, that's enough questions for now. How about buying a girl something to eat?"

The price for not cuddling, I suppose. "I might consider it if you wear something short and something uplifting," I say followed by a shit-eating grin.

She smiles. "Like my work clothes, huh? Candy told me you have a thing for short skirts. Will tiny shorts do?"

I pout. "I guess..."

"You know my cheeks hang out. I won't embarrass you?"

"Do I look like I embarrass easily?"

"I guess not. You look like the blond-haired, blue-eyed, All-American type. Maybe with the exception that your hair is a little long and you're a little battered at the moment."

"With my hectic schedule, haircuts are not high on my priorities and I heal fast."

Sandra laughs and traces the clotted gash in my brow. "Then maybe you should take a few days off to heal some."

Now there's a thought. Emotionally, I'm healing right proper and if you overlook the bullet holes, I've managed to fare well physically, too. I mean I have managed to consolidate the past week's three consecutive head injuries to one brow. Now that's got to be worth something, don't you think. Subconsciously, I like to keep at least one good profile for the cameras, you know? Well, I guess, some of you don't know yet.

"What are you grinning about, Steven Paul?"

"Oh, how lucky I am to have been shot only once this week..."

"Annnddd?" she asks poised and ready to pluck.

"And to have you here, of course."

She smiles. "Good answer. Candy warned me you were very good with good answers. Hey, did you kill Dom 'fucking' Pedro?"

"Nah, I blew his foot off and a good chunk out of his shoulder, but Miguel actually killed him by shooting him in the head."

"Wow! You're kidding? Wasn't Miguel the name of his right-hand man?"

"Yeah, he changed teams. In fact, he parachuted out just west of Cancun after I sold him a $40,000 parachute."

"Forty-thousand dollars! I've never even seen that much money in my life. The most I've ever seen is the nine grand that you had stuffed in your boots. Why would he pay so much for a parachute?"

"Well, I kinda had a monopoly on the 'chutes. Hey, are you about ready to go and have some fun?"

"Hell yeah. It doesn't include us getting shot at, does it?"

"Nope, hurry up and get ready."

"You got it. I'll be ready in a flash."

For those that don't know, Dom 'fucking' Pedro was not a nice guy. He was what they called a Cariocas, or a Rio dweller, an arrogant bastard and the person holding the woman against her will that the crew and I ultimately rescued. The only positive thing that can be said about him is he was opposed to Brazil's long-ruling military regime. Too bad, too sad. They're going to have to come up with a new leader.

Miguel, his right-hand man, actually turned out to be okay. At the very last moment, the moment of truth, he had the opportunity to shoot me, but he didn't. He defied the dying Dom Pedro's order to shoot me and turned his gun on Dom instead. What made him turn? I would like to think all my amusing antics over the previous few days swayed him at least some. Then there's the fact that I didn't kill him when I had the chance and, finally, Miguel had three hundred thousand reasons in his satchel to catch a flight out of Brazil in the DC-3 I was piloting. The piloting part I'm throwing out there, not to trick you into believing I'm a pilot because technically, I'm not. Well, I guess better put is, "I'm very technically not," but that's not the point I'm trying to make here. The point is I'm a versatile and resourceful youngster. To break it down even further, I tend to wing most everything. I may even be kind of a fuck-up in ways, but let's keep that our little secret, shall we?

Sandra enters the bedroom and does a spin for me. "Well, how do I look?"

"Hot, hot, hot," is what runs through my mind. What I come up with is: "Like I want to order a pizza."

"What?"

"To show you off. You're sexy as hell and I like the boots you girls picked out." All true statements, but a theory I'm working on is that one becomes all the more attractive to the women out there when accompanied by a beautiful woman.

With that in mind, there's an extremely beautiful woman by the name of Brandy, who works at Conan's, my favorite pizza joint. She also works part-time as a waitress at a titty bar on 51st and Guadalupe to help pay her way through college.

Anyhow, having been spotted with two beautiful women in the past week, she's sort of getting the impression that this is a daily occurrence for me and I should surely hate to disturb that impression. Well, with Sandra at my side, that might very well be the icing on the cake, the very move that will make me irresistible to her. Who knows? Crazier things have happened.

Not that I can't be satisfied with one woman at a time, mind you, but that's another theory to be tested another day. I'm a firm believer in testing only one theory per day. Make sense, doesn't it?

"Earth to Steven Paul: Candy told me when you get that look as you have now, you're probably up to something." She grabs a foot and tugs on it. "Come on, get ready already. I'm getting hungry."

I admire her again for a few seconds. I wasn't kidding when I said she looks hot, for she does, in her short-shorts, low-cut simple blouse, pushup bra and high-heel cowboy boots.

For those that don't know me, I'm right partial to women in high-heel cowboy boots and short skirts. Some would go as far as to call it a fetish. Hell, I'll cop to that and Sandra's short-shorts are close enough for me.

I ease myself from the bed and I'm still rewarded with a stab of pain in my side. During Sandra's cleaning and changing of my bandages, I noticed the entrance and exit wounds looked inflamed. I, fortunately, have acquired some penicillin, so I vote that I live.

The pain in my side, however, reminds me that in the kitchen there is a bag full of hundreds of number ten valiums. We acquired these along with three ounces of uncut cocaine by relieving the mobster pair, Tony C and his muscle Vinnie, of their personal stash of dope. Well, in all fairness, they were caught off guard while trying to abduct one of my family members, so they deserved to forfeit their dope, wouldn't you say?

I know. Things are getting stranger and stranger for those that don't know what transpired the previous nine days. You may even be starting to form a picture. See a pattern here? Well, as we know, life's not all fun and games. There are perils in all professions. But more on that later.

"Sandra, would you rinse the blood from my boots?"

"Sure, give me a few," she says and disappears from the room. I'm right partial to my new, fine, hand-stitched Nocona ostriches and they have already saved my life once, so they now have sentimental value as well. Yep, I'm partial to a lot of things. Okay, I'll fill you in some. It's like this: When I accidentally came into possession of the hundred sequential German bearer bonds, I did what any true American would do in my situation: I cashed a couple, ordered up a limo, gathered up my crew, stopped and picked up Cheryl from where she works at Allens Boots on South Congress and proceeded to the aforementioned titty bar where we shared the love by passing out hundreds of ones, several twenties and a handful of fives.

As fate would have it, I met Cheryl earlier in the day at Allens Boots and literally talked her right out of her jeans. Yep, I bought her a skirt. Cheryl turned out to be a lot of fun. She partied hard and held her own. She's a long-legged, blond cowgirl and right easy on the eyes. I hope to see her again someday, I do.

Where was I going with this? Oh, yeah, as fate also would have it, the mob pair discovered that this new man about town, me, was frivolously spending what they believed to be rightfully theirs and this pissed them off. I further pissed them off when they confronted me in front of the Holiday House, a small mom-and-pop Tarrytown eatery and I challenged their claim to the bonds, busted Tony C in the nose and barely avoided being nabbed by the bruiser Vinnie. You see, I was literally collared by the brute when the Chinese sweatshop stitching on one of my favorite Izod shirts gave way. I got free for a second, only to be snagged by my fleeing right boot. What are the odds? Well, I'm here to tell you the odds must have been pretty good, but my boots saved me when the one came loose in Vinnie's hands and I was out of there like a scalded dog. One couldn't run any faster if one was being chased by the law and that, my friends, is some kind of fast. As previously noted, being right partial to my new boots, I bravely retrieved my boot when Vinnie learned he was no match for my superior speed and he sent the boot whizzing past my head.

Thus, my friends, you can now see why my boots have such sentimental value."

"Honey, I got most of the blood off them. It will have to do for now," Sandra informs me upon returning to the room. "Honey" huh? So now I'm honey. I can only conclude: I must have been good to her. Just kidding. I don't profess to be the world's greatest lover, but I am a work in progress and dammit, I'm not going to give up trying until I get it right. I step into my boots. Ah, never underestimate the comfort of a well-made boot. "I'm ready girl." I say as I glance in the mirror and realize I'm a handsome fucker...

"Come on handsome, let's go then." Sandra says. Huh, caught that, did you? The prosecution rests.

Chapter Three

I grab Bonnie's string from the kitchen junk drawer and grab a partially open 12-pack of Bud.

"Come on Bonnie girl. You can go. Sorry, Smokey and Rosie— you'll have to stay behind." I set the beer down long enough to scratch them both good behind the ears. Just looking over the dogs reminds me how much I love animals and how I believe every family should own a pet and preferably adopt. There's no denying that through thick and thin, animals give unconditional love.

We step out into the early afternoon day. It's a smoker. Not a cloud in the sky and not a leaf can be seen to stir. Opening the car door, I'm greeted by a furnace. I opt to crank her and let the AC cool her down some. I like my latest ride—she's a '69 Pontiac Bonneville with a big block 428, 4bl Quadrajet carb and factory duals. She's a boat but she has muscle. I bought her for two large and I'm very happy with her so far. I imagine in their next life, Tony C and Vinnie are thinking, "Yeah, with our two fucking large, you fucking punk." I smile at the thought but I'm not sorry their ticket got punched. They were headed for hell anyway. We just got them there a little sooner.

I join Sandra standing in the lee of the house.

"Candy told me you had a nice Trans Am, but totaled it last week," she says.

"Yeah, but actually it was a Formula 400 with all the TA trim. She looked like a Trans Am with a double-scooped hood. You'll get to see what's left of her sometime. She's stripped and up on blocks behind Andy's now."

"Speaking of Andy, weren't you supposed to help him explain to his parents how their house got shot up?"

"Yep."

"Well?"

"Well, what?"

"Well, are you going to help him or not?"

"Well the sun is kinda high in the sky right now and you are hungry and all. And then there's the tacit understanding we have, Andy and I."

"Tacit understanding?"

"I tell him something, he wants to believe it and I ultimately let him down. That's our understanding." I smile.

"Okay, I guess." She smiles. "And you're right, I am hungry." We both laugh.

I step to the passenger door, open it and push the seat forward. "Come on Bonnie Girl, let's load up." Bonnie loads right up. I let the seat fall back into place and hold the door for Sandra.

"A true Gentleman, I see," Sandra comments.

"Absolutely, I wouldn't have it any other way."

I close the door and join her on my side. The AC blows cold. There's no question about it, my ride is big and comfortable. "Sandra, before we get something to eat, I need to stop by Austin National Bank and conduct some quick business with my International Correspondent Banker, William."

"Ah, it's like that, is it? International Correspondent Banker. Pretty important, are we?" Sandra teases.

"I would like to think so," I say in mock seriousness. "Actually, I think he's going to enjoy today's surprises." I leave it hanging like that. She's in for a surprise as well.

We cruise through the neighborhood that takes me right past my house. No cars in the drive tempt me to stop but I only point the house out and keep going. At the bottom of the hill, I turn left to head up Hillview. I point out Casis School where I attended the sixth grade after we migrated from South Austin. Like the Jeffersons, we moved on up.

"Look, you can see where the grass is tore up," I say. "That's part of where I converted the schoolyard into my personal motocross track."

"They let you tear up the school ground like that?"

"Only until the law shows up."

She laughs. "Of course."

We take a right on Exposition. Everything west of Exposition is the heart of Tarrytown and mostly old money, the nouveau riche and the aspiring. We fall into the aspiring category, so we get by right proper. I'm not really sure and really don't care what the address is to Austin National Bank because, being the tallest building in Austin, it's impossible not to find. We take a left on Windsor and cross under the soon to be completed Mopac, which will span Austin running north and south.

I punch the stereo's power button to catch mid-song Foghat's "Slow Ride." I can't sing so I bump the volume and sing along with Sandra. Well, at least the parts that I know. "Slow riding woman you're so fine." We laugh as the song comes to an end.

"You see that tall building," I say pointing the bank out. "That's where we're heading."

"Cool," is all she says.

Well, it's "cool" with me too. I smile as I watch her rub the goosebumps on her arm raised by my ride's cold AC, but that's not what actually makes me smile. What makes me smile are her ever-pert nipples struggling to pierce the cloth layers that enshroud them. I shake my head and think such a sight makes me realize there is a God.

"What are you smiling and shaking your head about, Steven?"

"I was thinking if you can maintain that pert look for the viewing masses, our trek into the bank will be all the more entertaining."

She looks down at herself and laughs. "You're a nut, you know that?"

"As William Blake once said: 'If the fool would persist in his folly, he would become wise.'"

She scrunches her face before saying, "I don't know who he is and I'm not sure what you mean?"

I shrug. "Nothing. I just like the way it sounds."

"Candy told me about that too, that you're big on sayings and clichés and such and you throw them out there for no particular reason."

I shrug again. "What can I say, I try." I pull into the bank's parking building and take the machine's tendered parking stub. "Don't let me forget to validate this parking stub."

"Anything else I need to remember?"

"Keep the nipples pert and follow my lead?"

"Roger that, Captain Kirk."

I pull into an open spot on the lower level.

"Bonnie Girl, you have to wait here for us, but since you're in the shade and I'm going to crack the windows, you'll be fine." I crack the windows before killing the engine. I look over at Sandra and grin. "Are you ready girl?"

She grins back before pinching each nipple. "Yep, now I am."

That's my girl. I open my door and exit. She meets me at the back of my ride and waits on me to pop the trunk.

"What's in the trunk?" she asks.

With a show of effort, I lift the black briefcase from within. "This, Sandra my dear, is our deposit."

I slam the trunk and take her hand. Being on the lowest level, I lead her out the way we entered the parking garage, so we can make our grand entrance from the street and right into the normal bustle of the prodigious lobby.

I check Sandra once more for pertness. Passing my rigorous standard, I release her hand long enough to open the door for her. For those that don't know me, I'm big on standards. I happily retake her hand to proudly traverse the seeming eternity needed to reach the elevators necessary to convey us to our desired second-floor destination. Oops, sorry, didn't mean to think in so many words.

Anyway, what I mean is our jaunt to the elevator did not go unnoticed. The cute, but mousy teller that I've previously hit upon does a double-take. I reassure her it is me with a wave and a shit-eating grin. The gawkers we encounter, we part like Moses parting the Red Sea. Isn't life grand?

The opulent elevator quickly delivers us to the second floor. Business on the second floor is more reserved. Or should I say, reserved for the more affluent? Well, however one chooses to see it, I announce our visit at the front desk. I inquire about the availability of William and say that Steven Paul requests his assistance.

If I'm not mistaken, I believe the lovely secretary colors some. Noticing such, I realize the errors of my ways: we should have stopped for chewing gum. Nevertheless, she heralds our arrival. Okay, maybe "heralds" is not the right term to describe our arrival. But, dammit, it should be.

The impeccably power-dressed Williams almost trips in the deep shag when he beholds the sight before him. We match his blush with our endearing smiles.

"Ah, William, there you are. So nice of you to be available on such short notice."

He stammers. "Steven... Steve, nice to see you. How... how may I assist you today?"

"William, I'd like you to meet my baby sister, Sandra. Sandra, this is my esteemed banker I spoke so highly of."

William's eyes nervously dart up and down. He runs a finger around his tight collar.

"Sssandra. Nice... Nice meeting you."

"Yeah, you too."

"Isn't she just the cat's meow, William? I really have to keep an eye on the little rascal, you know, seeing how she's my baby sister and all." I drop her hand and playfully pinch her cheek.

"I ...I suppose. If... If you two would so kindly follow me."

"Why certainly," I say in my best Curly imitation. Sandra giggles and elbows me in the side.

We follow William to his office where he ushers us in and we're shown to seats noticeably lower than the plush leather chair behind his desk. All the better for cleavage-viewing pleasure, but if intended as a psychological advantage, it ain't working.

"Steven... Steve, how, how again may I assist you today?"

"Well, William, it's like this, I've come to make some deposits, up the ante, so to speak, in our ever-budding banker/client relationship." I smile, cross my legs and steeple my fingers.

"Well, I suppose that should be easy enough," he says with a weak smile.

I don't know about Sandra, but I'm enjoying myself. Upon first meeting William, we soon established the pecking order. My secret, oh, of all of about one-and-half weeks, is to maintain assertiveness when it comes to banking and bankers. I set the briefcase on William's desk, spin the combination numbers to all zeros, push the latch release button and open the case with a flourish. There's a collective gasp as the case's contents are revealed. To both Sandra and William's astonishment, stacked neatly within rests $104,000.

William is momentarily taken aback. Upon first meeting him, I presented German bearer bonds to cash and now this. He's no doubt now wondering exactly what I'm involved in.

"Umm, Steve, this amount of cash is highly unusual," he manages to finally say.

"Isn't it? Doesn't it make your heart sing, William?"

"Steven Paul, this is highly irregular."

"Different way of saying the same thing, William." I re-cross my legs and re-steeple my fingers. "I think we've established that. Can we move forward with this transaction? My baby sister and I have a late luncheon to attend."

"I... I suppose. Let me summon my secretary with the proper declaration forms to fill in and sign."

I raise a hand. "Not necessary, William my friend." I reach in the briefcase, retrieve four individually wrapped $1,000 stacks and then remove another stack from a bundle of ten. "You see William, your time here will be better spent by counting and making my desired eleven, nine thousand-dollar deposits."

"But…"

I throw my hand up to cut him off again. "Ah, ah, no buts, William."

"But, Steven, to do so would be unethical."

"I think 'illegal' is a better term. Previously dealing with a minor, me—now that could be viewed as 'unethical.' And I'm not a lawyer, mind you, but perhaps 'illegal' as well."

It takes the now flustered William a moment. "But, Steven, you told me you were emancipated."

"Not 'told,' William, 'lied.' I lied to you."

William takes out his pocket-handkerchief and wipes his brow. "But what about the long-term substantial relationship with your S&L you spoke of?"

"William, William." I wave a finger before him. "Tsk, tsk. It's generated roughly 60 cents since its inception four years ago. Granted, the initial deposit did seem substantial at the time."

He audibly releases his breath and wipes his brow once more. "Anything else I can assist you with today?"

"Now that's the spirit Williams and since you're so kind to ask, we're in a wee bit of a rush, so if you don't mind please hold my briefcase here and I shall retrieve it at a later date."

"As you wish, but I…"

"Not a problem William. I trust your count. Now, if you would be so kind as to validate our parking stub, we shall be on our way. No need to show us out, and you a good day, William."

I wink at the front secretary en route to the elevator. Safely ensconced in the elevator, we both break out in laughter. It takes Sandra a second to push the ground-floor button.

Catching her breath, she finally manages. "You are fucking crazy. Your baby sister—I almost lost it! Did you see how he was stealing glances at my tits?" She laughs again. "That was fucking fun."

"Yep, wasn't that the shit? Ain't life grand?"

"Yeah, but all that cash. Wow! Now that was cool. Was that the pay for rescuing Melissa, the oil tycoon's daughter?"

"Only 25 of it is mine, but no, it was money I tricked Dom out of. He actually believed we were going to deliver a shipment of small arms to him. That was the deposit." I take her hand again as we exit the elevator.

"So, you guys have more coming?"

"We don't know how much." I wave again at my favorite teller. "But knowing Wallace, it's going to be substantial."

We step out into the heat of the day. All the birds but the pigeons seem subdued. That shan't damper my mood. We rejoin Bonnie at the Bonneville. She's in the driver's seat, ready and waiting to roll. She hops over the seat to the rear as we open our doors. The interior remained relatively cool in the shade of the garage.

"And now we get to eat?" Sandra asks as she pulls her door shut.

I smile. "Yep, eat, drink and be merry. I'm taking you to Hansel & Gretel's, a German place right off the drag. The owner is a friend of mine." I neglect to tell her less than two weeks prior I was employed as a lowly busboy there. Looking back, I can't imagine how I endured the indignity of working at such a job. I shudder at the thought. I crank my ride and turn all available vents on Sandra. Hey, I like the look.

She catches me grinning. "You are a shit, aren't you?" She says as she turns to face me with her own grin. "What's the drag?" she asks.

"It's the section of Guadalupe that fronts the University of Texas on Guadalupe. The street, not the river, that is."

"Oh, cool. Hey, you know you made me blush earlier in the bedroom, but I was serious when I said that I like you."

I put my ride into reverse and back out of our space. "And I think you're special too."

She playfully backhands me on the shoulder. "You better."

I put the big Bonneville in drive. We have to circle up before being able to circle back down to the exit. With Sandra's nipples still pert, the booth attendant gets an eyeful before taking my offered validated stub and opening the crossbar blocking our exit.

I check the temperature of our open 12-pack before pulling out into the heavy downtown traffic. Cold enough for comfort. I remove one, pull the tab and offer it to Sandra. I remove and pull the tab on one for myself as well. A meaningful sip assures me all is well. We are now officially en route to H & G's. The drive is a short one. H & G resembles something transplanted straight out of the Alpines—white with dark trim and steepled roofs.

We park on a side street in the shade of a giant pecan. After exiting, for show, I tether Bonnie with her walking string. She recognizes H & G from her one and only visit and leads the way. Bonnie is one smart dog.

Chapter Four

We enter through the back door and into the bustling kitchen. A number of new faces are present. It makes me wonder exactly how many they had to hire to replace me... Not. A few stop their hustling long enough to pet and coo over Bonnie and then rush off to wash their hands and get back to work. Right. The Peruvian wife of the owner who routinely dotes over me is not to be found, so I lead the girls into the dining area where we're greeted by my favorite waitress, Elizabeth—Liz to friends.

"Steven, there you are. I wondered what happened to you. You haven't been around in a few days and we haven't spotted you on the news lately." She smiles. "So naturally, we've been concerned."

I return the smile. "And rightly so. I've been trying to fly under the radar lately, you know."

"Yeah, right. I seriously doubt that." She bends to pet Bonnie, exposing her cleavage. Liz is a big, strong German girl who—I don't know how she manages it—has yet to succumb to my charm. Hmm, she must have some kind of will power.

"Who's your newest friend?" Liz asks rising back up.

"Sandra. Sandra this is Liz." I wink at Sandra. "Liz is rather sweet on me." I confide in her.

"Like most women, Sandra, have him tell it." She laughs. "You better watch this silver-tongued devil."

She only doles out such advice because she wants to keep me all to herself."

"I figured as much," Sandra says and laughs.

I pull out a chair at the employee's table for Sandra to sit. I take the seat next to her. The table is set before H & G's lone TV. For the moment, Sandra and I have the table to ourselves.

Liz pulls her tablet from her apron. "The usual, Steven?"

"You got it, girl. Hold the lettuce on Bonnie's."

Liz knows the routine. She jots down my favorite: roast beef, swiss and lettuce on a sourdough bread with ranch dressing, to be washed down, by the initial pitcher of Miller Draft. Liz rushes off to get the beer and iced mugs. Sandra looks around taking in the mostly UT crowd. "This seems like a nice place. How did you ever come across this place?"

"Hey, I hope you like Miller Draft," I say as Liz places the mugs before us and expertly fills them to near headless perfection.

I lift my mug. "A toast: to cold beer and good livin'."

Sandra bumps mugs with mine. "Amen."

Yep, Sandra may be somewhat crass, but she's a sport. I watch her take a pull from her beer, wipe her mouth with the back of her hand.

"So, Steven Paul, how long have you been quote"—she does the two-finger quote (or Nixon wave?)— "rescuing damsels in distress?"

"Oh, about four-and-a-half days now. I've found it to be," I smile, "rewarding."

"Candy told me an Austin detective set up the deal."

"Not officially. Hey, good. Here are our sandwiches. Thanks, Liz."

"Why? Why would he do something like that?"

I shrug. "He thought Wallace, Melissa's father, was running out of options. Plus, I believe he's a fan of my crew and our recalcitrant, but successful, ways."

"Recalci... What?"

"Unorthodox," I say before taking a big bite of my sandwich.

"Oh, okay... Success in what?"

I take a pull from my beer and top off both of our mugs. "Let's just say that we made most of Candy's worries disappear."

"But not her fuckhead estranged husband. He still calls the house at all hours. You guys going to make him disappear, too?" she asks in all seriousness.

"When Candy returns and if he still persists in fucking with her, we may have to give him, like Hank Jr. sings, 'an attitude adjustment.'"

"Have you always been so wild?"

"Liz, another pitcher, please. Anyway, beer is the answer, what was the question again?"

She smiles. "I said, I mean I asked, have you always been so wild? Hey, these are some good sandwiches."

"Not really. Other than terrorizing the neighborhood on my motocross bike, smoking a little reefer and drinking a few beers, I'm mostly harmless." I tear off a chunk of Bonnie's sandwich for her.

"And the girls in your school think you're harmless?"

"Only the ones who don't know me. Anyway, what about you? Here you go, Bonnie. Yeah, you're a good dog."

Sandra frowns. "Oh, I don't know. I don't much like talking about myself. I had a shitty childhood, being in foster care from the time I can remember. Some of them abusive. I ran away several times only to be found and returned. I've been on my own the past couple years..."

"And no boyfriend."

She turns her chair to face me more. "Yep, you."

I emote, letting out a big breath. "Well, at least that's settled." We both laugh. I told you I was easy.

We while away a few more hours. In the lull of the afternoon business, Liz joins us to knock back a few mugs of her own. Liz gets Sandra laughing when she recaps for her my television debut and ascent to the top-of-the-hour news' spot.

Actually, the newscast was funny, at least to me. You see, after our Tarrytown shootout, I waited for the news to go live before I gave my statement to my favorite Channel 7 reporter on the scene, Stacey Keys. In doing so, I may have accidentally mentioned (falsely) that Andy, during the shootout, was cowering under his bed. Plus, I managed to plug the NRA, squeeze in a couple of curse words and regale 7's viewers with my heroic actions in defense of la casa. Yet another example of "I do what I can."

In reality, however, it was some scary shit. Vinnie—I suspect it was Vinnie—unloaded a couple of 30-round clips into Andy's house. In my defense, though, I did manage to unload a seven-round clip from my Colt 1911 and in the process, I nicked one of the pair enough to leave traces of blood behind.

Liz knocks back the last of her beer and rises. "I need to wait on those two new customers that just came in. Steven, tell Sandra about your other recent news-making stunt?" She smiles. "Maybe it will help you get a better picture of what you're dealing with here, Sandra."

I refill both of our mugs. We're starting to feel no pain. "What Liz means is 'whom' you're dealing with and she means it in a nice way."

"I'm sure. So, what did you do this time?"

"You make it sound like a bad thing."

"It wasn't?"

"Maybe to the FAA, some Tarrytown and West Lake residents and perhaps the local police, but for me, it was only another day in the big city."

"Okay, what did you do?"

"We took Candy's plane on a maiden flight."

"And what's wrong with that?"

"We forgot to take a pilot."

She laughs. "Okay, I can see where that could be a problem."

"Then we buzzed Andy's house a couple of times, skimmed Town Lake and then buzzed my friend Alan's house in West Lake."

"Too cool."

I raise my hand. "Hold that thought, the news is coming on. Let me turn up the volume." I do so, change the channel to 7 and retake my seat.

Liz spots my actions and hurries over to stand by our table. "Steven, why do I feel like you may be expecting something on the news?"

I take a stab at it. "You're suspicious by nature?"

"Nooo. Well, maybe if I suspect you're involved."

"Now, Liz, what you just said defies logic. Hey, okay, everybody, it's coming on."

"Good evening, I'm Ted Collins. Thank you for choosing Channel 7 news at five. For news at the top of the hour we go live to our affiliate correspondent, Joanne Douglass. Joanne?"

"Thank you, Ted. Hi, I'm Joanne Douglass joining you live on the scene. I'm now standing at the entrance of Texas oil Tycoon John Wallace's ranch just north of San Antonio. Earlier today, law officials including the FBI descended upon this remote property when a DC-3 registered to Mr. Wallace illegally entered U.S. airspace and failed to heed orders from pilot Captain T.F. Riley to alter course and land at Houston's Hobby Airport.

"The information released from state and federal officials is sketchy at this time. What we have learned is the aircraft in question was intercepted while flying at a low altitude often consistent with attempts to avoid detection, a practice commonly employed by smugglers.

"The Captain reported the aircraft only acknowledged his order in a single radio transmission. The DC-3's only transmission was, quote: 'Sorry Charlie, only the best tasting tuna gets to be Star Kist.'"

Joanne pauses for effect. Sandra and I fill the void with laughter.

"I knew it! I knew..."

I raise my hand. "Hold on, Liz."

"Captain Riley went on to report that upon landing, a number of people were spotted exiting the plane and then fleeing in a brown station wagon. The Captain reports he lost visual somewhere in south San Antonio.

"Additional information we have received at this time indicates there were search warrants issued for Mr. Wallace's plane and the Wallace compound. It has, however, not been disclosed if any evidence was seized in conjunction with the execution of the warrants.

"We do know at this time that no arrests have been made, though the investigation is still underway. Live, south of San Antonio, this is Joanne Douglas. Back to you, Ted."

"Thank you, Joanne. Join us again at nine for an update on this case as it continues to unfold. In other news today..."

Liz thrust her hand to her hips. "Okay, one of you two better give me the down-and-dirty on this story! Steven, I know you know something. The 'sorry Charlie' bit is enough to convince me of that."

Liz's seriousness sparks a new round of laughter in Sandra and me.

"Liz, Liz," I say, "can't we two enjoy a simple pitcher of beer without your intense scrutiny and insinuations?"

"Like you've ever been falsely accused," Liz counters. "And that's you guy's fourth pitcher of beer, so give it up, pronto."

"And I suppose I'm supposed to feel guilty about that, too?" I say about the number of pitchers. "Okay, I'll acquiesce to your petulant pertinacity."

Sandra giggles.

"In English," Liz demands.

I take that as a threat straight from the beer tap, therefore I have no choice but to capitulate. "If I were to hazard a guess, I would say Robin Hood and his merry men had to fly to a foreign land and rescue Wallace's daughter, Melissa, from the clutches of some dastardly villains."

Liz's mouth drops. "Uh-oh, Steven, I hope you're kidding."

"Nope," Sandra and I manage in unison, before breaking into a fresh round of beer laughter.

"Oh shit," Liz says.

"And now Elizabeth, since your inquisitive mind has been sated, Sandra and I are going to polish off our last beer and head to la casa. If you would be so kind, call us in a large pizza so we won't have to go out anymore tonight."

Liz shakes her head. "Okay, but I hope you're not in trouble."

"Liz," I say, "what in the world could possibly go wrong?" I'm famous for saying famous last words. They come easy to me after sharing four pitchers of beer.

We finish off our beers, pay our tab and tip Liz my customary tip of $20 dollars. Customary all of about a week and a half. Being now dime-store rich, this also comes easily to me. I help Sandra to her feet. Actually, she didn't need help and seems to hold her beer well enough. I do it for the benefit of the ever-growing crowd, leaving no doubt in the female patrons' minds that I'm single once again. Just kidding. I do it in the name of science and the long-term study I have underway. You know the one, the theory where one in the hand attracts the two in the bush. Of course, that's not how it goes, but it does remind me of what Anthony Burgess said long, long ago: "Reality is what I see, not what you see." It makes you wonder, doesn't it?

Chapter Five

We step out into the early eve. The air is still hot and now balmy as well. A number of heavy clouds threaten to obscure the ever-rising full moon. Bonnie leads the way.

"What in the world made you think to say the 'sorry, Charlie' thing?" Sandra asks as we approach the Bonneville.

I open the passenger door and Bonnie loads up and jumps to the back before I can even say anything. I hold the door for Sandra. "Who said I said it?" I ask as Sandra slides in.

"I just assume you said it."

I wink at her, shut the door and move around to enter my side. "And you assume right," I say. "Why I said it, well, that's better left to the professionals."

"So, what now?" she asks.

"We're going to stop by Conan's long enough to pick up our pizza, then we're heading home and I'm going to eat a Valium and sleep awhile. Trust me, it's a long flight down there and back."

"You didn't sleep at all?"

"Yeah, a few hours here and there. Conan's is right up the road. They have the best pizza in Austin. Maybe we'll roll us a big fat one, smoke it up, get naked and you can feed me pizza."

"Cool."

Cool, huh? A woman truly after my heart. Plus, there's this other little thing going on here: I fall in love easily and always have since the ripe old age of 13.

I find a spot a block away and park. Guadalupe is bustling with college coeds. Lots of tan legs and Farrah 'dos.

"Here we are. Bonnie, you have to stay again."

After exiting our ride, we stroll hand-in-hand the short distance to Conan's. Yep, if you haven't guessed, I'm the romantic and protective type. Proud as a peacock, I open the door to the pizzeria and allow Sandra to proceed me. We don't go unnoticed.

Brandy spots us right off and makes her way over. "Steven Paul, why haven't you called?" That pulls Sandra up short.

"I'm playing hard to get," I say.

"What?"

"I lost your number."

Brandy blows the bangs from her eyes. I instantly think of Candy. "Nobody has ever lost my number. Who's your friend?"

"Isn't she the cat's meow?" I get to say for the second time today. I beam.

"Actually, I could get her a job in a second." She reluctantly offers her hand. "Sorry if I came off wrong, I'm Brandy. It's been a long day for me." She offers a weak smile.

"That's okay," Sandra says while taking and shaking Brandy's hand. "I'm Sandra and it's nice to meet you."

"This is one unusual guy you're hanging around with," Brandy comments. "Definitely has me guessing. I believe your pizza is ready and I'm going to write my number down again." We follow her to the counter, where in fact our pizza is ready. I pay the mere ten bucks and take Brandy's number for the second time. Now I have two copies. Never can have too many copies where Brandy is concerned. I'm definitely in love with the girl.

We step out onto the walk. "I can't believe you don't call that one," Sandra says. "She's beautiful."

She's definitely on my to-do list. I only met her a week and a half ago and my initial thought is still vividly recorded: "I'd give my left nut for this one." For the sake of civility, I shan't share the thought with Sandra. Instead, I opt for: "Perhaps someday I will."

"Well, if I were a man, I know I would."

"But I'm so content at the moment." The operative word being "moment." I'm often content moments at a time.

Sandra stumbles on a crack in the walk. "You're a smooth one, Steven Paul."

I smile. I liked the way her boobs jiggled when she stumbled. I pride myself on my ability to observe. "I try," I tell her.

We find Bonnie once more in the driver's seat and ready to roll. I open the passenger door and let Sandra in. I set the pizza in her lap, before rounding the car and joining her. Bonnie hops the seat to make room for me.

"What now, Steven Paul?"

"One final stop at the 'we'll sell to anyone with a car' Beer Barn, which is only a few blocks over on 29th. Then, as I said before, it's to la casa."

"Cool."

I crank the big Pontiac and rev the engine once just because I can. I love the throaty sound of the big block. The whole car rocks with power as I rev her again. Sandra slides to the center of the seat and leans her head against my shoulder as I put our big ride in gear and back into a gap in traffic. Her hand falls into my lap—I like the feel of her closeness.

I take the first two rights I encounter, which takes us to 29th and almost directly in front of the Beer Barn. I spin the tires some as I shoot across and turn in.

The regular longhaired and goateed attendant comes out to take our order. I roll my window down so he can serve us.

"Groovy man, new chick?" He chuckles. "Hey man, I really like that weed you gave me. Got any more?"

"Nope, not with me. Give us a case of Bud and a case of Tecate."

He chuckles again. "Oh, I get it, only you two tonight. Where're your crazy army buddies?"

"Laying low. Hey, hurry." I wink at him. "I got to get this young'un home and tend to her."

He gives me the thumbs up. "Groovy, man. I gotcha."

He hurries back and passes the beer and bag of ice through the window. I pass him a $20 and we're off once more. Sandra pinches the inside on my leg.

"Got a young 'un you got to attend to, huh?" she says and giggles.

I throw my arm across her shoulders. "Yeah."

I punch the stereo on as I pull out into traffic. Golden Earring's "Radar Love" greets us from the mostly rear speakers. I crank her up so we can sing along: "No more speed I'm almost there, got to take rhythm, got to take care."

I get in the throttle. That's how us motocross riders say it. The thought reminds me how much I miss riding my new Yamaha YZ 250 mono-shock. I whip out and shoot past three cars before having to whip back in. Something about this song brings out the need for speed in me.

"Sandra, dig out a couple of beers for us," I say as I remove my arm.

She slides the pizza out of her way and reaches across the back seat to open one of the twelve packs. She retrieves two, pulls the tab on one and places it in my hand. I take a deep swallow—much better than the Miller draft.

"Radar Love" fades and is replaced by another good sing-along: Foreigner's "Double Vision." Man, I love this whole album. I have this one on 8-track. I've been meaning to replace the Bonneville's stereo with the 8-track from my late Firebird but have been too busy rescuing. Damn the luck.

"There's that smile again, Steven Paul."

I lean over and give her a big smack on the lips before replacing my arm across her shoulder. She leans in even closer. We're acting like a couple of love-struck teenagers. It's not my fault she can't act her age. AC/DC's "TNT" gets us home. Got to love it, man.

As we pull into the drive and exit our ride, Smokey and Rosie can be heard from within the house. Bonnie beats us to the door and joins in on the ruckus. I let the girls in and go back to retrieve the beer. As I approach the door once more the phone within begins to ring.

Sandra sets the pizza on the counter and answers it. "Hello? ... Oops, it's Andy and it's for you." She hands me the phone and giggles.

"Hello," I cheerfully answer.

"Thanks a lot. Somebody wants to talk with you."

"Hello," I cheerfully repeat.

"Steven, my son tells me you might be able to shed some additional light on our house being shot up."

"Oh, Mr. J, nice of you to call—"

"Actually, we've been trying for hours. The house?"

"Isn't that the strangest thing? Out of all the houses they had to choose from, they chose yours."

"They?"

"Figure of speech. But the point is, Mr. J, none of us kids got hurt. What a blessing, huh?"

"Yes, it is a blessing," he stammers. "But—"

"I bet it raised some eyebrows with your insurance adjusters, huh?" I chuckle.

"Steven, we haven't turned it into our insurance—"

"Well, the boys and I decided it's only fair that we pitch in and help Andy pay for the damages, seeings how you left him responsible for the house while y'all were gone and it got damaged under his watch."

"I suppose, but my son has no money and as you know we don't believe in allowances.

"I mean his savings from work. We'll add to it."

"He's never saved a dime in his life."

"Mr. J, you'll be happy to know that Andy took my advice months ago and has been putting back 50 percent of his earnings each week."

"But..."

"No need to thank me, as a friend I thought it the responsible thing to do. I do what I can."

"Steven, we're talking about my son, Andy, right?"

"Yep, doesn't it make your heart sing?"

"I... I... He's been saving?"

"Ain't that the sh... I mean, neat?"

"I suppose. So, if I have this straight, you boys do not know why they chose our house to shoot up?"

"Bingo."

"Steven, it's my understanding that you made the news a second time this past week."

"That would be I. Anyway, Mr. J., that was a result of a total miscommunication between the owner of the plane and me. It was a real trip when I learned she, Candy, the owner, wasn't a licensed pilot. Imagine the shock."

"I suppose. Well, it looks like you really can't shed any additional light on the subject. I hope you boys are not into something you shouldn't be."

"Well, Mr. J., have a lovely evening and say hello to the misses for me."

"Very well, I'm putting my son back on the line."

"Hello," Andy says.

"No problem, I straightened everything out for you."

"Yeah, thanks. And where have you been? You were supposed to help me explain things hours ago. I finally gave up waiting."

"And I really feel bad about that, but things came up. Oh, and I was fixing to call anyway. I picked us up a large pizza."

"You were going to call, just now?"

"Yep, wanted to smooth things over with your folks and tell you about the pizza."

"Somehow, I find that hard to believe."

"That I picked up a pizza?"

"No, you know what I'm talking about—that you were fixing to call and smooth things over with my parents."

"Would I lie to you?"

"Among other things, yes, but I'll be right over."

Sandra giggles as I hang up the phone. "Do you think his dad—I am assuming you were talking to his dad—bought any of that?"

"Much like Andy, he would like to. Hey, Andy will be over soon, might as well prepare." I pull an oven sheet out and set it on the kitchen table.

"What are you doing?"

"Hiding all but the two pieces that you and I intend to eat right now. Let's see what Andy's reaction will be when he discovers an empty pizza box, shall we?"

She laughs. "You're rotten. Okay."

I smile as I slide the whole pizza on to the baking sheet. "Grab a piece." I grab one myself and then stash the oven sheet and pizza in the oven. I turn the knob to warm. I'm not totally rotten. "Grab us a couple of beers woman and then to the living room." I stow the bag of ice in the freezer and place the rest of the beer in the fridge.

In the living room, I set the empty pizza box on the coffee table fronting the couch, turn the TV on and settle on the couch. Sandra sits down beside me, hands me a Tecate and leans in close. "Cool, the Carol Burnett Show. It's been a long time since I've seen this," she says before stifling a yawn and taking a big bite of her pizza. "Hey, this is good." She chases the bite with a pull from her Tecate. I'm liking this woman more and more.

My musing is interrupted when the dogs break from their fierce pizza adoration and scat from the room in a chorus of barks. I finish chewing and swallow my last bite. "Andy has arrived."

"Wow. That was fast. The promise of pizza, huh?"

I laugh. "You're a quick study. Follow my lead."

"Roger that, Captain Kirk."

The front door can be heard slamming and the dogs precede Andy into the living room. He eyes the pizza box hard. "So, what came up that was more important than helping me explain the house to my parents?"

"I had to take some time out to pleasure Sandra." I grin. "Tell him, Sandra."

"He had to take some time out to pleasure me, Andy," she says maintaining her composure.

He shakes his head. "You too caught up in his web of deceit?"

"It would seem so," I answer for her.

Andy flips the box top to the empty pizza. "What the fuck?"

I shrug. "You took too long to get here. Besides, the dogs were hungry."

Exasperated Andy says, "It took me three minutes! Thanks a lot. I should have known better."

"Yep," I say. "Life is a learning experience. So quick to judge Andy, when like usual I'm only looking out for you."

"Yeah, always looking out. Thanks again."

"Andy, Andy—so pessimistic. Sandra and I thought it would be a nice gesture keeping the pizza warm for you since we had no idea as to how long it would take for you to get here."

"Oh."

"At a minimum, Andy, I think you owe Sandra an apology."

Andy reddens.

"Well?" I probe.

"Sorry," he manages before grabbing up the box and disappearing from the room.

Sandra and I laugh. "Man gives monkey gun, monkey shoots man, don't blame monkey," I say and we both laugh some more. "Andy," I yell, "bring us both a beer while you're in there." Sandra yawns once more. "What's on next, honey?"

"Hee-Haw."

"Cool."

"And then the nine o'clock news."

Andy returns eating double-decker pizza slices. He sets the remaining 12-pack before us. Between bites, Andy says, "Heard anything from anybody? I caught the news. I think the shit's going to hit the fan."

I pull the tab on a fresh beer and take a big pull. "Probably, but the beauty of it is that we're still minors." I neglect to inform him, though, that as ridiculous as it may seem, in Texas they can try you as an adult at the ripe old age of seven. I shit you not. Well, I resign myself to the fact, I can't change the laws, only break them. Such is life. That has me thinking, too, as Shirley Conran said last year in Superwoman, "Life is too short to stuff a mushroom." I know, makes you wonder, huh?

"You two look like you've been drinking beer all day," Andy says.

"And rightfully so, seeings how my new sidekick here and I are the brains of the operation," I say.

Andy downs his beer and grabs another. "Whatever," he says before plopping down on the loveseat.

The dogs bark and burn off again. "Looks like we've got company Andy, why don't you see who it is?"

"I hope whoever it is, they're not hungry. Not much pizza left."

The doorbell chimes, confirming the dog's suspicion. Andy gets up to answer the door. I shrug—I don't know who it is.

Detective Williams steps into the living room, followed by Andy. He does a double-take when he realizes the woman beside me isn't Candy.

"Steven Paul, I figured I would catch you here."

"Detective Williams, what brings you to our neck of the woods?"

He pulls a six-pack of Bud from the brown paper bag he's carrying. "I talked to Wallace earlier today. He's been keeping me apprised." He nods in Sandra's direction.

"She's cool," I say, "grab a seat." Andy looks on in puzzlement, even though he's privy to the fact that Detective Williams and I have come to some kind of strange understanding. "Andy, put the beer in the fridge. Detective Williams this is Sandra—Sandra this is Detective Williams."

"Sandra," he says before taking Andy's former spot on the loveseat. "Well, you said if I was ever in the neighborhood to stop by and have a beer, swap some war stories."

"That I did. Anyone willing to contribute to my delinquency is always welcome."

He chuckles. "Well, this visit again is strictly off the record."

"As long as the beer is cold," I say and salute him with my beer.

He pulls the tab on his and salutes me back. "I talked to Wallace moments before the law swooped in on him. Despite that fact, I don't think I've ever heard him so excited and happy." He laughs and salutes me again. "I'll be damned if you boys didn't pull it off. You've made a friend there for life, I assure you."

"Yeah, they're good people," I say. "You look like you're holding back something, Detective."

"Yeah. Wallace is an obstinate old fellow and there's no doubt in my mind he'll hold his mud, but since the Feds are now involved, expect some heat coming down. If needed, he's going to hook you boys up with the best lawyers and I know I don't need to say this, but I'm going to say it anyway: remain silent."

"If it makes you feel any better, that's an area I excel at, pleading the fifth."

"I imagine. Something else, as soon as the smoke clears, I have some other people I'd really be grateful for you to talk to. I don't know if you'll be willing to help, it's more or less a pro bono case, but they're good people and in desperate need of help."

"Similar case?"

"Yes and no. Legally at this point, no laws have been broken, but that doesn't make the parents any less desperate. I'll let them explain it to you if you're willing to hear them out."

"Well, it is what I do—it is who I am." I smile. "Supposing this is another damsel-in-distress case."

Sandra's head falls to my shoulder.

"Long day?" Williams asks.

"Yeah, something like that. It's hard to hang with the big boys sometimes."

"I hear you." He takes a swallow of his beer and pauses for a minute to collect his thoughts. "Candy seems sweet." He nods again in Sandra's direction. "Does she know about this one?"

"Yep, Candy is one of a kind. I wouldn't do anything to hurt her. She's decided to take some leave—time with a big sister she's never had. For now, I'm going to hold down the fort."

"To each their own. This one dresses kinda provocatively, not that I'm complaining."

"Nor I," I say and we share a quiet laugh.

Williams downs his beer and Andy goes to get him another one. "With the mood Wallace is in, he may very well wish to sponsor your next mission." He smiles. "Should you choose to accept it."

"Mission Impossible fan, are we?"

"Guilty." He takes the offered beer from Andy and pulls the tab. "Last year's Charlie's Angels as well. It's not the same without Farrah, though."

"I'm not happy about that either. Lee Majors is an idiot. Spent plenty of quality time with Farrah, I did. I have her iconic, red one-piece bathing suit poster, I do."

He chuckles. "You and millions of others. She's going to make a few guest appearances, I understand," he says and goes to stand. "It's been fun, but I need to get on down the road. I hate to say it, but your eye is looking worse."

"Yeah, I bumped it again. Later, Williams."

"I'll stop by or call. I have Candy's number. Andy."

Andy nods as Williams takes his leave. He waits for the sound of the front door closing. "What was that all about? Cops make me nervous."

"He's all right. Letting us know to expect the Feds. And, as you heard, he has someone he wants me to talk to."

"Well, I don't like the idea of doing anything for free."

"Very noble of you, Andy. Ever heard of doing something for PR or GP?" PR for me, meaning personal reasons in addition to public relations.

"Um, rescuing one person doesn't necessarily mean that's who you are—what you do."

"Maybe, maybe not, Andy. But so far it's put a bunch of beer on the table and food in your stomach." I pat Sandra on a tan leg. "And it does have its perks," I say and smile.

Andy scowls. "For you."

"And for you, too, Andy. You now can afford to buy a blowup in every color."

"Aw, fuck you," he says and downs his beer.

I laugh. Life is good at the moment at least. Hmm, where did that doubt come from? I'm not big on doubts, self-doubts, that is. I'm quick to doubt others. Just kidding. Giving people the benefit of the doubt is so instilled in me it is often viewed as a fault by others.

Andy stops his pacing. "I guess I'll take the last of the pizza, some beer and Smokey and Rosie to the house now that you smoothed things over for me and I'm allowed to return."

"And to show my appreciation, Andy, I plan to retire early with a real woman."

"Whatever. Someday she'll wake up and smell the roses."

"But not today," I say and smile. "Today it's nothing but good lovin'."

"Come on, Smokey and Rosie." Both get up to follow Andy from the room. Bonnie looks on, then at me for confirmation.

"Yeah, Bonnie girl, you get to stay." She gets up, rounds the table and places her head in my lap so I can scratch her behind the ears. "I bet you miss mama," I tell her. "Yeah, I miss her too, girl." I nudge Sandra. "Wake up, sleeping beauty. It's time to go to bed."

She stirs with a big yawn, a stretch and a slow smile. "Sorry, too much beer."

"Just the facts ma'am."

She giggles as I pull her to her feet. "I'm going to have a hangover." She smiles, "But not until tomorrow. Let's stop at the kitchen and grab a few cold ones."

"Your desire is my wish," I say.

"You're a nut, you know that?"

From the fridge, I pull the open 12-pack that now has only four remaining in it. Andy must have taken Williams's remaining Buds. I'm still not sure why Williams has taken a liking to me. I can only assume that as a cop, Williams, like the crew and myself, knew the mob pair was responsible for Kelly's torture and murder and knew that they likely would never be able to do anything about it, so at the time he decided to see how things played out between the pair and us, having rightly concluded we were engaged in an ongoing conflict. Williams came to this simple conclusion after learning my late Firebird was involved in an earlier accident where Vinnie was taken in on a firearms violation. The evidence pointed to the pair as the persons responsible for shooting up Andy's house. From these circumstances, our relationship ensued.

I can't complain. It's better than going to jail, Williams being in the position to influence certain outcomes and a little inside information now and then sure won't hurt my feelings either.

I turn on the TV as I watch Sandra shuck her tiny outfit down to panties and bra and climb into bed. Oh, the joys of being young and irresponsible. I'm talking about me, of course.

"What are you staring at?" she playfully challenges.

"You girl," I say as I toe off my boots, kick them to the corner and shuck my own clothes down to my boxers. Yep, no tightie-whities for me. No catch-me-fuck-me. No, sir. I'm a boxer man all the way.

I plop down beside her and the foot of the bed collapses with a bang, sending Bonnie scampering from the room. Between chuckles, the head of the bed crashes down with a bang and the headboard falls on top of us. I wrestle it free and like a real man, toss it to the side. "Shit, I guess my repair job didn't hold up very well," I say. Not getting into the unnecessary details, I inform Sandra, "I've straightened the rails once before."

"Forgot the duct tape, did ya?" she jokes.

"The proof is in the pudding, girl." I like to say this despite having no clue what it means. "But I've got the next best All-American cure for this situation: I spotted two pairs of jack stands in Candy's garage. Hold that thought, I'll be right back."

Within minutes, I have the situation remedied and I have adjusted our bed to a height fit for royalty. "How does that repair suit you, woman?" I ask.

"I like it—I can almost see the floor from here," she says and laughs.

"And as long as you don't forget where you're at in the middle of the night, or roll out of bed, you'll go unscathed," I say and join her in laughter.

Wayward

56

Chapter Six

Sandra unfastens her bra, works it free and tosses it into the void as I look on and build a pup tent in my boxers by sheer concentration alone.

Life sure is good, I'm thinking, as the ringing of the bedside phone interrupts my musing. I answer it with a joyous "Hello."

"Let me speak to my wife," a gruff voice demands.

"And whom may I inquire is calling?" I gleefully counter.

"Her husband, you moron," he screams.

"Sorry, we're in bed and she steadfastly refuses to speak with a mouth full," I say and pull the phone away from my ear far enough so Sandra can listen in.

"What, asshole? She refuses to speak?"

"Wait a minute, she's nodding... Oh, my bad. She's bobbing and unable to speak," I say and chuckle. Sandra giggles quietly beside me. I imagine him glowing on the other end. Flaming the fire is entertaining, I'm here to tell you. When done at a safe distance, of course.

"I saw you on TV and when I get my hands on you, I'm going to kill you... Better yet, let me give you directions and I'll kill you now."

"Hmm, very tempting. Let me see if I've got this right. You're going to give me directions so you can kill me? Well, after careful consideration, I think not. But being open-minded and all, seeing how you're kind enough to share your wife, if you're still willing to give me the directions, I'll be glad to forward them on to a couple Vegas' greaseballs that sure are looking hard for you."

He stammers. "Who... Who?"

"Now, now, no need to play dumb, of course you know I'm talking about Tony C and his muscle, Vinnie."

"How... How do you know about that?"

"I'd rather talk about your wife and my girlfriend."

"How do you know?" he screams in the phone.

"Well, it seems you ripped them off for a stack of sequential German bearer bonds and they now want them back. Oh, enough to say, well, enough to torture and kill you."

"But... But I don't have them anymore!"

I shake my head even though he can't see me. "Well, unfortunately for you, you know that and I know that, but being the nice guy that I am, I convinced them you still have them."

"You motherfucker! I'm really going to kill you now."

"Not if they find you first. Well, it's been a pleasure talking to you, but in order to come, I really need to go now."

"You BASTARD!"

I hang up on him and reach down and unplug the phone.

"Whoa! Steven Paul, I think he's really, really mad."

"You think?" I say and we both laugh.

"Are these guys, Tony C and Vinnie, really looking for him? And who are they?"

"Well, they would be if they weren't dead. They were a pair of mid-level Vegas mobsters who Candy's husband ripped off for a half-million plus of German bearer bonds."

"Candy told me her house got ransacked. I guess these guys did it, huh?"

"That and tortured and killed her dog sitter, Kelly, a UT freshman and her close friend. It was all her husband's fault."

"Man, that's terrible. She didn't mention that. And you killed them?"

"Now that I'll have to take the Fifth on."

"That's wild," she says. "I'd take the Fifth too."

Actually, I didn't quite kill Tony C. I tried to snap his neck as you see on TV and the movies so often and it simply wouldn't break. Imagine that. They make it look so easy. He ultimately died of a friggin' heart attack of all things. Maybe I scared him to death. Well, it's a theory anyway.

Anyhow, Williams correctly concludes the pair are no longer with us and seems perfectly fine with that. I doubt anyone is losing too much sleep over the pair. Knowing they so willingly killed a defenseless young woman, the world is better off without them. Not that I'm judge, jury and executioner, mind you. In fact, as little as a week and a half before, I never even imagined I'd be shot at, much less shot. Funny how time changes things.

"You're a strange one, Steven Paul," Sandra concludes.

"And beauty is in the eyes of the beholder."

"And silly," she adds.

I silently concur. "Hold the foreplay, the news is coming on."

We watch a recap of our story. Nothing new of significance has been added. I take that as a good sign. We sip our beers and watch on.

"In world news today, for a story out of Rio de Janeiro, Brazil, we go to our affiliate correspondent, Tom Dowl, in Brazil. Tom."

"Hi, I'm Tom Dowl, live in Rio de Janeiro. This evening the country is again in a festive mood, celebrating Festas Juninas, one of the most folkloric festivals in Brazil. As you can see by the crowd, it's a joyous occasion but not everyone in Rio and Brazil is celebrating today. Some are in fact mourning the death of a Rio resident and suspected leftist, Dom Pedro.

"The government earlier today confirmed the death of Dom Pedro. The government reports that he died yesterday evening in a military-style raid on his villa west of Rio. It has further been reported that no one survived the raid. No group has claimed responsibility for the assault as of yet, but many locals are quick to place the blame on the country's military regime. The government meanwhile remains adamant that it was not involved in Dom Pedro's death and claim a thorough investigation is underway.

"This is Tom Dowl reporting live from Rio de Janeiro, Brazil."

"Shit. Made the world news, Steven Paul."

"Yep, may have sparked an international incident."

"That doesn't sound good, put that way," Sandra comments.

"No, it doesn't. But what can I say? Other than come here, you sexy little tramp." I pull her in tight to my good side. She feels nice and warm. We continue to watch the news in domestic bliss if there is such a thing.

"Hey, Steven Paul, you better not fall asleep on me."

"Huh? What?"

"Hey, I can't believe it, you fell asleep on me."

"Oh, to the untrained eye it may appear to be so, but I assure you that was not the case." Am I slipping or what?

She smiles, peels off her panties and they join the bra in another dimension. Her hand snakes its way into my boxers. "Does the little rascal want to come out and play again today?"

Maybe I should hold out until she can come up with a proper adjective. At 17, I think not. "I believe you'll find the one-eyed monster compliant," I say.

"Hmm, I think so too," she says as she pulls my boxers down and off and discards them.

"Yep, having his own head, he performs on command."

Sandra straddles me once again and guides me in. "Ah," she says.

"Like a moth to a flame," I tell her. I like that saying for some reason.

She playfully thumps me in the chest. "Yeah, right."

Mindful of my injuries, she starts moving in a slow rhythm. The only complaint from me is a moan of pleasure. A single bark from Bonnie makes me wonder if we have company again. Not enough, however, for me to give up my advantage of being pinned to the mattress.

I hear, "I'm going to kill you, you motherfucker!" which shatters the bliss.

"Uh-oh! We forgot to lock up!" I yell, as our newest golf-club-wielding guest bursts through the bedroom door. With an adrenaline-fueled thrust, I eject Sandra from her pleasurable perch. Well, at least pleasurable for me. She disappears from sight and lands with a thud as I roll in the opposite direction, glass and wood splinters raining down on me. I narrowly avoid being whacked because the ceiling fan came to my defense. Divine intervention? I would like to think so. Somewhere between fight and flight, I manage to miss my holstered Beretta and take the nightstand's lamp to the ground with me. I won't chalk that one up to divine intervention.

He re-cocks for another swing. "You're dead, motherfucker!"

He's already established that, but I opt not to take the time to point it out to him. Instead, I bravely sling the lamp at him and thanks to the bed's elevation, I manage to duck his latest par-five tee.

The iron's head momentarily buries and hangs in the dry¬ wall. The lopsided ceiling fan and remaining bulbs cast an eerie and pulsating light as I instantly sum things up: I'm dead.

"Go with the plan, Son," I hear my dad's voice tell me. Plan? My only plan was to get laid. "Not that plan, Son." Thanks.

I do the smart thing: use my head. Yep, literally.

I scramble to my feet, charge, plow into him, lift him off his feet and drive him into the edge of the open bedroom door. He grunts as the air is expelled from him but manages to draw his knees up as we tumble to the floor. A knee catches me in the side and the stab of pain causes me to yell out and roll away. We both hustle to our feet and square off.

I remember now, when Candy told me to kick her husband's ass, she forgot to remind me how much bigger he is than me. He's rather big and sports a three- or four-day beard. I come to the conclusion that things haven't been going too well for him. Yep, intuitive, huh? He also looks mighty unhappy with yours truly, too. Who would have guessed?

If he weren't so blinded by rage, he'd notice that the naked woman in the room isn't Candy. I point that out to him with a straight right to the nose. I feel something give and I know it hurt. I know it hurt because I yell out in pain again. "Shit! I broke my fucking hand."

He drives forward, we clinch and he drives me into the dresser, causing the TV on top to crash to the ground and explode in blue sparks. He manages to get both hands around my throat, has me bowed backward over the dresser and is doing a right good job of strangling the life out of me. I can't use my head, already did that, so I thumb him in the eye. It's his turn to yell out in pain and up to me to suck some needed oxygen.

In my peripheral, I see Sandra scramble across the bed. As we stare at each other and gather our breath, I get mad when I realize who he's fucking with—me. He could get into some serious trouble fighting with a minor. His good eye tells me he's not considering that. Any chance to reason with him is out the door. Could it have been something I said? Nah.

He swings and misses. I attempt to kick him in the nuts, but only manage to stub my toes on his shin. Damn the luck.

A deafening boom shakes the room. Drywall dust showers down on us. We both turn to see Sandra with my 9. Lucky for Candy's estranged, he takes the opportunity to escape.

Shrivel-dicked, I grin as I dust my shoulders. "Right when I had him right where I wanted him," I joke.

"Shit. That scared the shit out of me, Steven Paul. I thought he was going to kill you with that golf club," she says in a shaky voice.

"To an untrained eye, it might have appeared so. Now you can let the hammer down nice and easy." Safety first is my motto—my safety when someone else is holding the gun, that is.

A bead of blood runs into my eye. I blink it out. I look down at my bandages. Fresh blood is seeping through.

"You're bleeding again," she says confirming my diagnosis. "We're going to have to fix you up again."

I look down at the floor and see Bonnie's nose poking out from under the bed. "Bonnie girl, we're going to have to come up with a better early warning system. Oh, say, bark twice if my life is in danger."

Bonnie only stares, she's not ready to come out yet. Actually, she did her part by letting out a single bark. I should have interpreted that to mean someone's here who she knows.

"Well, I got to meet Candy's estranged. Seems like a nice enough fellow," I say. "You know my gun looks bigger in your hand."

"Both of them," Sandra adds and we laugh. Laughing only helps with the pain when you're not the one hurting. I look down at myself and realize pain doesn't help your pride much either. Maybe Sandra hasn't noticed?

"Why do men's things do that?" she asks out of mock concern.

Of course. "What, play turtle? It's a defensive move."

She laughs. "Looks like you've been playing in the cold."

"Well, you do have a cure for that."

"Oh yeah, what?" she playfully challenges.

"The dreaded O-ring smile."

"As in speak into the mike?"

"Bingo, big girl." We share a laugh.

I hit the switch killing the ceiling fan's skewed rotation and survey the room's destruction in the spillover light from the hall. "Well,

65

woman, it looks like we're going to have to pull up stakes here and mosey on over to another bedroom."

"Uh-oh," Sandra says, "it looks like we have some more bad news. Look at your hand."

I think she means "my throbbing hand." I take a tentative look: the second knuckle is pushed back and out of place. I would like to say, "it looks worse than it feels," but I don't think I'll buy it. I grit my teeth and push it back into place. A wave of nausea washes over me. "Duct tape, please," I squeak. I wonder how long my ears will ring. Sandra seems to have fared well if her laugh is any indication. I've moved on, so I wonder what she still finds so funny?

Well, we live and learn, right? Or as Harry S. Truman so elegantly put it, "never kick a fresh turd on a hot day." I know, pretty deep.

I survive the re-bandaging ordeal and this time I actually do eat one of the blue valiums. As luck would have it, I didn't receive another head injury, merely lost some of the existing scab. Does it get any better than this?

Bonnie finally decides to join us. We take our fun and games into the living room, which now houses the last remaining operable television. Tomorrow we'll hit the "Big-O," and purchase a new Curtis Mathis for the living room and move the living room's TV into the bedroom. Since I've been entrusted with the house, I see no reason not to upgrade some things. It's called living large and I have the strong belief I was born to live large and perhaps even as a Mormon. If so, I've been kept in the dark about the Mormon possibility. Fundamentally, I could learn to live with multiple wives. That falls right in line with my ingrained belief in sharing—in sharing me, that is. Yep, I'm just the sharing kind of guy.

Sandra waves her hand in front of my face. "Hey, Steven Paul, are you still in there? You want me to fold out and make up the bed?"

"Sure, I think I'm close to being down and out for the day," I tell her, which is true. Even without the Valium, I've pretty much had it for the day. I have just enough strength left to practice some safe sex—sex in which I remain safely and firmly on my back.

I get off the couch and pull the coffee table out of the way. Always eager to do my part. That and watch over Sandra's nude efficiency. To watch her repeatedly bend over, however, almost kills my resolve for the safe sex.

The more I watch the more I think, which has me thinking of something Lord Chesterfield said hundreds of years ago, "The pleasure momentary, the position ridiculous and the expense damnable." I'm not sure exactly what he meant at the time, but it seems to apply here. I can afford the expense. Ah, to be young and impressionable. I go to the kitchen and return evenly balanced. Yep, a beer in each hand.

Sandra straightens and surveys her work with a smile. I pull the tab and hand her a Bud.

"Thanks," she says.

"And thank you," I counter.

"And here's Johnny," the TV announces.

Well that settles it: the safe sex is out. I mean, how am I going to watch Johnny at the same time? Just kidding, the sex can hold for a while. Now I am really fucking kidding and that, my friends, is some degree of kidding.

I assume my subservient position safely centered in the foldout bed and—though I'm not one to kiss and tell—I endure the pleasure and surrender to the Valium and beer. After an appropriate amount of cuddling, of course.

Bonnie's bark wakes me. I reach for a pistol that is not there. It takes a second to orient myself. "You're in the living room, big boy," I tell myself. Sandra is curled up in a fetal position next to me and doesn't stir as Bonnie again announces we have company.

The chime of the doorbell kicks me into gear. I have no intention of getting caught with my pants off two days in a row.

"Hold your horses," I yell out and continue on into the bedroom to don clean jeans and a red pullover Izod. I have about every red shade of Izod ever made. I acquired the same after reading an article about how women are unconsciously attracted to men in red shirts. How true it is, I have not a clue, but I'm not willing to leave anything to chance. I take a second to glance in the bedroom mirror and decide I'm not going to win beauty contests this morning. I make it to the front door as the bell's chime is followed by a knock.

I open the door and there, standing before me as radiant as ever, is Melissa Wallace, the young lady that the boys and I rescued. My first thought is she's recovering beautifully.

"Melissa, what a surprise." A pleasant, pleasant, surprise.

"Steven Paul, Dad said I would likely find you here. I hope I'm not interrupting anything," she says blessing me with a smile.

"Not at all. Come in, come in." I lead her to the kitchen. "I must say, Melissa, you're looking very well."

I pull out a seat for her. She thanks me and sits.

"I wanted to come and thank you again in person. I don't know how I'll ever be able to thank you properly."

I grin, I do. Yep, but that would be unethical. Damn the luck. She giggles.

"Some other way," she says, "Although I do find you interesting. Perhaps if I were a few years younger or you were a few years older."

I get the picture, no need to pour salt in the wound, prolong the no. "How do you know what I was thinking?"

"Your grin, but you seem to do okay in the women department. The two you brought to Dom's were beautiful."

"Thanks, I think so too."

Sandra steps into the kitchen, naked. "Steven—oops, I didn't realize we have company... I think I'll go put something on."

"Yet, a third one, Steven Paul? She's pretty too." She smiles. "I do have a couple of surprises for you and unfortunately some bad news as well," she says and frowns, but then smiles again as she dangles a set of keys with a Pontiac emblem before me.

"And the good news?" I joke.

"Good one," she says as she excitedly gets up. "Follow me." Not hard to do, the view from behind is a nice one too. Melissa was an aspiring model before her trip to Rio and she has the looks to succeed. A tall brunette that now sports a pixie cut. A cut that I'm sure was at Dom's hands, but the cut is still becoming. Melissa could make most anything work.

We step out into the mid-morning sun. "Ta-da," she says as she points to a blue Trans Am in the drive and tosses me the keys. "I hope you like it."

"You're kidding, right?"

Now she grins. "Nope, not at all. It's a '70 model that my dad got me for graduation. I added some headers and a Mallory ignition. So, what do you think?"

"I still think you're beautiful."

"Thanks, but I meant about the car."

"To tell you the truth, it's awesome and I've always wanted one. It's very kind of you, but I can't accept your graduation gift." Not without a fight... Not.

She scowls. "But you have to. Dad and I talked about it and I want you to have it."

I give her a hug and a quick kiss. It takes all my effort to hold back. "Thanks."

I open the Pontiac's door and look in on the all-black interior, with the exception of its unique chrome bezel dash. "Badass" is the only way to describe her, meaning the car as well. She has less than 20,000 miles on the odometer.

"Dad sent you guys something as well. It's under the spare tire. You guys really impressed my parents. You know they'll always be grateful. Me too, of course."

Sandra steps out. "Here you are. Wow. Melissa, right? Is this your Trans Am?"

"Was. It's Steven Paul's now."

"Too cool," Sandra says as she comes to peer over my shoulder. Bonnie loads up and we all laugh.

"She must want to go somewhere," I say.

"Perfect then," Melissa says, "because I need a ride to the Cadillac dealership." She shrugs. "I have to have something to drive, might as well be a Cadillac."

We all share a laugh. Melissa mellows. "Here's the bad news, Steven Paul. The shit hit the fan back at the ranch. The Feds were all over the place. They bagged up evidence from the plane. Dad and his lawyers think the Feds will be finding you very soon. The Feds told them they were subpoenaing my dad's phone records. Did you watch last night's news? The story on Dom Pedro?"

"Yeah," I say, "we saw it. Can't do much about it except do as your dad says, 'weather the storm and remain silent.'"

Melissa frowns. "Sorry to be the bearer of bad news."

I match her frown. "It's not your fault," I say.

"But yes, it is. I was the naïve one to take off to Rio to spend time with someone I didn't know."

"Well, it's water under the bridge now. What's done is done and I'd do it all over again if need be."

"Thanks. I hope I never scare my parents like that again. Yeah, dad did tell me to tell you to 'remain silent.' He already has a couple of Austin lawyers on standby for everybody."

"Fuck 'em if the Feds can't take a joke is what I say. Hey, do you already have a Cadillac picked out?"

"The new Seville."

"You're going to love it," I say. "It comes with a fuel-injected 350 and it's got all the bells and whistles. I like the built-in CB. Melissa, do you mind if we make one stop along the way?"

"No, of course not."

"Well, ladies, I say let's rock 'n' roll."

Sandra sticks out her hand. "By the way, I'm Sandra." They shake. "I'll ride with the dog in back, you can ride with the one up front... I'm kidding, Steven Paul is actually sweet... Sometimes."

Personally, I wouldn't have qualified my sweetness, but I've said this before, "why rock the boat?" Especially in light of the fact I'm down to one in the hand and well, a couple possibilities in the bush.

Chapter Seven

We load up in my new ride and I'm in love with everybody and the Trans Am. I lovingly pat her dash, although I have no doubts about this one cranking. My previous Firebird I sometimes had to give a little encouragement to, talk to her just right and throw in an occasional roll-start now and then.

I depress the clutch and turn the key. She fires off with a rumble and idles down to a decent lope. "Yeah, baby, that's what I'm talking about," I tell myself. I back her into the street and spin the tires some. Yep, I'm like a kid in a candy store. I put her in first and rev the engine once. The car and the hood's shaker rock and for a split second, the vacuum pulls the cowl induction open. "Too cool," as Sandra would say.

I like the way the car feels. The seats are low slung and it feels like being in a large enclosed go-kart. With a little throttle, I ease the clutch out. She effortlessly spins and we're off with the AC blowing cold.

A block up the hill is an S curve. A pair of plain, blue Plymouths come out of the curve toward us. I casually shift the Pontiac into second. The faces within stare at us as we pass. In my mirror, I see brake lights flare.

"Ladies, I believe the Feds have arrived. Time to buckle up."

Melissa looks over at me with concern. "You're not thinking...."

I get in the throttle, as us motocross riders do, remember? Melissa buckles up as the tires break traction and roil. My new ride shoots forward. Out of the second curve, I put her into a hard left, narrowly avoiding the attempts of a third car to block us in.

Melissa grabs her heart. "Oh, shit!"

Sandra bangs on my shoulder from the rear. "Go! Go! Here he comes!" This one does have moxie. I like that.

I catch third in the course of three short blocks and then lay heavy on the brakes as I steer into the slide making a hard right.

"Hell yeah!" Sandra screams in my ear.

The chase is over almost before it even starts. These are my stomping grounds and the Plymouths are no match for this Trans Am's roughly 400 horses, four-speed and 4:10 posse. We make it to Enfield and out of Tarrytown.

"Why did you do that?" Melissa asks. "Why did you run?"

"Too early to be questioned. Besides, I haven't had my first beer of the day yet."

"I bet they're going to be mad," she concludes. "Probably already have an APB out on you."

"Well, in that case, we should make our beer stop first," I say and smile.

Sandra leans in between the buckets. "Wow. That was too cool."

I pat Melissa on the leg. "About that stop. I need to run by Conan's really quick and as luck should have it, the Beer Barn is on the way."

"You're going to buy pizza? You're kidding, right?"

"I don't think he kids much," Sandra says.

I look over at Melissa. "Actually, we're not going to get pizza, I just need you to go in and ask Brandy, you'll know her when you see her. Ask her if she's seen me today."

"What? Why?"

"I'm working on a theory."

"Oh, okay, I guess. Don't forget there's a bunch of money in the trunk."

"I assumed that's what you meant. How much money are we talking about?"

"A hundred thousand."

I whistle. "Pretty good chunk. We'll have to stop by H & G's too then, put it in their office safe."

Sandra works herself even further between the seats. She's nearly up front with us. "We haven't seen that much money since yesterday," she says and laughs. "We dropped it off with Steven Paul's International Correspondent Banker, William."

"H & G's, you talking about the German Restaurant? You're going to leave a hundred thousand there?" Melissa asks.

"Yep, Melissa, the owner's wife dotes on me."

She shakes her head. "Well, that makes sense then."

I take an obscure route to the Beer Barn, through an area that consists of fraternities and sororities. The usual attendant does a double-take when he realizes I'm driving a Trans Am now. He scopes out Melissa as well.

"Man, I want your job," he says as I roll down my window.

I feel my pocket and realize I put on clean jeans and have no money. "Shit, I forgot to bring money."

"No problem, man, I'll front you."

"Well, a case of Bud will do it for us then."

"You've got it like that, do you?" Melissa says.

"Some say it is true, Melissa."

"No one is safe from his charm," Sandra says.

We all laugh as the stringy hair attendant passes the Bud through the window. It helps to be able to speak the local language too. "Groovy, man. Catch you between court dates."

The girls giggle.

"Far out, man. See ya."

I'm sure if the attendant is not naturally baffled by life itself, my unique appearances must leave him guessing. We lay some rubber leaving the lot. Hey, it's beyond my control. I'm a typical American consumer—I consume a lot of rear tires. The few short blocks to Conan's I drive in style, window down and ready to wave at any and all of the steamy coeds we pass.

"I'll let you out and I'll circle around," I tell Melissa as I pull short of Conan's entrance.

"I'll be right back," Melissa says as she bails.

Sandra punches me in the shoulder. "You'll be irresistible to her after this one."

Someday I'll figure out why almost all women are inclined to punch me in the shoulder, but not today. "Which one?"

She laughs. "Probably both of them."

I laugh with her as we circle the block. I pull up short again and we block traffic for a minute waiting on Melissa's return.

The grinning Melissa jumps back in the car. "I'm not sure what you're trying to do, but it's working. She looked exasperated. She said, 'no I haven't seen the gigolo and tell him when you see him, he better call.' Then she said, 'but tell him in a nice way.'"

We all laugh as a horn causes me to spin the tires. Sandra pulls the tab on one of the Buds. I grab it between shifts, take a decent pull, point the tab out and stick it between my legs.

"Want one?" Sandra asks Melissa.

"Sure, why the hell not," she says and takes the offered beer.

We come upon H & G's and I park in the shade of an old pecan. Is it pecan or pecan? I'm never sure. I leave the motor and AC running.

"You going in there without any shoes?" Melissa asks.

"Boots and yeah," I wink at her, "I like living on the edge."

I work the trunk key from the ring and exit my ride. Bonnie bails before I can tell her to stay. She knows where my favorite sandwiches are served. I let her tag along. I open the trunk and dig out a brown lunch bag from beneath the spare. I casually glance in—all hundreds. I wish it were all mine. Easy enough to divide since there were ten of us. So that's $7,500 apiece. It's a pleasant thought, but unfortunately, it's $10,000 apiece by my calculations—still, a nice chunk of change.

We enter by my customary way, through the rear kitchen door. The only difference is Bonnie's not a puppy on a string this time.

"¡Hijo! ¡Dios mio, Esteban! Your eye," the owner's Peruvian wife says as she takes me in arms and plants kisses on my cheek. "Your eye, ¿qué pasó?"

"It's nothing," I assure her. I could spend all morning telling her all the ways I busted my eye in the past week and a half. They flash through my mind: the steering wheel when I played derby with Vinnie in my Firebird, getting knocked out by the world's largest bouncer when Sandra quit her job at the night club in Rio, busting it on the yolk of the DC-3 when I failed to calibrate the altimeter and came in for a hard night landing, and finally, scraping part of the scab off in last night's skirmish. Let's see, three of the four involved a woman somehow, so that should tell me something. I'll be damned if I can figure out what, though.

"Is this your dog, Hijo?" she asks as she reaches down to pet Bonnie.

"Hey, I need you to do me a little favor."

"Sure."

I hand her the bag. "Put this in your safe."

If she's curious, it doesn't show. "Okay. Hijo, everyone do lot talkin'. I hope you no get in trouble." She frowns.

"Nah, not me. I'll see you in a couple of days."

"Liz say you bring more beautiful women." She pinches me on the cheek. "No make husbands mad, ¿sí?"

"I won't. Got to run. Adios."

She hugs me again before we're able to take our leave.

"That's a mighty fine car you got there, big boy," I tell myself as we approach the car. The girls have the stereo going and are singing along to Charlie Daniels and "Long Hair Country Boy." The Trans Am has an 8-track in it. It makes me wish I had some of my recent purchases with me, like Willie's "Red Headed Stranger" album and the "Outlaws" 8-track with Willie, Waylon, Jessie Colter, Chris Christopherson. Then if you want to rock, I have Van Halen's Van Halen album and Peter Frampton Live, to name a few.

I get in and close the door. "All set ladies. To the Cadillac dealership. Country music, huh? If I wasn't wanted by the Feds right now, I'd take you to my boot store, Allens Boots."

"He buys all his women boots," Sandra interjects.

"And short denim skirts," I add. "I have a thing for women in short skirts and cowboy boots," I inform Melissa.

We shoot over to I-35 South and I manage to merge with traffic by passing everyone in sight. Melissa grabs the dash as I wind my new ride up to 120, where she edges close to redline. Man, I love this car. I can't wait to drive it to school each day for my senior year. Since school is only a month and a half away, she only needs to last two weeks longer than the Firebird did. I can manage that. I chew on the inside of my cheek. Maybe.

We make it to our exit in minutes. Melissa looks tense and in the rearview mirror, Sandra looks gleeful. Personally, I'm giddy with joy. Short of arrest, nothing shall spoil my day today.

We pull into the dealership and I drive through the lot until we come upon the row of Sevilles for sale. Bootless, I shall have to view them from the air-conditioned comfort of my new ride. The day is already showing signs of being another smoker and my bare feet shall not touch the heating asphalt.

I stop at a Seville that is the same color, a bluish-grey, that Vinnie was driving the evening we played derby. The derby came to an end when the Caddy was T-boned at an intersection a block from my house. Miraculously, he survived the wreck with minor injuries. Unfortunately, his reprieve was a short one and now he's safely ensconced along with Tony C, in their second vehicle, a big Buick Electra, at the bottom of a Lake Austin cove. It just keeps getting better and better, doesn't it? They'll ultimately be found, for Lake Austin is periodically lowered to kill algae, but that's beyond my control.

I point to the Seville. "If I was to choose, that would be the one."

"It is pretty. Yeah, you know what? You're right, that one will work for me."

"Well, that didn't take long. Perhaps I should go into sales when I grow up," I say and smile. What are the chances? That I'll grow up, that is? I recently spotted a bumper sticker that said, "He who dies with the most toys wins." Tending to agree, there is a strong possibility I may never grow up. At least I'm realistic. Hmm, introspection makes me thirsty. "Sandra, another beer, pronto."

She pulls the tab on another beer and passes it to me. "Here, Daddy," she says.

Well, that's a first. I've been trying forever to get my crew to call me the endearing term of "Daddy" to no avail. Could this be the beginning of a new phase in my life? One can only hope.

Melissa hops out of the car as a salesman approaches. Lucky for the salesman I don't have my boots on, or I'd be out there playing hardball with him, cut into his commission. On second thought, I wouldn't do it. I'm in one of my generous moods. I'm just that kind of guy, generous. Especially when it's someone else's money. Hey, I do what I can. I roll down my window and turn the stereo down so I can overhear what's being said outside.

Melissa points. "I want this one. I'll give you $1500 over invoice... cash. Take it or leave it."

Not bad.

"I... I'll have to talk to my manager, of course."

"You'll still make a few hundred for the easiest sale of the month."

"I promise I'll do the best I can," he says.

"I'll meet you in the showroom then," she says before climbing back into the Trans Am. It's her turn to wink at me. "You can drop me off at the showroom. It's a done deal." She laughs. "My dad knows the manager and has already called."

I take a pull from my beer before depressing the clutch and putting her in first. Man, I love this car. I've thought that before. I let out the clutch and let her lope along at her own speed of ten miles an hour. I stop in front of the showroom. Melissa leans over and gives me a kiss. "Thanks."

"And thank you," I say. Did she linger a little on that kiss? She must be lowering her guard. Yep, that's got to be it. Sandra climbs between the seats to the front.

"I believe she's weakening. She's a hot one too."

That she is.

I accelerate from the lot. "You think it's too soon after rescuing her, you know...."

"She didn't lose a husband, silly," she says and we both laugh.

"I like the way you think, woman," I say.

"Good, then I'll keep you all to myself."

Damn the luck. I clutch her some to catch decent rubber in third. Sandra buckles up. Bonnie sticks her head between the seats and grins. Yep, grins, I shit you not. I scratch her head after hitting fourth. The speed reminds me of the Commander Cody 8-track I have, "Lost in the Ozone Again," and the "Hotrod Lincoln" song where he sings "the lines on the road look like dots." We pass cars like they're sitting still. I swear Bonnie's grinning.

"What now, lover boy?"

"I thought I was 'Daddy' now?"

"Daddddyyy," she stretches it out. "What now, Daddy?"

"Better. I guess it's to the Bat Cave to see what the Feds want."

She takes her time thinking it over. "That sucks."

"Maybe it would be safer if we alerted the media? Less likely to beat me with the cameras rolling."

"Yeah, you think of everything. Candy told me you weren't camera shy. She had me laughing." She smiles. "They'll catch you with your boots off."

"Damn, I wonder if Allens will front me a pair of boots? I could always plug the store for them."

She reaches over and straightens my hair somewhat. "You will still be adorable in your red Izod and blue jeans."

Now it's my turn to pause and think things over. "Maybe I'll even relate better to my fan base out there. I'll be seen as more 'earthy.' Yep, appeal to the common masses, I will."

Sandra laughs. "Where do you come up with this shit?"

"The long periods between medication," I seriously say.

"Oh...." She hits me again in the shoulder. "Really, no... I think you're fuckin' with me... I can never tell."

"Keep 'em barefoot, naked and confused," someone once said. Or did I just make that up? Sometimes my conceptualization even boggles my own mind. Perhaps this year will be my "annus mirabilis." All right, get your head out of the gutter. I know it sounds dirty, but it's only Latin for "year of miracles." Now, where was I? Oh, yeah, I need to stop and make a phone call.

I whip around a car and take the 38 Street exit and loop back around. I'm not taking the shortest route, but who would? I pull into the gas station on my right to use the payphone. I reach for my pocket again. Damn.

Sandra digs in her rear pocket and pulls out a small fold of money. She peels off a five. "Here, honey," she says as she slaps it my hand.

I lean over and kiss her. "You're a real sweetheart," I tell her.

"Don't I know it," she says.

And it's true. I'm really starting to like this girl. That's on top of already loving her, for as we know, at this delicate age, I love all women. It's a big responsibility to represent my generation and I take my loving responsibility passionately. Is there any other way?

I scramble across the hot asphalt and into the coolness of the store. My request for change is countered with an offer that I buy something. I offer to buy a brick, but they don't sell them. I settle on a ribbed condom in their largest size. Hey, I'm an optimist, I could still grow into it or make a pool toy out of it. I request a brown paper bag for my purchase. Not because I'm embarrassed about my purchase, it's because the phone's outside and I need something to stand on. Fortunately, there's still a phonebook attached to a cable by the phone. I quickly look up Channel 7, drop a dime in the slot and dial the number. They're quick to answer.

"Channel 7, how may I direct your call?"

"News desk."

"Hold, please." I endure a moment of elevator music. I'll have to talk to Stacey about that.

"Desk?"

"Stacey Keys, please?"

I love Stacey Keys. She's 30ish and gorgeous. We're starting to build on that. She's close to coming around. She just has a funny way of expressing herself, but I can see through her transparent disapprovals. I'm right keen on seeing through things when the need arises.

"I'm sorry, Stacey is out with the news van. May I ask who is calling and what this is in reference to?"

"This is Steven Paul and I have a scoop for her." I smile even though she, the person on the other end, can't see me.

"Ah, *the* Steven Paul," she laughs, "as in Stacey's nemesis?"

"I prefer the term 'future lover,' but, yes, it is I."

She laughs again. "I'm not sure she's ready to go live with you again, but we are talking Steven Paul and you do represent entertainment value for our viewers. What do you have?"

"The Feds are fixing to pick up the suspected pilot for questioning in the John Wallace story."

"No... Get out of here! You're the pilot?"

"Some say it is true. Anyhow, a source close to the investigation suspects that the DC-3 was used in a daring and heroic raid in Rio to free John's captive daughter, Melissa, who was being held by a Brazilian dissident, the late Dom Pedro."

"Get out of here! Oh, if Stacey gets the scoop on this one you might be right about the future lover."

"One would hope, but I would only hope I remain anonymous at this time, as the source close to the information, that is."

"You got it—where and when?"

"The house next to Reed Park in Tarrytown at straight-up noon."

"You're kidding, not the house involved in the UT student's abduction and murder?"

"The one and the same. I smell a Pulitzer."

"Get out of here! Stacey's going to love you for this one. It's 25 minutes to noon, I have to go."

I hang up and whistle an uplifting tune. The one from The Andy Griffith Show. Hey, it's one of the few I know. The government would like you to believe it's short-term memory loss associated with smoking weed, but I forgot why they want you to believe that. I forget most things that are not germane to my existence.

The paper bag blows away in the wind as I scramble back to the Trans Am.

Sandra hands me another opened beer. "How did it go?"

"Like clockwork, woman. I suspect we'll make the 12:00 news."

"I'm not sure that's a good thing, but what do I know, I'm along for the ride... Hey, you don't think they'll take me in too, do you?"

"Nah, but if they do, just play dumb."

"Okay, but that will be hard to do," she says and we both laugh. We bump cans, Bonnie grins. Life's grand.

Chapter Eight

I hand Sandra the condom and change. She looks it over. "Yeah, right," she says.

I like a girl with a sense of humor. "I thought you might object to the ribs, but I'm still young and adventurous, oh and compulsive, so I bought them anyway."

She smiles. "Did you note the size?"

I shrug. "So, I'll use it as a stage prop. As the Feds wrestle me to the ground, it will sling from my hand, Channel 7's cameras will zoom in, the whole world will know and as they say, the rest is history. Yep, my phone will be ringing off the wall."

"You're stupid," Sandra says before leaning over and giving me a smack on the lips. "So, what are we waiting for?"

"Timing. It's all about timing." I put her in first and pull alongside the clerk's window where I rev the engine gaining his attention. I down my beer and toss the can out of my window and across the hood bouncing it off the store's window. I give him a little wave and lay some rubber leaving the lot.

"You really like your new car, don't you?"

I hang a right on 35th Street and head west.

"Yep." Aside from being pulled over, I determine we should be right on time. Oh yeah, I remember now, I'm not one prone to pulling over, especially if the car is not registered in my name and I feel I have a good chance of getting away. I base my determination on 50 percent car and a 100 percent driving ability. Although some, perhaps my family, would question my driving ability on the sheer number of my cars that are in heaven now. Despite their belief, there's plenty of evidence to support my position. Take Richard Petty, for example. He's crashed more cars than I. The prosecution rests.

I shift her down into second and blow past a number of cars before 35th turns into a four-lane. Why wait to pass and take the fun out of driving?

Sandra turns the stereo on. "Any good rock stations?"

"KLBJ, 93.7. If Lyndon is looking down on us now, he's not happy with the direction that his radio station took."

"Cool," she says as she finds the station. Alice Cooper's "School's Out" pumps through the speakers. At least that's who I think it is. Off the Billion Dollar Baby Album. I'm not much of a Cooper fan. Sandra seems to like it, though, and I can't think of anything witty to say, so I let it ride. I point out Camp Mabry as we pass by. "Camp Mabry, my former playground. I got caught with the general's German shepherd in one of their Jeeps and believe it or not they had the audacity to suspend my playground privileges."

Sandra eyes me. "Really?"

"A true story," I say as we come upon Exposition and I point to a secluded drive on the right that abuts Camp Mabry. "Straight up that drive, you can barely see the house...." I take a left.

"Yeah?"

"That was my friend Alan's house. They moved to Westlake Hills and it's their house that we buzzed in Candy's King Air."

"Cool, but I still can't believe you pulled that stunt." She giggles. "Forgot to bring a pilot. Hey, I can picture it though. If I were a guy, I'd done whatever I could to impress her too."

I slow to take a right off Exposition. "Okay, we're almost back to Candy's. Time to fortify ourselves."

"Fortify?"

"Another beer, woman! Another beer!"

She shakes her fist. "One of these days, Alice. Pow! Right in the kisser." She opens and hands me another beer. Nothing like teamwork when it comes to confronting the Man.

I down my beer in one continuous gulp. "Ah, fortified and ready."

"If you say so."

I take a left leading to the park and Candy's. I spot one of the Plymouths in my rearview pulling out of a private drive. We're officially beyond the point of no return.

"Here we go," I say as we come up to Candy's drive. Couldn't have timed it better. The Channel 7 van pulls up to the curb opposite of the house. Another Plymouth descends from the S curve, followed yet by a third. I turn into the drive. We're abruptly blocked in. I wonder if being blocked in constitutes detention and an arrest subject to the Supreme Court's opinion in Terry v. Ohio? I mean I am no longer free to move about the cabin. I step out of my ride and into the grass as a half a dozen similarly attired blue-suited, mirror sunglass-shaded agents descend down upon me. Across the street, Stacey and her camera and sound man scramble to get into filming position. A Fed is attempting to discourage them, but it appears Stacey is having none of that. Good for her. I wave over a Fed to her. She acknowledges me with a nod and I believe a lustful smile. Okay, maybe I'm imagining that, but then again, it is my imagination and the First Amendment protects my right to imagine. I take up my good profile position. You know the one, the unmarred one.

The most prodigious agent steps forward, effectively blocking my right to be filmed unobstructed. "Steven Paul?"

"Oh, you must be looking for my twin brother. Have a good day, see you later."

"Steven Paul, we know you don't have any brothers."

"Then why are you asking?"

"What? Never mind, we need you to come with us downtown to the Federal Building and answer some questions."

"Hmm. And my other options?

"None."

"Well, that settles it, dammit. I'm going."

"Step back ma'am, please," another agent addresses Stacey.

"I'm Stacey Keys with Channel 7 news. Where are you taking Steven Paul and why? Are you Federal agents? Does this have anything to do with the ongoing investigation of John Wallace?"

That catches the agent's attention. He looks over at her incredulously, no doubt wondering how she came to that conclusion. "No comment, ma'am. Please step back." The sound man extends his mike over the agent's shoulder.

"Any comment, Steven Paul?" Stacey asks.

"Love your hair, Stacey."

She grunts. "Not that. Where are they taking you, Steven Paul and why?"

The agent attempts to hustle me to the car blocking mine.

"Meet me for dinner and I'll give you the exclusive."

She stomps her foot.

I shake loose of the grip on my arm and turn to address Stacey. "Sometimes individuals must step up to the plate when the government refuses."

"Does this have anything to do with Wallace's daughter? Is this tied to the story in Rio De Janeiro?"

"Trust your anonymous sources, Stacey. Later." I look over at the now concerned Sandra. "I'll call you later."

The agent helps me duck into the back of the Plymouth and then goes around to join me on the other side. They sure are considerate, aren't they? The lack of cuffs is encouraging. I attempt small talk. "Lovely day, huh, agent...?"

"Agent Ford."

"You related to Gerald?"

"No."

"You look like Gerald."

"Would you shut up until we get downtown?"

"Jeez, Agent Ford. I'm only trying to make conversation." I wait for him to respond. He remains mute. "I mean, don't get your panties in a wad."

He removes his glasses and glowers at me. If looks could kill.

"Has anyone ever told you that you have beautiful eyes?"

His face turns crimson red. He's fixing to explode. I try to defuse the situation.

"You know it's a felony to hit a minor. Even thinking about it should be."

"Would you shut the fuck up already!" he shouts.

I relent. "Okay, but this is going to hurt our chance of being friends."

"I have no desire to be your friend," he smugly says.

Some people. I guess I rubbed him the wrong way. I don't know what it is about authority. I'm all for authority. Well, as it applies to others, that is. I sometimes have problems with this recurring thought. Perhaps it even clouds my judgment. Nah, unlikely, Gerald's just not a patient guy.

Our Plymouth pulls up to the curb in a no parking stop in front of the Federal Justice Building. Gerald smiles at me.

"We're here. Now you'll be able to do some talking."

A beer fart slips out. Oops. An unavoidable consequence of drinking beer on an empty stomach. It's silent and deadly. No better way than getting all four doors open at the same time.

"Agent Ford, couldn't you have waited until we were out of the car?" I go with Agent Ford, not wanting to confuse the other agents of the source of the misdeed.

"It wasn't me, dammit!"

One of the agents up front snickers. The air outside is stifling hot, but at least it's not methane. They allow me to follow the big agent toward the building. He still seems to be fuming and he curses as he stumbles on a crack in the sidewalk. He's probably so shallow he'll hold his misstep against me too. Or is it I'm the one that's so shallow? One could only hope not.

The cool interior is instant relief to my burning feet. I must be slipping—caught with my pants off last night and now bootless. I'm sure I'd be much more imposing in my Nacona ostriches—all 17 years and 170 pounds of me. I gained five pounds in the past ten days. I chalk it up to good living.

In my defense, I used to work out almost daily. The only things holding me back now are my hectic heroic schedule and the bullet wound in my love handle.

We take the elevator to the fourth floor. The agents parade me through hushed silence. I bet the onlookers weren't expecting someone quite so dashing, so daring looking? Or could it be they were not expecting someone quite so young? I discount the latter as improbable. I would, huh?

Of all the lovely offices we pass, they take me to a barren room with a scarred table with embedded cuff rings, wooden chairs and an overflowing ashtray. They shut me in and leave me to my own devices. I check the doorknob first. Yep, locked as expected. I'm here to tell you that it's hard to amuse yourself in a mostly barren room. The operative word being "mostly."

Didn't someone once say "necessity is the mother of all invention" or something to that effect? I twiddle my thumbs for a couple of minutes. That doesn't quite do it for me. I slide the ashtray a little closer. I've violated one of my own golden rules that I learned in my one day of Cub Scouts: always carry a friggin' lighter. Oh well, no roaches in the ashtray so it wouldn't have done me much good anyhow. I sigh out of boredom. It seems like I've been in here for days. This third estimated minute has been a grueling one. I thump a top butt out of the tray and devise a plan. Not a plan to get out of here, mind you, but a plan to amuse. Pavlov would have been proud, for I whip up an ash paste and continue to salivate over the progress of my undertaking and the necessity for continued progress. Having whipped up an unhealthy batch, I encounter a quagmire—what to do with my lovely paste? Well, it's not Ash Wednesday, so that's out. I scan the room and yep, the doorknob calls to me like a beacon. Who would have thought?

I hurry—don't want to get caught—and liberally apply the paste. Voices in the hall have me scurry back to my seat. I set the ashtray down, slide it to the far edge of the table and revert to my timid, angelical self, right before the door opens.

Agent Ford steps in. "Been keeping yourself amused, wise guy?" he says as he pulls the door shut, then looks down at his hand in confusion. He reddens and puts his fist through the closed door. "You little bastard!" he adds, unsolicited. Okay, there may be some room for interpretation here.

I shrug. "I think my parents would take umbrage to that."

"I'd strangle your little ass if I thought I could get away with it." He puts his fist through the door again.

"Well, you can't, so get over it. Let's get on with this."

Another agent sticks his head in the door. "Is everything all right in here, Ford?"

Ford bounces a chair off the wall. "Yeah," he mumbles. He rights the chair and takes a seat.

"You know violence never accomplishes a thing, Gerrrralllddd," I remind him.

He backhands the ashtray off the table. He clearly has some anger-management issues, wouldn't you say? Surely, I'm not the catalyst—I dare think not. I chuckle at the stupidity of my thoughts.

He leans forward. "We know all about you, Steven Paul, or is it Esteban Pablo? Well? Cat got your tongue?"

I remain mute, granting his earlier wish that I "shut the fuck up." He can't have it both ways.

"Your blood is all over the plane, I suspect. By the way, what type of blood do you have, Steven Paul?"

Okay, I'm not good about remaining silent for long periods of time, so I capitulate. "The presence of a common type of blood proves nothing, Gerrallllddd."

"Ah-hah, now we're getting somewhere. What kind of blood did you say you have?"

"I didn't, I don't know even, but I suspect it's the most common one."

The door opens again and an agent passes in a fingerprint card, a plate of glass, a roller and a tube of ink. Ford smiles. "You know there were all kinds of beer cans in the plane, plenty of prints. Not to mention some of the cans were from Panama and some were from Paraguay and of course the Tecate and the additional domestic cans and bottles," he says and smirks.

I lean forward. "Here's some news for you, Agent Ford. The fifth Amendment says I don't have to give you any prints unless I'm subject to arrest, but I don't want to hurt your feelings so I'm going to put this nicely: go fuck yourself. If you're not part of the solution, Agent Ford, you're part of the problem. The government apparently wouldn't do their job, so I suspect some others had to do it for them."

The door opens for the third time. "This interview is over," a distinguished silver-haired older gent says filling the doorway.

"Unless my client is under arrest, we're out of here, Agent Ford." He says Ford's name like it's going to leave a bad taste in his mouth. "Take this to the bank, Agent Ford. I called ahead and informed your office I was en route. There will be a formal complaint lodged and anything my client might have said in your presence you can stick up your ass."

Well if that ain't telling him.

"Ford frightened me, too, counselor, when he ran his fist through the door." I gulp. "Twice."

I step out of the way as Ford rams the desk into the wall. Two agents step in to restrain him.

I wink at Ford as I step out of the room. I have a terrible feeling I'm not going to get the last laugh.

Out of earshot my new attorney leans in and whispers before snickering, "what in the world did you do to Agent Ford to get him so riled? By the way, I'm Buzz Townsend. John sent me."

I stick out my hand. "Nice to make your acquaintance, Buzz."

The elevator opens and we step in. Buzz waits for it to close. "You boys may be in a heap of trouble," he says.

"It don't sound so good, Buzz, when you say it like that."

"I reckon not, but don't you worry none, we're going to give 'em a run for their money."

"That's the spirit, Buzz, a run for the old money."

Buzz steers me to the right as we exit the elevator. "We're going out the back. Channel 7's news van is out front. I don't suppose you know anything about that?"

"Well, I can't lie to you Buzz, Stacey and I go way back."

He snickers again. "She is a fine-looking woman, that one is."

"Buzz, I suspect she's right sweet on me."

Buzz stops in his tracks and eyes me over. "You're a mite young for her, Son, don't you reckon?"

I mimic him. "I reckon not, Buzz."

He laughs as we make it to the exit. He hands me his card.

"Williams is going to give you a ride home. Call me if you need to... And this might be hard for you but try to use your head when it comes to Stacey Keys."

"I have every intention to, if she ever gives me the chance, Buzz." We share the laugh as we step into the afternoon glare.

I high-step it across the hot pavement to reach Williams's undercover ride. He reaches over to unlock the door and lets me in.

"Detective Williams, can't get enough of me?"

"Good to see you too, Steven Paul. Actually, I still want you to meet and talk with the folks I told you about." He sighs. "Didn't take the Feds long to get on your trail. The rumor around the office is they have plenty of evidence tying you to the plane." He shakes his head as he puts the car in reverse. "Mostly in the form of beer bottles and cans. They also found a forged pilot's license that John had intended on giving you but forgot. The good news is it didn't have your picture on it and it wasn't found in the plane. There's lots of blood, too. By the way, your eye is looking worse. I've been watching the news, too." He pauses long enough to put his car in drive and pull away. "Did we lose anyone on our team?"

"Only one of our Rio recruits. Must have been a Claymore that got him. They had at least one tripwire set."

"Hmm, no one else hurt besides you? Melissa told John you took a round in the side. You okay?"

"Yeah. It was a steel-jacketed .22 round and it went right through me, lucky huh?"

He takes a moment to ponder that. "I guess that's a youthful way of looking at it."

"Well, you can look at it this way too: Dom Pedro got off a lucky shot."

"Or you were unlucky and got shot."

"Yet a third possibility," I say and smile.

We come up on IH-35 and we take the southbound on-ramp. "The parents we're going to meet are Cuban, will that affect your decision?"

"You going to arrest me because I'm white?"

"Nope. Good point. They live on the east side. Good hard-working family. Living over in Tarrytown. I wasn't sure how you would react to the fact they're Cuban."

"I only judge a book by the cover if I plan to sleep with her."

Williams smiles. "That superficial?"

My turn to smile again. "Absolutely."

"You do know that's why they make light switches don't you?"

"Wow, Williams, your first joke. There may be hope for you yet."

He takes the Riverside exit. "Thanks for the vote of confidence."

He takes a right after passing the Back Room, a popular billiards and live music venue. He soon takes a left and then a right into a recently completed low-rent apartment complex. He parks next to a rusty and fading single-cab Ford F-100.

"We're here. Lock up," he jokes. Two in a row. Under my wing, the sky's the limit.

I hop over to the grass and then follow him up the stairs to the second floor where we stop at apartment 203B. Williams's knock is instantly answered, surprisingly, by a plump middle-aged white man with thinning hair. Behind him stands a younger, tall and slim woman with long raven hair and deep, alluring brown eyes.

The contrast between the two is striking. With the wave of a hand, the man motions us in. The apartment is small and modestly appointed, but spotless, almost to the point of obsessiveness. I'm often guilty of maintaining such cleanliness. Yeah, right.

"Steven Paul, I'd like to introduce you to Mister and Misses Eduardo Dos Santos Lopez."

I shake with each in turn. "Nice meeting you," I say.

"Thank you. Please, call me Ed and my wife Marie Anne."

I'm taken back for a second, flashing back to my own home on Maria Anna. I shall have no problem remembering these two's names.

A velvet Jesus watches over us. Comforting. Ed shows us to a threadbare couch partially concealed under a colorful patchwork quilt. On the coffee table sits a tray and tea set.

"There's coffee if you prefer," Marie Anne offers.

The pair seems very formal and polite. Polite enough at least not to mention my bare feet. My age definitely doesn't inspire confidence. Adding to the picture is my busted eye.

"Ed and Marie Anne, time to plead your case. Don't let his age fool you. I've found him to be quite competent and resourceful," Williams says, "even if he isn't much to look at," Williams adds with a smile.

Joke number three—he's on a roll. I might have created a monster.

Ed scoots to the edge of his seat. To still his hands, he wedges them between clenched thighs. He's momentarily at a loss for words.

Marie Anne comes to his aid. She lets out her held breath. "It's about our daughter, our oldest daughter, Monique... We fear for her safety. She's fallen in with a bad sort," she says in decent but broken English.

"Okay, I'm not sure how I can help you. Hanging with the wrong crowd is not a crime. There are probably a bunch of people that think I hang with the wrong crowd." And even more than that, they probably feel that I'm the worst of the bunch. I keep the thought to myself.

Ed takes a stab. "They're corrupting a young impressionable mind, giving her drugs—"

"And my friends and I smoke pot and drink beer."

Ed rises from his seat, goes into the kitchen, retrieves a bag from under the sink and returns. From the bag, he produces a small pipe and passes it to me before retaking his seat. I look it over and smell the bowl. It smells burned but flowery—not like the burned pot odor I was expecting.

"Opium," I conclude.

Williams nods. "It gets worse, show him, Ed."

Ed passes the whole small bag over to me. A disgusted but desperate expression morphs his face. I reach in and remove a simple tablespoon, its bottom blackened by an unclean flame. Also, from the bag, I remove a piece of tubing. My simple nod says it all. I replace it all in the bag and set it on the table.

"I'm still not sure how I can help. I guess the boys and I could threaten them, tell whomever it is to stay away from your daughter. It probably wouldn't change anything and likely only get us arrested and put in jail. Too, people that fuck around, um, excuse my language, but people that mess with heroin probably don't scare easily." I look over at Williams. "Why don't you get your narcotics people to come down on them?"

"I would if it were that simple." He frowns.

Marie Anne gets up and removes a framed family photo from a simple mantle above a humble fireplace and brings it to me.

"This," she points out, "is Monique. She's 18."

She's stunning. Takes after her mother. "Pretty."

"Yes," Marie Anne concurs.

"Williams?" I question, still not understanding why he can't help.

"I would if I could believe that. The problem is, we don't know where she or they are at the present, but they're not in Austin."

"Please, Steven Paul, we need you to find her," Marie Anne says as she kneels in prayer. "Please find her and bring her back."

"Whoa, okay. I can't speak for my friends, but I'm inclined to take a shot at it. We need to start at the beginning." Dammit, I'm a sucker for pretty faces, I admit to myself. Another damsel in distress. Williams has spotted my weakness.

Chapter Nine

Ed decides to take the reins.

"We fled Cuba in 1960, shortly after Castro came into power. With the uncertainty ahead, there was a mass exodus, mostly those well-to-do. My family was part of this group. Castro nationalized all industries and promised to redistribute the wealth—that everyone would share and prosper. That everyone from here on out would be equal. Discrimination was over with. Life was going to be rosy.

"Anyhow, Monique was two at the time. We, like most, fled to the States. The States at the time were very receptive to our plight, U.S. citizens being the biggest losers in Castro's land and property grab. We were immediately granted asylum and the States, by and large, have been good to us.

"We choose to live humbly and most of our income goes to organizations that help those left behind and those who live in exile here. Our money we feel is well spent. We also love our children and of course provide for them.

"We've taught them to be proud of their heritage and who they are and we've shared with them our desire to someday return to a free and democratic Cuba.

I pour myself a tea. Maybe, I shouldn't have said "let's start at the beginning."

Ed pours himself a tea as well. "Monique went to Travis High and this past year she met and befriended another Cuban student there. Her name is Sophia, a very pretty girl as well. At first, we were ecstatic she made a new friend of her nationality. Shortly, however, we began to see changes in Monique. She started challenging some of our core beliefs. We at first chalked it up as a typical teenage rebellion. Shortly thereafter, we began discovering printed socialist propaganda. Communist writings praising Castro and U.S.S.R.'s founder, Lenin. When we tried to question her, she would clam up and storm from the room, or tell us we 'are peons of capitalism.' Hurtful things such as that.

"Anyhow, it didn't take long to discover where this literature was coming from—Sophia's parents or, more accurately, the father and his girlfriend. His name is Gerard de Cuvaz. We never learned the name of the woman.

"And the drugs, when did they come into play?" I ask.

"We never knew for sure until we discovered the bag after we last saw her on May 15, but there were signs prior to that. Unexplainable lethargy, long periods of time spent alone in her darkened room or bathroom. As parents, we didn't want to believe—she was always such a sweet girl, a helpful girl, pleasant to be around." Ed dips his head. "And... And we want our daughter home and safe again."

I imagine so. "No contact from her? Any leads?"

"Only one," Marie Anne says as she hands me an envelope. "We received this in the mail three days ago."

I look it over before pulling the enclosed letter out. It's from the Sheriff's Department out of Key Largo, Florida. I pull the letter out and shake it open. It's an impound notice giving Eduardo Dos Santos Lopez 30 days to retrieve one 1973 Ford Maverick. Said vehicle will be deemed abandoned and subject to county auction if necessary action has not been taken by such time.

"Okay," I say. "It's a lead. A starting point." Way down in fucking Florida is what I'm thinking. "The Sheriff's Department have any information about the impounding of what I assume to be Monique's car?"

Edward shakes his head. "Not much. I finally reached the impounding officer. He told me the car looked lived-in and he suspects it was abandoned after the engine blew. That's it, nada, nothing else. Please say you can help?"

Williams chimes in. "I spoke with John and he'll happily sponsor the undertaking."

I feel they're really putting me on the spot. Even if we find her, what then? "It's who you are, it's what you do." I hear my dad's voice say. Thanks, Dad.

"I'll talk to my crew. See what they say. I know Andy will be gung-ho about going up against some commies," I think out loud. "I'll give you a tentative yes for now."

"With the Feds breathing down your back right now, it may be a good time to head out of town for a few days."

"I'm not sure that will keep the Feds from thinking about me, Williams."

He smiles. There is no rebuttal.

"I'll need pictures," I say.

Marie Anne gets up and heads into one of the bedrooms. She returns with a school portrait of Monique and a Travis high yearbook. She hands me both. "There's several of Sophia in the yearbook. I've marked the pages."

I flip to the first marked page. The caption names Sophia third from the left. Yes, she's pretty too. Pretty enough to make the cheerleader squad. It flashes through my mind, she's pretty enough to rescue as well. Yeah, I know, my age is poking through again.

"Well, let me go talk to my crew and we'll go from there. They're a pretty adventurous lot, so it probably won't pose much of a problem to convince them to tag along. I'll be in touch. Williams, you ready?"

He stands with me. We all shake hands again. Ed hands me his business card. "Here's my card, I've written our home number on it as well." The card lists him as a general contractor. I slide it in my rear pocket.

Williams and I step back into the early afternoon furnace.

"What do you think?" he asks as we make our way downstairs.

"They seem nice enough." I superficially add, "The girls are definitely pretty enough."

He laughs as we reach his car. "I figured that would be a big selling point for you."

"And you figured right, Williams," I say and grin. "I'd hate to disappoint you." We enter his car. "I'm fucking with you, Williams. I'd probably rescue the ugly ones, too." I throw in a faux shudder. "I just wouldn't be able to accept a kiss in thanks."

He cranks his Ford and puts it in reverse. "I think there's more substance to you then you let on. How serious were the Feds earlier?" he asks as he puts the Ford in drive and we pull away.

"Serious enough to drive Plymouths."

He chuckles. "I hear Ford is involved. He's not as dumb as he looks. Speaking of dumb, my boss is our liaison officer in your investigation."

"Jacob."

"Yep. The one and the same. I imagine you enjoy hearing that."

"It doesn't hurt my feelings none," I say and we share a laugh. Jacob is dumb as a box of rocks.

"They're probably going to try and shake down your close friends too. Andy, they definitely know about because of his house being shot up. Wallace tells me Candy is back in Rio, so they'll have a hard time talking with her. I don't think it was a very smart move on her part going back."

"I hear you."

"By the way, I never did congratulate you on rescuing John's daughter. The way it sounded on the news made it seem like it took a commando raid on his place to get her out."

"Something like that."

We ride in silence the rest of the way. I'm dismayed to see my Trans Am missing when we arrive at Candy's. My heart skips a beat and I'm hit with a hot flash. "Shit. The Trans Am is missing. Did the Feds impound it?" I ask despite the fact this is really not what I'm concerned about.

"Not that I'm aware of. Some advice though, if you have anything incriminating in the house, you might act on it fast. No telling what the Feds are up to. Where did you get the Trans Am, anyway?"

"Melissa gave it to me." I wipe perspiration from my face.

He nods in understanding and reaches to shake my hand. "I'll be in touch, try and keep you apprised of things the best I can."

"Thanks. Later," I say as I shakily get out on the car. From inside the house, Bonnie's bark does not greet me. "Not good, not again, big boy," I tell myself. Surely Sandra wouldn't do me like that and I hate myself for even thinking like I'm thinking, but I don't really know her and almost $10,000 in cash in the house may have been too tempting. "Surely not," I mutter.

I enter the stillness of the house. As I step into the kitchen, my eyes are drawn straight to the partially open kitchen drawer that held the dope. "Fuck! Not fucking again!" I yell at the silent house. The sight instantly takes me back in time to the discovery that the then love of my life, my little south Austin Jewish girl, had absconded with the nearly half of a million in the bearer bonds that were in my possession. I'm here to tell you that it took the wind out of my sails. It was a hard pill to swallow. I ultimately chalked it up to easy come, easy go. What else could I do? I sure wouldn't call the police on her.

I feel the beat of my heart in my ears as I slowly approach the drawer and ready myself to pull it open. A rumble from the drive distracts me. I pull up short as the quiet is broken by the slamming of a car door and the scratch of someone wanting in.

I didn't realize I was holding my breath. I release it, only to take another deep, calming breath. Another scratch at the door beckons me. I make it to the front door and yank it open.

Bonnie comes bounding in followed by a grocery-laden Sandra. She leans in to kiss me as she passes by. I follow her into the kitchen.

From over her shoulder, she tells me, "Your lawyer, Buzz, called. Said you were on the way home, so I thought I'd go out and pick us up a few things." She smiles and bumps the partially open drawer shut with her hip and sets the bags on the counter. She turns back toward me. "Hey, you okay?" she asks, her face suddenly etched in concern. "You don't look so well."

Now I do feel like a heel for thinking what I was thinking. "Yeah. I'm fine. Thanks. You need some help putting the stuff away?" I ask as I reach down and absently scratch Bonnie behind an ear.

"No. There are more groceries in the car, though. You know, it was the first time I ever drove a stick. It was fun."

"You didn't stall her none?"

"Nope. Spun the tires like you always do. Stopping at the top of Hillview was a trip. When I let off the brake the car began to roll back. I kinda panicked." She laughs. "I spun the tires good there! Think I even scared Bonnie."

Bonnie wags harder at the mention of her name.

Sandra tucks a strand of hair behind her ear. "How did it go with the Feds?"

"I may need to work on my communication skills. I've got at least one Fed extremely mad at me."

"You? How is that possible?" she jokes. "Hey, the news crew took off as fast as they could. I think what's-her-name..."

"Stacey Keys."

"Stacey Keys will be back. She's pretty, by the way."

"Yes she is and I vow that someday she will be mine."

"You're terrible, you know. Are you going to get the rest of the stuff out of the car?"

"Yes, honey," I say but first I make a detour to the bathroom to rinse my feet off and then to the bedroom for socks and boots. My feet have been burned enough for one day.

I bring the rest of the stuff in, set it on the table and get a cold Bud from the fridge. "Williams tells me I need to stash the dope in case the Feds get a warrant for the house."

"Hmm, he actually said that? That's cool of him."

"Well, not in so many words. I'm not going to worry about the pot, though—this is Austin after all."

She rises on her tiptoes to put the last item on a top-shelf. "I want you to take me to a movie. I haven't been in years. Please, pretty please." She gives me her "pretty please look."

"The last time I went to a movie was with Jim, Andy and James. We went for the midnight showing of Reefer Madness. From all the beer and pot earlier in the evening, Andy fell asleep. After the entire theater cleared, we all hid and sent the usher to wake him to tell him 'sir, the movie's been over for hours, we're going to have to ask you to leave.' Andy jumped up, looked around and just knew we had left him. Of course, we laughed our asses off."

She laughs. "I can picture poor Andy. You guys are kinda mean to him. I know I've said that before."

"But in a nice way," I say. "Push comes to shove, we've got his back and he knows it. One day he will be immune to our shit and will be a stronger person for it."

"Your way of saying you're doing it for his own good?"

"Absolutely. So, what's showing?"

"There are All the President's Men with Robert Redford and Dustin Hoffman and there's Carrie with that Sissy Spacek chick. It sounds really scary."

"Hmm, does she get naked in it?"

"Probably."

"Deal."

"But what if Robert Redford gets naked in his movie?"

"Carrie sounds good," I say.

"You'd make a good actor. You've got the looks and the gab."

"Thanks. A movie it is then. Let's take a walk, shall we?"

"Is your romantic side trying to peek through?"

"Yep and while I'm being romantic, we can hide the dope in the woods."

She punches me in my permanently bruised arm.

I pull the drawer open and retrieve the dope from right where it was supposed to be. Imagine that. I still feel somewhat guilty about my runaway imagination. I'll secretly make it up to her later—I'll pleasure her. What I won't do for the women in my life. And if I curl my toes in the process, so be it. Sometimes sacrifices have to be made for the betterment of mankind. I know, I'm just that kind of guy.

"Okay, are we going to stand here all day or are we going to go?" Sandra says poking me in my good ribs for emphasis.

I stuff the dope in my pants under my shirt, down my beer and grab another. I'm officially ready to go. Without Andy to tote a cooler, we'll have to make it a short trip.

It's still smoldering hot when we step back into the day. I take Sandra's hand. Might as well kill two birds with one stone, right?

Reed Park, next to Candy's, is a quaint little park with a lush green fescue lawn, hundred-year oaks, clear-running creek, a tiny pool and a small playground for the kids. The park abuts roughly 300 acres of woods believed to belong to Lady Bird Johnson herself. This is our playground and we know every inch of it. Only three entrances to the land. The Park being one, an entrance off Scenic Drive being another and, finally, the third going right between Andy's and his neighbor's house. It's an ideal place for me to play on my motocross bike too, for back in the woods I'm impossible to catch.

Some of the kids at the pool wave and yell out Sandra and Bonnie's name as we pass. Mostly the little boys for Sandra. Some of the Tarrytown's beautiful wives wave as well. Money attracts beauty is evident by the slim and tanned Tarrytown mothers. Life is good for these people. Well, life is actually good for me too. The opportunities are here for me, should I choose them. That's the reality of the situation. Sandra squeezes my hand in thought. It makes me realize something else: I don't want to hit anyone with this hand for a while. The hand's throbbing and swollen. The area around the knuckle discolored. Not that I go around hitting folks, mind you. In fact, I've confined all assaultive behavior to the past ten days and prior to that only to my heavy bag workouts. Sandra squeezes my hand once again in thought.

"What, woman?" I ask.

"This is nice."

"Stashing our dope?"

"Noooo. You know, going for a walk," she says leaning her head onto my shoulder. "No one has ever taken me for a walk before."

"Not even in the woods to get some, because I was...."

"No, not even for that. Seriously."

I swat a Texas state bird that has alit on my neck and by the look of the blood in my palm, it had doubled in size after landing, and prior to its ultimate death.

"Yep, swell," I say but I have to confess to myself it's not that bad, for most of the dirt road is shaded. Bonnie seems to be enjoying herself as she blasts by us chasing nothing. She waits for us before chasing nothing again.

The little creek to our right begins to widen as we near Scenic and Lake Austin. Halfway along, we come upon a small steel and wood bridge that would have toppled years before, save for a tree that keeps it mostly upright. It's steep and rail-less and 15 feet higher than necessary. We stop on top and look down on the shallows. Small bream can be seen guarding their spawning beds and hoping something to eat will come their way. I spit in the water and cause the nearest one to strike the surface.

"The cute little fish are hungry, huh?" Sandra comments.

"And I'm horny. Your point?"

"I won't let you keep your good hand warm during the movie if you keep it up and no late-night dessert either," she says.

"Good point," I say and down my beer. I hand her the can. "Here, hold this," I tell her. I know when to throw in the towel.

"Why are you handing it to me?"

"I like these woods, don't want to litter. Come on, let's stash this dope, so we can get back."

She shakes her head but smiles. I give her hand a small tug and we descend to the other side. The ground becomes a steep incline and the mosquitos form a hovering cloud around us.

We've gone far enough. I drop Sandra's hand and rock a fallen timber loose from its soft impression in the ground. I pick up a flat rock and dig a spot deep enough to hold the gallon Ziploc bag. I remove half a dozen Valiums before resealing the bag and dropping it into the created space. I allow the log to fall back in place and fan out the excavated debris.

I look up to see Sandra desperately fanning at the mosquitos that are attempting to make a meal out of her. I dart off.

"Run!" I yell out and we're off like two laughing school kids.

We scramble over the bridge and come to a laughing halt on the other side.

"Fuck this walk," she manages to say catching her breath. "These fucking mosquitos are eating me up. I'm out of here. Fuck this."

I laugh at her fleeing figure. "Get her, girl," I yell at Bonnie. That's all she was waiting for—she's out of the gate and streaking after Sandra. I'd run after them, but it hurts to laugh as is. Running is clearly out of the question. Besides, I've decided long ago that I'm not cut out for running. Well, unless someone is chasing me, that is. I smile, remembering again how I narrowly escaped Vinnie's grasp when my boot pulled loose in his hands. He was one mad motherfucker and I was giddy with relief having gotten away.

I fanned the fire after my hurled boot went flying by my head and yelled at him. "The next time you touch my boots it better be with a rag and a can of saddle soap." I'm good at fanning the flames, remember? But a little advice to the wise: sometimes it comes back to bite you. When I yelled at him, I included a couple of "you fucking Guineas." Or was it "you fucking greaseball?" Anyhow, he got the message.

I dry-swallow a couple of the Valiums as I head off after the girls, who are no longer in sight. Maybe, I should have only taken one. Too late.

I catch up with the girls near the pool, where they have garnered quite the attention. Everyone loves Bonnie and some preteens are snickering as they stare at Sandra's ass. They clam up as I approach like they got their hands caught in a cookie jar. The heat of the day is relentless and I merely nod at the mamas in passing. My girls fall in beside me. I like that thought, "my girls." I've had quite the turnover in girls the past couple weeks and in my love life. My sex life has improved exponentially every three days or so. Does it get any better than that? The love life, not the turnover. Well maybe....

"Did you talk to the people the cop wanted you to yet?" Sandra asks as we near the house.

"Yep."

"Another damsel in need of rescuing?"

"More like a wayward child, but essentially the same. She's apparently run off with dope-shooting commies."

"Is she pretty?"

I stop at the entrance to the house. "Candy asked the same thing about Melissa. Does it make a difference?"

I open the door to let her in.

"I guess not," she concedes.

I pull the door closed behind us. Being pretty shouldn't make a difference, but I have to admit to myself that it makes it easier, somehow. I know the media finds the beautiful more newsworthy. I wonder where Stacey Keys is? She should have backtracked by now. I get a beer from the fridge, pull the tab, and take a refreshing swallow.

"I'm going to make us sandwiches," Sandra announces. I smack her on the ass.

"Groovy, man. Hey, don't forget to make Bonnie one. Hold the pickles, onion and tomatoes on hers. I'm going into the living room. I'm sure Bonnie will keep you company."

Bonnie breaks her concentration long enough to give me a dismissive glance. She licks her snout, swallows and returns to her sandwich-watching vigil.

I find my way to the living room and remembered we had intended on going to the "Big O" for a new Curtis Mathis console TV. Too bad, too sad. We'll have to work with what we've got for now. I believe the saying is "put off till tomorrow what you can do today." Or is that the weed smoker's version? Whichever, I believe Jack Benny said it best when he said, "age is strictly mind over matter—if you don't mind, it doesn't matter." How does that apply here, you wonder? It's an old TV.

I turn the TV on. Dr. Smith is fucking somebody over in Lost in Space. Someday I hope to possess the level of wisdom Zachery does. Only kidding, of course.

Sandra brings me a halved sandwich, some chips and a fresh Bud. She presents it all with a smile. She's endearing herself to me at a rapid pace. Beyond the love at first sight, that is. Yes, I've said it before, "to be so young and vulnerable." I hope I never outgrow the two.

We watch some mindless television as the afternoon wanes. The valiums cause me to nod for a while. I'm surprised when I wake that the phone has yet to ring all afternoon. Disheartening is the fact this includes calls from Candy. She has yet to call, so all I can do for now is hope she remains safe while in Rio. Not a good time for anyone associated with me to be there. Too much evidence of us staying at the Copacabana Palace to be ignored.

Sandra stirs and stretches from her reclined position at the other end of the couch.

"What are you thinking about, honey?" She groggily asks.

"What time's the movie you want to go to?"

"Seven thirty or nine forty-five."

"Okay, let's take a shower and try and make the seven thirty show."

"Works by me. I need to clean and change your bandages too."

How could one not love her?

Chapter Ten

I'll never shower alone again is my New Year's resolution. I decide to apply it retroactively, for it surely wouldn't make sense to wait six more months to do so. Sandra proves to be vigorous and thorough in her soaping. She manages to get my attention and I end up insisting she rinse her hair for a long, long time, as I support her from the hips from behind. Another pleasurable first for me. I can only come to one conclusion: I've matured tremendously in the past ten days or so.

The redness around my wounds has abated some. The penicillin seems to be keeping the infection at bay. Lucky, huh? I would like to think so.

The clock in the bedroom indicates we have a little time to kill, which will give us an opportunity to stop and grab something to eat first. The prices at the theater tend to rip you off. I smack myself in the head when I remember I'm now rich and a man about town. A position in which I seem to be born to excel.

I pull on a fresh Izod and check myself in the mirror.

Even without my twin shoulder holsters, the mirror reflects an imposing, handsome devil. Well, maybe not quite so imposing, but there is no denying, "you're one handsome devil."

"Are you talking to me?" Sandra asks from the bathroom.

Oops, I must have thought that last one out loud.

"Only wondering how you're coming along," I appropriately answer.

She peeks her head in the door and catches me still before the mirror. She playfully scrunches her face.

"You think this outfit makes me look fat, honey?" I ask.

She throws a hand on her hip and shakes her head. "You're something else, you know it? You were talking to the mirror, weren't you?"

"Noooo," I say and we both laugh. She has a nice laugh. Our laughter reminds me that what can make you laugh can make you cry. The pain in my side cuts my laugh short. "I'm going to let Bonnie out to take care of her evening constitutional since she can't come with us." Bonnie wags her tail at the sound of her name. "Now, Bonnie, remember what I told you about going in other people's yard?" Bonnie's wag picks up. "Yep, she remembers—that's a good girl."

"What did you tell her?" Sandra asks.

"That she's a 'good girl' when she forsakes our own yard."

That renews Sandra's laughter. I let Bonnie out the front door and then check the fridge to see what else Sandra bought. That's my girl. I eye a family pack of prime ribs. I didn't even realize they came in family packs. No sense in wasting motion, I grab Sandra and myself a beer.

"Hurry up," I say. "The news will be coming on. I wonder where the media is?"

"Maybe they didn't feel their anonymous source is credible?"

I chuckle at that one. It doesn't hurt to chuckle. "Like my veracity would ever be at issue. For example: if I tell you this Bud is good, you can by God take that to the bank."

"Don't have to convince me, come on it's almost on. Let's see if you're even newsworthy."

We settle on the couch just in time.

"Hi, I'm Ted Collins, thank you for joining Channel 7 evening News at five.

"Today in the news, a local teen Steven Paul, a familiar face to our viewers and one not known to shun cameras, was taken in for questioning by federal authorities in the ongoing investigation of Texas oil tycoon John Wallace.

A file photo of a grinning, shoulder-holstered me briefly fills the screen. Sandra and I laugh.

"Wallace came under investigation yesterday when a DC-3, registered to Wallace illegally entered U.S. Airspace and failed to heed U.S. Air Force pilot Captain T.F. Riley's order to alter course and land at Houston's Hobby Airport. Wallace's plane landed on his remote ranch north of San Antonio and the pilot and passengers were able to flee before authorities descended upon Wallace's property.

"Search warrants were issued and some evidence, we have learned, was seized in conjunction and the execution of the warrants. Information, however, is still sketchy at this time and the investigation continues. No arrests to date have been made.

"A Channel 7 anonymous source has named Steven Paul as the pilot of the DC-3 and that the plane in question was used in a raid to free Wallace's daughter, Melissa Wallace, who was alleged to have been held captive in Brazil by the late Dom Pedro, who died in the commando-style raid on his villa west of Rio de Janeiro two evenings ago.

"Channel 7 News has yet to receive independent corroboration of its source and federal authorities and the state department are playing their cards close to the vest. No official statements have been released at this time.

"Stay tuned to Channel 7 for updates as this case develops.

"In other news today...."

"Wow, cool." She grins. "Nice file photo. Your gun really makes a hell of a statement. You look... Well, you look so daring," She pauses in thought. "So daring, but yet happy."

"You think," I say and we both laugh. "My hair was a little mussed, you know, from being in a major gun battle and all, but the words you were searching for were 'so daring and dashing.'"

Sandra hits me with a couch pillow. "You're crazy, you know that?"

"Some say it is true, Sandra. Some say it is true. Let's let Bonnie in and burn off."

"Cool."

I pull Sandra to her feet and lead her to the front door. I open the door and the name Bonnie dies on my lips. I watch in shock as Bonnie, a half a block up and in front of the park, jumps into the passenger side of a late model Ford LTD. The door slams shut and in a spin of tires the car takes off.

I slap my pocket—no keys. "Shit!" I yell and push Sandra out of the way to get back in. I snatch the keys off the kitchen table and blow by the frozen Sandra.

I look down in horror as I realize I grabbed the wrong keys.

The keys are to the Bonneville. Too late to correct the mistake. I jump in her and no sooner than the engine catches and I'm smoking the tires backing out of the drive. I slam on the brakes, bounce off the opposite curb and in roiling tires reverse course.

I fly through the S curve and three blocks up I see taillights and watch the Ford turn left. I stay on the pedal and close the gap. I don't believe the car that took Bonnie realizes I'm after them yet. I lay hard on the brakes and steer into the slide as I make the turn. I let the Bonneville have her reins and she eats up some asphalt. She's a boat, but the LTD is no match for her power, weight and speed. I come up hard on the Ford before the driver discovers I'm on his tail. He makes a run for it. I ram him in the left corner trying to pit him, but he doesn't spin and I end up beside him as we hit 60 coming into a blind right curve. One glance and I recognize the driver instantly—it's Candy's husband.

"Motherfucker!"

We come out of the curve side-by-side and banging metal. A half-block ahead sits a parked car. We both lay hard on the brakes, but in a protracted squeal of tortured rubber, there's no place for him to go and he disappears from sight in a sickening crash of steel. I slide to a stop and throw her in reverse. I pass through a cloud of smoke before screeching to a stop.

The cars are totaled: mangled piles of scrap. What's left of the parked car bursts into flames. All I can think of is Bonnie as I scramble from my car.

The LTD is nearly folded in half. Candy's husband is dazed and bloody. There's an imprint in what remains of the windshield where his head tried to go through it. A second glance at Candy's estranged tells me he didn't fare very well.

My adrenaline kicks me into overdrive. I yank at the damaged door. It won't budge. The heat from the burning parked car begins to intensify—the LTD begins to catch from the licking flames. In my peripheral, I become aware of people coming out of their houses. I have to get Bonnie and get the fuck out of here like right fucking now.

I put my boot and back into it. It takes several attempts, but suddenly in screeching protest the door gives and opens. Thank god. I grab Candy's husband by his rapidly soaking shirt and drag him to safety.

I go back for Bonnie. She's cowering in the rear floorboard.

"Come on, Bonnie, we've got to get the fuck out of here!"

She doesn't move—she only shakes. I lean into the driver's seat with my shoulder and push forward as far as I can, reach in, grab her by her front legs and drag her out. Clear of the car I scoop her up, round my car, toss her in and flee. Can't say I didn't render aid first though, right?

Not good. No witnesses to the wreck, but the twin sets of rubber on the pavement says it all. "Shit, big boy, not good," I tell the still quivering Bonnie.

I take a right and two blocks over I take another right. I look at Bonnie. "You okay, girl? You look okay. We'll stash the car behind Andy's."

I didn't get a chance to survey the Bonneville's damage. There's no doubt in my mind she's sporting some of the LTD's gold color. Well, my relationship with this ride was short and sweet, but it's time to ditch her. One of the beauties of never registering her is that she could belong to anyone.

I pass Andy's, pull into the easement that leads to Lady Bird's acreage and park my big ride 50 yards in by what remains of my Firebird. At least I didn't total this one.

I pull Bonnie to me, look her over more thoroughly and scratch behind her ear. She seems fine. I slide out of the car.

"Come on, girl." She inches toward me. "That's a good girl, come on."

She hops to the ground and leads the way to Andy's.

Sirens can be heard approaching in the distance. Smokey and Rosie's barks let Andy know he has company. His room is toward the end of the house leading to the carport. His mighty Pinto indicates he's home. We wait him out. Within moments, the door to the carport opens and Smokey and Rosie rush out followed by Andy. He cocks his head toward the sound of the sirens and looks around for my ride.

"I know you didn't walk here. You wouldn't walk to the store if it were across the street. What's up?"

"And nice to see you also. Bonnie and I were out on a therapeutic walk and decided to drop by. How's it hanging with the parents since I smoothed things out for you?"

"I hear the sirens. What did you do this time?"

"Funny you should ask. I'll tell you about it on the drive back to Candy's. I see you haven't bought a new car yet. Too bad, the one you got really sucks." I open the Pinto's passenger door. "Load up, Bonnie." She's hesitant to get in. "She doesn't think much of your car, Andy." With the added snap of the fingers, she loads up and hops to the back.

"How about I give y'all a ride," Andy offers.

"Hey, that's mighty white of you, Andy. Just to show you I have no hard feelings about riding in the rat mobile, I'm going to invite you to go to the movies with us. We're going to see Carrie, the new Sissy Spacek movie."

Andy pulls his keys from his front pocket. "I don't think so. You'll somehow turn it into a bad experience."

"Andy, sorry if I might have traumatized you in the past, but I've matured a lot since then." I toss in a smile before ducking my head to get into the rat mobile.

I named it that because viewed from the side, with its extra-long CB antenna, it looks like a giant blue rat.

Andy gets in on his side. "It's only been two months," he reminds me.

"True, but now I recall it was that little shit James's fault. It was totally his idea to pretend we left you behind.

He cranks the mighty Pinto and I involuntarily grab the dash. "Buckle up, Bonnie." Andy drives his four-cylinder with road rage flair. Somehow, he's managed to avoid accidents, but I rue the day he has additional cylinders.

Andy spins the tires, as best he can, leaving his drive and with a jerk, we're in second. He catches third before the end of the block. We're almost to Candy's before he can ask, "So, what did you do this time?"

"Would you hurry, Andy? We'll be late for the movie."

He looks at the Trans Am and then at me as he pulls into the drive. Sandra stops her pacing as she realizes I'm in the car as well. Relief washes over her when she sees Bonnie hop out of the car.

Sandra cuts off Andy's "where did the Trans Am come from?"

"Thank God you got her back." She looks down. "Is that fresh blood on your boots? Tell me it's not."

I follow her eyes. Sure enough, there's fresh blood on my right boot and pant leg. "It would appear to be. I believe we should go ahead and go. Andy, if you're not going with us, could you look after Bonnie for us?"

"I guess. Did you talk to the people Detective Williams wanted you to?"

"Yep. It looks like we're headed to the Florida Keys. Oh, by the way, I have another ten grand for each of us and expect the Feds to pick you up for questioning any time now."

Andy frowns. "Wonderful. That ought to go over well with my parents."

"Don't tell them about the money."

"That's not what I was referring to. Hey, how do you know the Feds are going to pick me up for questioning?"

"Williams," I say as I dig in my back pocket and remove the lawyer's business card. I hand him the card. "Here, call Buzz when they do."

"Buzz, huh? Sounds like a wrestler's name."

I smile as I throw my arm across his shoulder. "Inspires confidence, don't it?" Andy likes it when I talk to him like this. "Anyhow, we need to roll, in case the local cops come looking."

"You never did say what you did this time?"

I give him a squeeze before releasing him. "I thwarted Candy's estranged husband's abduction of Bonnie."

"Of course. You didn't shoot him, did you?"

"Hold that thought," I say before hurrying into the house to get the Trans Am keys from the kitchen table and a mostly full 12-pack of Bud from the fridge. Note how I used "mostly full" to describe the 12-pack? I always see the glass half full. Who would have guessed?

"The car?" Andy probes.

"Gift from Melissa—wasn't that sweet of her?"

"I suppose. So, what does she look like?"

"Who?"

Andy sighs. "I thought you were in a hurry. I'm talking about the girl. Doesn't somebody want us to rescue a girl?"

I toy with him. "Boy, girl, looks, what's the difference?"

Dejected-looking Andy tells Bonnie to load up. I snap my fingers and she does. She's getting the routine down.

"Andy, it's a beautiful 18-year-old, but I left the pictures in Williams's car by accident. I'm sure he'll realize it and bring them back tomorrow. For the record though Andy, I'm disappointed that gender and looks are an issue for you. What do you say, Sandra?"

"Disappointing," Sandra says in an equally disappointed tone.

"Whatever, I'm out of here. Sandra, don't let him ruin you for the rest of the world."

We laugh as we enter the Trans Am. Life is good. I love the throaty sound the Trans Am emits. I like all the different gauges she has too and I also note the clock appears to be correct.

We drive the couple miles to the Holiday House—one of the few eateries in Tarrytown. Despite the wealth of the area, it's a mom and pop joint that mostly serves burgers and fries. It's a popular place for us teens to eat as well. We have yet to smoke a joint, but Sandra assures me she's hungry and I tend to stay hungry once I've started drinking beer. I recommend we order chicken-fried steak dinners and a couple of large cokes. You guessed it—they don't serve beer here. Sometimes a coke does a body good. Hmm, that would probably make a good slogan for a milk commercial, wouldn't you say? Nah, too simple.

We attract the attention of a number of diners. We're being discussed in whispers and giggles and behind menus, but one braves the pack and approaches our table. A girl from my school I recently met and hit on. That didn't pan out—her dad forbade her to see me and she told me that "if we were caught, Dad's liable kill one of us." I wasn't born yesterday, I figured out right off who that one would be: me. Despite the threats, she tells me she can do what she wants on her 18th birthday. I interpret that to mean I have a one-year reprieve on my ultimate death sentence. She's on the high school tennis team if that tells you anything. Firm and tasty, it tells me. Ultimately, I'm doomed.

Anyhow, her name is Jennifer, we go to Austin High and we're "Maroons." Got me, I don't know what the fuck a Maroon is?

I'm not sure, but I believe I just became more interesting to Jennifer, having been caught with a pretty girl. We finish our meal, I invite Jennifer along, she begs off and to Sandra's relief, we're off again. Actually, Sandra was a good sport about it and she knew I was only kidding, kind of.

I finally decide to ask where the movie is playing. Turns out to be at Highland Mall. Another popular teen hangout in north Austin. My driving skills make it for a short two-beer trip. I believe I was born to drive. Actually, I'm a decent motocross rider and the skills carried over. Of course, my parents and insurance companies would beg to differ with me, but they couldn't possibly know everything, could they?

Despite having eaten, we still load up on the goodies. The movie turns out to be a damn good one. Sandra squeezed the life out of my good hand throughout the movie and a couple of scenes gave me a start. Especially the one at the end when the hand comes out of the ground and grabs the girl by her leg. Man, that was some scary shit.

Stepping back into the world, the afternoon heat has abated to a tolerable level. Unfortunately, the beer's temperature went the other direction. I opt to make a stop. I'm too much of a gentleman to subject Sandra to drinking hot beer. Luckily, I can now buy beer anywhere—I have Sandra with me.

That's kinda ironic. I'm now 17, which is the age of consent in Texas, so legally Sandra can fuck me, but legally she can't buy me beer. Maybe it's time to kick the Dems out of state government and introduce some sensible legislation. If you're old enough to shoot a gun, by God you're old enough to buy beer. The only other angle that comes to mind is, I could have Sandra adopt me so then she could legally buy me beer. Nope, that won't work either—she wouldn't be able to fuck me then. Hmm? Maybe we need to keep the government out of our bedrooms and coolers, now that sounds like it would work.

"Hey, you just passed the store. Weren't we going to get more beer?"

"Sorry, kinda was wishing I was old enough to vote," I say as I pull into the next gas station. I dig a rumpled $20 from my front pocket and pass it over. "Pick your poison, woman."

Sandra snatches the bill from my hand. "You buy, I fly. I can live with that arrangement," she says with a smile.

I wonder if Sandra realizes how rapidly she's growing on me? I have to be careful and not cede her too much power. She can already lead me around by one head. "So many women, so little time." Whoever said that has got my vote.

The ever-smiling Sandra jumps back in the car with a 12-pack of Corona and a half dozen dried-up-looking limes. She tears into the 12-pack and hands me a beer.

I open my door, ready to pop the beer cap on the door's lower hinge when from a hip pocket Sandra produces a bottle opener. She shrugs.

"A habit carried over from work," she says. She pops the cap off my beer and then her own. Like a seasoned gunfighter and a pistol returning to its holster, the bottle opener returns back to its pocket.

I pull my Uncle Henry from its sheath at my side and with a well-practiced whip of the wrist snap it open. I keep my knife well-honed and oiled. I slice one of the shriveled limes into fours and squeeze the life out of one of them to produce a few drops for Sandra's beer.

"It's the thought that counts," Sandra assures me.

"Yep. That's why I'm not upset about you buying dead limes." I emphasize my point by bouncing the wedge off her head. Bursting into giggles, she retaliates by bouncing a whole one off mine. She's clearly regressing in age to match mine. Although Sandra is probably only four or five years older than me. Older women—got to love 'em is my motto. I have many such mottos. Who would have guessed, right?

I spin the tires leaving the lot just because I can. Life is good, at least for now.

"You're going to get tickets in this car someday," Sandra remarks while buckling up as we roar down Burnet Road. I sure love my new car, I think for the umpteenth time.

We sing along to an Allman Brothers' song from their '72 live album and make short order of our drive back to Candy's.

Chapter Eleven

I take a route that drives by Jim's house. He's in the drive washing his '64 Riviera with its 430 H.O., four BL and dual exhaust. It originally came with a 455, but we blew that engine one day seeing how much of the big roller-dial odometer we could get her to reveal.

I pull to the curb and rev the engine.

Jim shakes his head when he realizes it's me. Where I'm concerned, he shakes his head a lot. He likes to tell people I can piss into the wind and not get wet. Here's another one he uses: "You feed them shit and they come out of their panties."

I rev the engine again and realize I can live with the accusations. I kill the engine and we get out with our beer.

"Watch your beer, my parents are at home." His parents aren't against beer, per se, but they are against us drinking beer.

"Okay," I say down my beer and discard the bottle in his yard.

Jim frowns as he moves to pick up the bottle. "This isn't Andy's yard, you know."

"Right, Jimbo, my man," I say as I reach in the passenger side and retrieve a beer. Sandra whips out her opener and pops the cap off for me. I grin.

Jim's frown returns. "Not you too, Sandra?"

My grin broadens. "Well, Jimbo, you know my policy about kissing and telling, but where this relationship will differ is, we're starting on a sound foundation." I take a contemplative sip of my beer and wipe my mouth with the back of my hand. "Right, honey?"

"Yep. Sound foundation," Sandra says and matches my grin.

"Yeah, right. Steve-O's idea of a sound foundation is when he's on the bottom. Where'd the car come from?"

"Gift from Melissa."

"Of course. Did it also include her gift wrapped in a teddy?"

"Now, Jimbo, you know that would have been unethical on my part, beings so close to her rescue and me taking a bullet for her and all. I made myself perfectly clear in that respect."

Jim laughs. "Yeah, right, Steve-O," Jim says again. "The last thing that I would expect from you is trying to discourage one like Melissa from shedding her panties. Sandra, you better watch him, he'll probably use you as bait to attract others."

My turn to laugh. "Jimbo, Jimbo. So young, but yet so cynical. There is more to life than getting laid and someday you will realize it too. But as true as that is, there's not much."

"Thanks, I'll keep that in mind. Heard from Wallace?"

"Yep. He sent a hundred grand with Melissa, so you have ten more grand coming. Heard from the Feds too, they—"

"I know," Jim interrupts, "they picked you up for questioning. I saw it on the news along with my parents. They sure were asking questions after that. I had to lie to them the best I could. I told them it must be some kind of mistake."

"With that haircut," I point out, "I doubt they believed you."

"My hair has nothing to do with it. They're my parents."

I shrug. "I'm just saying it looks like a cop cut to me."

"There's nothing wrong with my hair. It's my friendship with you that makes them suspect. Not to mention, you've become a regular in the local news."

"Well, you should tell them that guilt by association is not a crime."

Jim huffs. "Well, it sounds like an offense to me. Plus, that doesn't even make sense."

"Perhaps to someone unschooled in law."

"Right, Steve-O. That just happens to be you too."

"So, your theory is that I just pull my legal theories out of the air?"

"Absolutely."

We all laugh.

"So, what did the Feds want?" Jim asks.

"I'm sure what I wouldn't give them: a confession. I may have really pissed one of them off."

"You? How could that be possible?"

"Yeah, gets me too. Anyhow, Jimbo, our next mission should you choose to accept it...."

"I might be missioned out for a while, thank you."

"Involves two, beautiful 18-year-olds and a sunny trip to the Florida Keys."

"I'm in!"

We all share a laugh again. Jim, being young and eternally hopeful like myself, is quick to capitulate. I understand where he's coming from, so I surely can't hate on him. Jim's very astute to say the least and by far the smartest of the bunch, so he was quick to calculate that, since there are two young ladies involved, there could quite possibly be one left over. Well, I can give him advice and wish him luck, but I personally wouldn't bet on it.

"Steve-O, I still have this trunk full of guns—too many to try stash in the house."

He's not kidding either, there's a hell of an arsenal in his trunk: ten AR-15's, an assortment of pistols, at least one Mossberg 12 gauge and the cream of the crop, a full-auto MP-5.

"I feel you, Jimbo. Call Alan and see if we can store them in the escape tunnel to his bomb shelter. I'm sure he won't care, especially if you stop by Candy's and pick up a couple of lids of weed and maybe a case of beer to give him."

"Yeah, he likes his weed and peanut butter and jelly."

"Don't we all?" I say and Jim and I share the laugh. My mom always knew when we'd been smoking because we'd go straight to the kitchen and the peanut butter and jelly.

"All right, I'll call him. When are we leaving and how are we getting there?"

"I thought we'd take the Bonneville since it's not registered to any of us."

"Makes sense. Again, when are we leaving and who all do you think is going to go?"

"Hell, you, Andy and me for sure. Possibly Felix as well. Oh, and Wallace decided to sponsor the mission."

"Good deal... Hell, give me a couple of your beers."

"That's the spirit, Jimbo," I say. "I'll try and let you know something later tonight."

Sandra opens one of the two beers I hand Jim and we say our goodbyes. Candy's house is only about five blocks away. I'm tempted to spin my tires, but then remember we're not in front of Andy's. The street in front of his house looks like a drag strip going in both directions. As we come down the hill from the north, we spot William's car in the drive, but fortunately no other city cars and no Feds.

He gets out as we pull in and Sandra and I join him.

"Steven, I've been waiting for you for two hours. What did you do, go see a movie?"

"And that's why they made you a detective. Here, have a beer and the name of the movie is Carrie with Sissy Spacek. I recommend it."

"It's scary as hell," Sandra adds. "Here, let me open that for you, detective."

"Pretty quick on the draw, ain't she, Williams? Easy on the eyes, too, among other things."

Williams smiles. "Don't let him get your goat, Sandra."

"Don't worry, detective, I've been waitressing in one of the busiest bars in Rio for the past year. I know how to handle his type."

"So far TLC seems to be working well for her. Maybe we should take this inside, Williams. You stick out like a sore thumb out here."

William raises an eyebrow. "Because I'm black?" he jokes.

"Because you're a cop and I have an image to uphold."

He chuckles. "Gotcha."

He opens the door to his ride and retrieves from within the yearbook, photo and large envelope. He passes everything to me.

"You forgot the pictures and the yearbook in my car earlier. I've added a little something to it as well."

I take it as we pass through the front door that Sandra has opened for us. We take it as far as the kitchen where we all pull up a chair. I put the beer in the fridge before taking a seat.

I pass the family photo over to Sandra and pull the contents out of the envelope and view the two sketches within.

"I had our staff artist do composites. I took them by and showed them to Ed and Marie Anne. They both agree: the resemblances are uncanny."

"She's definitely pretty enough," Sandra comments. "What's her name?" She asks in reference to the photo in her hand.

"Monique and her friend's name is Sophia. Here, check it out," I say as I flip through the yearbook until I come to the first picture of Sophia.

"Wow. She's pretty too. I like the name Sophia. I wish I was named something like that."

"I like your name just fine," I say, "It's easy to remember and easy to spell.

Sandra scowls. "Thanks."

"And to eliminate any confusion, I'll call you 'honey.'"

Sandra lets that one pass. Williams conceals his smile with a pull from his beer.

Williams sets his beer back on the table. "Have you talked to any of your crew yet?"

"Yeah. It looks like we might leave as early as tomorrow."

He nods his head in approval. "The Lopezes will be glad to hear that. They truly are good people," he says before polishing off his beer. "I came unprepared—can I talk you out of another one of the Coronas?"

"We have limes you can play marbles with. Would you care for a wedge of one of them too?"

"Sure, why not."

I get up and retrieve the whole 12-pack. I remove a Corona, dig out one of the limes that Sandra had dropped in among the beer and unsheathe and snap open my Uncle Henry.

"Case?" Williams inquires.

"Uncle Henry, but they use the same steel. It has a Shrade blade," I say as I quarter one of the dead limes. I toss him two of the quarters. "Good luck."

"By the way, Steven Paul, it probably won't surprise you"—he checks his watch— "that about four hours ago an ambulance picked up Candy's husband about a mile and a half from here. Seems he hit a parked car at high speed. Last I checked he's in the ICU right now in critical but stable condition."

I nonchalantly shrug. "I'm not going to lose any sleep over it, as you might well imagine. To put it bluntly, he's a piece of shit and, as we know, it was his shit that got Kelly killed."

He takes a long moment. "I know, although I don't know exactly what the Vegas pair were after and how you boys got involved. I can't say I'm upset about the way things played out. Perhaps someday you'll be comfortable enough with me to share the story."

"Possibly, but as you know, there are others involved and I can't breach their trust."

"Noble," William comments.

"Well, perhaps there is hope for me after all. That's the first time a cop has ever accused me of being noble."

He chuckles. "I imagine. You're damn good at rubbing some of them the wrong way. The office gossip is that FBI Special Agent Ford has a hard-on for you. Watch your step. Although I don't personally care for him, he's actually a respected agent."

"Besides being in the ICU, what's the skinny on Candy's estranged?"

"Unfortunately, there's not a whole lot we can do about him. I'm going to run a few things by the D.A. Impeding an investigation perhaps, who knows. There's no law against being an asshole. We're going to try and make his life uncomfortable. Fortunately, there were no witnesses to the actual crash, but a number of the post-crash gave statements to the effect that Candy's husband was pulled from the wreck and dragged to safety by a person who then retrieved a dog from the wreck and fled the scene in a large coupe of an unknown color."

"Poor lighting, huh?"

"Poor witnesses. There was a lot of extra rubber on the pavement, but nothing but a totally engulfed wreck by the time police and fire arrived on the scene. It seems like we have a hero somewhere in the area that saved a man's life."

"Probably saved by someone who is a victim of heroic genes, driven by an instinct to save lives," I say in all seriousness.

We all get a laugh out of that.

"Yeah. That's probably it," Williams muses.

Ironic. I saved someone I actually wanted to kill. Not literally, of course, but you know what I mean. I hate to see my worst enemy die in a fire. Death by fire must be one of the most excruciating ways to die. I involuntarily shiver at the thought. Yep, my siblings and I were raised to respect life in all forms, big and small. In that respect, I'm also a firm believer in rescue and adoption programs. I also like to advocate for the adoption or sponsorship of the hard-to-place animals.

"You still with us, Steven?" Williams asks breaking my reverie.

"Yeah. Sorry, I spaced there for a minute."

"That's okay. Look, I need to be running along now. It seems like every day is a 16-hour day. Don't worry about the locals and this latest incident. I was assigned to the investigation, so it dies with me. Sorry, you don't get credit or news coverage for your latest rescue."

"Damn the luck," I say with feeling. We all share the laugh.

William rises. "Later, I'll see myself out."

"Later," Sandra and I echo.

Sandra reflects on the latest Williams visit. "Cool. You have like your own guardian angel. I've never had a cop do anything for me besides harass me and try some way or another to get in my pants. Even when I wasn't of age and I'd be taken back to a foster home after running away. It kinda fucked me up, you know?"

I can't think of anything other than something lame to say, "Sorry, but you turned out just fine after living through such a terrible ordeal."

Sandra offers me a weak smile. "Thanks."

I return her smile with a grin. "Like a diamond in the rough, I'm going to polish you till you shine."

"Hmm. That sounds exciting. To orgasmic bliss?"

I pretend to ponder the situation. "And what's in it for me?"

She laughs and smacks me in the shoulder. "You shit. 'What's in for me?'" she parrots. "Why me, of course!"

I reach over and tuck a few strands of loose hair behind an ear and brush my knuckle down her cheek. Sandra leans into the soft stroke and turns her chair more toward me. "Are you going to take me with you to Florida?" she faintly asks.

I'm not sure, but her eyes have enlarged. They darken as I turn to face her. I'm a sucker for alluring eyes.

"I won't get in the way, I promise."

I let out my breath in resignation. I shake my head no. "I'll write you in the script somehow... Provided you can talk James into watching Bonnie for us."

"Deal. That won't be a problem. James is very sweet," she says with conviction.

"You mean 'pushover?'"

Sandra bounces to her feet. "Yep, much like you. You caved in way too easy."

"And my penchant for getting laid every day of the week has nothing to do with it."

Sandra straddles me like she did the day before in her bikini and wiggles around until she makes herself comfortable and me uncomfortable. "Maybe it had a little to do with it," she squeaks out. Sandra plants a big kiss on me. "I'm going to call him right now."

I grab her arm as she tries to stand. "Not from this phone. If the Feds are monitoring it, we don't want to announce that we're going out of town for a spell."

"Well, then," Sandra says as she drops on her knees before me. She lays one hand on my crotch and with the other pulls my shirt up.

"We have something here we need to take care of," she seductively announces.

I involuntarily swallow.

To my dismay, Sandra pops up and pats me on the head. "I'll just be a minute getting a clean washcloth, salve and bandages."

My dismay is as palpable as her joy is tangible. "She who laughs first doesn't necessarily laugh last," I remind her.

She puckers her lips and makes a face. She throws her hands to her hips, further emphasizing her thoughts. "You're easy to fuck with. I'll save the laughter for the bedroom," she teases and barely avoids my grasp. She flees the room, leaving a trail of giggles in her wake.

I smile to myself. I'll show her. I'll limit her to multiple orgasms. That will teach her to fuck with me, don't you think?

I get up and locate a mop bucket from under the sink and wash it out with dishwashing liquid. I put the remaining few Corona in the bucket, add a few Buds, then top the bucket off with ice from the freezer. What I won't do for love. Or is that what I won't do for lovin'? I'm not sure, but when you're 17, they're one and the same.

I head down the hallway and intercept Sandra coming out of the bathroom. I block her path and maneuver her the short distance to the bedroom. She backpedals until her legs make contact with the bed. I set the bucket down and push her to a sitting position on the bed.

"I'm going to teach you to fuck with me," I sternly inform her.

I reach behind me and flip on the light switch. The bandaging items in her hands fall to the floor. "Oh, please, please don't," she pleas.

She may be playacting, but it works for me. She sealed her fate when she chose to straddle me. Now she'll get the tongue-lashing she deserves. There's no room for leniency. I shall mete out this just punishment swiftly and accurately. Hey, I've been practicing, okay?

I push her flat to the bed and reach down and snatch up a one-booted foot, tug the boot loose and toss it to the corner.

I repeat the action with the other, before reaching for the zipper of her jeans. With one skilled pull, the zipper comes down. Yep, I've done the same thing a million times with my own jeans.

It takes several tugs to free her skintight jeans. She watches me as I toe one boot off and kick it to the side, then the other. For efficiency, I shuck jeans and boxers in one swift move. The sight of her firm legs and prominent mound shielded by the simplest of white cotton panties has me hard and throbbing. I push her to her back before spreading her legs and kneeling between them. I grasp her above each knee and begin kneading her tan and toned legs, ever so slowly encroaching on my goal—on what I know will be hot and wet. I track my hands upward, replacing each as I go with slow kisses. I can feel her body tensing with each kiss.

I spread her legs a little wider and allow my left thumb to ever so lightly brush the protruding spot evident through the sheer fabric.

A gasp escapes her—I settle my hand firmly above her sex and use my palm to begin a circular massaging motion as my free hand pushes the crotch of her panties to the side. My kisses and tongue move dangerously close. I can sense the rise and fall of her chest and feel her heat on my face. Sandra works her T-shirt off, tosses it to the floor and pushes her bra up to free herself. One hand falls to cover my circling hand—the other pinches a nipple. A moan escapes her throat. "Please," she says without pretense.

I lift up to find a flush face. "Um, your bikini trim is slightly off-center. I believe I can straighten it out, shouldn't take more than five minutes or so."

She hits me with a pillow and I laugh.

"Just kidding, honey," I say before diving back in with abandon. I work two fingers in her as she arcs to meet my tongue. A hand grabs my head to pull me in tighter. I alternate a circling tongue with kisses, tender nibbles and a gentle suction of lips plus tongue. I arc my fingers in an effort to tickle my circling palm above—the only thing separating the two is her desire. She responds with a shudder, a fresh round of moans and repeats my name: "Steven Paul!"

I've found the combination that takes her to the place she wants to go. She arcs higher and convulses against my eager mouth. My hands drop to grab her by the cheeks of her ass and I squeeze and pull her in tight. With one final arc and shudder, her body collapses in my hands. I hold her in place a moment longer. My reaction to her reaction has me throbbing. I have to have her now.

I drop her to the mattress and hurriedly work her panties down and off. She spreads her legs and invites me in. I enter her without a guiding hand and bury myself deep inside her. She responds by wrapping her legs around me. We lock fingers and I push her hands above her head. I kiss her hard. A tear slides down her face. She returns my kiss with passion. Sandra feels like every young man's dreams. She contracts against my every thrust—the sensation is more than I can handle. It's my turn to call out her name: "Sandra, right now."

Sandra frees her hand and with legs and arms, she engulfs me tight. In a gush, I explode inside her.

She whispers in my ear, "Thank you."

I kiss her, catch my breath and roll off of her. I pant beside Sandra for a moment. I may have discovered what makes her tick. If sex gets better with age, I resign myself to the fact I may not see 18.

She wipes the sweat from my face with her retrieved shirt. She then wipes herself and laughs. "Ugh. Look, it's coming out. How much of your demon seed did you put in me?"

"Enough to tide you over for a little while."

She smiles. "I like the way your mustache tickled me."

I lay my hand protectively over her mound and gently stroke her clit. She hugs my arm.

"I hardly noticed," I tell her.

Sandra giggles. "I was really gettin' into it, huh?"

I believe I have just found the elusive and mystical G-spot. "Yeah, I started to panic, I thought for a minute there that you were not going to let me up for air."

"Sure you did," she says, "And by the way, my bikini trim is perfect... You play dirty, too. I wanted to scream when you pulled up short. You better be glad you got back down there, or you would have witnessed what a frustrated woman is capable of."

"I can imagine and after careful tongue measuring, I believe you are correct: your bikini trim is perfect."

Sandra sighs contently. "I'm glad you brought me back from Rio."

"And I can honestly say I am too. How about a beer?"

Sandra hops up. "Ten-four, captain."

We sip our beer as the ceiling fan in the spare bedroom dries our bodies. Totally sated, I drift off to sleep.

Chapter Twelve

A tickling foot rouses me. I groggily open my eyes to find Bonnie, with front paws propped on the bed, licking my left foot. I snap my fingers and Bonnie joins us on the bed. She excitedly inches forward with her rear in the air and her entire back half wagging.

"I see you made it home, Bonnie girl," I tell her. Bonnie nudges and works her nose under my hand, determined to have me scratch her behind the ears.

"Okay, girl, you win," I tell her.

Sandra stirs. "Huh?" she says as she yawns and stretches all the way down to her toes. "Oh," she sleepily comments, "I see Bonnie made it home. Where's Andy?"

"After catching you with the lights on in the nude with your legs spread, he fled."

"Huh?" She smiles. "No, he didn't."

"Scout's honor."

She stifles a yawn. "Yeah. Right. You probably weren't ever in the Scouts."

"That's where you're wrong, woman. Much like my judo lessons, I attended one time. The scouts taught me a valuable lesson, though, one cannot build a fire without matches, lighters, or magnifying glasses. Plus, my Judo robe makes a fine winter robe."

"So, that explains why you carry a lighter in almost every pocket. Hey, you know, we still need to change your bandages."

"You got it, girl. I imagine Andy's in the living room. Let's tell him we plan to leave tomorrow. We'll get him to call James in the morning about watching Bonnie."

"We still need to change the bandages. Or, that's why you carry lighters?"

I jump up and work my boxers loose from my jeans on the floor. I slip into my boxers and I'm attired. "You coming?"

Sandra rolls off the bed for an answer. "I'm going to jump in the shower first."

"You're not going to wait for me?"

"I'll take another one. I feel like dried sweat and icky."

She picks her clothes up from the floor and uses them to shield herself for the few steps necessary to make it to the bathroom.

"Don't forget to brush your teeth," I call after her. "I might decide to kiss you again later."

Sandra sticks her hand out of the bathroom and gives me the one-finger salute. She giggles as she pulls the door shut. I grab a beer from the mostly melted ice, change my mind, put it back in and take the whole bucket.

I find my bottle-opener Andy in the living room watching Johnny Carson and chewing on some beef jerky. I cringe just thinking about him opening bottles with his teeth. I've broken him of that habit, but I've given up hope of stopping him from crushing beer cans with his forehead. Anyhow, the first I solved by giving him a nice, key-chain opener. Even after that, though, it was challenging. I mean, how do you convince someone it's wrong to leave your keys in a Pinto. Now, I'm not exactly sure of this, so don't quote me, but I don't think you can even report a Pinto stolen.

Andy finally acknowledges me with a mouthful and a nod.

"Where did you get the jerky, Andy?"

He takes a minute to finish chewing. "I stopped at the store on the way over."

"You live three blocks away, Andy, and there are no stores on the way."

"Okay, so I found the jerky in a kitchen cabinet."

"So, you just lied to me."

Andy shrugs. "Yep, just like you always lie to me."

"I mostly only steer you wrong. There's a big difference. Plus, we have this tacit understanding that it's to be expected. You know the reason."

"I know your reason, to build my character. Well, the character you built just lied to you," Andy smugly says.

Hell, don't that suck. Could all my work be for naught? Should I try a different approach? Nah, I'll just have to hide my jerky better.

Having made an important decision, I make another: to drink another beer.

"You going to give me one of them beers?"

I smile. "We're out of beer."

He gets up from the recliner and gets his own. "So, when are we leaving? I told my parents that I, Jim and James are going to spend a few days at the beach."

"Tomorrow. Let's meet up around ten. When you leave, go to a payphone somewhere and call Jim. Tell him we'll meet in the woods behind your house. Also, call James and tell him that we need him to watch Bonnie if he can't go—"

"Why can't I call him from the house?"

"Can't chance the Feds listening in."

Andy downs most of his beer in one long pull and belches.

"Oh yeah. That makes sense."

Sandra enters the room wearing a long T-shirt she found somewhere. "Hey, Andy," she says while running a comb through her wet hair. "Why didn't you wake us?"

"Y'all looked like you were sleeping good."

"He was peeping, Sandra," I falsely accuse.

"Andy!" Sandra exclaims.

"I... I was not," he stammers and reddens some. "The... The door was open and the lights were on."

Sandra and I laugh. "It's okay, Andy," I say. "You were bound to see some real pussy one day. And it didn't even cost you a $20."

His "whatever" gets Sandra and me laughing again.

"Andy, you may not win any races, but you're still my dog." I like saying that. Actually, I like saying anything that has entertainment value.

"Is Big Blue still at your house, Andy?" Big Blue is the name of my big blue Igloo cooler.

"Yeah. Hey, I better head to the house. What are we taking with us?"

"Some clothes, pockets full of cash—if you intend to eat—our pistols, my good looks and charm and the lovely," I wink at Andy, "Sandra, since you now know what she looks like in the nude."

Andy hides his face behind his almost empty beer for a second before turning away and mumbling, "Okay."

"Oh, since we'll be in Florida, don't forget your Speedos."

"Very funny," Andy says as he snatches another beer from the bucket. "See you tomorrow," he says before stepping out of the living room entrance.

I eye Sandra suspiciously. "What do you have on under that T-shirt?"

She smiles. "Nothing."

"Damn. That's what I was afraid of," I say but mean "isn't life grand?"

For sanitary reasons, I have Sandra join me in the shower. Sandra makes sure I do not leave the shower until I'm squeaky clean and 300 calories lighter. Sandra re-bandages me and we return to the living room to snuggle and catch the day's late programming. Is it just me or does the word "snuggle" sound sappy? "Snuggle" to me almost implies payment for a bill owed. Just kidding. As a helpless romantic, I don't mind curling up with a warm body. Yes, I know it's "hopeless romantic," but you get the idea.

Chapter Thirteen

I awake to the morning sunshine in the eyes, with a crick in my neck and my back plastered to the vinyl couch. A thousand dust mites separate me from the source of the light. I have to piss like a Russian racehorse and that, my friend, is having to take some kinda piss.

I extricate myself and barely disturb Sandra in doing so. She groans and rolls to fill the void. Her T-shirt rides precariously high. I may have to wake her yet.

I water the horse and find one remaining clean Izod, yesterday's crumpled jeans, a pair of clean socks and boxers, my Nacona ostrich boots and Candy's Bud cap to round out today's attire.

I catch myself in the mirror and am reminded once again, I'm one handsome fucker. I grab my empty suitcase, throw in my Beretta 9 and Colt .45 and a toothbrush and toothpaste. With that my packing is done. I stuff my pockets and boots with nearly $9,000 in cash. My front pocket is reserved for a roll, as Cheryl would say, "that could choke a horse." Somehow, I now feel complete, but also wonder what Cheryl is up to? I really need to call her. I mean she did fulfill this young man's fantasy by giving it up on a well-lit billiard tabletop. It just doesn't get much better than that, now, does it?

I feel a stirring. Perhaps I should wake Sandra for her own good. I want her to have plenty of time to pack. Girls tend to take longer, you know. My guns clunk to the bottom of the suitcase as I pick it up and proceed to take it out to the TA.

Bonnie has been patiently eyeing me since we got up. "I see you, girl." I take a moment to scratch her behind the ears. She yawns and stretches with her rump in the air and then shakes it off. She bounds after me into the kitchen, where I proceed to dish her out a bowl of Alpo.

Chore completed, I continue to the car and nearly collide with Stacey Keys as I step out of the house. She pushes me back into the house.

"Going someplace, Steven Paul?" she asks as she kicks the door shut behind her and wraps her arms around me. "You're going to tell me everything, one way or another," she purrs in my ear.

I drop the suitcase. "Another," I croak and swallow.

She pushes me away and changes her tone. "But not that way." She says with a penetrating stare. "Where do you think you're going, Steven Paul?" she rephrases her question.

"I was going to say, to enter the foray that is my love life, thou shall have to take a number, Stacey," I say meaning I'd give my left nut to get a shot of that. I maintain my poker face.

Sandra walks in with a surprised look. "What's going on?"

"Stacey thought she could pick my brain by offering me a piece," I'm quick to point out.

Stacey's mouth drops open. "I did not—he's lying."

They eye each other for a minute, so I fill the void. I'm right partial to filling the voids. I offer my solution: "Y'all can fight over me."

Stacey reddens. "That's ridiculous, I'm not about to—"

Our laughter cuts her short.

"He's fucking with you, Stacey. I'm fixing to make some coffee. Would you like a cup?"

Stacey sighs and regains her composure. "Yes, please. He seems to always say the most inappropriate things."

I peek around to check her backside. "You know, you look pretty good in jeans, for an older chick."

She takes umbrage. "I'm not that old."

"Nor too old," I remind her with a grin.

"Should I choke him for you, Stacey? By the way," Sandra sticks out her hand, "I'm Sandra."

They shake.

"Whoo, I need to sit down for a sec," Stacey says. "I'm racking my brain trying to figure out what is going on. This is the house of a recent abduction. Steven Paul was in a shootout a week ago. Days ago, he's buzzing houses here and in West Lake in a plane without a license. Yesterday, he's taken in for questioning in conjunction with a millionaire's plane illegally entering U.S. airspace and now that same Steven Paul, our station's anonymous source, tells us that the plane was used in a raid to free the millionaire's daughter from a Rio de Janeiro villa that resulted in the death of the owner and others and sparked an international incident." She lets out her breath after such a long sentence. "I mean, excuse me, but what the fuck?"

I pretend to think it over and rub my chin. "Hmm. Put that way, Stacey, it does give one pause."

Sandra giggles. "I'll sum it up for you, Stacey. He's crazy."

"Yet, all these things are happening," Stacey continues. "And yes, it does give one pause." Stacey rubs her temples. "Where are you going? Should I dare to ask or just wait until it becomes news?"

"On a secret mission Stacey and if I told you, I'd have to kill you." I never get to say that enough.

"Figures."

"Actually, Stacey, we're off to try and find a wayward child and attempt to bring her home. I doubt it will be newsworthy and what are the odds of sparking another international incident?"

Little did I know, pretty good.

"Well, I guess you're right," Stacey concedes. "I don't see how you can get in trouble doing that."

I open my palms to her. "And there you go, Stacey."

The microwave pings to indicate the water in the cups is ready. Sandra retrieves them along with a jar of instant Folger's and sets it all on the table.

"Milk and sugar, Stacey?"

"Please."

I take my cup and pull up a protective chair next to Stacey, forcing Sandra to take another. "I like my coffee like my women—"

"Hot and black. That's an old one, Steven Paul."

I shake my head and tsk, tsk her. "I was going to say sweet, Stacey." Although hot and black will work too, possibly?

She fumbles with her spoon—it clinks against the cup. "Oh." She hides her embarrassment by taking a drink of her coffee. We wait her out.

"What?"

"I imagine under that tough newswoman exterior, you're as sweet as can be and that's why I'm kind of sweet on you, Stacey. I can see our relationship continuing to blossom."

"He does talk about you quite a lot, Stacey. Ultimately, you'll come around to his way of thinking. We all do." Sandra manages to say with a straight face.

Stacey does a double-take and focuses back on Sandra. "You for real? You're setting women back a hundred years thinking like that."

"But the sex is so, so rewarding." Sandra takes a sip of coffee.

I shrug and pretend to shyly pick at a nail. "Some say it is true, Stacey."

Stacey looks like she's watching a tennis match, looking from one of us back to the other. "Okay, I guess. When will you be back and when will you grant me a non-live interview?"

"We still have to find time to squeeze in our first date. We'll play it by ear from there. You know a non-live feed will wreak havoc on my spontaneity."

"Havoc on his spontaneity," Sandra echoes.

"You're having fun with this, aren't you, Sandra?"

Sandra and I laugh. A small smile creeps up on Stacey's face. Yep, I feel her defenses are in jeopardy. Hey, crazier things have happened. Mostly in the last week and a half, but I take things in stride and I'm one quick to mature, remember?

"Well, ladies, I hate to break this little shindig up, but I have a damsel in distress to locate and snatch from the clutches of evil. It's what I do, Stacey—it's who I am. Sandra, get dressed and packed, so we can hit the road."

"I thought you said something about a wayward child," Stacey says correcting me.

"Nothing gets by you, does it, Stacey? If you must know, she's a beautiful 18-year-old, so she does qualify as a 'damsel in distress' by my definition. As all beauty does."

"You're too much," Stacey says but this time she laughs good-naturedly. Her laugh and subsequent smile light the entire kitchen.

"Nice meeting you, Stacey. I'll leave you to your fate while I pack and dress."

"You think I'll be safe?" Stacey jokes.

"Well, he's already undressed you with his eyes and you lived."

"Thanks, that's reassuring."

We all share a laugh before Sandra takes her leave to pack and dress.

"She's very understanding," Stacey comments.

"Yep," I concur. "Not bad for a baby sister."

"What! Baby sister, but she said—"

I hold up both hands. "I'm fucking kidding, Stacey."

Stacey wipes imaginary sweat from her brow. "Whoo, thank God."

We hear laughing from somewhere in the house and Sandra yells out, "He's probably claiming right about now that I'm his 'baby sister' or something."

"She knows you well. How long have you two known each other?"

"Platonically for several days now. I found her in Rio and brought her back."

"Platonically, right. I'm not biting this time."

I turn my chair to completely face her, cross my legs, steeple my fingers, place them over chin and mouth and contemplatively look her over for a long, long minute. She begins to fidget under my intense scrutiny before I lower my hands, cock my head some, lean into her space and whisper, "What really brought you here this morning, Stacey?" The fact is that I don't believe I could ever get anywhere with the woman sitting across from me who's spawned many a fantasy. But, on the other hand, I'm not too old to hope.

She nervously tucks hair behind an ear that doesn't need tucking. "You know... You know. For the scoop."

I lean back, smile and totally bluff. "Stacey, Stacey. I don't believe you."

Her too-fast response sparks real hope in me. "It's true. I swear, Steven Paul."

Yep, I believe the glass is half full. Maybe it's time to take her shopping. That and ply her with plenty of drinks so I can continue to hone my special art of seduction. Hey, don't knock it if you haven't tried it. Here's a failsafe method I truly believe in and espouse: if you ask ten and only one will go, ask 20. Play the odds enough, people, and you're bound to literally come out on top. Well, that is, if that's the position that floats your boat. Yes, I know, the wisdom I've amassed in so few short years. Case in point, as Francis Bacon so wisely put it hundreds of years ago, "a wise man will make more opportunities than he finds." Deep, huh?

"Steven Paul, you're staring. You're making me nervous."

"Well then, never let them see you sweat, that's the ticket." I don't know who might've said that, but it sounds like something Patton would say. If he didn't, he should have.

"What?"

"Never mind, but, Stacey, you are beautiful in your uncertainty."

Sandra cheerfully rejoins us toting two suitcases.

"Done. I found another suitcase in the spare bedroom."

"Thank God. But how did you manage to squeeze everything in only two?" I ask in mock seriousness.

"Well, actually one's completely empty, but I'll be needing it for souvenirs, of course. You know how we women are, always planning ahead." She says it as if that somehow explains things. It must because Stacey nods her head in agreement.

"We can shop for souvenirs on our downtime from rescuing. You know, maybe even between meals and in lieu of sleep," I say summing it up the best I can. I might as well be talking to myself for all the good it does.

"Well, hopefully, the extra suitcase will be sufficient," Sandra continues.

"Hello, anyone home? I was being facetious, sarcastic," I say knowing all the while that Sandra is far from being dense. I put my hands to my knees and rise. I don't move, which causes awkwardness as Stacey goes to stand. I can feel the heat coming off her firm body. Well, I might be imagining that, but I'm not imagining my enhanced cleavage view. Some fine viewing, I'm here to tell you. I notice things like this. It's what I do—who I am. You know, as a fallback career. I am not imagining this either. Whatever kind of perfume she's wearing, it's mighty enticing.

Stacey pulls a card from her hip pocket. I watch the movement, getting stuck on the crotch area until Sandra nudges me.

"Here, I wrote my home number down," Stacey says.

It's my turn to say "Of course," and smile. She hands me her card and it goes straight into the must-do file in my left rear pocket. It fits comfortably with the other cards and numbers, in my must-do file. Are they accumulating, or what? Pretty lucky.

Somewhat flustered from our nearness, Stacey steps back. Well, okay, maybe it's my imagination that she looks flustered, but I get to tell it as I see it.

"Well, now that you know where I live, don't be a stranger," I say with longing.

"Sure, call me when you get back. Sandra, it was nice meeting you. Well, I'm off. Be careful, Steven Paul. You too, Sandra."

"Likewise," Sandra says with sincerity. Man, you got to love this girl, I tell myself, thinking of Sandra again. Can't neglect thinking about the sure one in the hand. Overall, though, things are looking up. Wait till the boys hear about my latest visitor. They'll be mightily happy for me in a begrudging kind of way.

We follow Stacey out and wave goodbye as she pulls away. She's driving what I consider to be a classic: an early '60s Buick Wildcat, which I believe has a 340 under the hood. It amazes me just how fast those cars actually are.

"What did you do to her to get her so flustered?" Sandra asks.

Flustered? Did I hear that correctly?

"You noticed too, did you?" I say. "The sexual tension in the air was so thick you could cut it with a knife." She might have noticed the bulge in my jeans, huh?

"That's what I was thinking," Sandra says and we both laugh.

I pop the trunk and toss our luggage in. I round to the passenger side, open the door and tell Bonnie to load up. She jumps straight to the back. "Good girl," I tell her, wishing we could take her along. She's one good dog. If it weren't for her, my life wouldn't have taken the fortuitous change for the better that it has. Well, excluding the gunshot wound, a couple cracked ribs I barely notice anymore, the gash in the brow and the still throbbing broken knuckle. Pretty lucky, huh, that none of the injuries are life-threatening. Man, I'm on a roll, on cloud nine. Does it get any better than this?

I close the door for Sandra, jump in on my side, slam the door and crank and rev my Trans Am. I back into the street, slide to a stop and roil the tires heading into the S. I note Sandra grabs the sissy strap above the glove box. Believe it or not, it's a rare option on the Trans Am that you seldom see. In 60 seconds, we're turning into the easement next to Andy's. I pull us in next to the Bonneville, which is of course parked next to the late Firebird. I get out and readjust the bulge in my jeans. Somehow, my choke-a-horse roll of cash and two Bic lighters shifted uncomfortably toward the front. Huh, I wonder how that happened? I hope Stacey didn't notice and misconstrue my obviously inadvertent oversight.

"I was wondering if you were ever going to straighten your pocket out," Sandra says before we go to join the awaiting crew.

"Daddy's home," I gleefully announce and deploy my shit-eating grin.

Jim shakes his head. "Sandra," Jim says, "whatever you're doing to him needs to stop. That Bud cap he's wearing is already on its last notch."

"And, children of the corn, good morning to you as well," I say. "And, Jimbo, the look of envy is not becoming. I believe Wendell L. Wilkie got it right when he said, "We hate no people and covet no people's lamb."

"And I'm the lamb," the grinning Sandra chimes in.

"Oh, boy, she's lost to us already," Jim says and everyone laughs as Bonnie, Smokey and Rosie sniff each other's asses like they haven't seen each other in days. Boys will be boys—girls will be girls, and I guess dogs will be dogs. It makes sense, doesn't it?

The ever-timid James makes his own announcement with downcast eyes. "I can watch Bonnie, but um... I can't do it at Candy's. My parents saw the latest news and they decided...."

"We can't play together anymore," I finish for him.

"Well... Um... They said you were... You know... Trouble."

"Misunderstood, but trouble? Jeez, James, that really hurts. I hope you set them straight."

"I... I wanted to."

We all laugh at his discomfort.

"Will I get a cut this time?" James is brave enough to ask.

"Not likely," Andy volunteers. "He decided we'd take on this mission per boner."

Incredulously, we all stare at Andy.

"Andy, it's 'pro bono,' and it's for a good cause."

"'Cause she's 18 and foxy as hell, is what I think and I still think Steven was thinking like he usually does, 'per boner,' like I said."

"Wow, not bad, Andy. You actually put together a decent joke." I'm not quick to give praise. It's contrary to the chain of command.

"Show James the pictures, Steve," Andy says.

"Shit. I left the damn things at the house."

Sandra smiles. "While you were entertaining Stacey, I put them in my suitcase."

Everyone keys in on "Stacey." The cat's out of the bag. I puff up proud as a peacock. I ignore their curiosity.

"And being so mindful is why I decided to make Sandra our treasurer."

"But you barely know her," Andy objects.

"But I know her bare, Andy," I counter.

"And you've known me for years," Andy finishes.

"Well Andy, my friend, sometimes it's not who you know, but who you blow." I smile. "Still want her job?"

"Fuck that!"

We all get a good laugh at Andy's expense.

"Um... About Bonnie?"

"I hear you, James," I say. "How about $100 a day or about $50 more than you'll be earning after you graduate from junior college."

"Like he'll ever graduate," Jim says with a grin.

"I'll graduate. From a real college, that is."

"Well, if you girls are all ready, I say we roll out. Hit the hammer, boys."

From a huddle, we all bump fists including Sandra. Our mission is officially underway.

Chapter Fourteen

Sandra shakes the Bonneville's keys before me as we all cross the short distance back to where the cars are parked. The woods are dense enough in cedar, scrub and stunted oaks that my vehicle will go undetected. For the most part, we're some of the few that venture into the woods at all. Andy flushes a covey of quail, scaring the shit out of us all. The little fuckers wait until you come right up on them.

"Shit. That scared the shit out of me," Sandra says clutching her heart in one hand and passing me the keys with the other.

"Forgot these keys too, didn't you?"

That I did. I take them and pop the massive trunk on my ride as Jim checks out the scrapes and recent damage to the passenger side.

"Didn't hurt the girl much at all, did it, Steve-O?"

And, in fact, it hadn't and everybody now knows how the damage was done, so I don't bother with a reply. I retrieve Sandra and my bags from the TA and add them to Jim and Andy's carry-ons. I pet and say my goodbyes to Bonnie and promise her I shall return. We all pile in my big ride. Jim opts for shotgun, Sandra centers between us and Andy gets to ride in the back with Big Blue. He will dispense from within when Big Blue is properly stocked.

The Bonneville fires right off. I turn the AC to the max to deal with the stagnant and suffocating hot interior.

"Steve-O, the cops aren't looking for this vehicle, are they?"

"Nah, Jimbo. Williams drew the investigation and the investigation officially hit a dead end."

In gear, a spin and we're off. "Cool. Williams turned out to be all right. I don't know how in the fuck you managed to get a cop to watch your back, but you fucking did it."

Sandra punches the stereo button and cranks up "L.A. Woman" by the Doors. Some decent jam. We stop at the Safeway on the corner of Exposition and Lake Austin Blvd and the sight of the "strawberry douche" incident. Needless to say, it was funny as shit and it involved Andy. I'll have to tell those that don't already know the story about it sometime.

"I'll wait in the car," Andy says.

Jim turns to eye him. "Chances are no one will even recognize you. Hell, it's been a week now. What do you think, Steve-O?"

"Long forgotten," I say in my most reassuring voice. A break in the brief conversation makes me wonder if Andy actually believes us.

"You think?" He nibbles at the bait.

Using my most revered question, Jim asks him: "Would I lie to you, Andy?"

"Umm... I've never actually caught you, but Steve's been a bad influence on you."

"Andy, if Steve-O told me which stock to buy, do you believe I would listen?" Jim says dangling the bait again.

"Nah, I guess you're right. Fuck it, let's shop."

Andy swallows hook, line and sinker.

We all exit the big Pontiac. Out of earshot, Sandra whispers, "Recognize him for what?"

I nudge her and whisper back, "Later."

I take her hand as we near the store's entrance, for her appearance's sake. Wouldn't want the store's patrons and employees thinking she's easy just because she accompanies a group of male teens. I'm always mindful of others' appearances.

I maximize Andy's exposure. "Go fetch a buggy, Andy."

Sandra squeezes my hand inquiringly. I wink and mouth "patience."

Even though it's a different time of day than before, I notice some familiar faces. We may be in luck. We cruise the snack aisle. I snatch items off the shelf and blindly toss them over my shoulder for Andy to catch as he trails us. I clear a whole row of peppered Jerky and snatch up a glass jar of Penn-Rose pickled sausages. I hear the cart crash as I lob the heavy jar the way of the other items. Who says shopping isn't fun? Sandra giggles at my side and tosses a couple of items of her own. We round the corner and buzz the beer aisle. This could become perilous. Only kidding. Wouldn't do for me to throw an arm out on such a heavy item. One often needs two good arms when it comes to rescuing. "Stay focused on the cause," is one of my mottos. Another is "Only high-dollar beer from here on out." Being a wine connoisseur and aficionado, I select a couple bottles of this year's vintage, with fizz and with an undemanding twist-off cap. Yep, it's Boone's Farm "Strawberry Hill" for the crew and me. Does it get any better than this? Sparing no expense, we load up on Bud and Tecate as well.

Still leading the way, I steer Sandra and the rest of the trailing crew of two down the personal hygiene aisle. I peruse the items. I feel tension behind me. I bring us to a stop and turn to face Andy. His face has begun to redden.

"Andy, perhaps you have a recommendation?" I nod toward the array of douches. "Which do you find to be most effective?"

"How... How would I know?" Andy stammers.

Jim and I laugh. Sandra giggles but has no clue what the inside joke is. Still, she wants in on it.

"Can't you help a girl out, Andy?" she asks in all sweetness.

Andy barrels past us with the cart and rounds the corner. I snatch up a strawberry-scented douche and give chase. Sliding past the mouth of the aisle I yell out, "Andy! You forgot something!" Yelling out "all help to aisle three," wouldn't have garnered more attention. I let loose of the douche with a high-arching lob. Andy looks like a deer caught in the headlight as the douche seemingly in slow motion turns end-over-end only to bounce off his shoulder and land prominently displayed in the cart on top of our other purchases. Laughing, Sandra and Jim come to a stop behind me.

"Andy!" I yell out again, "bring the cart and douche over here. This looks like the shortest line."

A resounding chorus of laughter fills the store as Andy abandons ship and flees. Sandra doubles over in laughter and falls to her knees beside me. Jim staggers off to catch his breath. I shrug and ask the onlookers, "Wonder what got into him?"

I pull the only adult among us from the floor and we grab our cart and join the nearest queue. I wink at the cashier who's around my age. I'm rewarded with a blush. I pluck one of each of the displayed news rags and add them to our purchases. Got to keep up on the world news. I remember one of my favorite Sun articles: "Two-Headed Man Sings in Stereo!" Doesn't get more informative than that. I peel off a crisp hundred from my roll and pass it to our in-house contributor to the delinquency of minors so that she may pay. Jim informs our still blushing cashier we need two bags of ice as well. She rings us up.

"You're that guy from the television, aren't you?" Tami asks. Her nametag reads Tami.

I wink. "Some say it is true, Tami."

She giggles. "Would you like your trading stamps, sir?"

"In lieu of your home phone number? Never."

With a shaky hand, she mistakenly returns the change to me. "I get off at noon," she softly says.

"Sorry, not today, Tami. See you around," I tell her.

Sandra tugs at my arm. "Come on, lover boy. Tami, I just can't take him anywhere with me these days."

Another tug gets me started in the right direction. I whistle an upbeat tune, one of the only ones I know—The Andy Griffith

Show tune. I snag the two bags of ice on the way out. We head to the car.

"Does Andy have a douche phobia or what?" Sandra asks in earnest.

"Not until we convinced him that it would remove black shoe polish from his face. Before you ask: he blackened his face for a night mission."

"Oh. Did it work?"

"Surprisingly, yes."

We come up on the Bonneville. "There you are, Andy. Where the hell did you go?"

"Thanks, very funny. I can't go anywhere with you."

Hmm, I think that over. I believe I've heard that somewhere else, but I'll be damned if I can remember where. "Look," I say, "I did it for you so you'll already have a douche if we go on another night mission. Plus, it's better to be embarrassed by people you're liable to run into regularly than to be embarrassed in front of total strangers."

Andy looks over at Jim. "Makes sense to me," Jim says.

Andy scowls. "Well, you'll never convince me of that."

"All right, Andy, I'll try from here on out to be more sensitive to your feelings. Now would you hurry up and ice the beer. After your latest spectacle, I'd just as soon not be seen out here in public with you," I say, using a nice variation of his own words.

"Aw fuck you," he says as he pulls Big Blue from the rear seat and begins to ice the beer. I stow most of the mountain of snacks in the trunk and out of harm's way: Andy. I keep out several bags of jerky for a late breakfast and a healthy source of protein. Now, I didn't make this up, but breakfast is said to be the most important meal of the day. And, as we all know, "a beer a day, will keep the doctor away." You can quote me on that.

"Andy, don't forget to return the buggy."

"I don't think so. Have your treasurer return it."

"Gosh, Andy," I say. "So hostile. With that tone, one would almost think you blame Sandra for waking up last week with panties on your head and your nails done!"

"Do you have to tell her about that too?"

"I guess not. Well, children of the corn, onward through the fog." "Onward through the fog" is the slogan of Austin's landmark and finest head shop, Oat Willies. Speaking of which, as we get into the car I ask, "I hope someone remembered to bring the weed?"

Sandra raises her hand as she slides to the center making room for me to enter.

"I just don't know what I would do without her, Andy?"

Andy mumbles something unintelligible but I'm sure it's another "fuck you." One of his more astute phrases.

I crank her up and back out. Okay, this time we are on the way for real. It's nice to wake up each day with such a noble purpose in life. And a car full of camaraderie is refreshing as well. I hear the "pssst" of a can being opened. It must be noon somewhere and beer is an important part of a balanced diet. And by God, an "abstainer is a weak person who yields to the temptation of denying himself pleasure." Ambrose Bierce said that. Thus, I shall not abstain today. "A beer, Andy, my friend." See, I can play nice when need be.

"Fuck it," Jim says, "give me one too."

"Fuck it, me too," Sandra says as she pulls a small bag of weed from her pocket.

I pull out on Lake Austin and we head east. Soon on our right is Lake Austin and the hike and bike trail. It always amazes me the number of people out during the week and during work hours. "Don't these people have jobs?" I ask no one in particular.

"Technically, none of us have real jobs now, Steve-O," Jim observes, "but I can't complain about our earnings."

We come up on I-35 and take the north ramp to 290 East. We could have taken 71 to Houston but I prefer 290—so, 290 it will be.

Andy taps me on the shoulder. "Did you bring a map, Steve?" I tap my head. "It's all up here. We're going to hang a left on I-10 after Houston and then a right on IH-75 south. You want someone to write that down for you in case I let you drive at some point?"

I punch a preset on the radio and change the station to goat-roping CASE FM and we sing along to George Jones's "White Lightning." The Possum—got to love him. Sandra works on rolling a joint as I take the exit leading to 290. Weed's falling out of each end and it's evident we'll end up with a "humpback." I smile at the sight of her concentration. The tip of her tongue is sticking slightly out the side of her lips as she puts the last of the roll to her creation. She licks the gum. Somehow, she manages to make rolling a joint look sexy. I brush her thigh free of debris and then lay my hand there.

I take a right and soon we're merging with the 290 East traffic. The Bonneville, the tank, is a cruiser and I open her up some. Not much between here and Houston. We could make a quick stop at Manor Downs and place a few bets, but I'm not into betting on the ponies. Put a pool stick in my hand and the betting's on. I've also been known to be mean with a deck of cards, whatever the game. The card gene I inherited from my dad and I grew up playing with the adults from as far back as I can remember.

I take her up to 90. The road is straight with only an occasional hill or two. The sky is clear and bright. Up ahead, the heat rises in waves. The AC blows cold. Sandra fires up the doobie from the car's lighter. Blue smoke swirls away from the AC Vents as Sandra exhales a choking lung full. She wipes the tears from her eyes after blindly passing me the joint. I thump her on the back as she doubles over trying to catch a new breath.

We all laugh at her because we've all been there before. In her defense, it is a decent grade of Mexican that I got from my high school buddy, Felix, who was also part of our Rio crew.

The doobie burns slow and it slowly turns brown with all the resin the burning weed produces. It doesn't take long before we're a car full of giggling idiots tearing into packages of beef jerky. Life is good—the miles blur by.

We make it to nearly Brenham before needing to make a fuel and piss stop. I don't know what it is about beer. I can hold a few before nature calls, but once I've taken that first leak, we will be having to stop every 30 minutes or so. There's an antique shop next to the station and it is more than us curious can stand. Actually, there are a number of antique shops along this stretch.

We enter the old clapboard house. We find the place musty and packed to the ceiling in places with antiques, mostly of the western era. An old and cobwebbed moose mount catches my eye. I want it as bad as I'll want to make the next piss stop. The only place it will fit in the car is Andy's lap. He spots the glint in my eye.

"Oh, hell no, forget it," Andy protests. "I'm not riding with that thing."

As much as I hate it, I have to let him make it this time. I settle for a set of multi-colored longhorn bull horns and enough baling wire for Andy to mount it to the front of our ride. Still high, for now, it makes for a hell of an accessory. I'd go out and help Andy wire it on if it wasn't so damn hot outside. Since there's no nuts and bolts and instructions involved, I think he'll be fine. With approving stares and a round of laughter, we hit the road again.

"You did secure the horns?" I ask Andy out of curiosity.

I hear a huff behind me. "Of course."

We make good time, albeit for the frequent piss stops. After a long stretch filled only with music and the periodic scanning for new stations, Jim finally decides to broach a subject that's probably been eating at him since we met up this morning.

"So, what's up with Stacey? I'm assuming Sandra was referring to Stacey Keys this morning?"

"Well, of course, the one and only," I say with pride. "She nearly tackled me at the door, wrapped her arms around me and huskily whispered in my ear 'I'll get you one way or another.'"

"Nah. No way," Jim says. "Sandra, did she say that?"

"Well, I'm not sure what she said before I walked in on them, but she sure seemed flustered when I did. Even then, my presence didn't stop her from giving him her home phone number and telling him to call as soon as he got back."

I can feel Jim shaking his head on the other side of Sandra. "I don't fucking understand it. I mean, I wouldn't even buy a used car from Steve-O and someone like Stacey Keys stops by and gives him her home phone number."

I dig in my back pocket as we hit the Louisiana state line, dig out my ever-growing stack of four phone numbers and wave them in Jim's face. "Don't forget Brandy's, Cheryl's and Jennifer's. Not to mention Sandra here, whom I need not call, but merely follow to the bedroom."

"Merely follow to the bedroom," Sandra echoes.

"And ruin for all mankind," Jim says.

Sandra and I laugh. The uneven rectangles of cement that make up Louisiana's roads create a rhythmic thump that reverberates throughout our ride as we continue to roar along. We hit a bridge that must be 40 miles long. The Spanish moss-laden cypresses make for some interesting viewing. I imagine all the fish in the gator-infested water, the nutria and all the other flora and fauna found in the Louisiana swamps.

"Who the fuck is Jennifer?" Jim finally asks.

"Nobody of import, just some hardy, tanned, lithe, soon-to be-senior at our high school. Oh, you might recognize her, even though you're not part of our clique, as playing on our school tennis team."

"That Jennifer, you're kidding? And, you're not part of that clique either."

"Well, keep your head buried in the sand if you must, but she happens to be dying to go out with me too." Actually, as you may recall, she's waiting until her 18th birthday, because her dad threatened to kill one of us if he caught us together. I felt it prudent for her sake to wait out the year. This is of course on a need-to-know basis and Jim need not know.

"God have mercy on her soul," Jim pronounces. He must feel strongly on the subject.

We exit the bridge down to the tiger station to fuel up and to empty our bladders. I remind Andy to keep his hands out of the tiger cages. I'm just the protective type. Plus, he needs both hands to cipher. I have to be ever mindful of his future, as well. It might be right difficult to bus tables with a hand missing.

We buy a half a dozen dried 'gator heads and strategically place them throughout the Bonneville's interior. I buy myself a small 'gator-claw key chain just for the hell of it. I find it too bad they don't have a 'gator briefcase for sale to hold all my money.

We hit the road smoking—smoking another joint, that is. I forget why we needed to smoke another joint. I believe the government might have a theory on that.

We hit straight open road between bridges. I step on the gas a bit more. The sound of the open road is soothing. Sandra goes to pass me the joint when in a flash of an eye the horns disappear from view followed by a bang and the steering wheel being wrenched from my hand.

Sandra pierces my ear with a hair-curling shriek as I lay into the brakes and in a protesting scream of rubber, we go into an all-out, uncontrollable spin. Unbelted, we bounce off each other like pinballs as the spin takes us across the medium, the wheels throwing up a cloud of dust, grass and debris.

Still spinning, we careen through oncoming traffic, but somehow manage to cross unscathed, finally coming to a dust-settling stop in the far side ditch. My heart's thumping. Man, what a ride.

A chorus of expletives fills our ride. The mood quickly changes to one of exhilaration upon the realization we somehow narrowly avoided death. Upon further reflection, we all turn toward Andy, who's wearing most of the cooler water and has one crushed beer can in his hand.

I sum up our thoughts: "Wonder what happened, Andy?"

"Low-grade baling wire," he offers.

"Sounds logical to me." My ear is still ringing from Sandra's screams. The interior of the car smells like burned rubber. The cars on the highway keep whizzing right on by. Well, that's one quick way to lose a buzz: spin out of control at 90 mph plus. Luckily, we weren't on the bridge. My lucky streak continues.

"Well," I say, "look at the bright side, Andy, you won't get much wetter changing the tire."

Still clutching her heart, Sandra says, "that scared the shit out of me. I saw my life flash before my eyes when we bounced into oncoming traffic and I knew that was the end."

We all step out to survey the damage. The left front tire is shredded and the rim is fucked, but otherwise we're okay. I look up under her after opening the trunk for Andy. Clumps of dirt and grass are wedged throughout the underside. No big deal. It's all biodegradable and will disappear over time.

"Double-time, Andy, we need to get out of here before a cop rolls up on us. I'd hate to see you get a ticket."

He leans into it and breaks one of the lugs loose. "Why would I get a ticket? I wasn't driving."

"You know that, I know that, we know that, but it's what the cop believes that counts. This is a democracy and we remember you were driving."

Andy wipes the sweat from his brow and mumbles something.

"We'll be in the car," I tell him. "It's hot out here."

Still relieved to be alive, we laugh at Andy before climbing back into the car. What are friends for?

"Shouldn't you help him?" Sandra asks.

"I did already. I made sure he was turning the lugs the right direction."

"I'm going to double check the lugs just for the hell of it," Jim decides. Jim leans over the seat. "Who wants a beer?"

"I do, I do," Sandra and I echo, both raising our hands. We sip our beer and enjoy the car's cold interior.

"Jimbo, how did you like the way I avoided the oncoming traffic?"

Jim smirks. "Right. We got lucky. You had nothing to do with it."

"To an untrained eye, I suppose, maybe." I honk the horn to speed Andy up. "But I called for divine intervention and the big man upstairs came through for me. I clearly remember saying 'Oh, God,' but believe what you will, Jimbo."

Jim takes a pull from his beer. "I will."

"You know, Jimbo, I believe the Feds are going to do another round and lower the prime rate another half-point to try and jumpstart the economy. If this economy doesn't start to show gains this third quarter, I believe we'll be seeing a peanut farmer as our next president."

"What are the odds of that?" Jim asks.

"Vegas is giving 12-to-1 right now. I'm thinking really hard on dropping a couple of grand on it just for the hell of it."

The trunk slams. Andy comes over to rap on my window wanting in. His hands are black with brake dust and a long streak divides his left cheek. I reluctantly let him in. I shake my head disapprovingly.

"Did you have to get so dirty, Andy?" I disgustingly spit out "Andy."

"Fuck you."

We all laugh.

I launch dirt and grass as I get in the throttle to take the ditch at an angle and take advantage of a break in traffic to shoot across the double lanes, then the medium. We hit 10 East with wheels spinning. We're en route once again.

Chapter Fifteen

We cross the mighty Mississippi into Mississippi. Looking back, it's one of the longest words I ever learned to spell—in the first grade, that is. After that, I just sat next to someone I believed could spell well. I've been a strong B student ever since.

"That was a badass bridge," Sandra comments. "Hey, I've got to hit the lady's room, like really bad."

"We'll stop in Biloxi," I say.

"I don't think I can make it that far."

I was only kidding. I exit and pull into the first station. There's a small fish shack next door. After relieving ourselves, fueling and buying some "I love Mississippi" mugs, we go to check out the shack. It sure smells good. I order ten pounds of fried shrimp and a basket of fries and we take the time to eat at an oak-shaded picnic table. The food is delicious and sating. We make mincemeat out of the grub.

I let Jim take over driving for a while. I'm not quite yet ready to see what Andy would do with more than four cylinders. Statistically, he's a better driver than I, but that's not very comforting.

"So, what's the plan, Steve-O?"

"We can drive all the way through, or stop a little over halfway, say Lake City, Florida. Rest up there and head out again in the morning."

"I vote we stop," Sandra says. "That Louisiana uneven pavement got my ass numb."

I squeeze her thigh. "I believe I can massage that back to life."

"He almost sounds like he's doing you a favor," Jim says.

I shrug. "I do what I can. If it makes you feel any better, Jimbo, I'll derive no personal pleasure in restoring Sandra's glow."

"My glow," Sandra says.

Jim shakes his head. "A match made in heaven."

We laugh at Jim's sarcasm.

"So young, yet so cynical, Jimbo," I say. I love saying that.

"Jimbo, Woody Allen said just this year, 'the lioness and the calf shall lie down together, but the calf won't get much sleep.'"

"Hmm, okay, I'm not sure I'm following you?"

"I'm the calf," I say.

"And I'm the lioness," Sandra says.

"Oh, brother," Jim says

Actually, I took a little liberty with the saying. Allen really said "lion," so I had to adapt it to work. Work how, you wonder? Me too.

190

I poke Sandra in the side, causing her to jerk. Ticklish, I conclude. To fuck with Jim, I poke her again in rapid succession and start her into a giggling fit. She goes into a defensive mode. Despite a stab in my own side, I pull the struggling Sandra into my lap.

"Time to sit in Daddy's lap," I announce.

Jim groans. Sandra and I lock lips as she squirms sideways in my lap and her feet kick Jim in the leg. I think we're embarrassing Jim.

"Geez, get a room, already," he says before turning up the radio.

Sandra is having as much fun with it as I am. She comes up for air and screams "Oh God!"

It's too much for even me. I break into a fit of laughter to which Sandra joins in. Life really is good. Sandra moves back to the center. I lift my shirt to make sure I haven't sprung a leak. Sandra answers my unasked question.

"Yes, I brought the stuff to deal with your gunshot." I forgot most everything this morning, I realize. Perhaps, it was I that was flustered this morning? Nah, I was too busy focusing on the big picture to worry about the small details. I'm big on focusing on the big picture.

Traffic in Biloxi and a pit stop slow us down some, but we're soon back to burning up the open road. Not long thereafter, we hit the Alabama state line and the traffic associated with Mobile. Mobile is supposed to have a hell of a nightlife. Someday I hope to check it out. The beer is going down well and none of us are feeling any pain. We collectively decide to forego another joint. For me, that would be the nail in the coffin. Jim brought along some of the cocaine with him that was left over from our Rio adventure, but we didn't do any of it then and are unlikely to do any this time around either. I'm hesitant to get back on that horse. Our one, all-night binge proved to me that it might be too easily liked.

It seems like it takes forever but we finally hit the Florida line. We let out a hallelujah and bump cans. I know one thing: it makes me appreciate the convenience of flying. Perhaps, subconsciously, that is why I took up flying? Nope. That wasn't it. I remember now—I took up flying to impress Candy. It was a spur of the moment decision that almost landed me in jail, but for Detective Williams's intervention. I'm still liable to receive some FAA fines over the incident. Well, Candy has the kind of beauty that one would put out his own eye to impress. And that, my friends, is some kind of beauty.

We piss-stop in Pensacola, fuel and re-ice the cooler. We buy some "I Love Florida" mugs. Yeah, I know. I blame it on over-imbibing. I blame a lot of things on that. At least I haven't woken up with a "two" yet. I shudder at the thought, figuratively. I'll save the literally for if and when that ever happens. "It wasn't my fault, she followed me home." I try the excuse in my head. I'm not sure, but that one seems a little lame.

"You're zoning, Steven Paul."

Sandra's voice brings me back to earth. "It's called 'introspection' Sandra, and I use it to channel my thoughts."

Jim chuckles. "He's full of shit, Sandra. He's probably working on lame excuses to get out of something he's likely to do in the future."

Dammit, Jim is sometimes uncanny in his perception. Could I be that shallow? Nah, it was a lucky guess. He was just throwing something out there to see if it would stick.

I chuckle with him. "Jimbo, you're so naïve. Why use a lame excuse when a perfectly good lie will suffice? I'm merely internally honing my skills should I ever decide to practice law without a license."

Jim chuckles again. "Now that I can believe."

"He's good at lying," Andy pipes in from the peanut gallery.

"Sandra," I say, "Andy's still hoping he'll turn 18 before the election so he can vote for Jimmy Carter. Andy's a closet 'peanut farmer.'"

"I am not," Andy protests.

"Well, I know it's a 'closet' something or another. Give me a minute. It will come to me. Andy, tell Sandra your excuse for having hundreds of 'Vote Carter' signs in your yard."

"He also had so many Carter stickers on his car that you couldn't even tell what kind of car the Rat Mobile was," Jim adds.

"They weren't mine."

"Save it for the jury, Andy—save it for the jury," I say.

We all laugh, except Andy of course.

Actually, very few 'Vote Carter' signs are to be found in Tarrytown and dammit if the vandals won't stop pinching ours. We might be too young to vote, but one's never too young to be politically active. Mother Dearest is right proud of her NRA sticker on her car—until she notices it, that is.

We're eating up the highway and coming up fast on IH-75, also known as "Cocaine Alley" and Lake City, Florida. The dash clock says 10:00 p.m., so it's now 11:00 in Lake City. If we check in quickly, we'll have enough time to catch the last call plus somewhere. Now that's what you call planning ahead. We locate a Budget Inn right off 75, pay for two doubles and are given quick directions to a hole in the wall, a popular country dive named Tom Cat's.

The clerk was correct. The place is hopping, but I wonder why they need two bouncers. A $20 gets us in the door and another $20 gets us served. The bartender tells me she's a single mother and her name is Mitzi. She's right easy on the eyes and I tip her another $20 for the information. You never know when information like this comes in handy and did I mention "she's right easy on the eyes" as well?

A few pitchers later we all leave alone, but I've added another phone number to my collection should I "ever make it down Florida way again." Her words, not mine.

Back at the hotel, Sandra and I tussle and she successfully pins me to the bed.

"Damn the luck," is all that I can say. Sleep comes easy and it's a deep, dreamless, rejuvenating sleep.

I awake to the sound of a hairdryer and the view of Sandra's still wet and glistening backside. The muscles in her legs, back and shoulders are well defined. She also has an ass tight enough, as I like to say, to bounce a quarter off of. Such an inspiring sight so early in the day. My just desserts are finally coming home to roost, I muse. No, I don't know exactly what that means, but that doesn't preclude me from thinking it.

Sandra turns to catch me staring—she smiles and goes back to drying her hair. She sure has a strong personality. She's quick to join in on my nonsense and doesn't seem to rattle easily. Well, then there's the loving, too, which is always rewarding.

Sandra turns again and this time turns the hairdryer off and approaches the bed. She yanks the spread off and tosses it to the floor. She throws her hands on her hips.

"I suppose you need me to take care of your little problem there?" I chalk her observation up to dim lighting and a poor angle. From my perspective, it's a mighty large problem.

"What was your rhetorical question again?" I ask.

She climbs in bed and without preamble guides me in or as I like to say "Hooommmme."

"Should I count backward from ten or should I just let it happen?" I humbly ask.

She doubles up on her action. "I doubt you'll last that long, but if you must," she says with her hands pressed to my chest and all business-like. I succumb to the inevitable and hide it well with a bead of sweat rolling down my temple.

"You came, didn't you?" she accuses.

"Noooo," I lie.

She pats me on the chest. "Sure you did. Now maybe I can finish drying my hair and we can get this day started.

"What gave me away?" I weakly joke.

"You fell out," she says before we burst into laughter. Her patting me on the chest reminds me so much of Candy, who did and said nearly the exact same thing. So, I still have a little bit of work to do in the early morning lovemaking department. I vow to myself to keep up the practice. My morning prayer: "God keep 'em coming."

I shower, brush my teeth and kiss Sandra good morning before she applies new dressings to my wounds. The area looks less inflamed each day. I seem to be healing right properly. Soon I'll be able to start working out again. I have to dress in yesterday's apparel. I need to put shopping way up there on our to-do list. I ring Jim and Andy's room and then knock on the dividing door to wake them. I hope they slept as well as I did—not really.

Sandra puts on her bikini and then dons the short denim skirt and the women's high-heel cowboy boots I bought her. She knows how to treat her man... me. Maybe, I'll give her a bonus tomorrow morning—I'll count backward from 20. Thoughtfulness just comes naturally to me. I open the door to our side. Jim and Andy's door is already open. Andy's still in bed and Jim's apparently in the shower.

I stealthily move into the room, empty Andy's jeans of cash and stash it in his carryon satchel. I rejoin Sandra in our room and watch a bit of the local news on cable TV. Nothing much happening locally. I take a moment to admire my fine hand-stitched Naconas. I need to find someone to clean them with saddle soap, seeing how it's becoming more and more evident I may never get around to doing it myself.

Jim pops his head into the door. "Everyone dressed?"

"Yep," I cheerfully announce. "Doesn't Sandra look just as fine as wine this morning?"

"I hope you're not referring to the Boone's Farm you swill?"

"Yep. She's just as sweet and tasty."

"Just as sweet and tasty," Sandra echoes.

We laugh at Jim's momentary discomfort.

"You two are some sick puppies," Jim concludes.

"And some healthy carnal-consenting adults," I assert.

"A few days back, Sandra, you could have been charged with statutory rape by messing with this one." For emphasis, Jim points at me like I'm somehow at fault.

"And next year, I'll be allowed to vote," I say. "But I fail to see your point, Jimbo."

"That's because I was pointing the fact out for her, not you."

"And being a chick magnet has its rewards, Jimbo," I say. "Did you get Andy's lazy ass up by chance?"

"Yeah. He should be ready any minute. Let's catch a quick breakfast at the Waffle House. It seems like there's one at every exit. Must be a reason for it. Probably due to all the seniors living here in Florida."

We gather up our things and check out. The food at the Waffle House turns out to be satisfying. Where else can you get a $5.99 T-bone breakfast? It's only a quarter of an inch thick, but I'm sure you get the point.

We gas up before hitting the road—I'm back behind the wheel.

Yep, only one accident per trip is my motto. Now that breakfast is out of the way, I opt for a beer. If you don't start in the morning, how else are you going to drink all day? Something to ponder. Eighty miles later we pass Ocala and expensive horse operations with barns costing more than the average home.

"Steve-O, how do you suppose we're going to find this girl?"

"Shit. I don't know. With old-fashioned gumshoe work. Most of the Keys are less than a mile wide. We'll get some copies of the pictures made in Florida City and then fan out when we hit Key Largo. There's a chance that the guy and quite possibly the woman are heroin junkies, which might make them easy to find. We may have to get our hands dirty to find them."

"I hear you, Steve-O. We find them, then what? If this girl took off with them on her own free will, how are we going to convince her to come back with us?"

"Good question. It may be we have to convince the guy it's unhealthy for him to keep Monique around."

"I say we kick the commie's ass when we find him," Andy pipes in. "Shove his commie propaganda up his ass."

"Nice plan, Andy," I say. "Maybe somebody can test the water first this time. I've almost met my threshold of pain."

Jim's jaw drops in mock astonishment. "You mean God placed limitations on you after all?"

"Sadly, Jimbo, it is true, but fortunately they're few and far in between. I make up for any shortcomings in the bedroom, no pun intended."

"I'll vouch for him," Sandra says as she slides in closer. I throw my arm across her shoulder for a loving hug. Jim shakes his head and stares out his passenger window.

We come upon a section of IH-75 not yet completed and the detour takes us through the industrial outskirts of Tampa. Twice we have to wait on freight trains to clear their tracks before we're able to proceed. We soon find ourselves on old Highway 41 and we once again get up to speed. Not much to see besides palmettos and billboards and an occasional egret or two. Andy thinks they're miniature cranes. Close enough, I don't bother to correct him. I'm determined to fill his head with only important stuff—stuff that I feel is important, that is.

We stop and take a piss in Sarasota and top off our tank. Not many gas stations along this desolate stretch. At least we're making good progress. We begin to see billboards advertising North Fort Myers's Shell Factory. According to the billboards, the Shell Factory has it all. That almost seems too good to be true but, taking no chances, we decide to check it out.

True enough, the Shell Factory has everything a tourist might want. I buy tri-colored comfortable flip-flops for my feet, a half-dozen Florida T-shirts and a pair of funky, surfer's swimming trunks. Everybody buys something, except Andy, who's discovered that he was robbed in his sleep and none of us find him creditworthy enough to float him a loan. I really begin to feel for Andy when we go to leave and approach the Shell Factory's sub shop.

"I bet one of the black maids took it," Andy concludes. I back him in a corner and bet him a hundred that it will likely turn up and that he most likely stashed it in a drunken stupor. I also remind him it's not nice to stereotype people, unless you're talking about commies, of course. Got to keep his anger honed. Because I'm a nice guy, I buy him a small sub. We all laugh at the size of his sub, as we make our way back to our ride. Andy finishes his sub in two disgusting bites.

Cruising right along, we soon find ourselves on Alligator Alley and screaming toward Miami. We light up another fat joint in celebration for the sheer heck of it. Thought I was going to say, "hell of it," didn't you?

We're soon a car full of laughing idiots. Every now and then we spook a sunning 'gator back into the Everglades. I watched a show on PBS about the Florida Everglades, the diversity of life its ecosystem supports and man's steady encroachment. I agree with the environmentalist when it comes to the preservation of the glades.

"They also have what's called 'key disease' down in the Keys," I say to no one in particular.

"How do you catch that?" Jim asks.

I chuckle. "By digging in the cooler when you wake up in the morning. Drinking and other vices is a 24/7 lifestyle in the Keys. There's also the coconut telegraph, which consists of local gossip about any subject, person, place or thing. If they're still down there we'll find them."

"Where do you learn about all this shit, Steve-O?"

"People, places and things. Oh, and I watch a lot of TV too. Andy, hand me another beer."

"It sounds like you'll fit right in, Steve-O."

Chapter Sixteen

The glow of the Miami skyline comes into view as the sun slowly sinks in the west. Sandra's excitement is contagious. I've also never been to Miami before, much less Florida. She's squirming too because she needs to use the facilities. She refused to get out of the car and be bitten by something on the side of the road. Us boys had no such qualms, but the mosquitoes out here can carry you away. The little bastards seem to love me. To them, it's like going to a free keg party. Our windshield and grill are plastered with the bugs we've hit. Every now and then we hit a cloud of love bugs. They're called such because they fly joined in mating. I've heard that if you hit enough of them it can cause your car to run hot on hot days like today. The day's heat is finally waning, though the evening remains muggy. I decide to forego Florida City and drive straight through to Key Largo. I'm feeling the need for a cool shower and some fresh clothes.

"Do you know the way, Steve-O?"

"Not really. Miami has a bypass and there will be signs to Homestead and Florida City. From Florida City, we take 1 to Key Largo. Should be as easy as that."

"Honey," Sandra says, "stop at the very first place you can."

"Back teeth floating? I hear you, girl. I saw a billboard for a Texaco truck stop ahead. That ought to work."

We exit and pull into the mega-stop. Sandra races to find the ladies' room. I find a five-pack of tube socks and a three-pack of men's boxers to purchase. Everyone's hungry again, especially Andy, even though it's only been a little over two hours since we left the Shell Factory, so we decide to eat right here.

It's truck-stop fare but palatable. It seems we're the only English speakers present. That will change when we get beyond Miami, I'm sure.

Back on the road, the traffic picks up along with the speed as we enter Miami city limits. Safety in numbers is the mindset and only now and then is a car pulled over. We drive straight on through. We pass some exotic rides along the way, including a pair of Roll's convertibles. One of Miami's claims to fame is the well-known fact Miami is the cocaine hub of the United States. Our excitement continues to grow as we pass Homestead and Florida City and we officially have 25 miles to go. Any lodging concerns are quickly quelled by the numerous billboards. Azul del Mar, Marriott Key-Largo Bay, Tarpon Flats Inn and the Sunset Cove, which looks interesting.

We finally hit the long-awaited causeway to carry us over. With some "Hell yeahs" and the bumping of cans, we hit the island and Key Largo proper. I spot and follow the small signs pointing us to the Sunset Cove.

"Oh, hell yeah," Sandra excitedly says. "Check it out: tiny cottages. I hope they have some available."

Kind of a dive, but cool. Sporadic throughout the grounds are concrete elephants, tigers, camels and leopards. Centered is a chickee, or thatched hut, with a stone waterfall that gives the appearance of the place being its own small island. I pull into the office to make inquiries. Sure enough, they have two vacancies with full kitchens at $75 a night. I'm told for the guests, there are lounge chairs and barbeque pits on the beach. There are paddleboats and canoes available at no cost. I'm sold and the older lady finally accepts my cash after I assure her that we have no intention of trashing the place. In a show of good faith, I let her hold a couple of crisp hundreds as collateral.

With keys in hand, we locate our cottages. The interiors look like something left over from the '50s, but everything looks clean and tidy. Even more charming is the fact that one wall sports a mural of exotic flora and fauna. Sandra is ecstatic. Looking around, it's easy to forget we're actually on a mission.

We share a quick shower to spark some life back into us. I manage to suppress most of my urges. Sharing showers is still relatively new to me and nothing I shall ever tire of. I don one of my new tees, add the trunks and flip-flops and tuck my Beretta in the back. A little more color and I'd fit right in. Sandra dresses in her bikini, adds a sheer wrap and rounds out her ensemble with a pair of hip, low-cut white Converses. She meets my approval—Sandra looks sexy as hell. For a final touch, she pulls her hair into a ponytail and caps her head in Candy's Bud cap. I give her a thumbs-up and a whistle of approval.

We catch up with Andy and Jim at their cottage. Andy appears much the same: jeans and a drab brown pullover. Jim, on the other hand, wears jeans, a Hawaii Five-O tropical shirt and a pair of light brown penny loafers without socks. I give him a thumbs-up as well.

"Book 'em, Dan-O," I say and we all laugh. "If you and Rockford over here"—I nod in Andy's direction— "are ready, let's rock 'n' roll."

"Where first, Steve-O?"

"I saw a sign for Snapper's Waterfront Saloon & Raw Bar. That sounds like as good a place as any to start. Until we get copies of the photos made, we might as well stick together."

Everyone nods their agreement. We load up for the short drive. Finding the ocean-side bar is easy enough, seeing how it's located on Oceanside. The place is pretty hip. We find us a spot on the waterside deck under palm fronds supported by seasoned cypress. I order up four dozen oysters on the half shell and a pitcher of Bud. Andy requests a menu.

"Steve-O, I think Andy has something he wants to tell you," Jim says suppressing the urge to laugh. I raise an inquiring brow.

"I... Um... I found my money."

"Probably the black maids hid it from you. Anyhow, you lost a bet it would seem. Being a sport and all, I'm going to let you off light. I'm going to allow you to buy tonight."

"But..."

I raise my hand. "Ah, ah. No buts, Andy."

"But I don't eat oysters and they're expensive."

"And I didn't eat the sub I bought you earlier, but I still paid for it."

"It wasn't even a real sub. It pissed me off. I ate it in two bites."

We all laugh at Andy.

Our waitress returns with our pitcher and mugs balanced on a round tray and with menus in the other hand. She's actually cute as a button. Petite like Candy with a dark tan and deep brown doe eyes. Her exposed mid-section is flat and firm. Quite the number with her Farrah cut and lively too. As she bends near me to pass the mugs around, I catch an intoxicating whiff of her. "Refreshing" comes to mind.

"My name is Sarah and I'll be back in a sec with your oysters and to take your order."

I return her smile. Sandra accidentally steps on my foot, but it doesn't hurt.

The beach is mostly deserted at this late hour, but a few couples stroll hand in hand. No doubt Sandra finds it romantic.

"Isn't it romantic how they walk hand in hand?" Sandra comments.

I can be romantic too—I lay my hand near Sandra's warm crotch. "Sandra, let me see the composites."

Sarah returns with a large iced platter of oysters and a bottle of Louisiana hot sauce. She centers them on our table. The composites draw her attention.

"Sarah, have you by chance seen either of these two?"

Sarah doesn't hesitate. "Yep. I've seen them both. Why?"

"There's a couple of young ladies associated with the pair and we're trying to get one of them home. When's the last time you saw them?"

"Day before yesterday, but they weren't together. The woman kept nodding off. We finally asked her to leave. Now that I think about it, the guy left about the same time."

"Know where they might be staying? Anything else that might help us?"

"Not that I can think of. Maybe she was here trying to be picked up. She was pretty enough. If it had been later in the day, she probably would have been. There was something strange about her. She was wearing long sleeves and that's one reason I remember her so well."

I peel a $20 from my roll and hand it to her. "Thanks. You've been helpful. My name is Steven Paul and we're staying at the Sunset Cove in rooms nine and ten. If you spot them, please call."

Sandra opens the yearbook and points to Sophia and then points out Monique in the family photo. "If you see either of these two girls, give us a call as well."

Sarah nods her understanding.

"Sarah, where's the nearest Radio Shack?"

"Florida City."

"You working tomorrow?"

"I work five till closing."

"Beautiful, we'll eat here tomorrow evening."

Sarah nods again. "Can I get you guys anything else? Something from the menu?"

Andy's engrossed in the menu. I smack him on the head to get his attention. The thought of food makes him immune to his environment. "Now's your chance to order, Andy."

"Um, I'll have two prime rib dinners, baked potatoes with them and no salad."

"Sir, the steaks are thick and quite heavy."

"That's why I'm only ordering two," Andy smugly says.

I shrug. "We ate an hour and a half ago," I say by way of explanation. "The steaks sound good though. I'll split one with my sister. Make ours medium-rare and burn Andy's. Bring us each a chef salad as well, Italian on mine. Sandra?"

"Italian is fine." She adds another toe stomp.

"Jimbo, you want something?"

"Nah, I'm fine. Another pitcher of beer when you get a chance," he tells Sarah.

"Coming right up," Sarah says and bounds off.

Jim sighs. "Nice."

"I hope the steaks are as thick as she claims," Andy says.

Sometimes Andy quashes all hope in me for him. I fork an oyster, splash on some hot sauce, add just the right amount of black pepper and after a few savoring chews, down the hatch, it goes. Now that I know the value of vitamin E and can afford oysters, I'm going to buy them and eat them at every opportunity. Why risk a deficiency? Must I ask?

I down my mug, refill and pick up the composites to show some of the other patrons. I start with the most weathered. I receive several bites, but no new leads. A couple of the locals tell me to check out Coconuts Restaurant & Lounge. It also happens to be located on Oceanside. It's Wednesday night and ladies' night there and will be hopping.

I make my way back to our table. Sarah delivers our steak and, sure enough, it's fat and juicy. It just doesn't get any better than this—outside the bedroom, that is. I'm quick to qualify that. Andy's steaks arrive about ten minutes later, lifeless and shriveled to half their original size. I smile—she just earned a hefty tip. I don't have my trusty Uncle Henry with me, or a hacksaw, so Andy will have to fend for himself. We eat our steak and drink our beer. I cop a cheap thrill under the table and am back in good graces with Sandra. She's soon wet and juicy. It's tempting to forego our mission and resume in the morning, but then we'd miss ladies' night. Can't have that—can't pass up the opportunity to save one admission price.

Andy grumpily pays the bill and I add another $20 to it. One thing I'm good at is greasing palms. Actually, I'm more of the easy-come, easy-go type. We say our goodbyes.

Before leaving, I ask Sarah where the cheapest places to stay on the key are? I'm surprised to learn that we're already staying there. Then there's the Hungry Pelican Motel that is right next door to us on Bayside. Well, if our accommodations didn't impress Sarah, perhaps my choke-a-horse roll of bills did. Hell, it impresses me, but I'm young and impressionable. I'm keen on reminding people of that.

We stroll the short distance to the Coconut Restaurant & Lounge. Fifteen dollars later plus $20 in gifts and we're through the doors. The large dance floor is already packed.

With no place to sit, I sidle up to the bar and order us a round of Buds. We huddle up and decide to hold off on showing the composites until we've toured the place and made sure they aren't currently present. We haven't quite worked out our approach, but our first sortie will not be Andy's preferred commando-style raid, at least until that action is deemed necessary after careful consideration. Sounds pretty good put that way, huh? What I really mean is we will likely wing it if we spot either of the two. Why depart from a formula that so far seems to be working well for us?

Sandra and I are not the only ones present that look like they have recently left the beach, but despite that, Sandra garners her fair share of attention. I notice a number of other hard bodies present with an appreciative smile. Sandra, with a beer in hand, steers me onto the dance floor. Not my forte, but I'm game. A strobe light adds to our moves. I'm well enough down the road to over-imbibing to have some fun with it.

I nod in Jim's direction and circle a finger in the air to prompt him to circle while I keep a keen eye out for the pair from the dance floor. It's decisions like this one that make me the natural leader.

Andy stares off into space. Wait, no, he's staring at a snack rack on the side of the bar. Figures. He causes Sandra and me to laugh.

If those that laugh live longer, there's a good chance we may live forever, in addition to being immortal, that is.

It's hot on the crowded dance floor. There's some serious gyration going on. Some pretty hot stuff. A bead of sweat in my eye tells me enough is enough. I lead Sandra from the dance floor and we work our way back to the bar for a fresh round of Buds.

The pair is clearly not here, so we huddle back up with Jim and Andy.

"I've shown the composites," Jim says, "and the doorman remembers seeing both of them, but not together. He said he remembers seeing the woman leaving with an older tourist. He remembers her because they appeared to be such a mismatched pair. All three of the bartenders recognized both of them as having been in here, as well, but had nothing of importance to tell me."

"Hmm." I scratch my scalp. "You think this woman is turning tricks to support their drug habits?"

"That's my guess," Jim says, "Either that or they're setting up people to rob."

"If that's the case, Jimbo, it wouldn't take them long to wear out their welcome on this small key. Maybe, we should talk with the local law tomorrow, see if anything unusual has been going on that they are aware of."

"Sometimes johns don't report the crime," Jim comments. "If they are in fact johns."

"That's something they don't teach you in high school," I say and we all laugh.

"But they did teach you how to bowl, sort of," Jim adds.

As an elective, we all took bowling as a course but we weren't actually given any pointers—only a ride to the nearest bowling alley for what amounted to a social hour. Now, in gymnastics, I actually learned something. I learned what some of the finer girls looked like in leotards. A pleasant lesson on female anatomy. Inadvertently, I learned how to walk on my hands too. That ought to be worth something, wouldn't you say? The only issue I had with the class is they wouldn't allow me to spot the girls. Who would have thought? They need to get with the program, join the rest of us in the '70s. School is no place for discrimination—that's my belief.

The day finally wears on us and we decide to call it a day. We might not have accomplished much, but there is a pattern starting to emerge. We also know they have recently been on the key. If they are still here, we'll find them by starting our search at the cheapest lodging, which we now know includes ours. Cheap or not, I still believe our lodging is pretty cool. We'll also have to learn where some of the less desirables hang and start beating the bushes there. If they're doing heroin as we suspect, they have to get it somewhere. From what I've read, heroin is a hell of an addiction and not one easily kicked. They don't call it "a monkey on your back" for nothing.

We ride the short distance back to our lodging and collectively agree to sleep in. Recuperate from the long trip in getting here. Despite being tired, I'm a light sleeper and regardless of my intent, I'm sure I will still get up early. After our goodnights, we go to our separate cottages.

Sandra backs me to the bed and pushes me to a sitting position. "Playing with me under the table got me hot, could you tell?"

"Nope," I say and smile. "But I'm sure you're going to make me suffer the consequences and impose upon my sensitivities."

Sandra laughs. "Sensitivities, right." She pulls my first flip-flop loose and tosses it to the side. "You're silly," she says freeing and tossing the second to the side.

I'm not sure what it is about women and them pegging me as being silly, but it seems like I'm accused of that a lot lately. It seems to get me laid a lot too. If one could bottle and sell the stuff, I'd be a rich man, I think and chuckle when I realize I am a rich man, sort of. I frown. I should have been a much richer man, but my little Jewish South Austin girl, the only one at the time who would let me wet the whistle, so to speak, told her father where I so thoughtfully stashed approximately half a million in the German-bearer bonds that Tony C and Vinnie were so desperately trying to retrieve. They're now off living the American dream. Well, one can dwell on it like I am now or one can move on. I hand Sandra my pistol. I choose to live—to move on.

She tugs at my trunks. "You better not be laughing at me, Steven Paul."

I fall back and make it easier on her. Sandra frees me of my trunks and I spring to life. "Does it look like I'm laughing at you?"

She drops down and strokes me a couple times before taking me in her mouth. I feel my toes curl. Nope, I'm definitely not laughing.

Sandra halts what she's doing and takes the time to shed her wrap and bikini. I forget the question. She's hot. Sandra climbs onto the bed and sprawls out beside me.

"Your turn to do the work."

"But what if I blow a stitch?"

"You don't have stitches," she reminds me. "You've been milking that injury long enough."

I touch her between her legs and feel the heat coming off her. I'm starting to see her point. I mean, it's only a gunshot wound and what has it been now, days? And she's either aroused or the room's cold AC has her nipples hard. Probably aroused, so it must be for her own good, I reason.

Sandra rises up on one elbow. "Well? It's not like you'll be jumping into a frigid pool."

Her dirty wordplay convinces me. I climb aboard and bask in her heat and wet tightness. She lets out her breath as I enter and gently bites me on the shoulder. I take it slow and easy until her whisper in my ear tells me to stroke harder and faster. Saying no to that request would be like ordering one's own execution. When Sandra shakes below me: I'm all chips in. I explode inside her. When you're 17, one "explodes" inside, okay?

I don't know what Sandra does for the rest of the evening, but it must have been lights out for me moments after rolling off because that's the last thing I remember. Though the odds are that I snuggled some first.

Chapter Seventeen

I awake chilled to the bone and having to piss again like a Russian racehorse. Sandra's wrapped three times in the top sheet and seems to be faring well. Like "snug as a bug in a rug" comes to mind. Where, when, or how that saying came about, I haven't a clue.

I ease off the bed as so not to disturb Sandra. I don't know what time it is, seeing how my last watch, a scuba watch good to a hundred meters, fell off while I was taking a bath and went kaput.

The tiles are cold to the feet. I tiptoe in a hurry over to the AC and cut it off. After relieving myself, I take a long hot shower and dress. The warmth helps and I actually feel decent. Must not have over-imbibed yesterday, I conclude. A Coke would really be refreshing. They have a soda machine outside the office, I recall. I gather up the composites and head that way. Might as well clock in while I'm at it. The early bird gets the worm, someone said. My internal dialogue is full of clichés this morning. A lazy man's way of thinking? Some would argue clichés are substitutes for original thought. Something to ponder? Only if you have nothing else to waste your time on.

I borrow enough change out of Sandra's snap purse to buy us each a Coke in case she wants one too. Probably up to 25 cents now. Highway robbery.

I flip-flop my way the short distance to the office. The same little old lady is working this morning. I show her the composites.

"Yep, I recognize them. Checked out yesterday morning after being here a week. Stayed in the same cottage as you. The Gonzaleses and daughters. Nice family."

I could smack myself in the head. Why didn't I ask yesterday?

Her smile turns to concern. "Why? They're not in trouble, are they?"

"No, ma'am. Nothing like that. My friends and I go to school with the daughters and we knew they were down here somewhere. So, what are they driving?"

"They were driving, I believe, a Maverick or Pinto. I get them confused. They must have had trouble with it because for the past few days they've been driving a rust-bucket Olds. A local car. I see it all the time."

"Any idea where they were heading from here?"

"Only an impression. I got the impression that they were going to continue south."

"We'll head south too and try and catch our friends."

She frowns. "I guess that means you young people won't need the cottages for another night."

"Yes, ma'am. We'll stop and see if any cottages are available on the way back though."

"Well, good luck catching up with your friends."

"Thank you, ma'am."

I buy the two Cokes and suck the bottom out of mine on the short trek back to the cottage. Maybe my body's telling me something. I suddenly have a craving for a tall cold glass of milk. That and a big, country-style breakfast.

The cottage has lost some of its chill. I find Sandra still down for the count. I give her sheet a tug. Sandra is so ensconced that she comes with it and she's unable to free herself before she thuds to the floor. Giggling, she's still unable to free herself as I give her another good tug.

"Up and at 'em, girl. I bought you a Coke."

Sandra gets up rubbing her ass. "Thanks. Hey, you bruised my ass."

"I've already showered, so hurry up and get ready. I found where they've been staying."

"Really? Where?"

"Right here, in our cottage to be exact."

"You're fucking kidding?"

"I fucking kid you not."

We laugh.

"That's a trip, man," Sandra says.

"Ain't it? Now hurry up and get ready."

She salutes me.

"Aye, aye, Captain," she says and looks damn hot doing so. It's only right that I help speed things along by washing her back. And what if she drops the soap? Hey, it could happen. I'd be there to hold her steady as she bends to retrieve it. It's considerations and personal sacrifices like this that keep me smiling. It takes me all of ten seconds to undress and join her in the shower. Well, if nothing else, I make a handy towel rack. Okay, maybe only a face towel rack, but there is no denying that showering has taken on a whole new meaning for me.

Showered, refreshed and sated, I dress and watch Sandra as she prepares for the day. Sandra's a low-maintenance type of gal and takes little time to prepare. I have to give her credit—she pulls it off well.

We stow our stuff in the Bonneville's trunk and go and wake the boys. I quickly run down what little I've learned about our quarry. Not much, but it is further confirmation that we've picked up the spoor.

I have Andy use the shower in our cottage to expedite things. Soon we're off and running again. We settle on the Hobo Cafe on Oceanside. We soon learn it's a local favorite. The menu is simple and the food is good. We breakfast on a pile of scrambled eggs, fried potatoes, crisp bacon and an assortment of fruits including Mango. I end up drinking two tall glasses of milk and eat enough to feel bloated. Our new battle plan includes backtracking to Florida City to locate a Radio Shack and to get copies of our composites so we can branch out if need be. The ordeal takes us most of the morning, but we get our copies made and we buy six of Radio Shack's best walkie-talkies. We ought to buy stock in Radio Shack considering all the gear we've bought from the chain in the last couple weeks. Oh, well. The only budget I'm comfortable with is spending. I'm right good at that. On the way back, we decide to eat lunch at Snappers. Besides eating, I want to leave Sarah a note explaining our necessary departure, a $20 for the minimum tip she would have earned and a number and open invitation to visit Texas.

Sandra and I dine on onion-encrusted grouper roulade and Key Largo crab cakes. Jim gets the yellowtail and Andy three burgers and fries. We opt for a couple of pitchers of Bud to wash it down and three dozen oysters, of which I eat most. I'm simply not willing to take any chances at this stage of the game.

We restock and re-ice our cooler and buy a Florida Keys map. The next logical stop is Key Largo, a mere five miles down the road. Hell, I didn't even know there was a Key Largo until I opened the map. I'm beginning to believe there is a learning curve involved in rescuing damsels in distress or in this case a wayward teenage girl. Returning her is almost consistent with my long-term life goal of opening a home for wayward teenage girls. If all else fails, I believe I'd make a good cult leader. That may derail my aspirations for being president someday—they told me I could be president in grade school—but sacrifices are necessary for the betterment of mankind, am I wrong? Whatever course I'm going to take in life, I'm sure it beats pumping gas and drilling a peephole in the bathroom wall for entertainment.

The road is all ours—I wind her up to 90. The water is turquoise on both sides. I'm surprised how clean the water looks on the gulf side. Nothing like the murky gulf water on the Texas coast I'm used to. Despite the color of the Texas gulf water, I shall not forsake it for you can't beat Padre Island on spring break or the Texas women.

At 90, our trip takes all of three minutes. Not even enough time for Andy to ask, "Are we there yet?"

"Well that was fast, Steve-O," Jim says. "What now?"

"Well, Jimbo, I say we keep our eye out for the rust-bucket Olds. The nice old lady didn't say what year it was, but it doesn't take long for a car to turn into a rust-bucket down here. A total guess, but I'd say '68 or older."

"That sounds reasonable to me," Jim says.

Andy leans forward almost to my ear. "Our maid has a '67 Olds Ninety-Eight." He chuckles. "One time when it wouldn't crank, I suggested that we roll start it and she said, 'everyone knows you can't roll start no hydromatic.'" He mimics his maid well.

"Well, Andy, I hate to rain on your parade, but it just so happens that the two-speed automatic in the '67 Olds is called a hydromatic."

"Yeah. Like I'm going to believe you and our maid."

"Two minds are better than one," I remind Andy.

"Not when one's our maid's and the other is yours," Andy smirks.

We spend 30 minutes cruising the small key. No Olds rust-bucket to be found. We decide to take our search farther down the road. We spend the next two hours searching blips on our radar along the way: Tavernier, Plantation Key, Upper Matecumbe Key,

Islamorada, Lower Matecumbe Key, Layton, before stretching our legs at Long Key State Park.

If one were to do some camping, this would be the spot. All the sandy sites are right on the water. Half of the 60 sites offer water and electricity and all offer picnic tables.

One thing that I do not find appealing is the fact that dogs are not allowed in the park. That fact alone would keep me away, especially now that I've been entrusted with the care of Bonnie. The concession stand's lack of beer doesn't win me over either.

We relieve ourselves and hit the road again. Hit the road again, as in the next stop five miles down the road. We search Duck Key, Grassy Key, Key Colony Beach, but Marathon poses a bit more of a challenge. Heavily developed in the '50s, Marathon's canals make it difficult to search. Difficult, but not impossible. I make a mental note of the fact Marathon hosts a general aviation airport, along with refueling capabilities. We strike out and head out again. We pass Bahia Honda State Park but roll on.

Big Pine Key is a bird of a different feather. Vast and mostly uninhabitable, it apparently serves as home base for many Marathon and Key West workday commuters. Our search takes us near the National Key Deer Refuge where we spot many of the diminutive deer.

Andy taps me on the shoulder. "What the hell are those, wild dogs?" he asks.

"Andy, it's 'better to be silent and be thought a fool than to speak and remove all doubt,'" I say.

"And what smart ass said that, Steve? Probably made it up."

"Abraham Lincoln said that, Andy."

"Fucking Yankee! It figures you'd quote him."

"She speaks, yet she says nothing," I retort quoting Shakespeare from Romeo and Juliet from my amplitude of stored knowledge.

"Aw, fuck you," Andy says and we all laugh—excluding Andy, of course.

We come up dry once again. Unless we miss them going north and assuming they're still heading south, we'll find them. We pull into the Big Pine Restaurant & Coffee Shop and the place looks like it's been around for a long time. Lots of older Floridians and snowbirds sitting around shooting the breeze and sipping coffee. We take a table. The menu lists cheap American fare including chicken, steaks and ribs.

An older, bee-hived, gum-chewing waitress straight out of the '50s saunters over to take our order.

"What can I get y'all folks?" she asks between smacks.

I defer to Sandra. "Whatchya want, honey?"

"Oh, I don't know. How's the baked chicken?"

"The regulars seem to like it."

"Okay, I guess. Give me mashed potatoes and gravy, the corn and salad."

"And you, sir?" the waitress asks me.

"I want the sirloin, medium rare, baked potato and the corn and salad too."

Jim and Andy order the same, except Andy is back to his old habit of ordering his steak well done.

I take the opportunity to show the waitress the two composites.

"Seen either of these two?"

"Yeah. I served them and their daughters a late lunch. They pulled out about three hours ago." She blows and pops a small bubble.

"Did you happen to notice what they were driving and which way they went?"

"Nope. Hey Ralph, did you notice what kind of car and what direction the couple with the teenage daughters went?"

"They were driving a rusted out white late-60s Oldsmobile and they went south."

"Thanks," I tell the man named Ralph. Yep, we're definitely onto their spoor. The latest information makes me want to up and go, but we've ordered and one must eat. The sirloin sounds good about now too. And if God didn't intend us to eat steaks, he wouldn't have made them meat. Fran Leibowitz said, "food is an important part of a balanced diet." I know, enough with the quotes today.

The food arrives and turns out to be plenty satisfying. Having to drink iced tea is a whole other ball of wax. I'll have to remember to repent in the morning.

I pay our bill and tip the waitress $10. That should buy her a can or two of hairspray.

We step out into the waning day. A northerly breeze is lowering the mercury. I wish we had a convertible. We load up and I roll my window down and enjoy the fresh air. I hope Andy doesn't catch too much air in the back—not really. I leave the AC on so us in the front will be able to enjoy the best of both worlds. I do what I can.

Back on 1, the sign tells us we have ten miles to go to reach Cudjoe Key and 15 to reach Sugarloaf Key. We search each. Noticeably, property values have increased. Totally gone are the mobile homes. Also gone are places to lodge. In stark contrast, I've seen no less than 20 advertisements for lodging in Key West. I've read some about Key West and Duval Street. On Duval Street, successfully drinking your way from one end to the other is known as the "Duval Crawl." Sounds challenging. It may become necessary to carry out the mission and we know how big I am on carrying out the mission.

The anticipation mounting in the big Bonneville is thick enough to cut with a knife as we roll into Key West.

Sandra squeezes my leg. "Too cool. I never thought I'd visit Key West."

I wink at her. "I hear you, girl. Boys and girls, keep your eyes peeled. They're around here somewhere. For the record, Andy, we're at the southernmost point of the continental United States."

"Steve-O, you don't find it strange that we're tracking Cubans and we're now 90 miles from Cuba?" Jim asks.

"Yeah. I just didn't want to vocalize it, but it surely has crossed my mind."

"Devil's advocate, Steve-O, what if they are—"

"Shit, Jimbo, we'll cross that bridge when and if we get to it. I hope not. I don't want to bump heads with the Cuban government."

"Fucking commies," Andy spits out.

"Honey! Honey!" Sandra excitedly shouts as she slaps my thigh. She points. "That's it! That's their car!"

I do a double-take. "Looks like a rust-bucket Olds to me."

"Fucking A!" Jim says as I turn right and pull in behind the Olds. "I don't see anyone though, Steve-O."

I throw the Bonneville into park and kill the engine. I tuck my pistol into my waistband in the back and remove one of the two ignition keys from my key chain and hand it to Jim.

"In case of an emergency. Everyone have their guns?"

"Mine's in the trunk," Sandra says. She answers my unspoken question. "I brought Candy's Smith & Wesson."

"Oookayy," I say. "Comfortable with a gun?"

"Of course, I lived in Laredo, remember?" she says.

I slap myself in the forehead. "What was I thinking? Shot a nice hole in Candy's ceiling too." Sandra kisses my cheek. We laugh.

Chapter Eighteen

I step out of the Bonneville.

"Andy, grab four of the walkie-talkies. Jimbo, notice anything about the Olds?"

"Yeah. There's an oil slick under it. This ride played out too."

"Which means they could be anywhere. Staying at any one of the 20 places right now or they could be out on the beach—Gulf or ocean-side." Though technically, ocean-side is Gulf too. I hand Sandra the keys so she can get the Smith & Wesson out while the rest of us look over the Olds. It looks lived-in.

"Andy, get out the tire tool and let's pop this trunk. That may give us some clues."

Andy returns with the tire tool and hands it over. There's pedestrian traffic at both ends of the block. "Y'all cover me the best you can. And, Andy, don't be so obvious."

It takes a number of tries before I knock the outer ring off holding the lock in place. I flick my Uncle Henry open, insert the blade into the hole and with a quarter twist, the trunk pops open.

"Nice work, Steven Paul."

"Thanks, honey."

The trunk is devoid of luggage and half full of trash that probably belonged to the previous owner. We all come to the same conclusion: they're packing their gear, which means they've likely sought lodging.

"All right," I say, "everybody takes a radio. Jimbo, take our ride and check out the ocean-side. Andy, you take the Gulf. Sandra and I will take Duval Street and check the businesses on Duval Street."

"Steve-O, the sun's fixing to set, most people will be off the beach or heading in. By the way, what's this Duval street you two plan to check out?

It's like the main strip. Okay, we'll check the beaches tomorrow if we don't locate them tonight. You and Andy start canvassing the places of lodging."

Andy stops his pacing. "It sounds like they're getting the better deal, Jim."

"Keep your walkie-talkie on, Jim. Andy, it's not about better deals, we're trying to save this girl from these commie bastards," I say playing to Andy's weakness. Jim merely smiles at my ploy. "Maybe with Jimbo's help you can handle them, should you find them first."

Andy knees a dent in the rusty Olds. "Come on, Jim, let's go."

I turn my walkie-talkie on, insert the earbud and clip it to my side. Thankfully, my shirt obscures it, so I don't feel quite so ridiculous or conspicuous.

"You kinda look like a Secret Service Agent," Sandra comments. "Hey, check out the little train coming our way."

I turn to look. Sure enough, a tour train is headed our way. We watch as it pulls abreast of us.

"Which way to Duval Street?" I ask the fake conductor as he slows to a stop.

"It begins two blocks over and one block up. Hop on, we can give you a ride."

"Cool," Sandra says. "We get to ride the train."

"Thanks," I say as we board the near-empty ride. We chug along at about four miles an hour, but it saves a whole three blocks of tough, sea-level trekking. We officially disembark on Duval Street in front of the Pier House Resort. The place is interesting and is made up of a consortium of businesses. The Havana Docks bar, the Beach Bar & Grill and even a piano bar called the Wine Gallery. Overall, the place's ambiance is too upscale for the group we're tracking but, out of an abundance of caution, at the Havana Docks Bar Sandra orders a couple of Hemmingway's Specials: two frozen daiquiris. One must be cautious and the daiquiris are quite tasty.

We mingle among the many patrons, but spot none of the four. We finish our drinks and move on. The daiquiris had enough kick that I doubt many people can drink them and survive the Duval Crawl. Perhaps only the brave and foolish? The street, blocked to traffic, has a French Quarter feel to it.

A pit mix wearing glasses and beads, sports a colorful parrot on his back. A weathered local sits on top of a large, three-wheeled bike that looks like it was built in Haiti and has two fading plastic Flamingos mounted on the front. Our next destination, Sloppy

Joes, has neon lights. The sun dips behind the buildings. Sandra squeezes my hand and pulls me toward it.

I have to admit, the place is exciting and the pedestrian traffic has picked up the short time we've been on the scene.

We enter Sloppy Joes with a young couple. The woman of the pair is happy to share with us that the bar has been open since 1933 and at this location since '37. Plus, she tells us it was Hemmingway's favorite watering hole. I wonder when he found time to write—the atmosphere in the place is contagious. We work our way to the bar and order enough frozen daiquiris for the young couple as well. Misery loves company. We bid our farewells and begin our search.

A live band plays Bob Seger's "Turn the Page," and is doing a damn good job of it. No search would be complete without searching the gift shop. In furtherance of our disguises, we buy Sloppy Joe's T-shirts and I add to my boxer collection. Sandra buys a pair of goofy, oversized sunglasses and props them up on her head. We listen to a little more of the band in case any of the four show up. You know the routine—it's all about caution. Drinks gone—we move on.

Across the street is Rick's Key West, which turns out to be four nightspots in one, hosting live entertainment until 4:00 a.m. One of the places, Durty Harry's—yep that's how it's spelled—doesn't open until 8:00 p.m. We find a spot at The Tree Bar to sit a spell and watch over Duval Street below. We opt for Buds, seeing how we don't have a clue as to how long Duval Street is. I find it prudent, being slightly buzzed by the two daiquiris already. Sandra looks on with a big smile. I hope Jim and Andy are as thorough in their search as we are. From our current position, none of the four will slip by us going back north, that's for sure.

Our bartender nods at our empties. I indicate two more. He pops the caps off the two Buds and places them before us.

"What's up with the earpiece?" he asks. "You look too young to be a cop and you're definitely not a cop from around here."

"It's called good genes, but no, I'm not a cop. My friends and I are looking for a couple of Cubans."

He chuckles as he wipes the table clean. "Shouldn't have many problems finding Cubans around here."

"I feel you," I say. "But we're looking for two in particular. They've got a couple of beautiful girls my age with them."

"Sorry, can't help you with that. You see that every day and all day around here. Have pictures?"

"Thanks anyway. We have pictures, but my crew has them and is checking the accommodations around the Key."

"Well, good luck," he says taking the $10 Sandra offered. I wave off the change. We sip our beers and watch the ever-growing crowd.

"This is too cool," Sandra says.

"Ain't it though?"

The sun is all but gone when we get up to leave. The arriving full moon lights the night. Somehow the moon appears larger than it recently did in Texas. Could we be closer? Surely not enough to make a difference.

"Look how big the moon is," Sandra says as we walk toward the Bull & Whistle. So, it's not my imagination. That's good.

The Bull & Whistle turns out to be another three-in-one. The downstairs is open air with live music. We buy a couple Buds and begin our search again. We work our way to the second floor, which houses pool tables, pinball machines and another good view of Duval. Seeing the pool tables makes me jones to play. The last games I played were in Rio, against the late Dom Pedro. I took him for a quick $500. The key to winning is betting on something that you know. And I know billiards.

I have our waitress, with her Florida tan and New York accent, break a hundred for me as I pay our small tab. I can't help but ask her where she's from. She tells me "New Jersey," which is the same to me as New York.

"Don't they say 'have a fucking nice day' up there in Jersey?" I ask her. She laughs as she gathers up our empties and her tip.

She nods. "Something like that," she says with a smile.

We're back on the prowl. Across the street and half a block down is Fat Tuesday, the name no doubt borrowed from New Orleans. The place is packed. It turns out their claim to fame is their 26 flavors of frozen drinks, including 190 octane rum runners and a drink called a "pain in the ass."

We end up buying T-shirts with their motto: "one daiquiri, two daiquiris, three daiquiris, floor." So as not to offend the establishment, we're back on daiquiris. I laugh at Sandra and all the shit we've accumulated for her to tote. I'd help, but I'm ever mindful that my hands are lethal and while on a mission, I must keep at least one of them free. For subterfuge, I tie up one hand with the daiquiri. Don't want to stand out in the crowd, now would I? Perhaps I was born a sleuth?

"What are you grinning about, Steven Paul?"

"I find the tourists amusing."

That one gets by her. I blame it on the drinks. Sandra snickers. "Me too." Sandra's all right. Got to love her.

"Maybe they have a backpack in the next gift shop."

"Or maybe a wagon that I can load and pull," Sandra says.

We bump glasses and share a laugh. Our prey is not present. We finish our drinks and like a pair of giggling teenagers tumble back onto the street.

Sandra wipes her face with one of the T-shirts. "Whoa, the drinks have some kick."

I know what she means. I grab her left bicep to steady her. Or is it to steady me? I always get the two confused at this stage of the game. Anyhow, we manage to part the crowds and cross back to the other side. Standing like a giant before us is the Crowne Plaza Key West La Concha, which as we soon learn is also known as the Top. The doorman answers our inquisitive stares.

"Welcome, friends. The Crowne Plaza is the first upscale lodging facility in the area. Hemmingway romanced both Ava Gardner and Marlene Dietrich here. At the Top, you have views of Key West Harbor and of course Duval Street as well."

I interrupt his spiel: "Sold! We'll take two of everything!"

"Wonderful, if you're meaning rooms. If I had to guess, I'd say you two have been working your way down Duval."

"What gave us away, our tans?" I ask.

He ponders that a long second. "Yes, perhaps your glow."

"Wonderful," I now say myself. "We're from Texas, by the way," as if that explains things. I look over at Sandra. "Well, honey, if it was good enough for Ava, I suppose it will do in a pinch."

I lead Sandra through the doors and into the reception area. I'm feeling "expansive," or is that "effusive?" Whichever it is, I settle for one of their best suites and a room less pretentious for the boys. If their parents ingrained in them a sense of frugalness, who am I to impose upon their beliefs? I know, always considerate of others. It's a curse I live with.

I pay cash for ours and tell the lady the others will pay for their room when they get here. Still feeling expansive or whatever, I order up a bottle of their best champagne and bill it to their room. I ask that it be chilled and waiting for them upon their arrival. Again, always looking out for others.

I have a bellhop relieve Sandra of her goods and tell him to dump it in our suite since we were going to the Top to check things out. I grease his palm with a mere five. Hey, I'm not the one drinking champagne.

We stroll hand-in-hand to the elevator. I whistle one of the few uplifting tunes I know. Yep, the Andy Griffith Show again. I don't want to draw attention to us by whistling something I don't know. Makes sense, huh?

The view from the Top is spectacular. We switch back to beer. I radio Jim, tell him where we're at and tell him their room number and inform him that they need to pick up their key at the front desk. Jim tells me that so far, they've struck out. I tell him likewise, but we're still beating the bush. He says something like "it sounds so," but I'm not sure, because far below I spot Sophia. I try to point her out for Sandra, but the person I spotted has disappeared in the crowd. Could it be my imagination? Why would she be alone if it was her? Good questions.

I leave a ten on our table to cover our two beers. I down mine in one large swallow. "Waste not, want not," isn't that what they say?

"Come on girl, let's roll."

Sandra does a decent job of downing hers and we're off and running again. Not literally of course. Perhaps "a fast, controlled stagger" is more descriptive.

Anyhow, we're soon among the crowds again. The place is reminding me more and more of New Orleans as we continue on. There are a number of bars and clubs right off Duval, but for now, I opt to skip them. I begin to understand the challenge of a successful Duval crawl. Sheer will propels me on. "Grin and bear it." That's my style.

On the same side of the street, we come to Cowboy Bill's. I like the sound of the place. It makes me wish I were wearing my ostriches. A true urban cowboy, I am. That doesn't stop me from spinning a decent yarn. Imagine that. The place is an urban cowboy paradise. County music blaring from the speakers. There are pinball machines and pool tables and the dreaded mechanical bull. I know, damn the luck. It beckons me like a cold beer. That's some kinda beckoning.

I sidle up to the crowded bar. Something else I'm good at: sidling. It's two Buds for me and the little missus. I like the efficiency of our bartender: cowgirl with a push-up bra. I graciously pay from my choke-a-horse roll. I tip her well. I feel eyes upon me and look along the length of the bar's backdrop. My eyes make contact with someone watching me in the mirror.

My heart skips a beat—it's her—it's the fucking woman we're searching for! She smiles. She's quite attractive, with a straight, white smile. She's the woman in the composite, I have no doubt. Her composite doesn't do her true justice. I make her out to be around 35. Surely this woman is not a heroin junky. I pass Sandra's beer back to her and lean over to whisper in her ear:

"She's here—the woman. No, no, don't look. Take the walkie-talkie into the lady's room and radio Jim. Tell him we're a block south of the Top, at Cowboy Bill's and that we've found the woman."

I casually pull the earbud free as Sandra discretely unclips the walkie-talkie from my side and moves off. I turn back to the mirror. The woman's eyes are still on me. She seems to be ignoring the chattering guy beside her. I lift my beer and wink. She raises her empty glass. The guy beside her would probably be making better progress if he would buy her a drink.

I make a judgment call—he doesn't look very intimidating. I signal the bartender. "The brunette down the bar nursing her empty drink, get her one of whatever she's drinking."

"Rum and Coke. That will be two-fifty, please."

I slide a five to her from my previous change. "Keep it."

"Thanks. She's a little old for you cowboy."

"Aim high and shoot low," I say and I have no clue why I said it or what it could possibly mean.

The bartender takes it in stride and hustles off. The woman in the mirror mouths a thank you. I wink and lick an eyebrow. Well, maybe I just winked again. I purposely ignore her for a minute but keep her somewhat in my peripheral vision. I don't want to lose her. It took a lot of drinking—I mean searching—to find her.

I feel a tug on my shirt. I turn to see who it is. It's her. So much for my peripheral vision.

She shakes her empty glass. "Buy a lady another drink?"

"Ply 'em with booze," I hear my dad say. Or perhaps I've forgotten to take my medicine again. But to the woman, I say, "I would have it no other way."

"Your girlfriend won't get mad?" She sticks out her hand. "My name is Pamela, but my friends call me Pam."

I shake her hand. "No, she doesn't bite. Besides that, she's my sister. Steven Paul, they call me. Nice to meet you, Pam." I catch the bartender's attention and indicate with my fingers that we would like another round. I turn back to face Pam. Her eyes are so dark and deep the pupils are indiscernible from the iris in the bar's dim lighting. Up close, her complexion looks flawless. She's actually quite stunning. I'm at a momentary loss for words.

239

"Steven Paul. Steven Paul. That has a nice ring to it. You here with your parents?"

I smile before turning back to pay for our drinks. I hand Pam hers. "Good one, Pam. No, actually I'm out scouting the older rob-the-cradle crowd. You know, to ply her with drinks and invite her up to my suite at the Top."

She returns my smile. "Oh, it's like that, is it? A suite at the Top? Impressive." She twirls the ice with her finger and then sucks the rum and Coke from it. I do the 17-year-old involuntary gulp. She laughs at what she believes is my discomfort.

"Will you excuse me a minute?"

"Sure."

"Now don't go anywhere. I'll be right back, I promise."

I shrug. It works for me.

The bartender stops before me. She grins.

"I see you, stud."

Chapter Nineteen

Sandra returns.

"What's up?" I ask.

"She's making a phone call from the ladies' room. Are you keeping an eye on her or what?"

"You mean Pam?" I innocently say. "She'll be back."

Sandra's mouth drops open. "You already know her name? And she's coming back here?" She points to the ground.

"Of course. Where else would she be going?"

"She must have spotted your roll of money. I got a hold of Jim. They're heading this way."

"Good work. Now get lost while I work my magic. I must discover the location of their lair. I may have to go deep undercover."

"Right. Remember, Candy warned me about that look. Hey, did you notice the large bandage in the crook of her arm?"

"Not yet, I haven't made it beyond the face and breasts yet, but rest assured, I'll allow nothing about her to go unnoticed."

"I bet. Look, here she comes. I'll be on the lookout for Jim and Andy. Try not to do anything stupid. She may be dangerous."

Pam slides up next to me. "Where's she going?"

"We have some friends here. She's going to go look for them."

"Oh. Where you from, Steven Paul?"

"Georgia. Dalton, Georgia. Ever heard of it?"

"Dalton... Dalton. Is that where they manufacture all the carpet?"

"Yep, you got it."

"And what do you do there?"

"Work for a man named Bob Shaw, of Shaw Industries. Philadelphia Carpet sales. We're the largest manufacturer in the world, even bigger than World Carpets."

"You seem mighty young, Steven Paul."

"As long as you do not carry me across state lines, you have nothing to worry about."

"Worry about?"

"It's called the Mann Act. Title 18 U.S.C. 421 et seq."

She cocks her head and looks at me appraisingly. "Whatever that is, how could you possibly know about it?"

"I read a lot." Actually, I believe it only applies to women and girls being transported across state lines for immoral purposes. It's also known as "The White Slave Traffic act." Somehow, I retain this type of nugatory trivia. Never know when knowledge like this is needed to carry the conversation.

She waves her empty drink before my eyes. My beer is still three-quarters full. "Damn, girl, you don't mess around, do you?"

"I thought you said your goal was to ply them with drink?"

"I believe I qualified that with an older, rob-the-cradle type."

"And your point?"

"Hmm. Okay," I say before again turning to signal another round. "So, Pam what is it that you do?"

"I'm a frustrated housewife."

"Hausfrau, hmm? Which means your husband won't kill me, exactly why?" I turn to pay for and retrieve our drinks. The bartender makes the sign with her hand indicating "a heavy drinker," before moving on. I turn back and replace Pam's empty. "You were saying?"

"Half the fun is not getting caught," she says stepping forward and rubbing her knee against my crotch. Did I mention that I'm a sucker for brunettes? Some say it's true. And this one's getting my attention. Somewhere in the back of my mind, I'm still focused on the mission. It will come back to me before long, I'm sure. Probably after I quit walking with a limp.

"So, what's our plan?" I ask.

She leans into me and whispers in my ear. "We finish our drinks and sneak out the back." With that, she downs hers in one swallow. Damn, she's not playing fair.

"Out back?"

"Yes, out back. In case my husband's trolling Duval Street searching for me."

Hmm, can't argue with that logic. "Let's roll."

243

She hands me her empty and I set it on the bar along with my empty longneck bottle of Bud. "Good luck, cowboy and come back and see us," the bartender tells me. Pam grabs my hand and gives it a tug. "Come on, this way," she says.

"You sure we're allowed to go out the back?"

"Of course, come on."

We pass through the crowd and past the bathrooms. The door is marked exit only and has the push-bar for opening. Hand-in-hand, Pam leads the way.

We exit to the outside and into a semi-secluded back alley. A lone bulb above the door lights the area. We step into the gloom when a "something isn't right" feeling comes over me. I bring us to a halt as the shadow before me inexplicably changes. Reflexes take over—I duck, but not fast enough and I take a blow to the shoulders hard enough to send me sprawling. Pam hits the ground with a thud. Shit. That's going to leave a mark. I'm instantly aware I only received part of the blow and the follow-through took out Pam. I roll to my back in time to see the outline of the attacker poising to strike again.

He lets out a curdling scream: "FUCKING NO!" and swings what I now believe to be a bat. I roll and attempt to snatch my pistol from behind me at the same time. The gun snags as the bat comes crashing down, narrowly missing me. I roll again and yank the gun free from my waistband, but I lose my grip on it as I avoid the next swing. The gun skidders out of reach and settles under a dumpster as the bat comes crashing down again, once again narrowly missing me. The bat splinters, leaving only the handle in his hand. It's then that I recognize him: Gerard de Cuvaz.

In his second of indecision, I make it to my feet and plow into him as he inverts what's left of the bat with the obvious intention of now wanting to stab me with what's remaining.

I take him off his feet and with momentum on my side drive him into the steel door with a bang. His breath audibly expels, but he manages to retain a bear hug on me as we tussle in circles before tripping over the inert body of Pam.

We both struggle to stand and I can't seem to find my footing, my flip-flops long gone.

He bites my shoulder—my turn to scream: "Motherfucker!"

I head-butt him and feel the cartilage in his nose give. Blood spews from his nose as we continue to struggle.

The bar's backdoor opens—our clamor apparently has not gone unnoticed. Strong arms engulf me and pry me loose. Gerald sprints into the night.

"Not him! Not him!" I hear Sandra yell. "The other one—don't let him get away."

Andy pushes his way through the gathering crowd and sprints off in the direction Gerald fled.

"Let him go, you morons!" Sandra screams. "Someone call an ambulance now! Let him go, I said."

The hands release me and I join Jim at Pam's side. He's checking for a pulse. "She's still alive," his panicky voice announces.

I look at Pam and have to swallow back the involuntary bile.

Pam's nose and forehead are caved in. I'm instantly sober.

"She's not going to make it, Jimbo," I say and again have to choke back the bile. "Everybody, stay the fuck back!" I manage to yell. "Give her breathing room," I add, knowing in my heart it's a moot point. Fucking shame.

I stand. My shirt, knees and feet are covered in blood. Some his, some hers and for once none of my own. I used the top of my head to butt. It must be less cut prone there. It didn't hurt at the time and it's barely noticeable now. What is noticeable is the thumping of my heart in my ears.

The bartender comes to stand beside me. "Sorry, cowboy, called the Monroe Sheriff's Department. Told them this one will have to be airlifted to Florida City. What happened?"

"Unfortunately, she set me up to get robbed. Made a phone call earlier."

"The cops will be asking a bunch of questions," she says and frowns. "I'll tell them the little I know. It clearly wasn't your fault."

Andy returns panting. He bends and places his hands on his knees. "The fucking commie got away."

Jim and I give him a stern look. "He got away," Andy repeats, omitting the "commie" part this time. He got the message.

A deputy sheriff steps through the back door, kneels by Pam and checks her pulse, careful not to get blood on his uniform.

"She's still alive, barely. A chopper is on its way. Can anyone tell me what happened," he asks basically directing his question toward me, the bloody one.

"She set me up to be robbed. It didn't work out as planned. I saw the robber's shadow and ducked—caught some of the blow on the shoulders. The rest of the swing she took head-on, no pun intended."

"Know her name?"

"Only what she told me. She said her name was Pamela and everyone called her Pam."

"She didn't tell you where she was from, where she might be staying?"

"When she began rubbing my crotch I kinda forgot to ask."

"And how did she get you to come out back?"

"Said she didn't want to run into her husband on Duval."

"Do you normally mess with married women?"

"Only when I get lucky and so far, that hasn't happened, but hey, I'm only 18. I still have time to grow."

"In the wrong direction, if you're not careful. Have any ID on you?"

"Nope. Left it at our suite at the Top. Name is Steven Paul, the suite's registered in my name."

"And if I run your name, what do you suppose I'd find?"

"I know what you won't find, you won't find I'm an A-plus student. I'm not trying to be smart—I'm still shaken."

Pam makes a rattling noise, which draws our attention. She quits breathing.

"Brenda, call the Sheriff's Office and cancel the chopper, tell them we'll need a wagon instead," the deputy tells my bartender.

"Yes sir, Marty."

"Deputy, you're not going to try CPR?" I ask.

"No, Son, I'm not. Too much blunt force. She's beyond help." His knees pop as he kneels down to check the pulse one last time. He looks at his watch, then back at me. "Can you give me a description of the assailant?"

"Not really, everything happened so fast, but I can tell you this, he'll be wearing shades by morning. I busted his nose good. This blood on my shirt is his."

"I suppose I need to ask for the shirt then. Can anyone else give me a description? Has anyone seen this woman around before?" He peels the large square bandage from the crook of Pam's arm and shakes his head. "It's a clue to finding her identity," he says more or less to himself. His knees pop again as he stands.

I strip my shirt and hand it to him. His eyes zoom in on my own bandaging. He taps his front tooth but asks no questions. He's the second person I've seen do that lately.

Brenda steps back out. "Done. Marty, I can vouch for the young man. This dead woman honed right in on him. She was already at the bar when he came in."

"I saw her make a phone call in the ladies' room," Sandra volunteers. "I didn't hear what she was saying though."

"Which means they likely have lodging somewhere on the key," the deputy deduces out loud.

"Or the guy was waiting for her call at some pay phone nearby," I offer.

"Shit. What a mess," the deputy says. "We'll be treating this one as a homicide since the death occurred during the course of another felony. Maybe we'll get a hit on the prints from the baseball bat, assuming there are some. Well, Son, I suppose you're free to go." That's better than him saying something melodramatic like "don't leave the key."

I pick up my flip-flops. They're also covered with blood. I find an outside spigot to rinse them off, along with my feet and knees the best I can.

My crew gathers around. Most of the gawkers are steered back into the bar. "Steve-O, why didn't you wait for us to arrive?" Jim rightfully asks.

"Hindsight is 20/20, Jimbo my friend. I thought I had things under control."

"You always think that, Steve," Andy says.

True. It's hard to argue with that statement. I keep that concession to myself. You know, for the morale of the troops. Hey, plus I've been on a roll lately—things have been steadily working out for me. Why would I expect things now to be different?

"Do you know who it was?" Jim asks.

"Looked a lot like Gerard de Cuvaz."

"Where's your pistol?" Jim whispers.

"It slid under the dumpster. We'll have to come back for it later."

Brenda steps out of the door with one of their T-shirts.

She offers it to me. It reads, "I rode it at Cowboy Bill's."

"It's on the house, Steven Paul. Yeah, I know your name now, cowboy."

"Thanks, times two."

She smiles. "Right."

I return the smile. You know, now thinking back, I'm still on a roll. That man tried to cave my head in, but the lone light bulb gave him away. That's pretty damn lucky, wouldn't you say? I wiggle my shoulders. Probably will be sore in the morning, but tonight I feel good enough to ride the bull.

"Hundred dollars says I can ride the bull for at least 30 seconds, regardless of who's at the controls."

Sandra laughs. "You're joking, right?"

"And misrepresent me by wearing this shirt? Surely you jest. Plus, we have to kill some time until the cops leave so I can retrieve my gun. Mission protocol: have gun."

"Killing some time doesn't mean you have to kill yourself at the same time," Sandra says. "Defying death once a day should be plenty. Hey, we better tend to that bite soon. Looks deep.

"Hmm, I almost see your point. Come on children of the corn, I'll buy. Sandra, the latest wound can wait."

"Do they serve food in here?"

"Of course, Andy. Now that I think about it, on a full stomach I'll weigh more and therefore stick to the saddle better. Good plan, let's order something to eat."

We head to the area mostly reserved for eating. Cowboy Bill's is rather large. In addition to the dining area, there's a game room and a large dance floor to do some boot scooting, if one so desires. The late hour allows us to find a table and we're soon approached by our waitress, a pretty cowgirl in tight blue jeans and red, high-heel ladies boots. Her tips are as good as made.

She passes us each a menu. "Hi, my name is Tracy. Excuse me if I seem somewhat nervous—I'm still shaken up about what happened out back. Can I get y'all anything to drink while you look over the menus?"

"Thank you, Tracy. A pitcher of Bud please."

I feel a little morbid and crass about even considering something to eat so soon after my ordeal, but as they say, life does go on and we still have to eat. Put something in our stomachs besides alcohol.

"Now what, Steve-O?" Jim asks.

"How many of the lodging places did you and Andy get to?"

"Half or better, I would suspect."

"Okay, we'll start back in the morning. We should split up. Gerard is going to be running scared. And what if I was to be his source of dope for tonight? The way he swung that bat, he had every intention of killing me. That sounds desperate and stupid."

"It sounds pretty desperate to me, Steve-O. We better cover the harbor first thing. Gerard may be heading to Cuba for sure now, having killed his woman. How accurate are the composites?"

"Hers didn't do her justice, but it was pretty damn good. I recognized her right off. As far as Gerard, I didn't get much of a chance to look him over, but I'm pretty sure it was him."

"Excuse me," Tracy says, "have y'all decided on what you want? The steaks are always good. The sirloin is huge." She distributes the mugs between us and centers the pitcher.

"Sandra?" I ask as I pour her a mug.

"Sure, why not, a sirloin, medium-rare and I think I'll have fries with that. Do you have Texas toast?"

"Yes, ma'am."

"Then some Texas toast with that too."

"Make mine the same," I say.

"Ditto," Jim says.

"The same, well done and times two," Andy says.

Incredulous, Tracy reminds Andy how big the steaks are.

"Sir, the steaks are huge."

Andy huffs. "I hope. That's why two should do."

"Very well." She gathers up the menus. "Anything else?"

I eye the pitcher. Four mugs knocked a hell of a dent in it. "Better bring us another pitcher."

"Very well, coming right up."

"That bite's bleeding through your shirt, Steven Paul."

I pull a napkin free from its chrome holder, fold it double twice and hand it to Sandra. "Stick this to it."

"Okay," she says doubtfully. "If you say so. I hope it doesn't get infected."

The blood adheres it to my wound. It's hard to feel sorry for someone that tried to rob you, but I can't help but think what a shame. She was probably a decent person at one time and got caught up in the drug scene. I hope she hasn't left any kids behind.

The steaks arrive in short order, at least three of ours, that is. The steaks are good—the conversation limited and subdued. Everyone's kind of off in their own world. At least I'm going to call it an early evening. Rest and regroup my thoughts. Andy's steaks finally arrive. Watching him saw into one makes me realize that I don't have my trusted Uncle Henry at my side. I wonder what I did with it? It must be back in the car somewhere. I can't even remember when I used it last.

"Jimbo, where did you park the car?"

"It's parked at the Top. As much fun as this day has been, I'm fixing to head that way as soon as I finish eating."

"I'm ready to call it a day," Sandra chimes in.

Andy garbles something, or perhaps it was only a grunt?

Our waitress returns. "Everything okay? Can I get y'all anything else?"

"No, thank you," I answer for our table. "Just the check, please."

"Yes, sir." She tallies up our bill and sets it upside down near me.

Not bad. Our bill's less than $50. I fork over $70. "Everything was wonderful."

"Thank you, sir. Um... Um, so you were the guy involved outside?"

"Sadly, yes. It sure put a damper on my day, too." I give her a weak smile and add a sigh.

"I imagine so. I would have died of fright."

"Has the body been picked up?" I ask.

"I think so. I heard they were taking pictures of the scene and they were going to leave after that."

"Thanks again. Have a nice evening."

"Thank you, you too," most of us manage. Andy may have a steak bone stuck in his craw. Either that or the shoe leather is actually slowing him down.

"Steve-O, why didn't we just let the police know what we know? If they pick Gerard up, the girls will probably have no place to go except back to Austin."

"True enough, Jimbo and good point. I'm going to call it in as an anonymous tip. I didn't want to draw attention to us. Right now, the Feds may very well be searching for me and Andy, at the least. I'm not ready to go to jail today."

Andy manages to swallow. "You think they're looking for me?"

"They have already been by your house looking for you," I say.

"Shit. My parents are going to shit." Andy runs a hand through his hair, before going back to his sawing.

"I imagine they will shit, Andy," I say, "but on their best day they could never shit as much as you."

We all laugh. It's scientifically impossible that all Andy consumes doesn't come out at least in large part at some point. I know Bonnie's current diet creates some major torpedoes.

"I'll smooth everything over for you, Andy," I volunteer.

Andy stops sawing for a second. "Gee, you'd do that for me?" We all crack up, including Andy. See, some of the lessons I teach do stick. Trust me, he'll be stronger for it.

Andy pushes his plate away and signals he's done with a belch. You might question my methods, but you see what I'm working with.

I knock back the last of my beer. "Jimbo, we'll catch up with you two back at the Top. We're going out the back to fetch my pistol."

"What's y'all's room number, Steve-O?"

I shrug and lightly step on Sandra's foot. "Oh, I don't know. I forget. I have to pick up a key, too. See you two there."

I tug Sandra to her feet. "Come along, dear. Call in the tip while I ask Brenda a couple of questions."

"Okay, see you guys," Sandra says. "What do you want me to say when I call?"

"Give them his name. Tell them he's a Cuban and until recently he was living in Austin. That he's likely an illegal and is traveling with two teenage girls. That he's also likely a heroin junkie. That the victim was his woman and that he had her turning tricks and setting up victims for him."

"Wow, okay. That should get their attention. That's it, nothing else?"

"That's it, girl. I'll meet you at the bathrooms after talking to Brenda."

Sandra nods and heads off. I work my way through the crowd and to the end of the bar to the flip-top the bartenders use to get behind the bar. Brenda spots me, finishes what's she's saying to a customer as she wipes an imaginary spot and joins me at the end of the bar.

"What can I get you, Steven Paul?"

I lean in close. "Brenda, if a man wanted to cop some heroin on the key, where would he look?"

That gives her pause. She shakes her head. "I wouldn't know and I would advise you not to find out."

I chuckle at her expression. "Brenda, I'm not trying to buy heroin, I'm trying to get a lead on the guy that killed his woman tonight. You didn't notice the large bandage on her arm?"

She neatly folds her bar towel and then shakes it loose. "Yeah. Now that you mentioned it, sure I saw it. I think you need to let the cops handle it."

"Thanks, that's good advice, but I have personal reasons for locating him. Another question."

"Shoot."

"Why do I always see bartenders wipe nonexistent spots on the bar?"

She smiles. "Guilty as charged. Boredom... Attempting to look busy. Hell, I don't know."

I share a laugh with her. "And you look damn fine doing it."

"Thank you. Try the harbor. Some of the rougher crowd work on the boats."

I peel off $20 and hand it to her. "Thanks for the information," I say. Here's a pointer: always keep them confused and guessing. It draws them in like magnets. And if that should not work, the constant tipping with twenties increases your odds exponentially. Don't you like that word: exponentially? It's not every day you get to slide that one in there. How long have I been practicing these theories you wonder? Practicing and perfecting more than two weeks now. Oh, you don't have the twenties to spare? Don't blame me, I didn't choose your occupation.

"Steven Paul, anything else?"

"Oh, no. Sorry, see you around, Brenda." Sorry, I went off on a tangent.

I work my way through the crowd and meet Sandra right as she's exiting the ladies' room.

"Done. They sure tried to find out who I am," Sandra says.

"Let's get my pistol then. I doubt anyone has used the back door since the incident."

I push the security exit bar and we step out into the night. No yellow crime tape, no chalked-off body spot. They must not be hip to the times. The blood is still readily apparent and it looks like even more now. Someone must have tried to water it down.

"Hurry up, I'm getting the creeps out here," Sandra says.

I watch her shudder and I smile. "Okay, okay, hold your horses, girl." I squat down and blindly feel under the dumpster, but don't feel anything. "Hmm, hand me your lighter, Sandra."

She digs in her purse and hands me a BIC. I put my head near to the ground and flick it. The lighter illuminates nothing.

"Shit. The damn thing is gone."

"Uh-oh," Sandra says. "That's not good."

"Said the little engine that could."

"What do you think happened to it? The cops find it?"

"I don't know, Sandra, but I seriously doubt it. I bet you Gerard backtracked and got it." I ponder the ramifications. I'm keen on pondering. This is what I come up with: "Not a good development, Sandra. Let's look at the bright side though. If Gerard got it, he only has one, 15-round clip. I still have my .45 with two, seven-round clips. With one chambered, that puts us at a dead heat. I win the tie because my .45 has more kick."

"But he can keep shooting at you while you take time to reload."

"Yet another consideration I failed to calculate into my best-case scenario. Thanks for pointing that out for me, Sherlock."

"You're welcome. Now can we get the hell out of here?"

"Okay, let's go. But maybe I'm a better shot? Then I have Andy. Well, maybe I'm a better shot—let's stick with that theory. But as we walk down this long unlit dangerous alley, perhaps you ought to pull your gun out in case he's waiting to ambush us."

I inwardly smile as I watch Sandra fidget. She pulls the pistol from her purse and thrusts it into my hands. "Here, you hold it and I'll follow close behind you."

I shrug. "Okay, if you insist, but where's your spirit of adventure?"

"Trust me, my spirit of adventure will be right behind you."

We laugh before heading down the dark alley. I whistle the best I can the music from the Night Stalker to keep us company and to uplift our spirits. Sandra clutches the tail of my shirt until we make it to the end of the block and we can see the pedestrian traffic on Duval.

Chapter Twenty

I hand Sandra her pistol back as we approach Duval. She quickly stashes it back in her purse. "You going to tell them about losing your gun?" she asks.

"Of course—not. Just kidding, but I'm not sure yet how I'm going to convince them that it was Andy's fault."

"Gee, I see your dilemma. That could be tough." We laugh as we enter the Crowne Plaza. "What's up with the added E on Crown?" she asks.

"Pretentious, isn't it? Thank God we're not pretentious."

"Yeah. If we were, we'd probably be drinking champagne, huh? Like Jim and Andy."

"Not much gets by you, does it?" I say and we both laugh.

We're still laughing as we approach the desk.

"Ah, Steven Paul, you've returned to acquire your key no doubt," the red jacket, white shirt and black bowtie-attired clerk says.

"That we would, my kind sir."

"Very well, your suite awaits you. I think you'll find it most comfortable... Oh, your traveling companions called down a minute ago and told me to relay a message to you. The caller said, 'tell them we'll be in our room.' He said to emphasize 'room.'" He chuckles before covering his mouth and regaining his composure. "He also said to tell you to 'ring our room, if it was not too much beneath you and if it was possible to humble yourself enough to invite them up to your suite.' He said to emphasize 'suite' too."

Sandra giggles next to me and it's beyond my control to suppress a smile. "Hell then, please ring their room and inform them that we 'politely demur.'"

We take our key and head toward the elevators. That ought to rattle Jim's cage. It's not all my fault. I mean if they could forgo the champagne every now and then they could afford the suite as well.

We step into the elevator.

"Gosh, you don't think they're envious about our accommodations, do you?" Sandra giggles as she pushes the top floor button. "Maybe you should remind them that envy is one of the deadly sins."

The elevator starts its ascent. "You're right and that's consistent with the ills of drinking champagne on a beer budget."

"You're so wise, Steven Paul."

"And no doubt why you're with me," I say as we reach our floor.

We burst into another round of laughter as we step out and turn in the direction of our top-floor suite. Life surely is good. Is there no end to my lucky streak?

I open our door and graciously wave Sandra in. "After you, my lovely lady."

Simply put, the suite is posh. A tiled entrance and a small chandelier greet us as we step across the threshold.

"Wow, this is nice," Sandra says as she takes it all in.

"Check out the sunken living room. Hey, and the terrace overlooks Duval. Cool."

And it is cool. I peek into the bedroom and take in the king-size bed. I step down into the living area and pull the doors open on a large, richly stained wooden cabinet. Located inside are a minibar and a small fridge. I pull the chart out.

"Hey, honey," I say, "look at this, this setup is based on the honor system."

"Then make mine a double," Sandra says and we both laugh.

"That's a good one, Sandra," I say and nod my approval. "Who inanely said 'homeschooling doesn't work?'"

Sandra pulls me to her. "They just didn't have the right teacher, Steven Paul."

"And how does it make you feel?" I ask.

"Horny," she softly whispers.

I give her the contemplative look. "Works for me. I'll call down to the desk and tell them to hold our calls."

"Then join me in the shower."

Ah, yeah. Visions of loofas and exfoliation run rampant through my mind. Yeah, right. What I'm really thinking is I hope she drops the soap again. Wonder what the odds are of that happening again? Only one way to find out. I hastily call downstairs, grab two miniature Malibu rums and join Sandra in the bathing room. I prefer to think of it as the "bathing room," for all its opulence and space. There's a large walk-in shower, with two heads and a large bathing tub with Jacuzzi jets big enough to fit four people. Sandra grins as the tub rapidly fills. I shuck my minimal garb. I smile myself—I'm more than happy to provide Sandra with a snorkel, or at least something she can hold onto so she won't get lost and drift out to sea.

"What are you grinning about, Steven Paul?"

"You. You're as fine as all get-out."

"Thanks, but I'm not sure what that means?"

"Splendiferous."

"Oh, okay. Hell, why didn't you just say so then, silly?"

Our bathing room even comes equipped with an antique cradle phone. Sandra eyes it at the same time as I do.

"Should we order room service?" she asks.

"And?"

"Bill to Jim's room, of course."

Don't you just love this girl? "Some bubbly it is. I shall do the honors and call it in," I say as I lift the receiver.

Sandra wags a finger at me. "Okay, but no skimping."

I have to finish cracking up before I can dial. Dom Pérignon it shall be. I'm informed it will be right up. Chilled and accompanied by two flutes.

"No need for the robe, darling. I shall don this bedizenment of the finest of hand-ginned cotton and meet thy yeoman in the foyer and retrieve our vin du champagne."

Sandra giggles. "Oh, I like it when you talk dirty to me," she says as she fans her face. "Hurry back, big boy."

The bell chimes to indicate our porter has arrived. I dig a $20 from my trunks to tip with and open the door to let him in.

He rolls in a service cart. "Some cut fruit, compliments of the house, to accompany your champagne, sir."

"Thank you. I'll take it from here," I tell him and pass him the $20. He bows and backs out of the room.

"Thank you, sir. Enjoy."

I wheel the cart into the bathing room and drop my robe. The tub is full and Sandra has the jets running. She's the vision of content. I hand her a flute and pop the champagne's stopper. It bounces off the gilded mirror before plopping into the lavatory. I pull the cart close and step into the tub. I fill her flute, then mine. "Cheers," I say and we bump flutes.

"We'll probably need to check out a few minutes before Jim and Andy, huh?" Sandra asks.

I take a drink. "Ah, so refreshing, but yep, that's what I was thinking."

We laugh and do the interlocking elbow move to take our next sip. Sandra reaches for me. "Oh, there you are, you naughty boy."

I grow rigid in her hand. She leans in for a kiss. Our flutes are momentarily forgotten. With her free hand, Sandra pulls me in tight and our kiss is long and deep. I slide my hand between her legs and quickly locate her button. Sandra responds with a sharp intake of breath. Our hearts accelerate.

The bell chimes.

"Shit. Let's ignore it."

"Yeah," Sandra decides, "let's ignore it."

We resume our kiss—the bell chimes. A pronounced knock accompanies it.

I throb in Sandra's hand. "Fuck! What does it take to get some privacy in this place?"

"A secret suite in another place," Sandra volunteers. "Sounds like a champagne-fueled knock if I ever heard one," she adds.

"Fuck it. I better answer the door or call security. They might not take too kindly to the second option, though. I'll be right back."

I step out of the tub, half-ass dry and don my robe. "Try not to start without me," I say.

Sandra grins. "Okay, I'll try, but the water jets have been known to be quite stimulating."

"I imagine." I take a pull right from the bottle, fill Sandra's flute and go and answer the persistent knock.

"Jimbo, my man. I thought I detected a knock. I see you brought trusted man-servant Andy, along as well." I smile.

Jim steps past me. "Nice robe and even nicer digs. Our champagne seemed so out of place in our double room."

"Should I have made it a single?"

"Right. And speaking of champagne, that was very considerate of you."

Andy pushes past me.

"Champagne?" I question with my most quizzical look.

"Steve-O, don't pretend you know nothing of the bottle of Dom Pérignon chilling in our room. This is not Andy you're speaking to."

"Hey! I'm right here, Jim, I can hear you."

We ignore Andy. "I'm shocked, Jimbo, that you would come to such a conclusion when Sandra and I were simply concerned about your guy's hydration. You know, because of the heat and searching all over the key and all. I ordered chilled water, Perrier."

Jim takes in the spacious living area. "Save it, Steve-O, at least you only ordered one bottle."

I clap Jim on the back. "That's the spirit, Jimbo."

"So, where's the other half of your conspiracy, Steve-O?"

"She's in the bathing room adjusting the jets on our Jacuzzi. I mean, she's in the bathroom filling the no-thrills tub."

"No stopping you when you're on a roll, is there?"

267

"Probably not. The pistol's missing too."

"What! Your pistol? You lost your pistol?" Jim asks.

"Only one of them. Hey, as soon as I get out of the bath, maybe you two would like to join us in the lounge for drinks." I wince at my statement. "Oh, yeah. No can do. The concierge lounge is restricted to guests on this floor. The guests with suites."

"Gee, Steve-O, just our luck. It was thoughtful of you to consider us though."

"Sure, what are friends for?" I shrug. "I do what I can. Now, if you boys will excuse me"—I give the man-to-man wink— "I shall return after freshening up. Make yourself at home. And, oh, no pay-per-views or pornos. Have to keep our costs contained."

I return to the bathing room and hope they don't discover the liquor cabinet. I smile as I enter and close the door. "Everything's under control. They don't know about the second bottle."

Sandra has a mischievous and sexy look on her face. She raises up onto her knees and scoots to the edge of the tub. With a finger, she beckons me forward. I drop my robe and step before her. She lightly touches me and I again spring to life. She makes a minute adjustment before the jet, closes her eyes for a long second and deeply sighs.

She slowly begins to stroke me before opening her eyes again. Her dark eyes find mine and she maintains the contact as she slowly takes me in her hot mouth.

I let out my breath, unaware that I was even holding it. She stops and runs her tongue around the tip, causing an involuntary shudder to course through my body. She picks up the tempo. I grow weak in the knees and steady myself by resting my hands on her shoulders.

"A little slower, baby," I tell her. "I want to come with you." And that I do, having only recently discovered this exciting component of sex.

Sandra slows. I feel her heightened pulse through my thumb that gently rests against her jugular—it matches mine. A moan escapes her lips. She cups my balls in her hand, gently massages them and picks up the tempo to a frantic pace.

I explode and shake at the knees. Her shoulders take my weight. She holds me deep inside her as a shudder racks her body and a moan again escapes her lips.

"I have to sit down for a second, baby," I tell her. "I need to catch my breath."

She gives me one last gentle squeeze before withdrawing.

She smiles. "Did you like that, big boy?"

I smile. "I won't lie, you had me by the balls." We share the laugh and I join her in the tub. I take her between my legs so she can recline against me. I stroke a nipple and stroke her center. Sandra hugs my arm and leans her head back against my shoulder and neck. She takes a pull from the bottle and then puts it to my lips for a drink. Now, this is living.

"What now, Steven Paul?" Sandra asks breaking the tranquility.

"I say run the boys off and call it a night. You took the last out of me."

She giggles. "You think?"

I nuzzle her neck. The warm jets are more than soothing. My eyes droop to half-mast.

"Thanks for bringing me back with you," Sandra says. "I mean from Rio," she adds.

"I know. And you're more than welcome."

"It may be selfish, but I hope Candy doesn't come back for a long time. Not that I don't like her, because I do. I know, too, she's also had a rough time. I may just be a blip on the radar, but I hope it works out for the both of you," Sandra says and turns and kisses me on the cheek. "You'll always be special."

You'll always be special. Doesn't that usually come at the end of a relationship? Along with it's not you, it's me? The thought fades as I slowly drift off.

The knocking on the bathroom door wakes us. It's Jim wondering if we're still alive. I really don't feel like moving. Sandra stretches in my arms and stifles a yawn. It's contagious—I yawn myself.

"Coming," I finally yell. We must have been in here for a while. The ice in the bucket is melted and the empty bottle lies on the floor. I poke Sandra in the side. "Come on, girl, let me up." My hands are wrinkled from being in the water for so long. Slowly we dry and don our hotel robes to join Jim and Andy.

"About fucking time, Steve-O."

"Yeah, yeah, I know," I say. "Achieving multiple orgasms takes time, Jimbo. Someday, perhaps you'll come to appreciate that."

I look over at Andy. "You too, outside a movie theater, that is."
Jim shakes his head, but smiles.

"What's the plan again, Steve?" Andy smirks. "Now that he has
your gun."

I correct Andy. "Only one of them and maybe the cops found it."

"Not likely, Steve-O."

"Then assume Gerard is armed and dangerous. I'm sure he's
running scared."

"Commie bastard."

"And, Andy, even though he's a 'commie bastard,' try not to shoot
him. The law might frown on it, us being from Texas and all.
Anyway, tomorrow we get up early, spread out, stay in radio
contact and find him, or at least Monique. Brenda suggested the
rougher crowd hangs around the harbor and boats. If he's
needing a shot of heroin, that's where he'll look. And with that, I
bid you a good night."

"What time in the morning, Steve-O?" Jim asks as he starts for the
door.

"Shit, I don't know. We need to get an early start just in case they
try to get off the key. Put in a wake-up call for seven a.m. We'll
grab a bite here and head out."

"All right. I hope we don't get shot tomorrow, now that Gerard
may have a gun."

I throw an arm around his shoulder as I usher him to the door.
"What are the odds, Jimbo?"

"Right. That's what I'm worried about. Later."

"We'll get that commie bastard tomorrow," Andy says in parting.

"That's the spirit," I say before slamming the door on him.

"Steven Paul, you want me to put in the wake-up call?"

I look at her with mock incredulity. "Are you kidding? Who wants to get up at that ungodly hour? Get with the program, woman."

Sandra laughs. "You are rotten to the core."

"Thanks. It does my heart good to be acknowledged." I offer Sandra my elbow. "Shall we?"

We lock arms and head for the bedroom. We drop our robes and I pull back the covers. "After you, my dear," I tell Sandra.

Sandra climbs in "Ahhhh. Is there such a thing as a bed feeling too comfortable?" she asks.

I climb in beside her. It is nice. We giggle like schoolgirls as I pull the cover over us. Sleep is soon to follow. And it's a sound sleep. I only stir once, when I wake to Sandra's mumbling.

I can't make out what she's saying, but it must be funny because she giggles. I smile and pull her in tight. Life is good.

Chapter Twenty-One

The chiming of the bell and the pounding on the door wakes us. I feel surprisingly well, although the banging on the door is somewhat irritating. Sandra yawns and stretches in luxurious pleasure next to me. She kicks the covers to the floor. Her body is hard looking but inviting. I really am a lucky fucker. The proof is in the pudding and is evident next to me. I pat her on her firm leg.

"I believe the boys are eager to get started. I think I'll dress for success today. I'll have to send one of the boys down to fetch our luggage."

"What do you want me to wear?"

"But for the mission, you're wearing it now." I sigh. "It doesn't really matter but wear your tennis shoes in case we have to beat a retreat. I'll get the door." I don my robe and head for the door. "Good morning, gentlemen," I say. Expansively, I wave them in.

"Steve-O, I thought you said we were going to get an early start?"

"Funny, now that you mention it. I do kinda recall saying something to that effect."

"Selective memory again, Steve?" Andy scornfully asks.

"Andy, if you're still upset about that misunderstanding about you cowering under your bed, I apologized for that."

"No, you didn't."

I scratch my chin, "You sure? If not, I sure meant to."

"Are you apologizing now?"

"Right. Hey, how about running down to the car and fetching our luggage while I order us something to eat from room service. Oh, and don't forget my spare pistol and holster. If you see my knife, grab it too."

"And why me?" Andy asks.

"Because you're hungry and I hold the purse strings. I believe we've been over this before."

Andy's straddling the fence. I can see it in his eyes. I employ my trump card. "Andy, the sooner we get our luggage, the quicker we get that commie bastard."

"Fuck it. Jim, let me see the key."

"Oh, and Andy, stop by the gift shop and pick up some tampons."

"Fuck that!"

Jim and I laugh as Sandra joins us.

"What are y'all laughing at?"

"Andy refuses to stop at the gift shop and pick you up some tampons."

"Andy," Sandra scolds.

Andy reddens before making his escape. The rest of us laugh.

"See what's on the TV, Jimbo, while I call us in something. Hungry for anything in particular?"

"Nah, just order a bunch of it."

"Sure thing, buddy." See, I can play nice when I want to, remember?

I step in the bathroom and close the door to order. I don't want anyone to overhear my billing instructions. It's impromptu decisions like this that make me the obvious choice for being the leader of the pack. Well, that, and as I reminded Andy, I kinda hold the purse strings.

I check myself in the mirror. "Looking good, big boy." The inflammation from the gunshot's all but gone. The brow scabbed over right proper, my shoulders barely throb, my ribs no longer ache and my hand hardly looks swollen anymore. It just doesn't get much better than this. I call in a hearty All-American breakfast—plenty of butter and grease.

I rejoin Jim and Sandra in the living area. They're watching the morning news. I take a seat next to Sandra. "Anything interesting?" I ask.

"This is a Florida City station," Jim tells me. "They mentioned the death here of an unidentified woman and they told it as you told it: an apparent robbery that went wrong. That they're now looking for the assailant. They mentioned Gerard as the suspect, but they didn't produce a photo of him. It's what they didn't mention, though, that worries me: the pistol."

"Nothing new then. Catch any world news yet?"

"Nope, but I won't be surprised if Dom's story is still in the news. That one may not go away for a while."

I frown in earnest. "Yeah. It wouldn't surprise me. At least we have Wallace in our corner."

"Steve-O, I'm sure they will tie me in sooner or later. Felix and his bunch will be harder. Speaking of which, you still need to pay them."

"Yeah, I'll call Felix later and also H & G's and tell mama to release the bag to Felix. They should be happy campers. Plus, you never know when we might need them again."

"Steve-O, as lucrative as it's been, you do realize this is not really a profession."

"Well, I'm still too young to buy a titty bar."

Jim laughs. "Now that I can see. Man, time's flying fast. One more year of high school and then it's off to college. Decided where you're going to apply yet?"

"If UT is good enough for Felix, it's good enough for me. You can't beat Austin either."

"You're right there."

Andy knocks on the door and I get up to answer it. Andy's huffing. "I didn't know which one Sandra wanted, so I brought them all."

"Good thinking, Andy. Likely saved you a trip." I hope the compliment doesn't go to his head. One can never be too careful, but I wonder why he didn't get some assistance?

"Hurry, Steve-O, here it is, the Dom story."

I hurry back and take my spot next to Sandra.

"In world news today, the Brazilian government continues to cry foul in what they characterize as the assassination of Dom Pedro, a prominent Brazilian citizen and known political dissident of Brazil's military regime. The Brazilian government has gone as far as suggesting CIA involvement, an allegation that the U.S. government vehemently denies. The State Department, as well as the F.B.I., report that they'll continue to investigate.

"For those new to this story, unofficially, Texas oil tycoon, John Wallace, has been linked to this story when earlier in the week a DC-3 registered to Wallace illegally entered U.S. airspace and failed to heed the Air Force's command to alter course and land at Houston's Hobby Airport. The Wallace camp continues to remain mute. Not yet confirmed is the story by Austin's Channel 7 New's reporter, Stacey Keys, who reported an anonymous source close to the investigation has informed her that the raid on Dom Pedro's villa was actually a private covert operation to rescue Wallace's daughter, who was being held captive at Dom Pedro's country villa. The raid was allegedly conducted only after both governments failed to act.

"As bizarre as this story seems, Keys reported that the raid was led by Austin's very own teen, Steven Paul, who appears to be no stranger recently to the Austin news scene or its cameras. Tune in this afternoon for an update as this story continues to evolve. In China, crews continue to dig through the rubble..."

"I think, Jimbo, the key to this story is no arrests have been made."

"True. Have you considered that they may not know where you are at the moment, though?" Jim's quick to point out.

"Nor Andy—don't forget Andy," I say. Misery does love company. I know I say that often, but some things are worth repeating.

Andy scowls. "Thanks, Steve, for reminding me."

I smile. "You're welcome. That's what friends are for."

A knock announces the arrival of our food.

"I'll get it," I say. "Andy, I hope you're not too upset to eat."

Jim shakes his head and smiles. "That will be the day I'll not live to see. Since you're being so generous, Steve-O, I'll get the tip."

"Sure, Jimbo, whatever makes you happy." I think for a second that Sandra's going to laugh and give me up, but she maintains. "Set it up on the dining table for us, porter," I say.

He does and it smells wonderful. With bacon, biscuits, eggs, sausage, gravy, fruit salad, milk and juice set out before us, Pavlov's dog just sang. We dig in and make mincemeat of the meal.

"So how do you want to tackle this, Steve-O?"

"How about you, Jimbo, take the car and kinda cruise around the key and try to spot them. Andy, you keep an eye on the harbor, take the composites and ask around. Hold on, let me think about this, there's a lot of food vendors down there, it could be dangerous."

"I can handle it."

"Okay, give it a shot then. Sandra better stick close to me since she's still in training."

"And, Steve-O, I suppose you two will keep an eye on Duval again?"

"Only out of necessity, I assure you."

"Right, Steve-O. Are we going to check out, or what?"

"If we don't have any luck by, say, 11:30, we better stop back by here and get our accommodations for another night."

"I haven't even paid for the first night yet, Steve-O."

"Right. Pretty trusting, aren't they? Hit the hammer and let's rollout. Make sure your walkie-talkies are on."

"Honey, aren't we going to dress first?"

I smile. "You see, Andy, and you wondered why I made her second in command."

"Second in command? You said she was the treasurer."

"On top of things this morning, are you, Andy? When I demoted you to bellboy, I decided to raise her status."

"Aw, fuck you. Jim, let's roll. Leave these two lovebirds to nest or whatever they do."

"Do I detect a gibe here, Andy?" I smile. "I believe I do." I turn serious. "Try not to get shot. Remember our real goal is to find Monique and convince her to come back with us. Be careful."

We huddle up long enough to hit the hammer and out the door Jim and Andy go. Sandra and I dress. I wear my loose tropical shirt in hopes that it will conceal my shoulder holster. To me, it looks obvious that I have a firearm under my shirt, but Sandra assures me it's not that noticeable—that I can tell because I know it's there. Whatever. It is what it is, as my dear mother likes to say. After last night, I do not plan to get my pistol caught up in my waistband again. Yeah, I'm a quick study.

I don blue jeans and my Nacona ostriches. Looking at them, one would never suspect they're only two weeks old. Still, they're some fine hand-stitched boots. I take a few extra seconds to admire the lifesavers.

"If you spent as much time with saddle soap and a rag as you do admiring them, they'd still look new," Sandra says.

Don't you hate it when someone intrudes upon a private moment?

"I can almost see your point. Are you about ready?"

"Yessss, honey, I'm ready." She gives me a quick peck on the cheek. "Can we stop at the gift shop and buy some sunglasses?"

"Are you a mind reader or what? I was just thinking we'd look good in matching Ray-Ban wayfarers." They're also good for disguising eye movements.

Sandra laughs. "You probably want them to mask your wandering eyes."

Woman's intuition. Why did God have to go and create something like that? I mean, he wasn't satisfied when he created Andy to vex me? Or is it I that vexes him? I always get the two confused.

Out the door and arm in arm, we stroll to the elevator.

"Do you think the breakfast will leave a bad aftertaste when Jim gets his room bill?" Sandra asks.

I turn to admire Sandra as we wait on the elevator. Under my wing, this girl could really go places. "A woman after my own heart, aren't you? But, if he decides not to pay the bill, the hotel will keep my deposit since I'm the one who registered the rooms."

"A flaw in an otherwise perfect plan," Sandra notes.

We laugh as we step into the elevator. The couple that joins us on the next floor eyes us suspiciously before stepping in. I goose Sandra causing her to squeal. I assure the pair, "It's okay, she's my sister," and they step clear to the back of the elevator. Sandra and I poke at each other all the way to the ground floor.

Through the lobby and out the front we go. It's a beautiful morning. Pedestrian traffic on Duval is already substantial for it being so early in the morning. So, into playing around, we forgot all about the gift shop. I lead Sandra past a group of Japanese tourists and across the street to Cowboy Bill's, where we step in to check out their gift shop. We end up with cheap imitation Ray-Bans. Oh well, think of all the money we saved. I plug my earbud in and turn on my walkie-talkie. I key the mike. "This is head honcho with a radio check."

"This is Andy, I can hear you loud and clear."

Hmm? I shake my radio. "You're coming in muffled. What are you doing?"

"Eating a hotdog to blend in."

"Andy, people don't eat hotdogs at nine o'clock in the morning."

I picture him swallowing. "Then they shouldn't sell them this early," he's quick to point out. Well, he's got a point there.

"Nothing yet on this end, Steve-O," comes clearly through my earbud.

"Ten-four, Jimbo, keep your eyes peeled," I reply.

I turn us southeast to head up Duval. Traffic's clearly picking up as we walk against the grain. When we get to the beginning of Duval, we hang a left and walk the ocean-side beaches toward the International Airport. There's really no other way to go because, if my memory serves me, Harry S. Truman Naval Station will be to our right. Can't go there. It's a pleasant enough stroll. If variety is the spice of life, it can be found here. I find people-watching interesting. The latest bikini fashions give one reasons to rejoice. Well, at least if you're a hormone-crazed teen like me. A number of hard bodies catch my eye. An occasional tug keeps me going in the right direction. If only they made the sunglasses with rearview mirrors. Wouldn't that be the shit? If I could only patent my thoughts, that would be even better. Just kidding, I know they've been doing that for years. We cross South Street and there we are facing the Atlantic.

A number of people are taking photos in front of the Southernmost Point Monument. It would make for a pretty cool photo, but of course, we're not tourists and we don't have a camera. Other than not being dressed for the beach, we don't stick out. Sandra sports a wonderful tan and I'm no stranger to the sun. As we stroll along, I keep my face slightly turned toward the ocean so the breeze coming off of it keeps my bangs from my eyes. I should have worn the Bud cap. Sandra seems to be enjoying herself. She swings our hands between us as we continue our search.

Static fills my ear—I bring us to a halt and indicate with my free hand to be quiet for a second. My earbud comes to life.

"I see him! I've spotted him!" blasts in my ear. I instinctively reach for the volume to dampen it. It's Andy and he sounds excited.

I key the mike. "Andy, stay calm, keep a visual. We're a mile and a quarter out and en route." Andy's keen on official jargon. "Jimbo, copy that?"

"Ten-four, Steve-O. I'm near the Blue Lagoon and headed toward Andy."

"Steve! I'm moving in!"

"Shit!" I key the mike again. "No, Andy, maintain visual only!" Now it's my turn to give Sandra a tug. "Come on, girl, let's make some tracks."

Sandra's excited too. "Has Andy spotted him? What about the girls?"

As fast as possible, we head back the way we came. At least now we're no longer heading against the grain. Still, the pedestrians impede our progress somewhat. All-out and we'd draw too much attention. I also hope we don't see any cops along the way. I imagine there is more than the usual number on the key today, but so far, I have yet to spot any.

A bead of sweat stings my brow before settling in my eye. I blink it out, half-ass wipe my forehead with a backhand, and we continue on.

We pass the Top—we're getting close. A gunshot rings out. The crowd scatters, a lane opens for us. I pull Sandra to a stop.

"Sandra, find the car and wait for us there."

"What about the girls?" she asks again.

"He didn't mention the girls—got to go." I try to radio Andy but there's no response. A rapid succession of shots ring out. A good five or more rounds. I pass Caroline Street. Ducking people are running toward me. I try but still can't radio Andy. Jim responds.

"I'm out of the car and I heard gunshots!"

I pass Emma Street and see water. It's Key West's Historic Seaport. I pull my Colt. I spot Gerard, but not Andy. The girls are ahead of him and in my line of fire.

I fire off a round above him. The big .45 booms. "Drop it, Gerard!" I yell.

He doesn't. He snatches Monique by her hair and yanks her in front of him. "Back off, or I'll kill the girl!" he yells steadily backpedaling and pulling wide-eyed Monique along with him. Sophia, all the while, maintains a safe cover behind them both.

Gerard drops his arm and squeezes off a couple in my direction. I dive for cover. I see Andy pop up a hundred yards to my right behind a hotdog cart. In my periphery, I spot Jim advancing. Gerard's backing himself and the girls down the dock. There's no way to flank him.

Gerard is waving his gun, forcing people to pass them, sending them fleeing in my direction. Gerard and the girls drop out of sight and onto a boat. I take the opportunity to advance at a crouch. Jim and Andy do the same. We converge at the dock as an outboard motor revs.

A boat swings into view. Sophia's at the helm. Gerard kicks an unwanted passenger off and into the boat's wake. Andy's .22 pops beside my ear. The last vision of Gerard is his middle finger.

I tuck my big Colt back into its holster and hastily re-button my shirt.

"Shit! Time to split up and beat a retreat. Everyone go in a different direction than the one we came and let's meet up at the Top."

We're alone on the dock and stick out like a sore thumb, though no one appears to have stuck around. The man ejected from his boat is nearing the shore. I get a good look at his face before turning and heading in the direction from which Jim and Andy appeared. I hurry off and do not look back. Slowly and cautiously, people are starting to return. I pick up my pace.

I turn to head up Simonton Ave. I spot my Bonneville, but not Sandra. I ignore my ride and keep on walking. Simonton runs parallel to Duval. There's little foot traffic on this road. Sandra rounds the corner as I approach Eaton Street. I take her hand and turn her to join me in continuing up Simonton.

Sandra's hand slightly shakes. "What... What happened back there?"

"Unfortunately, our rabbit flew the coop. Commandeered a boat and he and the girls headed out to sea."

Sandra frowns and squeezes my hand. "Oh, no. Just what y'all were worrying about."

We turn right on Southard Street enabling us to approach the Top from the Southeast.

"'Fraid so."

"Now what? And both girls were with him?"

"Yeah. The punk grabbed Monique and used her as a shield. There was nothing we could do. I'll get a call into Williams and ask his opinion. This may be our first failed mission."

"You're not used to failure, I can tell."

"I wouldn't go as far as saying that. I can honestly say, though, I don't like failure." In some worlds losing a half mil plus could be viewed as a failure. Like, in my world. I keep that thought to myself.

We turn right on Duval. A siren can be heard approaching. It sure seems like it's taken them long enough to respond. Things are returning to normal on Duval. We make it to the Top without anyone pointing us out as being the pair hustling toward the commotion. That's a good sign. We make it to the elevator unmolested. We find Andy and Jim waiting for us before our suite. I let us all in. We gather around the table. I tap my fingers as I eye Andy.

"So, what happened, Andy?"

"It wasn't my fault. He stopped to talk to this guy and sent the girls ahead. About the time they made it to the dock, Gerard pulled his pistol—pulled your pistol—and was going to rob the guy. I think he was ripping off the dope man…."

"And," I prompt.

"And, I pulled my pistol and yelled for him to drop it. Well, he didn't. He turned and shot at me. I had to take cover."

"Behind the hotdog cart, you were guarding," I say.

"Yeah, behind the hotdog cart."

I sigh. "Well, it wasn't your fault, then," I concede.

"Now what, Steve-O? You know where they're heading now, don't you?"

"Of course. Fucking figures too. What do you think about the way he grabbed Monique's hair and used her for a shield? You think she sees him now for what he really is, a piece of shit?"

"Yeah. That was a pretty fucked-up move," Jim says.

"Fucking commie!" Andy adds.

I stand, remove my wallet and dig Williams's number out.

"I'm going to give Williams a call, see what he says. Plus find out what the status is on the Dom investigation."

"I doubt it will be good news, Steve-O."

I step into the living area to place the call. Williams is not in his office. I call his Motorola voice pager and leave our phone and suite numbers. I call it back a second time, just to make sure he understands the numbers. I return and rejoin the crew at the table.

"I left him two voice messages. Until he calls, let's do some brainstorming of our own."

Chapter Twenty-Two

"Steve-O, they're probably halfway to Cuba by now. I don't think we have any options open to us."

"Brazil has a military regime and that didn't stop us," Andy points out.

"Andy," Jim says. "There's a big difference. Cuba is a communist country and we have an embargo against them. If we get caught over there, we're as good as fucked. We'll end up in one of Castro's prisons. Keep in mind we have a naval base a mile from here and the waters between here and there will be heavily patrolled by both sides."

"Andy, we also have another naval base, Guantanamo, on the other end of Cuba. The waters are probably infested with U.S. ships and boats," I say.

"Well, I still say fuck 'em. One of our citizens is stuck over there and somebody needs to bring her back."

I hate to say it, but I do. "I agree, Andy, but we don't know her status now. Will she willingly leave with us after what's happened in the past two days? That's a question we can't answer."

"Woman's intuition—I think she'll go with us," Sandra says. "Steven Paul, you guys, you can't leave her over there." Sandra grabs at straws. "You think the government will help on this one?"

Jim shakes his head no. "And risk another disaster like the Bay of Pigs? No way."

"You're right, Jimbo, that ain't happening." I start my tapping again, lost in thought. Or a semblance of lost in thought? Whatever, a plan starts to take shape. Now remember, I'm not saying it's going to be necessarily a good one. "Okay, here's how I see it. One, we need a boat to get there. Two, we need to arrive without getting shot. And three, we need to blend in when we get there. If we can pull off the three, we might just make it."

"You missed one, Steve-O. Four, we need to make it back without getting shot or captured."

I smile. "You see, that's why they call it brainstorming and I believe I know how we can accomplish our mission."

"Does it include getting shot at some more, Steve-O," Jim jokes.

"Like you're not getting used to it," I joke right back.

Andy scowls. "All his plans lately seem to include getting shot at."

"But this time, Andy, we'll have commies in our crosshairs."

Andy brightens. "You're right. I bet if Ronald Reagan was here, he'd say 'go for it.' The only good commie is a dead commie."

"That's the spirit, Andy. Kill 'em all and let God sort 'em out," I say to wind Andy up some more. Why I'm revving him, I'm not exactly sure. The phone rings before I can figure it out. I jump up to answer it.

As expected, it's Williams returning my page. I give him a quick rundown of what all's transpired. He listens without comment.

"And that's pretty much where we're at now," I tell Williams.

"Shit, Steven, I was afraid that was going to happen, I can't in good conscience tell you to pursue them into Cuba. It sounds like it's time to pack it in and head back home."

"Speaking of home, how is it on the home front, Williams?"

"The Feds haven't gone anywhere. They're still sniffing around. They've been looking for Andy to question and they want to take another stab at you."

"And the others?"

"So far they haven't discovered who all the others are."

"And they have no clue where we're at?"

"Nope. It's hard to follow a cash trail."

"If we don't pack it in, is Wallace still willing to sponsor this shindig?"

"Yeah. I talked to him this morning. You know he'll be forever grateful. He doesn't want to sit back and just count his blessings. He wants to get involved in helping others. This one might be beyond anyone's reach, though, even with his kind of money."

"I've been thinking, Williams, it might not be impossible. This is how I see it, but we have to get things going ASAP. We're naturally going to need a boat, but there are thousands around here. We'll find what we need. We're going to need three uniforms, the equivalent of privates in the Soviet army and one equivalent to a private in the Cuban army. All the accessories to make them look official. I'll also need four AK-47s with extra clips, either caliber will work."

"What size uniforms?"

"Make them all 30 in the waist, except one of the Soviets. Make that a 32 and all can be 32 in length. The shirts all large, but one of the Soviet's make it an extra-large. Hold on a second Williams—Jim, Andy? What size boots do you wear?" I holler out.

"Make mine a ten and a half, Steve-O"

"What for?" Andy asks.

"Just give me your fucking size."

"Ten."

"Okay, Williams. We'll need a pair of nines, tens, ten-and-a-half and a pair of elevens."

"Got it. We should be able to get everything out of Miami. Give us 24 hours. Anything else?"

"Yeah, I'm going to call my friend Felix right now. Enlist him, since he's fluent in Spanish. I'll need him to catch a ride from Austin. I'll give him your number. Oh, one last thing: I only have a little over $8,000 on me. I'll need additional working capital."

"Gotcha. Everything seems simple enough. I'm not sure I like what you're contemplating though."

"Me neither, but after what I witnessed on the dock, it may be Monique's only hope of getting back."

"Have to agree with you there. Okay, well, I wish you boys luck. Anything else you can think of, page me."

"Double up on the uniforms and add four duffle bags to the list."

"I hear you. Later."

"Later."

I call and reach Felix. Pass along William's numbers and tell him we need his help and that I'll fill him in when he gets here. Surprisingly, he doesn't inquire further. I also instruct him to pick up the hundred grand from H & G's and pay his guys for the last mission. He's glad to hear this because they've been asking about it. Can't blame them—it is a bunch of money.

Finally, I call H & G's and tell mama to release the money from the safe to Felix. If she's looked to see how much I put in her safe, she doesn't mention it. I'm still not sure why she chose me to dote on, but I'm not complaining.

I rejoin the crew at the table.

Jim raises a brow. "Well?"

"Good news. We're going to Cuba!"

Jim groans and drops his head to the table. He mumbles, "Of course."

Andy jumps up to pace. Endless visions of commie killing no doubt fill his head. He smacks his open hand. "Fucking commies."

"We're going after her then, Steven Paul?" Sandra asks.

"Not we. You've got to hold the fort down here. I can't put you in danger."

Sandra cast her eyes down. "I know. I figured as much."

I pull her over into my lap and kiss her on the temple. "I know you want to go keep your bikini on. We're going to go down to the harbor and see what we can learn and maybe also get a lead on a good boat."

Jim raises his head. "I better go down and pay for last night and another night."

"Um... Yeah, sure. We'll go down with you," I say. Not.

I go and put on my trunks, change into the Cowboy Bill's T-shirt and this time add the Bud cap. Hopefully, no one will recognize me from earlier.

"I'm ready," Sandra announces.

I lean over and whisper in her ear, "When we get off the elevator, we're going to beeline it for the exit."

She giggles the confirmation. I have to squeeze her hand to quell her giggles as we rejoin Jim and Andy. I have a hard time maintaining myself. We ride the elevator in silence. The door opens and we're out of the gate.

"Hey! Where are y'all going?" Jim yells.

I yell across my shoulder, "Tell them we'll catch them on the rebound!"

We break into laughter as we step out into the morning sun and crowded street. We dissolve into the masses and work our way toward the harbor.

Sandra laughs again. "I wish we could have seen Jim's face when he discovered the bill."

I have to laugh too. "Perhaps we should stay away for a while." I shake my head in amusement. "You would think he'd have seen it coming by now."

Sandra gives me a quick peck on the lips. "Wouldn't you?" she says and we share another laugh.

Everything seems to be back to normal. No sign of the police. We make our way onto the dock. There's no sign of the guy who lost his boat. There is, however, someone on the boat next to the empty slip—a man busy polishing the chrome cleats. I take a second to check out his boat. It looks to be about a 26- to a 28-foot Mako configured to mount twin 200 Mercurys. A nice sturdy boat and they are said to be unsinkable. Maybe with me at the helm, I muse.

The man finally stops what he's doing and looks up at us. "Can I help you, folks?"

"Where'd the guy who lost his boat go?"

"Old Mat." He laughs. "The last I saw of him, he was planning to get drunk. Don't see much excitement like that around here."

"What kind of boat was it?"

"Oh, it wasn't much. Just a little runabout with a 140 Evinrude on it."

"Was it big enough to make it to Cuba?"

"Now, what kind of question is that?"

"Just curious."

"Sure, it can make it, if the sea's not too rough and she doesn't run out of fuel."

"Interested in selling your boat?"

"Not today, Son. You sure ask a lot of questions."

"One of the best ways to get answers. Know anyone that has a boat capable of making it to Cuba and back? Let me qualify that: a fast boat capable of making it?"

"You're not from around here, are you, Son?"

"Nope. How about a boat for sale? I'm still asking."

"Yep. I know of one—a high dollar one. It's a late-model, 32-foot Scarab with twin 350s."

"Made by Wellcraft, huh? Chevys with Merc outdrives."

"That would be her. Know your boats, do you?"

I smile. "Some say it is true."

"You plan on smuggling Cubans, Son?"

"Something like that. How do I get in touch with the owner?"

"I don't know the number. I'll draw you a map to get you there. The Feds popped his boy, so you may catch him needing the dough. He was a smuggler—cocaine, the boy that is. It was his boat." He roughs out quick directions and hands it to me. "Can't miss the place. The boat's on a tandem trailer in the yard."

I reach in my pocket, pull out my roll and peel off a $20. "Thanks, mister. Let me buy you a beer."

"Thanks, Son. I do like my beer."

I salute him before turning and leading Sandra back down the dock.

"Is it a nice boat that he's talking about?"

"Yeah, it's a high-end boat. They call them 'cigarette boats' around here."

"Cool. We going to go check it out now?"

"Well, it's either that or go face Jim."

"Let's go check the boat out."

"And you wonder why I'm crazy about you."

We turn left and head toward the Bonneville. The key's not that large until you go walking it. I figured that out earlier. The sun's starting to beat down and the heat index is rapidly rising. Might as well enjoy the AC.

I unlock the Bonneville and open the passenger door. A blast of hot, stale air greets us. "We better let her cool off a second," I tell Sandra as I walk around to the driver's side and open my door. I insert the key and crank her. The AC is already set on high, so we eye each other over the top of the car while she cools. What a lucky find when I found Sandra.

"What are you smiling at?"

"You, girl. I'm smiling at you."

"Thanks. I'll take that as a compliment."

As is intended—I gingerly scoot my ass in, careful that no skin touches vinyl.

"Careful, honey," I warn Sandra, "the seat's still smoking." I slowly sit back until I can handle the heat. I dig in the back floorboard and find a sack I can tear and spread across Sandra's side. She too slides in gingerly.

We're off. The drive seems like less than a mile. The house is located on James Street and is built on stilts. A nice little inland beach house with a crushed oyster shell drive. Sure enough, there sits the boat—mostly under the house and she's a beauty.

"Wow. Man, that's a nice boat. I bet they want an arm and a leg for that one," Sandra says.

We get out. I leave the car running. A scruffy, weathered old coot stares down at us from behind his screen door.

"Whatchy'all want?"

"Heard you may be interested in selling your boat."

He opens the screen door and spits tobacco over the railing.

"I reckon it, like everything, is for sale if the price is right."

"All right, I'll bite. What's the right price today?"

He wobbles his way down the steps. "Thirty-five," he finally spits out. He wipes his tobacco-stained hand across his mouth.

I step up on the trailer and look in at the controls and gauges. The boat is showing less than 200 hours. For all practical purposes, she's new. I whistle. "Thirty-five? Thirty-two fifty," I counter.

"Get off my boat then, boy." He spits, barely missing his own barefoot. Wouldn't have made much difference if he'd hit it, I muse.

"All right," you old fucker. "Thirty-five it is then. We'll take it." I drive a hard bargain. I'd have bought it at 45. It's a dreamboat for sure and I never dreamed in my life I'd own such a boat. It's a shame I plan to paint it gunmetal gray.

I dig in the back pocket of my trunks and pull out 5,000 in hundreds folded in the middle. I unfold it and thumb the bills to show him that they're all crisp hundreds. "There's five grand here. If you have a bank account, we can wire the other $30,000 into it."

He spits. "I don't know nothin' about wiring."

"Your bank on the key?"

"Uh-huh."

"You got the title to this boat?"

"Uh-huh."

"Get it. Let's take a ride to your bank. When your banker says the other $30,000 is in your account, will you be happy?"

"Uh-huh." He turns and slowly starts climbing the stairs leading to his screen door.

"Weird old man," Sandra whispers. "I can't believe you're going to buy this boat."

After a good ten minutes, the old man rejoins us, clasping an envelope in his hands and a set of keys with a miniature red buoy attached. On his feet, he now wears grimy sandals. He grunts, indicating my car.

"I'll ride in back," Sandra volunteers. We pile in and he doesn't smell any better than he looks. He points with his fingers to give me directions. We end up at a small branch of Florida State Bank, not a hub of much activity this morning. The whole ordeal takes less than 30 minutes. After verbal confirmation with my own personal international banker, William—you know the cat—I had the whole $35,000 wired, opting to hang on to the five grand I was originally intending to fork over. Reluctantly, the old coot hands over the title, but only after his bank prints out a copy of his current account.

Well, financially, the transaction wipes me out, but hopefully, I'll be reimbursed by Wallace and wouldn't it be nice if I somehow managed to retain the boat? I'd be the pride of Lake Austin and Lake Travis. After restoring the original paint, that is. I feel Sandra sharing my excitement. We're both giddy with joy.

I work out a deal where I can paint it right where she sits, after, of course, we take her for a spin. Like a car, inside the dash, I find an operator's manual. We sit for a minute in the Bonneville as I look over some of her specs. Impressive. The 350s are 375hps and, with the 21 pitch stainless props that come with her, she'll do 85 at 4000 RPM. That, my friends, is moving out on the water. Especially, if it's choppy, I would imagine. She also, I note, burns

0.6 gallons a minute at 4000 RPMs and holds 120 gallons of fuel. She's exactly what I was looking for and then some. I toss the manual in Sandra's lap so she can look at the pictures. Just kidding. I don't know if the specs will mean anything to her not.

"We'll find someone to pull her down to the marina and drop her in the water for us. You know, take her for a test spin."

Sandra grins. "Are we going to take the boys?"

I smile. "Maybe we should. Suppose we break down. We'll need someone to paddle."

She slides over next to me. "You think of everything."

"I try," I say and we laugh as I point the big Bonneville in the Top's direction.

We pull into the lot designated for the Top and park. Sandra's still flipping through the manual and I grab the title to carry up with us.

We stop at the desk to pay for another night. The clerk smiles at us.

"Having a little fun with your friends?" he asks.

I return his smile. "I'm not following you?"

"Let's say they were shocked to get the bill. They made a very unusual request: that they not be allowed to charge anything else to their room."

"Unlike me and the little woman here, my friends are of limited means and conscious of their bottom line."

He seems suspicious of my explanation, but gladly accepts my payment for another night. I have him ring Jim and Andy's room and inform them we've returned.

Nothing Jim says will dampen my jubilant mood now that I've bought the boat of my dreams. The elevator stops at their floor and Jim and Andy step in. Jim takes the offensive.

"The two bottles of champagne and breakfast added almost $300 to my room bill, you know."

I shrug. "No, I didn't know, but I know now."

I pause for a long second like I'm actually contemplating something. "Hey, don't forget the tip, might as well count it too. But hey, that's not important—what's important is I bought us a boat and she's a beauty, so stop whining."

The elevator stops on our floor and we step out. "You two have been gone less than an hour and you've already bought us a boat?" Jim puts a heavy emphasis on the word "us."

Sandra hands Jim the manual. "She's a badass boat," she says.

"How much of our money did this set 'us' back?"

"It took some haggling, but I got him down to $35,000."

Jim stumbles on the lush carpet and juggles the manual almost dropping it. "Thirty-five!"

I throw my arm across his shoulders and give him the old buddy squeeze. "Yep. Hard to believe, ain't it? You know, Jimbo, if you look at it this way, that $300 you were whining about earlier seems almost trivial now, doesn't it?"

I give him another good squeeze before letting him go in order to open the door to our suite.

"I wasn't whining. I'm merely trying to bring to your attention that you have no respect for money."

"Gosh, Jimbo, said with such emotion, too. Maybe, you're in the wrong line of work, being my sidekick and all. You should take up acting."

"I'm not getting through to you, am I?"

"Probably not," I say. I don't like lying to Jim. We don't have that kind of relationship.

"Scarab. I've heard of this boat," Jim says. "She does look nice."

"There you go, Jimbo, what can I say? And just think, we can probably get by with a three-quarter-ton truck to tow her. It came with a tandem trailer. Lucky, huh?"

"Lucky, huh?" Sandra echoes.

Jim shakes his head. "Ruined for all mankind," he jokes again.

We all laugh. Andy reaches for the manual. "Let me see that, Jim."

"Well, if y'all ladies go change, you can join us for a test ride."

"Have you even heard the engines run?" Jim asks.

"Nope, too busy haggling to kick tires," I say slightly distorting how the events unfolded. There's a fine line between distortion and lying and I refuse to cross it. I've read there's a fine line separating genius and madness too. Perhaps I'm skating close to the edge. Something to ponder. "Anyhow, I didn't need to hear the engines—she's got less than 200 hours on her. She might as well be new. Hurry up and meet us down at the harbor. I need to find somebody to put her in the water for us." We step back into the hall. "Oh, one last thing. We're shy one adult life preserver. Andy, you'll have to wear the arm floats."

"Ah, fuck you."

We all laugh as we step into the elevator. Life is good.

"We should wait and see how the mission goes before I go out and buy a truck, huh, Jim?"

"It may be prudent if I went along also."

Prudence? I don't even know what that means. Andy and Jim get off on their floor and we continue on to the ground floor.

We stroll over to the harbor and find the same man as before on his boat. He's now sitting in the lee and shade of his flybridge drinking a cold one. He salutes us with his beer bottle. "How did it go with the boat?" he asks.

"We bought her."

He nods his head in approval. "You don't bullshit around. How much did you have to give for her?"

"Thirty-five."

He continues his nod. "Not bad. Step aboard and have one of your beers. You too, young lady. What brings you back? Need a way to get it to the water, I would suspect."

I step aboard and hold Sandra's hand to help her aboard. "You suspect right. I've got a case of Bud for anyone that can bring her to the water for me and another case to get her back out later. We want to take her out for a little while."

He twists the cap off of a cold Bud and passes it to Sandra and then does the same for me.

"I'll give you a hand. No need to pay me, but I would like to take that ride with you. In all my years of boating, I've never been on one that did more than 45 miles an hour."

I roll the bottle across my forehead before taking a pull from it. "Deal. By the way, this is Sandra and they call me Steven Paul." I extend my hand and we shake.

"Well, my name will be easy for you to remember then. My name is Paul as well. Good to meet you, folks."

"Likewise," I say. "A couple of my boys will be down here any minute."

He takes a pull from his beer. "Boys?"

"Couple high school friends. Speaking of which, I see them coming now."

I whistle and wave my hand in the air drawing their attention. They turn and start heading our way. Paul tosses his empty into an open crab basket and slaps his knees before standing.

"No time like the present. Let's drop that boat in the water."

I down my beer in one long pull and toss it into the basket. "Sounds like a plan. They sell beer at the marina?"

"Beer, ice, a little of everything."

We give Sandra an extra minute to finish her beer. I help her back onto the dock. "Jim, Andy, meet Paul. He's going to help us with the boat."

Greetings made, Paul leads the way. He owns a '70 Dodge, single cab, one-ton dually, its utility bumper mounted with three different size hitch balls. "It's got a 440 magnum. It will pull your boat. Not much room up front—you boys will have to ride in the back. Good thing I left the windows down."

Sandra and I hop into the passenger side as Jim and Andy load up in the back. Paul looks over at me. "Not that it's any of my business, but $35,000 is a sum of money for someone so young." He turns the AC to high.

"It is a piece of change. Word of advice, never bet against me in pool or cards," I say and mean it. I do have a good stick and I'm quite savvy when it comes to cards. I think I've mentioned that before. Hey, it's something.

"I'll keep that in mind," he says. We ride in silence the short ride over to James Street. Jim and Andy jump out before the truck even comes to a stop after spotting the boat.

"Fucking nice, Steve-O," Jim yells.

"Fucking A, Steve," Andy yells.

Nothing not to like. She is one badass-looking boat. I get out to guide Paul in lining up the hitch and trailer. I assume it's the largest of the three balls and line him up accordingly. I quickly ratchet the trailer tongue down onto the hitch. I plug in the lights and also the heavy connectors for the electric trailer brakes. The old coot watches us from his screen door. I wave and holler,

"We'll be back later!" He opens the door and spits over the rail in response.

I jump back into the cab. Jim and Andy climb in the boat.

"Ready," I announce.

He pulls out and to my surprise, he heads in the opposite direction. "We're going to drop your boat at the public launch on Stock Island and from there we'll go over to Garrison Bight Marina and get the fuel and whatever else you might need. I've been doing business with them for some time."

"It works for me," I tell him.

Stock Island is only a few miles away and the Dodge does pull the boat with ease. I'm sure it doesn't hurt that everything is level too.

"I'll probably be in need of a truck in a few days, too," I say.

"Can't help you there. Might fare better in Florida City or Miami. This trailer pulls easily enough and is well balanced. You can get by with a three-quarter-ton, but I'd still go with a dually if it was up to me."

I picture a big Chevy crew cab dually 4 x 4 with a big block 454 that gets about eight miles to a gallon. GM hasn't quite mastered a diesel yet, so I'll steer clear of it.

We make it to the ramp—there's no wait. Everyone has already put their boat in the water by this time of day. It's right at noon and I'm getting hungry and thirsty again.

Paul backs the trailer as if he's done it a thousand times. I jump out when he comes to a stop. I unclip the front U-bolt and climb on into the boat. I wave at Paul to indicate I need a minute. I want to check the oil, but I'm really more interested in what the engines look like.

We gawk at the pristine engines. Naturally, the oil levels are perfect. Likely the original oil and probably should be changed at the 200-hour mark. I let the shroud drop back into place and step up to the helm. I insert the key and turn the ignition on. I bump both throttles and push the port engine starter. She fires right off and rumbles as she blows bubbles. The excitement is so palpable you can cut it with a knife. I hit the starter for the starboard engine. She fires to life. I wave to Paul to back us a mite farther. I engage both Merc drives and throttle her enough to pull free from the trailer. Paul pulls away as I back her farther out. I engage the stern drives in forward to bring her around to the dock. I'm chomping at the bit. We truly are kids in a candy store. It seems like forever before Sandra and Paul appear on the dock. Jim grabs Sandra's hand and pulls her aboard. Paul simply hops aboard. I idle her beyond the no-wake buoys with outdrives down.

It's time. I put the throttles to her, she jumps up and her rear squats, but within seconds she planes out. I trim her until she clocks 87 miles an hour. There's a collective "hell yeah!" She slices through the chop and I turn to cross the wake of a bigger boat— crossing doesn't even register. The hum of the engines is invigorating. The salt, the wind and the sun—man, it doesn't get any better than this. Paul points us back toward the key and the marina. I look over my shoulder to appreciate the rooster tails we're throwing. You couldn't paint bigger smiles on our faces. I wave to the slower boats. Wouldn't you? Paul indicates the marina is to our left and to back her down a notch. I drop the engines to 3,000 and she's still registering 70 miles per hour. I turn to slice through another set of wakes before it's time to back her way down. I idle into the no-wake zone and pull her in next to the pumps. Paul jumps to the dock and quickly and efficiently secures us to the cleats.

Chapter Twenty-Three

Garrison Bight is a full-service marina and I have them top off my tank as all of us boys go in the marina to look around. Sandra decides to stay aboard and investigate the cabin. I barely take the time to glance in, but what I glimpse is nice enough to plug into the marina's utilities and spend a night aboard. Of course, that's not in the cards tonight. I don't have much time if I intend to stick with the plan.

Inside, Andy is grabbing food items like there is no tomorrow. I feel like spending some money too. I buy a quality Coleman cooler, a flare gun and flares, a first aid kit, inflatable boat and oars, a roll of duct tape, a small tool kit and beer and ice. Jim buys us all barbeque sandwiches. He's suddenly realizing money isn't everything. It only seems so when you don't have any.

I pay for all the gear and the 40 gallons necessary to top off the tank. Forty gallons—good thing OPEC doesn't currently have their panties in a wad. I remember before the embargo well—it took almost 30 cents to fill my first little motorcycle.

If it were up to Andy, we'd never suffer through another embargo, because we would go over there "and take them OPEC sandniggers' oil." And to think he'll be able to vote next year. Almost gives one pause, don't it?

With the agility of one truly happy, I leap aboard my boat. Secretly, I'm conspiring to keep the boat all for myself. It may even work better than my own personality as a chick magnet. Naw, not possible.

Sandra pops her head out of the cabin. "Steven Paul, you have to come check this out."

I follow her in. You can't stand up, but it's pretty damn neat. There's enough room to sleep two comfortably and there are even a diminutive sink and chemical head. I open the small fridge—the light comes on, but it's not cold. It only works when the boat is connected to a power source.

I head back up to the marina to gather up my remaining purchases. Additional things needed to be purchased, but we'll have a better variety at a grocery store.

Everyone back aboard, we hit the open water once again. As exhilarating as it is, I point us back in the direction of Stock Island. Our maiden voyage is short but sweet.

I drop Paul and Sandra back at the dock and idle around in circles while they get the truck. Paul again expertly backs the boat down the ramp and into the water. The breeze is to my back, so I'm able to line up on the trailer on the first try. I power her right up on it, before killing the engines and raising the drives. This is not my first rodeo either.

I climb down, hook the cable and winch her the last few inches. We're once again ready to roll. I join them in the cab as Jim and Andy climb into the truck bed.

"So, Steven Paul, where are you planning to store your boat?"

"Back at the old coot's, for at least tonight. I'll likely need your help again tomorrow, but I insist on paying you something the next time."

"Well, you do seem to be the one with money to burn, so I'm not going to argue with you. As long as I don't have a charter tomorrow, I'll be able to give y'all a hand. I don't suppose you're going to tell me what you guys are up to, are you?"

"You know these waters pretty well, don't you?"

"Yep. Been living here for almost 25 years. I also know to steer clear of Cuban waters."

"Maybe I'll run something by you tomorrow, Paul"

"If it involves smuggling, don't bother. I love my freedom too much. I've seen a bunch of them caught over the years and even knew a few of them. Nope, no thank you when it comes to smuggling."

"Smugglers we're not, Paul," I say as we pull back up at the James Street House.

Paul backs her back in. In all the excitement, I realize I haven't eaten my sandwich yet. I get out to unhitch the boat and climb in to retrieve my sandwich and to gather us all a round of cold ones. I have Paul drop us off behind the Top so we can get the Bonneville and get the show on the road. It's also about time I let the crew in on the beauty of my master plan. Jim will be happy to learn it's not another "wing it" plan—my specialty.

The Bonneville is not so hot this time because it's mostly parked in the shade. Before hitting the road, we dump the water from the Bonneville's cooler and restock and re-ice it. I'm really doing well on my drinking today. Of course, the day is still young, dammit.

I reveal the master plan en route to Florida City. Jim is so impressed he's speechless. I can't bear his silence any longer. "Well, what do you think?"

"You're insane, Steve-O."

I sigh. "Other than that, Jimbo?"

"You're going to paint that awesome $35,000 boat gunmetal gray and dress us like Russians soldiers and Felix like a Cuban, so we can search at will for Monique in the communist country of Cuba?"

I smile and take a pull from my beer. "Yep. You summed it up right nicely there, Jimbo, my man." We all laugh, including Jim.

"You're fucking insane, Steve-O," Jim repeats.

"Thanks, Jimbo, that really means something coming from you. What do you have to say, Andy?"

"I don't want to dress like a commie."

"Well, I do realize that you're slightly commie-phobic, but I'll let you wear the commie uniform and, if our mission is a success, I'll give the Polaroid picture of you that I have. You remember the one, don't you? The picture depicting you in all your glory—you with your painted nails and wearing the gladiator helmet you crafted out of Cheryl's panties. By the way, you did earn a ten for originality."

We all laugh—Andy huffs. "How do I know you even have a picture, Steve?"

"Are you willing to take that chance?"

"I hope you ordered the right size," Andy says and we all laugh again including Andy.

"Look at the bright side," Jim says. "There's always the possibility you'll get to shoot a commie."

I look in the rearview to catch Andy's frown. "There's a better chance that I'll be shot by a commie."

"And go down as a martyr for your cause," I say. "You're in a win-win situation, Andy. How do you do it?"

I catch Andy frowning again. "Somehow it doesn't feel like it," he says generating a fresh round of laughter.

We arrive in Florida City and stop to fill up our ride. I ask the attendant where the nearest hardware store can be found. His directions are easy enough. Exit 821, stay on the access road and we'll find one about a mile down the road. Sure enough, it's an Ace Hardware—and a decent-sized one at that.

We're going to do a half-ass paint job. We'll sand it enough for the paint to adhere and brush and roll on some exterior home enamel. Too bad there's not an Earle Shribe on the island. You know how it goes, "We'll paint any car for $39.95." There have been rumors for years that if you hit a certain speed in your ride, the Earle Shribe paint will come off in sheets. I doubt that will happen with our paint job. We'll be using top-shelf paint: Sherwin Williams.

In addition to the brushes and pans, I buy some wide clear tape, several packs of large letters used for mailboxes and such, a box cutter, a pack of poster board and a can of black enamel spray paint. Yes, there's a method to my madness. I routinely mention that, mostly for my own benefit.

"What else do you think we might need, Steve-O?"

"Non-perishables such as jerky and other nutritious, lightweight staples. We can pick that stuff up on the key. For now, we better get back and get to sanding and painting."

"Do you really think we have a chance in hell of finding Monique and bringing her back, Steve-O?"

"Of course, it's as simple as mind over matter." And it will only matter if we get caught, nags my thoughts. Much like cheating, it only matters if you get caught. I forget which wise man said that.

We pay for our painting supplies and hustle back to the car. The temperature is steadily rising. The perfect day to be on the beach or in the boat. Unfortunately, duty calls. I'm big on duty. Well, perhaps I'm better at delegating—been doing it for weeks now. Yep, a natural-born leader. Something keeps nagging at my side. Nope, not Sandra. She's yet to nag. It may be one of my cracked ribs, compliments of the Austin PD. They kicked me while I was down. Not until I explained my civil rights to them did they cease and desist. Or was it divine intervention?

I wonder what Stacey Keys is doing today? Will she ever succumb to the inevitable? I've recently discovered that stranger things have happened.

Sandra waves her hand in front of my eyes. "Earth to Steven Paul. You in there somewhere?"

I snap back to the present. "Only lost in thought."

"If that's the case, I've noticed you do a lot of thinking."

"Sandra, you mean scheming?" Jim says. "He does lots of scheming."

"Don't knock it until you try it, Jimbo, my man."

It's going on three o'clock when we arrive back on the key and back at the boat. I forgot to tell the old coot we were going to use his hose and water. Too bad, too sad, he'll have to get over it. Working as a team, we make quick work of the sanding. We're only going to paint that which is normally above the waterline. I take great care to remove the Florida registration and place it sticky side up in the boat's glove box. An hour later and she's gunmetal gray. It's almost enough to make you cry. All but one brush and the leftover paint go into the coot's trashcan. My other purchases I stash in the boat for later use with special plans. For the box cutter and poster board, I have big plans for them. They're key components of the master plan.

"What now, Steve-O?"

"Yeah. Anything else stupid you want us to do, Steve?" Andy says with a smirk.

"You mean like something you can understand?" I fire back. "Not really. Nothing left to do. I say we burn one, then go stuff our faces at Cowboy Bill's. I need to reload on the vitamin E. Ain't that right, honey?"

Sandra kisses me on the cheek. "Yep."

Life's grand.

Jim shakes his head and smiles. "Like two peas in a pod."

"Thick as thieves," Andy adds.

We laugh as we pile into the Bonneville. Andy breaks out a fat humpback from his wallet and works it back into shape. Andy lacks the patience and dexterity to roll a decent joint. No matter, for high and hungry we will get. We smoke in the comfort of the car's cold AC before heading back to the Top's parking area.

Stoned, the hot sun looks twice as bright. I don my cheap sunglasses and enter into another world. A slight bout of paranoia sets in. I check it with the downing of another Bud. The pot has turned everyone quiet. I park and kill the engine.

"Well, boys, I'm going to go up and change into my ostriches and jeans—go as a cowboy," I say breaking the silence.

"I'll change into skirt and boots," Sandra says. "Go as a cowgirl."

"A trampy cowgirl, I hope," I say.

She smiles. "Is there any other kind?" Got to love her.

"Oh boy," Jim says. "There's no rest for the weary."

"Hey, Jimbo, I like that, 'no rest for the weary.' Where have I heard that before?"

"You say it all the time, Steve," Andy says.

"Oh, you're right, Andy. To quote me is to love me."

With that, Jim pushes his door open. "Enough, I'm out of here. Meet you there. I'll see about getting us a good table."

"Great. Don't forget your chick repellant."

"I won't. Come on, Andy."

We all laugh except for Andy.

"Aw, fuck you guys."

Sandra and I stop at the front desk to see if we've received any messages while we've been away.

"Only one," says the clerk. "Mr. Williams says quote 'all's good, local airport at noon.' Kinda cryptic, isn't it, sir?" He adds a raised brow.

I slide a folded five across the counter and ring his service bell. "To the untrained eye, I suppose. Keep up the good work." I never get tired of saying that.

"Sandra whispers in my ear on the way to the elevator. "Do you think he knew we're stoned?"

I whisper back, "Why are we whispering?"

Sandra giggles. "Because I'm really stoned." She hits the up-call button. She looks around to see if anyone's watching. "I bet we smell like pot," she says.

The way he was eyeing your crotch, I think you mean 'pheromoned'. You smell of pheromones."

She punches me in the shoulder. "No, I don't."

"I think so. I've noticed others eyeing you too."

We step into the elevator and Sandra selects the button for our floor. She waits for the doors to shut. "It's because I'm in my bikini and my wrap is so sheer."

We ride to the top and step out. "You want me to wear the push-up bra I was wearing the night you met me?"

"Now why would I want you to do that?" I say. She punches me again. Enough affection. I bruise easily—not. "Of course, honey. And remember," I grin, "no panties."

I open the door for us.

She removes her shades and squints her eyes at me and puckers her lips. "I don't know. I might be too high to do that."

I kick the door shut and crowd her against the foyer wall. I cup one of her breasts while my other hand snakes between her legs. I feel the warmth through the fabric and know just the spot to rub. I kiss her long and hard. She knocks my hat off and works her fingers into my windblown hair. I grow hard. Not part of the plan—the original plan. At 17, I'm still flexible.

Sandra works a hand into my trunks and firmly grips me. I'm no longer flexible there. What was my original request?

As our tongues continue to explore, she frees me and gently begins to stroke me. I push her bikini to the side and finger moisture to knead her swollen clit.

A moan escapes her throat and my heart pounds. I drop the hand cupping her breast, grab her behind the knee and lift. She guides me home and she's as hot and wet as ever.

I drive her to the wall with my first thrust and pin her there. She responds with a grunt and expulsion of air. I feel her contract against me. She breaks our kiss for a second and huskily whispers, "do you feel that?" in my ear.

I answer her by finding her lips again, withdrawing only long enough to pound back into her. Sandra grunts again and pulls me hard against our kiss. I have to have her now—my instincts take over. With every thrust, I drive her back into the wall. I can no longer help myself—I'm lost in action and her response. Her moans only serve to spur me on more. The feeling is too intense. I'm beyond control now. My right hand grips her firm ass. This is it, no turning back now. My last thrust I intend to make count. Despite our impassioned kiss, Sandra manages to nod her assent. I drop her leg and grab her other cheek as well. My last thrust lifts her from the floor.

I cum deep and I cum hard. Sandra responds—her impaled body shudders. Her dangling feet quiver below her. I'm spent, but I somehow manage to hold her pinned to the wall until her body goes slack in my grip. Not until then do our lips part and we come up for air. I'm amazed—even Sandra's firm ass is now jelly in my grip.

"Whoa," she manages after a long moment. She wipes away a bead of sweat that rolls down from my temple and then gives me a quick peck on the lips. I stare into her deep eyes.

"Okay, you can set me down now," she finally says.

"Oh, sorry." I set her down and pull her bikini bottom back into place and smooth out the imaginary wrinkles. "There, that should hold you for a while," I say in my best condescending tone.

"Thanks," she timidly squeaks out.

We both erupt in laughter. Perhaps we are like two peas in a pod. Whatever the case may be, for an adult she sure is fun to be around. We head toward the bedroom to change.

"I squish when I walk. What did you put into me?"

"Some call it demon seed—I call it luck."

"I can see the 'demon seed,' but 'luck?' I don't see how it can be luck for me?"

"I didn't say you were the lucky one. I believe Samuel Beckett got it right when he said, 'we are all born mad, some remain so.'"

"What? Never mind. Hey, check the tan suitcase and see if my mini is in there."

I find the skirt and toss it to her.

"Thanks, we better hurry or they'll wonder where we've been for the last minute," she nonchalantly says.

"That long, huh? Not bad then. That equals six and a half eight counts. Which is also consistent with my policy of riding them hard and putting them away wet."

Sandra cocks her head and scrunches her face. "Yeah. Right," she says before we both erupt in laughter again.

"Ah-ah." I wiggle my finger at her. "No panties." I pause to think. "You know, I hope your moans didn't disturb the suite next door."

"Moans. Did you say moans?"

Now it's my turn to say, "Yeah. Right."

I pull on my boots. We're just having too much fun. I take a moment to brush the tangles from my hair. You are a handsome devil. I chuckle—mirrors don't lie.

"Get out of the mirror, stud and come on."

I transfer the wad of cash from my trunks and stick it into my back pocket. You know, when you're rich, wallets aren't very practical. I stop to think about that last thought. Since I bought the boat today, I'm actually deficit spending. I shake the thought off. I can always get a job high up in the government. Perhaps I should run for some type of office next year when I'm old enough to vote. I could start out small, like the mayor of Austin. Yeah, the mayor of Austin, that would work.

"Steven PauuuuuL, are you coming or what?"

"Yeah, baby girl, I'm coming."

I guess no one taught her that patience is a virtue.

324

Chapter Twenty-Four

Cowboy Bill's is already hopping as we step in from the early afternoon crowd that congests Duval Street. I spot Brenda waving at me from behind the bar. We mosey on over and sidle up to the bar. Yep, when in Rome, do like the Romans do.

"Steven Paul, how are you? Did you hear about all the excitement this morning happening down at the old harbor?"

I smile. "A little—what did you hear?"

"They say bullets were flying everywhere and people were scrambling for their lives. The scuttlebutt is that it was probably the guy who killed your date last night."

"Oh yeah. Who was he shooting at?"

"I don't know, but there was more than one."

I raise the Belushi brow, the one not scabbed in place.

"Hey... Hey! Your friends just came in a minute ago. You weren't by chance down at the old harbor this morning, were you?"

I shrug. "How about a Bud for me and the little missus?"

"Hi, Sandra. Right, I'm sorry, I didn't mean to ignore you. It's just we don't get many shootouts around here. Sorry, I'm rambling. Two Buds coming right up."

325

Brenda wraps a napkin around each and pops the caps with the opener she removes from her hip pocket. Brenda's pretty quick on the draw and she has a rather nice hip connected to her ass. I break out my wad.

She waves me off. "I got this round."

"Thanks, Brenda. It's still early, but we're joining the boys and getting us a bite to eat." I wink at her. "We'll catch you later."

Sandra pinches the back of my arm as we work our way toward the dining area. "I noticed you checking out her ass. What happened to your theory about 'one in the hand?'"

"Close, but no cigar. I believe the night that I met you it was 'two in the hand is better than one in the bush.'"

"Well, I'm better than any two in the bush," she says as we spot Jim and Andy.

I'm not going to touch that with a pole. I'm on the precipice of being pussy-whipped and shouldn't risk the one in hand. Uh-oh, I didn't think that did I? Shake it off, big boy, that was simply an errant thought and it shouldn't happen again.

I pull out a chair for Sandra and seat her. "Boys, boys, sorry— Daddy's running late. Daddy had to take time to sate the little missus."

"Y'all already ate?" Andy asks.

I pull out my own chair and sit. "Something like that, Andy."

Jim suppresses a chuckle. "We have Tracy again for a waitress."

"Great," I say. "Ah, and here she comes now. Tracy, how's it hanging?"

"Hanging?"

"Never mind. Two more iced mugs and a fresh pitcher. Add four-dozen oysters on the half-shell. Andy's buying."

"I don't even like oysters," he says in his objecting tone.

I motion Tracy a little closer. She inches closer. I motion her yet closer. I want to take her into my confidence. "They remind poor Andy of a part of the female anatomy. He says he can't eat them because they're ugly."

Andy reddens—Tracy's momentarily stuck. I throw up my hands. "Hey, he said it, I personally have no qualms about eating oysters. You can ask Sandra here."

"No qualms. I'll vouch for him."

"He's lying," Andy says. "I don't like the taste. That's all."

"Mugs, beer and oysters coming right up," Tracy says recovering nicely.

"Why did you have to go and tell her that lie?"

"'Cause it's for your own good. Perhaps someday, you'll decide to try some oysters."

"And some pussy," Jim adds.

"He who lives in a glass house shouldn't throw stones, Jimbo."

"How many times do I have to remind you, Steve-O, you are the one who lives in a glasshouse. And, unlike you, I'm too much of a gentleman to kiss and tell."

I shrug. I like shrugging. "From that, Jimbo, I must presume you've never had any pussy. Listen, it's nothing to be embarrassed about. A few years back, I was in the same situation. A bit of advice: do a little something about your hair."

"There's nothing wrong with my hair. You and your hair bit."

"You can't believe everything your parents tell you. Take Andy for example... Ah, hold that thought. Here comes Tracy with the beer and oysters." I rub my hands together in anticipation. Love my oysters, I do. "Look, Tracy even brought the hot sauce. Man, you're one fine waitress." Literally and figuratively.

"You'll have to excuse him, Tracy. He sometimes gets like this," Sandra says.

"It's okay," Tracy says as she places the oysters in the center of the table. She fills Sandra and my mugs. "At least he doesn't grope."

Sandra laughs. "Yeah. Right. Give him time."

I meekly smile.

"Okay, thanks for the warning. I'm a little confused. Are you two together?"

"Yep. Hard to imagine, isn't it?" Sandra says.

"Then what was he doing with the woman who got killed?"

I interject, since I seem not to be part of this conversation. "I'll field this one, honey. Sandra is very understanding and is secure in our relationship. It's a true sign of her maturity." I'm not shy when it comes to complimenting Sandra. I bet she appreciates it too, huh?

Tracy looks puzzled. "Okay, I guess." She chews the bottom of her lip. "Have y'all decided on what you want to eat yet?"

I decided the first time I laid eyes on her. I defer to Sandra, however. "Honey?"

Tracy is a right cute gal. Cute gals need loving too.

"Oh... I'm not very hungry, but a large chef salad sounds good. Maybe some peel-and-eat shrimp to go with that."

That actually sounds good to me as well. "I'll have the salad too. Bring us three pounds of steamed shrimp."

"You guys?" Tracy asks.

"I want two steak dinners like last night."

"Okay and you, sir?"

"Give me the fried pork chop dinner with fries instead of a baked potato. Can I get a side of brown gravy to go with that?"

"Yes, sir. I'll bring y'all another pitcher as well."

I told you she was one fine waitress.

We sate ourselves with the food and beer as the afternoon wanes to evening. Nothing better than the comradeship and getting lost in mindless banter. I love my friends in my own special way.

Maybe, with my riding them like I do, I make up for my own shortcomings. Yeah, right. I'll never cop to something like that. I give them a hard time for the sheer joy of it. But I know in my heart that push comes to shove, I've got their backs. The beer is making me mushy, it would seem. I pour myself another.

Tracy returns to check on us. "They're taking up a collection to see who rides the bull the best tonight. Ten dollars to get in—winner takes all."

I like the sound of that. "Winner takes all."

"Andy, here's a chance to prove yourself. Tackle some of the rumors head-on."

"Why don't you? You're the one with the $200 boots."

"Five hundred," I say. I'm quick to stand up for my fine hand-stitched, lifesaving Nacona boots. Someday, I plan to clean them too.

"How about you, Jimbo?"

"You're the one who wears the boots among us."

"I'll tell you what, I'll enter but if I win you two have to ride the bull too."

Jim looks up at Tracy. He grins. "How many do you think will enter?"

"At least ten, maybe as many as 15."

"Steve-O, if I understand you right, we only have to ride should you win."

I point my gun finger at him. "Bingo."

"Fuck it, Steve-O, It's a bet."

Jimbo likes the odds. Jimbo's good with odds. That doesn't fare well for me. "Andy, it's up to you now."

"Fuck it. Bet."

Jim's smile widens. "Hit the hammer then."

We do.

"I'll be cheering for you, honey," Sandra says with a smile.

Hmm, wonder why Sandra's smiling at the prospect of me riding the mechanical bull? She must be genuinely happy for me. Yep, that's got to be it. What a sweet girl.

"Thanks, Tracy, for bringing this winning proposition to my attention." I dig out my roll and peel off a $20. "This is for you, Tracy. Andy will pay the tab if you'll tally it up for him."

Andy huffs. "I'm still not sure why I have to pay for the whole bill?"

"Andy, it's like this," I say. "This is a democracy and we voted that you pay tonight."

"I don't remember taking a vote."

"All right, if it makes you happy, we'll do a revote. All those in favor of Andy paying raise their hand."

Sandra and Jim are quick to raise their hands.

"Well Andy, it looks like one might be straddling the fence." I don't feel like being the one that hangs the jury, so I belatedly raise my hand. "Sorry, Andy. It looks like a majority now that I've voted."

We all laugh including Tracy and, well, excluding Andy. It's the price you pay for living in a free society. Tracy tallies up and Andy reluctantly acquits himself of the cash. To the staging area of the games we go. The crowd is boisterous and I ante up my ten spot. In the back of my mind, I wonder if my half-day Colorado trail ride, where we didn't even break into a trot, will somehow qualify me to ride this mechanical beast. I believe it will and didn't someone once say "nothing ventured, nothing gained?" Could it be whoever came up with that had me in mind? Someone else also said "drinking clouds one's judgment." Hmm, that could be a good thing, for right about now the bull's looking mighty painful. That says something for procrastination—I'll mostly put off hurting until tomorrow. I know one thing for sure: too much introspection gives me a headache. I watch the first two riders get annihilated to the "oohs" and "aahs" of the crowd.

They pull the next rider's name from the hat. I roll my shoulders, not me. It's only a matter of time though. Time to prepare. "Woman, the shoulders: work your magic. 'One must remain nimble when riding such a beast.'" I come up with that on my own.

Sandra starts in on my shoulders. "A little tense are you, big boy?" she whispers in my ear.

I swallow and lie. "Noooppppe."

"You know the key doesn't have its own hospital?" Sandra says.

"Thanks for the info. You know, you'd make a great motivational speaker."

"I do what I can," she says and laughs. With the latest remark I'm beginning to believe that, when it comes to Sandra, I've created a monster. She seems to be morphing into a Steven Paul right before my very eyes.

"You want me to hold your money for you, so, you know, it doesn't fall out of your pocket or something?"

"Nope, but I'll hold your beer for you." I shake her hands loose and turn to face her. Sandra finishes her beer in one long pull and hands me the empty. "Order us another one, would you, honey?"

I cringe as the crowd roars and another one bites the dust behind me. I eye Sandra shrewdly. Another name is called.

Sandra straightens my collar. "Go get 'em, tiger."

"Sandra, correct me if I wrong, but don't I need to wait until they actually call my name?"

She deflates some. "I suppose."

Well, that mollifies me. I feel much better now. I catch the circulating waitress's attention and hold up two fingers and mouth two Buds." She acknowledges me with a nod.

"Nothing like liquid courage, huh, Steven Paul?" Sandra says with a laugh. "I can say this for you—you don't rattle easily."

"Nope, sure don't." At least not externally.

Another roar and then, in the lull, "Steven Paul! You're up!"

Brenda pushes through the crowd. "Go, Steven Paul! Show 'em how it's done in Texas!" Sandra pushes me forward. The crowd roars.

Great, now I feel like the whole state of Texas is on my shoulders. I don't even remember telling her we were from Texas. Tracy breaks through to stand next to Sandra. She waves with excitement.

I turn to Sandra, "Hand Tracy your pom-poms, would you?"

Sandra doesn't hear me because she starts chanting.

"Steven Paul! Steven Paul!"

The crowd joins in. They would, wouldn't they? I look around— where's my latest round of liquid courage?

"Go with the plan, Son," I hear my dad say. I should have a little talk with him about sending messages at such inopportune times. I hear you, Dad.

I step forward, or perhaps everyone else steps back? I crack all my knuckles, except the broken one and readjust my cracked ribs. Nothing left to do but perish, dammit.

I sling myself onto the bull, like it's the most natural thing in the world. I wiggle on my perch. Hey, you can't rush perfection. I bet they are all noticing the finely crafted boots that round out my attire. I take a second to admire the one without the bloodstains. The crowd quiets—I lean back and nod my assent.

All hell breaks loose! I instantly feel like a ball tethered to a paddle. I'm whirling and twirling and bouncing and banging. Somehow, I'm painfully holding on. The blurred crowd roars.

I look up—wrong move! As I start to slide to one side, the bull changes course and like a pinball being smacked with the rudder, I somersault through the air. To the crowd's cheers—and divine intervention—I land on my feet. I hop to pull my feet together, aping the gymnastic moves I'd witnessed in school and on TV. "Yep, pardner, you done Texas right proud," I tell myself.

I spin and wave to the crowd. The slack-jawed waitress hands me my Bud. I'm not a true believer in divine intervention, but something sure as hell saved me. The inside of my legs and knees burn as if on fire. I thought I made a conscious decision to procrastinate as to the pain. What the fuck happened to "mind over matter?" I guess it doesn't apply when the "matter" is pain.

Sandra reclaims me and gives me a wet kiss on the cheek. "Where in the hell did you learn to ride like that?" she excitedly asks.

I take a pull from my beer. "Hold the applause—you're distracting my admirers," I chide. The drunk judges give me a ten, and two nines.

"Touché, Steven Paul. Wow, that was far out."

The games continue. Someone tugs at my sleeve. I turn to find both Brenda and Tracy and two broad grins. Brenda is the first to speak. "You earned that T-shirt tonight. That was amazing. What are you, a gymnast?"

"Was it that obvious? Surely that doesn't disqualify me, does it?"

Brenda grabs my arm above the elbow. "No, of course not. What do you say, Tracy?"

"That was spectacular. You may win."

"How could I lose with you two lovely ladies rooting for me?"

The crowd roars, someone else buys the farm.

"I've got to get back behind the bar. Nice ride," Brenda says before she leaves Tracy by my side.

"Tracy, you don't have to get back to your tables?"

"No, I decided I made enough in tips tonight, so I gave up my last couple of tables."

I turn to Sandra—it's my turn now. "Sandra, order us a round. Tracy, would you like a beer or a drink?"

"Beer's fine, thank you."

I finally notice Andy and Jim off to the side. It's mighty dim in here, but if I'm not mistaken, they look a mite green around the gills. I chuckle at the thought and beam. Wouldn't you? Sandra orders three beers and possessively hooks her arm in mine. I wink at her—let her know I was only getting some payback.

We sip our beers and watch the last two riders crash and burn in seconds. The announcer waves for silence. "Ladies and gentlemen, it looks like we have a tie. Two top scores of 28. We have Steven Paul from Texas and our very own Key West resident and no stranger to Cowboy Bill's, Wayne. Let's give both of these gentlemen a round of applause... Come on you two, step up here. We can only have one winner, so we'll have to resort to a tiebreaker. My heart sinks as I step up. I won't survive another ride.

"Ladies and gentlemen, you decide the winner. When I raise their arm, cheer for your winner. The loudest cheers take the prize."

336

I smile now. What a lovely way to decide. "Jim. Andy. Don't forget to cheer."

He raises Wayne's hand first. He receives a nice round of cheers. I see Brenda has rejoined the girls. The announcer raises my arm. The cheers and applause are deafening. It couldn't have been louder if Jim and Andy had joined in.

"Ladies and gentlemen, we have a winner." He raises my arm again and I receive another round of cheers and applause. The announcer pulls off his Cowboy Bill's cap and hands it to me. Inside it has the collected entry cash.

I bow to the crowd and walk back over to the girls. I place the cap, cash and all, on Sandra's head. How could anyone ever be mad at me? Besides, I want to keep Sandra happy. I have a few new wounds for her to attend to. Resilience: the curse of the young and pure of heart. Well, maybe not the pure of heart.

I would like to say I took no pleasure in the short brutal rides that Jim and Andy take, but you'd probably see right through that. The truth of it is, I'm giddy with joy. We find us a table on the fringes of the crowd and share some beer with our new friend Tracy. Over the initial awkwardness, Sandra and Tracy seem to get along well. Which of course has me thinking, what are the odds of lightning striking twice? I inwardly smile and thank the heavens above.

We end up closing the place down. No big deal—we're a block from the Top and nothing will be happening until noon. We say our goodnights and stumble out into the night. The temperature along with the humidity has dropped. The moon is nearly full and the sky's filled with more stars than I've ever noticed. My knowledge of astronomy is limited to identifying the little and Big Dipper. I know it's hard to fathom that there's actually a limit to my knowledge, but it is true. Give me another year or two and I should know it all by then. Oh, and the North Star, which I point out to Sandra.

Sandra holds my arm and leans her head on my shoulder for the short trek back to our suite. The long day has worn me out too. Jim and Andy step off on their floor with hardly a word. Back in our suite, Sandra belly flops onto the bed—clothes and all. Looking down on Sandra, my resolve to crash and burn teeters precariously. And speaking of precarious, Sandra's short skirt rides precariously high and lo and behold her panty-less moose smiles back at me. Damn the luck.

I kick off my boots and shuck jeans and boxers. I lean over and spread her legs some. She moans and slaps at my hand. She rolls on her side and I slide in behind her. Sandra reaches behind her as if blind and takes ahold of my stiffening member. She guides me in before cuddling up to a pillow. She dreamily smiles as I do all the work behind her. Got to love this girl. I make slow and steady work of it. As always, she feels too good and it's not long before I release deep within her.

One happy camper, I fall asleep inside her.

Chapter Twenty-Five

I wake up after a hard sleep and need to piss something fierce. I'm no longer inside Sandra, but I'm poking her in the ribs. I take a second to get my bearings and conclude I'm not feeling so spry. Must have been something I ate.

I roll over and the top sheet comes with me. Someone during the night pulled it across us. The damn thing seems to be stuck to the inside of my left leg. Peeling it off enlightens me as to why. Some of the scab remains stuck to the sheet—the inside of both legs is denim burned. Damn the luck. Should have seen that coming. My cottonmouth is almost overwhelming. I scoot my way to the edge of the bed without disturbing Sandra. She's still down for the count. Despite the way I feel, I smile at her. Around her, like a halo, are last night's winnings that have spilled from the Cowboy Bill's cap.

I rub the sleep from my eyes and try to clear my mind. The red light on the phone flashes with a message. I wonder if it was flashing when we came in? I lift the receiver and punch zero. The desk answers on the first ring. The message I receive is simple and sweet. "All systems go. Felix en route."

I yawn and stretch. A sharp pain spikes through my side causing an involuntary groan. I twist at the waist in an attempt to work some of the kinks out of my back. Hmm, I stifle a yawn. I must have slept wrong. Maybe I should cut back on the sex some. I seem to be falling apart at a ripe young age. I smile to myself as I stand up to plod to the bathroom. Like Lee Majors, it's nothing that some good old American duct tape and baling wire can't fix.

I drain the lizard and brush some life back into my mouth. Fucking Lee Majors, keeping Farrah from the second season of "Charlie's Angels." I wonder if she misses me—I haven't seen her in nearly two weeks. Nothing like waking to her smile and pert nipples. I step into the shower and hope the rest of the scabs don't wash off. On a positive note, the bullet holes seem to be mending well. I'll chalk that up to good genetics and a string of good luck. The hot shower brings me back above room temperature. The suite is a might chilly this morning. I wipe the mirror free of fog—a world-renowned champion bull rider smiles back at me. I have to admit, I impressed even myself last night. Perhaps the leotard-attired female inspirations at my high school who forced me to sign up for gymnastics made it pay off after all. And to think that at the time I thought my skills were limited to walking on my hands. After last night's performance, I likely shall not doubt myself again. Would you? Yep, I bet you would jump at a chance to fill my boots.

I whistle an upbeat tune—you know the one—as I reenter the bedroom. Sandra is still down for the count and much in the same position she was in when she fell asleep. Hmm? I wonder if she's cold? I could do her a favor now that my body temperature is back up. You know, heat her from the inside out. If everyone had such compassionate thoughts, the world would be a much better place. Hey, but what do I know? Well, I know my towel somehow slipped from my hips. Perhaps I was brought into this world for this reason: to show others compassion. I almost feel duty-bound to start with Sandra. I shall tackle this world one woman at a time. I slide in behind her.

I would whisper sweet nothings in her ear, but upon awakening, she buries her head under her pillow to muffle her inevitable moans of pleasure and gratitude. Oh, to be young and manic, I bet you're thinking? You know, envy is not becoming of you.

Sandra sated, we cuddle for a while—15 seconds. Sandra is reminded that the early bird gets the worm this morning. She's so content that she's yet to move.

I jump up: I think I'll order a pitcher—a pitcher of milk and a large breakfast. Quick to judge, are you? Yep, someday they'll discover that milk does a body good. I know, only reminding.

I call my order in, reauthorize billing to Jim's room and plop down before the TV. Got to keep the old batteries charged. No telling what useful tidbits I'll luck upon. I chuckle—I'm easy to amuse. Even when I only have myself to blame.

Jimmy Carter's on the news. I turn up the volume. His peanut farmer's voice is hard to understand. Hey, but he's got a nice smile. According to the TV, he's steadily gaining in the polls. He's a few points away from a dead heat. That's something, else I didn't see coming. He's jabbering about world peace and Yasser Arafat, whose limousine appears to be an extra tall camel. I wonder how many miles to the gallon he gets out of that one? They ought to take up baseball over there. Some mighty good throwing arms available in the region.

Enough of the frivolous. I channel-surf to find something truly inspiring and luck upon Green Acres. Now there's a minefield of knowledge to reap from. Is there no end to my luck?

"How can you be up and watching Green Acres at this time of the morning?" Sandra mumbles.

I turn to look at Sandra. "Sleeping beauty, there you are. I trust you slept well?"

She moans in response, a residual effect from her earlier sating. She sure reached bliss easily this morning. I mean, she moaned from the second I entered her. The passion has yet to abate, her face is aglow. She plops down beside me and rubs her temples.

"My head's splitting. I think my blood pressure is going through the roof. Have anything for it?"

I pat her on her thigh. "Only advice. When you lie with the big dogs, sometimes you get fleas."

She dubiously eyes me through spread fingers. "What is that supposed to mean? Never mind."

I shrug. "Suit yourself. Only trying to help."

"Help by resurrecting me from the dead."

"When the moose calls, I go hunting."

"What?"

"You still didn't have any panties on. You were advertising like a beacon beckoning a ship in from the sea. Remember, as a minor, I easily succumb to your vixen ways."

"Well, that's enough schooling for one morning. I'll go and see if the shower will achieve what you couldn't."

"Now that's the spirit, honey. Holler if you drop your soap."

She scrunches her nose and eyes me through slits. "Did I ever thank you for rescuing me from Rio?" she says and attempts a smile. I collapse in laughter as she stumbles away. Women, can't live without them. You know Brendan Francis Behan was on to something when he said, "the most important things to do in the world are to get something to eat, something to drink and somebody to love." So, I'm a little out of sync this morning—can't hate on me for that.

A knock on the door indicates my room service has arrived. I hurry to retrieve my robe before answering the door. "Set it up on the table," I instruct. I peel off a $20 and pass it to him since Jim is not here to cover the tip. I'm not quite sure about the food yet, but I down two large glasses of milk right out of the gate.

The porter backs the cart back out of the suite. Do they do this for the appearance of servitude? It does seem like standard operating procedure. Oh well, as mom would say, "it is what it is." I wonder if she is thinking about us. She has difficulty in recognizing the entrepreneur in me. Well, she's obviously aware of my leadership prowess. There's no denying my ability to lead others into trouble. Let me qualify that: inadvertently. As you well know, all good deeds do not go unpunished. It's not my fault that's a law of nature. Here's a rule of thumb: "they only seem like bad ideas when something goes wrong." Viewed analytically, it makes sense, doesn't it?

The milk has helped. The food is starting to smell good. I ring the boy's room. I mean if Jim is kind enough to put food on the table, it's not beneath me to invite him to partake.

Jim answers after a dozen rings. He sounds somewhat subdued this morning. What's wrong with all these people? Can't they feel like shit and be happy at the same time? Or did they break the mold after me? Well, Cheryl too. Now that girl can party hard and wake bright-eyed and bushy-tailed. I wonder what she's doing while I pile my plate with food. I hope this small world gets smaller and includes her again someday. Your first pool top encounter doesn't fade from your mind easily. It will probably still be memorable a year from now. Only very slowly evolving maturity jeopardizes the memory.

Sandra returns death-washed over. She pulls up a chair across from me. "Well, you're looking better," I say. I turn to hide my cringe. Actually, I'm only fucking with her. She does look a tad better.

"I'm not feeling much better. How do you feel after your exciting ride last night?" She struggles to giggle. "Maybe you'll think twice before next time."

"Advice after injury, Sandra, is like medicine after death. I seem to recall you goading me on. It's was almost like you intended to find satisfaction at my demise."

"Well, it worked out fine for you, didn't it?"

"Yep and now I'm an experienced rider. For you see, Sandra, experience is what you get when you expected something else."

I smile, fill a glass of milk for her and slide it across the table to her.

She downs it in one swallow and wipes her mouth with the back of her hand. "Thanks. That hit the spot." She meekly smiles and reaches for a dry piece of toast. She nibbles a corner off of it as if she's testing the water. The doorbell chimes.

"I'll get it, honey." I dab at my mouth proper with a soft napkin before rising. "I figured they might want to partake since Jim was so gracious to treat us again."

She smiles. "You didn't?"

I grin back. "Oh, but I did." It's decisions like this that keep me at the top of the food chain.

I open the door and wave them in. "Come in, come in, boys, breakfast is served."

Jim eyes me suspiciously. He is moving somewhat awkwardly. Andy blows by both of us to get to the dining table. They don't make a hangover that could possibly spoil Andy's appetite. He mumbles a greeting to Sandra.

I retake my seat at the head of the table and rightfully so. No need for me to reiterate all my justifications—you know the spiel.

I slide some more over-easy eggs onto my plate and slather up a couple of pieces of toast. No shortage of butter in this kitchen.

Jim breaks the silence. "Why are you so cheerful this morning?"

"The mission is a go, Jimbo. Felix is en route and his ETA is noon."

"I'm not sure that's something to rejoice about, Steve-O. In fact, I'm having serious reservations."

"So did the Columbus crew and look at how it worked out for them. They went on to discover a new world."

"But unfortunately for us, Cuba's already been discovered and it's a communist country ruled by Castro."

"And perhaps our presence will sow that seed of discord that leads to the collapse of Castro's government and sends him into exile and hiding."

Andy speaks with a mouthful: "Like in exile on a Soviet nuclear sub, in the Port of Havana."

I throw up my hands. "You see, Jimbo, there you go. Andy maintains faith in my scheme... plan."

"That didn't sound like an endorsement."

"That's only because you don't speak Andy's language."

Jim chuckles. "Few do."

Andy stuffs a biscuit into his mouth. "What's that supposed to mean, Jim?" he garbles.

Jim sighs. "It looks like we're going to Cuba."

I supplement Jim, "And kill some commies!"

Andy grins and I speak for him. "One can only hope so."

We all laugh. Sandra chokes on a piece of dry toast. I pop the cap on an orange juice and slide it across to her. She takes a sip and clears her throat. "You're fucking crazy," she spits out before continuing to laugh.

We finish our breakfast and Jim and Andy head back to their room to shower and prepare for the day. I step out on the terrace to take in the view. Not a cloud in the sky. A hopeful seagull lands on the terrace next to us. "Sorry, seagull, I'm not going to feed you." To do so would bring hundreds of gulls out of nowhere and the people below might frown upon that. I know I'd hate to be shat upon. That's how we say it down here in the south: "shat upon." Sandra joins me out on the terrace and I throw an arm around her. She leans in close. "You are going to be careful, aren't you?" she asks earnestly.

"Yes, girl, I will. That's my middle name, 'careful.'"

"You'll pack plenty of bandages, won't you?" she meekly asks.

"Yes, honey, just for you," I comfort her.

"Hey," I hug her tight, "I know what we can do."

"What?"

"Bandage me up right proper for the road. Maybe we can add preemptive bandages—places I'll likely get injured."

Sandra kisses my cheek. "You're so smart. You think of everything." We both get a good laugh out of that. Ain't it the truth?

Back in the bedroom, I dress in trunks, my Cowboy Bill's T-shirt and the flip-flops. Might as well give my fresh wounds a couple of hours to air and scab properly. I peel off a couple of grand before stuffing the remainder in my rear trunk pocket. I toss it on the bed. A little seed money to cover Sandra should something happen to me. I toss Wallace's number on the bed beside it. He'd help regardless of the need. I hope the successful mission of rescuing his daughter wasn't simply a fluke. I mean, the way we went about it was pretty unorthodox. Still not sure what all the ramifications of that mission will be, but perhaps Buzz can keep the dogs at bay. Seems like a lot of "perhaps" today.

"What's the cash on the bed for?" Sandra asks.

"Make sure you're covered should something happen. Wallace's number is there too, should you get in a bind. He knows all about you. Melissa filled him in."

Speechless, Sandra falls back on the bed. Finally, she covers both eyes before speaking. "No one's ever done anything like that for me before." Her voice is raw with emotion.

I sit down beside her and take her hand. "Cheer up. You only get to keep it if I don't make it back."

She doesn't respond, only squeezes my hand harder. I feel for her, despite the fact I can't truly relate. My home environment has always been a stable one. The only instability introduced is by yours truly. Again, I have things astir. Sooner or later, I'll have to pay the piper—face the music. That realization sucks. Well, on the bright side, I shan't face it today. That's how us folks say it down south: "I shan't face it today."

Sandra brings me back to the present. "I don't want you to go— I'm scared."

All I have to offer is something lame. "It'll be all right. I'll make it, you'll see." I stand up and tug at her hand. "Come on, girl. Get up. You can hang with us until we head out to sea."

I pull her to her feet and she presses her face into my chest. I wasn't aware that I had made such a profound impact on her. Damn, I'm that shallow. The thought's a hard lump to swallow. How many times has Sandra been abandoned and disappointed in her young life? I know I've come to really care for her.

I brush her hair with my fingers. "I'll be back, quit worrying."

Sandra sniffles—crying no longer an option in her life.

"You promise?"

"Yes," I promise, not knowing if I'll be able to keep the promise or not. Totally sober, my grand plan seems more than foolhardy. An easy answer comes to mind, "have a beer, then." Wow, how's that for introspection? It seems to be my answer to most everything. Despite the foolishness, I resolve to bring Monique home. I internally sigh. I knew I would. As ridiculous as it is, my plan is in all likelihood Monique's only chance to see her family and freedom again.

I lift Sandra's chin bringing her face up and give her a soft kiss on the lips. Her eyes are teary, but no tears have fallen. I wink at her and give her the old Steven Paul grin. A smile slowly touches her eyes.

"That's the spirit, girl. Add a bikini to that smile and we'll be ready to roll."

Sandra tiptoes and kisses me. "Okay, but no peeking while I change."

Damn, now why did she have to go and say that? That's like telling me to keep my hand out of the cookie jar. "Okay, but can I help by holding your ankles?"

We both laugh.

A true smile lights her face. "You'll always be rotten, won't you?"

"Probably."

We maintain eye contact for a long moment. The moment finally passes. Sandra shakes her head. "Give me 30 seconds."

"Hey, girl, you stole my line."

She only smiles and turns. She totally forgets to say, "Yeah, right."

I smack her on the ass to speed her up. Or maybe because the temptation overwhelms me. And, hell, to mark my territory. Just kidding. I think.

The door chime sounds—the boys are back. I move to the foyer to let them in.

"Sandra will be out in a second, then we'll be ready."

"You're keeping the suite for Sandra, right?" Jim asks as he sets his suitcase on the tiled floor.

"Yep."

"We'll check out on the way out then," Jim comments.

"Okay," I say to myself. That ought to be interesting.

Sandra rounds the corner in her bikini and wrap. Her shades are propped on her head. "Ready," she says handing me my cheap sunglasses and Candy's Bud cap. "I'm hanging with y'all until you set out to sea." She grabs my hand and pulls me through the door. Jim and Andy follow in our wake. I must be born to do this. I'm already thinking nautical. "As any good captain should," I add to my thoughts.

"What, Steve-O?" Jim asks from behind me. Oops, I must have been thinking out loud again.

"How about this weather, Jimbo?" The art of misdirection. Starting to pick up on it, are you?

"How would I know? We haven't been out yet."

We step into the elevator. "My bad, Jimbo, I forgot your room didn't come with a terrace." It's hard to be wealthy and down to earth. In order to connect with the commoners, I chuckle. But I try—not.

"You want to let us in on what's so funny, Steve-O?"

The door opens. "I'll fill you in on it later. We'll go get the car cooled down—meet you there. Come on, honey."

Jim snags my shirt. "Hold on, what's your hurry? Why don't you..."

"No thanks," I pull loose. "Meet you at the car," I say joining Sandra in giggles as we speed walk it out of there. People eye us curiously as we up the pace and burst out onto the street. I'm reminded that sometimes it's the simple things in life that bring one joy. But, not as many as the good life, I concede to myself. If you can't be honest with yourself, with whom can you be honest? I'm sure somebody said that and if they didn't, they should have.

We round the corner. "Whoa, that was fun," Sandra says.

"I concur, baby girl."

I stop us so we can catch our breath from the sheer frivolity of our antics. We saunter the rest of the way to the car. I unlock her and crank her. The car's clock reads 11:45. Hmm, we'll either be right on time or an hour late. The message neglected to mention at which time they would be arriving—Texas time or Cuban Standard Time. No, I don't know if there is such a thing. I'm merely amusing myself. I'm probably cheating myself out of a joke. Not guilty of that often.

Jim and Andy come into view. Jim's scowling and Andy is grinning behind him. He stops before me.

"The car should be cooled right proper, Jim."

"Cool, huh? You had to go and do it again, didn't you?"

I point at Sandra. "It was her idea." But, yeah, I did. Why ask?

"Hey! It was not."

I make a pistol with my hand and finger and point it at her. "Got you," I say before turning serious. "It's like this, Jimbo. There are cost constraints for me to consider. When I present our bill for reimbursement, I don't want my bill to seem overly lavish. You see, a few more meals and maybe another bottle of champagne and things would have balanced out."

"Gee, Steve-O, I see what you mean. By maintaining a suite, you manage to balance things out."

I smile and throw my arm across his shoulder. "Not much gets by you does it, Jimbo? Sandra, any thoughts in furtherance of the conspiracy?"

She shrugs. "What's money between friends?"

"Did you catch that, Andy?" I say. "And you wonder why you're still a private in this army. Oh, and soon you'll be flying your true colors as well—commie colors."

We all laugh, except Andy.

"Load up, boys," I say. "They should be here any minute."

I raise the seat to allow Andy in the back. Loaded, we're off and en route. Key West International Airport is on the Atlantic side and only about two and a half miles away. We're there in minutes. For an international airport, it's a small one. Most fly in and out of Miami. I follow a route that takes me to the smaller hangers. We watch and wait.

Chapter Twenty-Six

I watch the minute hand click to noon. I snap my fingers.

"Beer, Andy." Noon Texas-time, a personal best. A solid nine hours of downtime.

I hear Andy slosh around in the cooler. "Still some ice," he says passing a beer to me. I pull the tab and take a long pull. Hmm, pretty damn refreshing.

"Have a beer, Jimbo, it's the least I can do, now that you've made me feel somewhat responsible for inflating your bill."

"Thanks, that will square us. Andy, hand me one."

Andy passes a beer to Jim. "Sandra?"

She vigorously waves her hands. "Oh, no. I might not ever drink again."

I squeeze her knee. "My little trooper. Hey, look, that's her I believe. It looks like Candy's Super King Air.

"Yep, Steve-O, that's her. Candy's plane."

We watch as she turns off the runway. "Wow, that's a pretty plane. That's the one in which you terrorized Austin?" Sandra asks.

"The one and the same," I proudly say. "Don't forget Westlake—I buzzed them too."

"No shame in his game, Sandra," Jim says.

"Nor should there be," I counter. I down my beer and toss it over my shoulder.

"Hey! You almost hit me with that!"

"Your point?" I say as I exit the Bonneville. Gary, Wallace's pilot, spots us and taxis our way. He has at least one passenger.

We walk toward the plane as her props come to a halt. The cabin door opens and the steps lower to the tarmac. Felix is the first out and he's beaming. "Esteban Pablo. How's it going, my friend?"

"Muy bien. ¿Cómo estás?"

"I'm doing fine. Depende."

"On the mission, no doubt."

Oscar steps off the plane next carrying two of the army duffle bags. Felix's uncle grins.

"Oscar, how's it going?" I ask.

He sets a duffle down and shakes my hand. "Okay, I talked Felix into letting me come along. Get in on some of this cash you're generating."

"Okay, but this might not be easy cash. You know Andy. That's Jim and Sandra over there."

They collectively nod at each other. Gary's last off the plane carrying two more duffle bags. He also has a bank bag tucked under his arm. His grin is a big one as well.

"Steven Paul, good to see you again. Jim, Andy, likewise." He sets the duffels at my feet and to my surprise embraces me and then Jim and Andy in turn. I almost laugh at Andy's discomfort. "Boys, I haven't had the chance to thank you for bringing Melissa home. I was stern and had my doubts, but y'all proved me wrong. I apologize for that and sincerely thank you. Melissa's like a daughter to me." He laughs. "Even made it back with the big bird DC-3. I noticed it has an oddball tire on it now."

"We're definitely happy we made it back. We had one hard night landing. I forgot to calibrate the altimeter and we stalled before we should have."

He hands me the bank bag. "There's $15,000 in here. Wallace didn't know how much to send, but there's always more a phone call away. He says if need be to contact Williams again and Williams will get the message to him."

"And the Feds?" I ask.

"Still breathing down his neck. They want another shot at you. And, oh Andy, they're very eager to talk to you as well." He laughs. "They're looking high and low for you boys."

"No chance they'll follow you here, is there?"

"Doubtful. I filed a number of flight plans by fax. I did a splash and dash in Austin and reversed direction. So, you boys are off to Cuba, are you?"

"Yeah, as much as I hate it. No other way short of throwing in the towel."

"By the way, Melissa sends her love. She says you're 'out there.' Is that what you young folks call 'far out?'"

"Something like that. Hey, good to see you again, but we really need to get going. They already have a 24-hour head start on us."

"Sure. Hey, at least you won't be flying this time. Later, boys."

He turns and waves before stepping into the cabin. Felix steps over and puts a hand on my shoulder.

"Nice guy, but talkative. He couldn't praise us enough. Oh, the boys back home never expected to see so much cash. To say the least, they're ecstatic."

He laughs. "They're all sitting around the phone right now hoping we may need them."

"Not this time, but I think I can write Oscar into the script."

"Thanks, Esteban," Oscar says. As our straw buyer, he only made a hundred dollars, whereas the rest of the Felix recruits made, as you know, $10,000 apiece. Of course, they got shot at, but at least none of them got shot.

Felix breaks my reverie. "I hope you have some cold Cerveza in that big Bonneville of yours. Gary has a rule about coolers on his plane." He laughs. "He says the FAA frowns upon it. He couldn't believe all the beer cans and bottles the Feds removed from the DC-3."

I smile at the thought. "I imagine. Well, we need to pick up supplies and make waves."

"You've already got a boat?"

Jim interjects. "It's a bad boy too."

"I'm sure. Esteban doesn't do anything at half speed. Sandra, how are you doing?

"Sad, afraid, hungover."

Felix frowns. "It will be all right, Sandra. Esteban has the luck of an Irishman." He looks over at me and looks puzzled.

"What happened to your legs, Esteban?"

Andy finally breaks his silence. "He's a bull rider now."

That really confuses Felix. "They have bulls in Key West?"

I smile. "Not just any bull, perhaps the world's meanest. Let's roll. I'll tell you about it in the car."

"Fucking Esteban, you're too much man."

I grab a duffle bag and head toward my big ride. We load them all in the trunk. Oscar and Felix join Andy and the cooler in the back. "Esteban, what's all that paint on the side of your car?"

"Candy's estranged tried to kidnap Bonnie and I ran him into a parked car doing about 60."

"No shit?"

"I shit you not. Hand me a beer, Felix."

"And what's up with this meanest bullshit? Pun intended."

I light up. "Mechanical bull and they pitted me against some of the state's finest riders...."

"The bar's drunkest he means, Felix." Jim clarifies.

I eye Jim. "Who's telling this story?" I take a pull from my beer and put the Bonneville in gear. "You wouldn't believe it, Felix! I was amazing! Needless to say, I took the grand prize—all the cash. My dismount truly wooed the crowd. A twist, half pike and full backflip. I scored a ten, and two nines."

"Come on, Esteban."

"What he means is somehow he landed on his feet." Jim says apparently happy to help out again.

"Well, my baby took the prize money," Sandra weighs in.

"This store over here will work," I say pulling into a small grocery store.

Andy adds his two cents: "Hear Steve tell it, he defied gravity."

I throw the car into park. "Which you and Jim didn't. Felix, they both lasted about one second."

"Jim, don't tell me Esteban talked you into riding a mechanical bull."

"Yeah. He suckered me into it. He bet me if he rode, he'd win. The odds of him winning were almost nil."

"I believe you failed to factor in your ardent and repressed desire to bet against me," I say and smile. "Had you done so, Jimbo, you would have realized you had no chance of winning."

Sandra chimes in: "My baby's got a point there."

"Yeah, I should have known better. Again, Steve-O managed to piss in the wind and not get wet."

"With that, let's do some shopping, boys," I say as I push my door open.

"Esteban, what all are we buying here?"

"Provisions. Anything that suits your fancy, but keep in mind Andy can only tote so much."

We all laugh, except Andy.

"Fuck that. Y'all are going to carry your own stuff." Andy chuckles. "Which means: better keep it light."

"Good one, Andy, you actually squeezed one in," I say.

We raid the aisles. While Andy's studying a can of pork and beans, I beat him to the beef jerky display and snatch up all the choice packs. I make a big show of sharing them with the others. Andy's look of disappointment is discernible.

"Fucker," he says. I don't know why I work so hard to keep him on his toes.

"Did you find the brand of pork and beans you were looking for?"

Of course, I plan to share mine, but his expression is worth a thousand words. We gather up everything we think we'll need. This also includes medical supplies. We'll have to stop in the liquor store next door and supplement our rubbing alcohol with some field alcohol—vodka. The good stuff that comes in lightweight plastic half-pints. I'm starting to believe Sandra: I do think of everything.

"What are you smiling about now, Steven Paul?" Sandra asks. She's getting pretty good at reading me.

"Nothing," I lie. She only smiles. Well, actually, since she knows I'm lying, it's really not a lie, now is it?

The sun is high in the sky and beaming when we step back out into the heat. This far inland, there's not much breeze in front of the store. Andy and Oscar take our carts to load up the Bonneville, while the rest of us walk over to the liquor store. I have Sandra buy us a fifth for each of the duffle bags and a handful of powdered Tom Collins mixes. With that, it seems like we're set. The moment of truth is fast approaching.

We make the short drive over to James Street to stow our guns and goods. The old coot eyes us suspiciously from behind the safety of his screen door. The ice in the boat's new Coleman cooler is mostly intact. We break a moment to drink a beer out of this cooler and give Felix and Oscar the opportunity to look over the boat. They're both rightly impressed. I still can't believe we own this boat. I mean, the exterior looks like shit now, but at some point, if we're successful, she'll be restored to her former glory. No more ifs. From here on, it's only when we'll succeed.

We load back up into the big Bonneville. Andy's getting tired of holding Big Blue in his lap, but, hey, someone has to do it.

We park back at the Top and this is where Sandra and I will part company. It turns out sad, but not tearful. I hand her the keys to the car and the moneybag with instructions to put it in the Top's safe. I have enough cash on me as it is. The people of Cuba are poor and a little bit there will go a long way. With some luck, it will be in and out. Yeah, famous last words, I know.

We walk the short distance to the old harbor and out on the dock where we find Paul sitting once again in the lee of his flybridge drinking a beer. He raises his beer in greeting—ushers us aboard. "Grab a beer, boys."

I hop onto the deck followed by the rest of my crew.

"Paul, good to see you again. You know Jim and Andy." I point to Felix. "This here is Felix and over here is his uncle, Oscar."

"Nice to meet you fellows. I guess you're determined to put your boat back in the water today?"

I help myself to a beer and move away so the others can get to the cooler. "Yes, sir."

"Have your recruitment pitch down?"

"I thought about it and I think we're going to wing it."

"You can't miss Cuba, so there's not much chance of getting lost. I'll show you how your LORAN works, if you don't know how to work it, that is."

"Thanks." I pull out the fold of bills and peel off $100. He tries to wave me off, but I tuck it into his shirt pocket. "That pays for some discretion too, should anyone come asking about us."

He nods. "Fair enough. I hope you boys know what you're doing."

"That's subject to debate," Jim says no doubt feeling the same cloud of apprehension that engulfs me. Felix and Oscar have yet to ask exactly what the grand plan is, but they obviously know it includes a trip abroad. With the arrival of Oscar, I've amended the plans. He'll come to play a vital role—our means of return to the states. I'll fill them in onboard.

Paul slaps his knee, before rising. "Let's put her in water, boys."

We toss our empties into the crab basket and follow him to his truck. Jim and I join him up front for the short trip.

The boat comes into sight—Paul's jaw drops. "What the fuck?"

"Yeah. Makes a statement, huh?" I say. "A real chic magnet now."

Paul rests his head on the steering wheel as we come to a stop and groans. "Steven Paul, such a beautiful boat."

"Thanks," I say and we all laugh.

"Back me to the hitch. I'm almost embarrassed to tow it."

"Yep. Be hard to plead the fifth after that," I comment before jumping out. The rest of the crew pile out and I back him up just right.

Paul gets out and explains the LORAN to me. It's simple enough. The LORAN (Long Range Navigation) system determines your position by analyzing the time intervals from pulsed radio signals from two or more pairs of ground stations of known positions. Makes sense, doesn't it?

I grab us a couple of Buds from the boat's cooler for the trip to Stock Island. The day is poised to be a beauty. We listen to Don Williams along the way. "I believe in love," Williams sings.

Paul expertly backs the boat down the ramp. Once again, not much activity at this time of day, but we raise eyebrows on the few present.

We bid our adieus and we're off. Despite some foreboding, there's an air of excitement. The deep-throated hum of the engines can be heard and felt.

I open her up and trim her out. There are smiles all around. I slow her as Garrison Bight comes into view. As we make some last-minute purchases, I set Andy to work drawing and cutting out a hammer and sickle stencil. He mumbles, but, considering his commie phobia, he's the most qualified for the task. To the purchase, I add a handheld ship-to-shore radio and batteries. In addition, a small collapsible cooler, a case of Bud in cans and two slabs of dry ice. With our purchases, I believe we've been accepted in Key West's wayward community.

As they say, the shortest distance between two points is a straight line. I set us on a course due south and run her at an optimum 2500 rpm for fuel conservation. We should have plenty of fuel. In fact, by my primitive calculations, we have enough to make the trip there and back twice. I love the boat and being at the helm— I'm a born skipper, a man and his boat, a mariner, a seafarer.

Andy's hammer and sickle stencil don't cut the mustard. It looks more like nothing and a banana. Oscar volunteers to give it a shot. I don't know what a Soviet gunboat looks like, but perhaps the people we encounter won't either—in other words, anybody other than the Soviet Navy. I don't expect the U.S. would tolerate Soviet war vessels in the waters on this side of Cuba. Or for that matter anywhere around our own naval stations. But we only encounter a smattering of fishing boats on our way out and no military ships or boats of any kind. Lucky, huh?

When I estimate we're 40 miles out, I cut the engines and let her drift. I have Andy pass out the duffle bags. It's time for us to change into our newest attire. As requested, there are two sets of each. My duffle also contains an AK-47 in .223s with spare clips and extra ammo, the boots and cap, a belt with a holstered Smith & Wesson 9mm and authentic insignia on the sleeves of the shirts. Hmm, better than I expected. Dressed, I salute Andy. He peevishly grins and salutes back. I believe he's officially come out of the closet. The AK's come with slings, an added bonus.

Deep down in the duffle, I find a spare clip for the 9, three boxes of Remington hollow points and a map of Cuba. Far out.

I take the shirt I was wearing and dry a section toward the rear of the boat above the waterline and line it with enough short strips of the clear tape to accommodate the stencil. I then spray it with the black enamel and transfer the stencil to the boat. I survey my work—not bad. And it can be stripped away within minutes. I repeat the process on the other side. To further my lovely disguise, I pick out a few random numbers and letters, align them upside down on a strip of the wide tape and apply it to the boat after the stencil.

Everyone silently watches my progress. "Not fucking bad, Esteban," Felix comments. Everyone else nods their assent. I wipe the sweat from my face and drink another beer while we drift for a moment.

Jim turns on the boat's stereo and dials in a Miami rock station. Eric Clapton's "Cocaine" courses from the speakers. The sound's decent, but most of the speakers are located in the cabin.

"Speaking of cocaine, Steve-O, we still have a bunch of it."

"I know, Jimbo," I say. "I haven't quite recovered from our first and only binge."

"Just throwing it out there," Jim says.

"I'll keep it in the back of my mind." The far back.

I loop my AK around my neck and over my shoulder so it rests at my mid-section. I retake the helm and crank the engines after allowing the blowers to run for 30 seconds. No sense needlessly blowing oneself up from the fumes trapped by the engine's enclosure.

I throttle her back up, turn my cap backward and don my shades. The wind softens the sun's edge. A calm comes over me.

I have Oscar take my position at the helm so I can start stowing my provisions in my duffle bag. The others do the same. I toss Andy the collapsible and warn him to limit the weight to the official amount he can reasonably tote for a long distance. No more than 80 pounds. On second thought, I add, "keeping in mind we'll be thirsty and they probably only have commie beer on the island." It almost seems like a patriotic thing now, don't it? I've effectively assured he brings the whole case plus some.

"The rest of us, let's divide up the bulkier from the light stuff." Boy, that was a close call. I believe my duffle shan't weigh more than 15 pounds or so. I hope I don't struggle too much with it. A perceived weakness would undermine my authority. It's a better policy to have Andy struggle. Um, patriotically struggle, I mean.

I toss Andy a pack of jerky. "Here chew this, build your strength." See? I've mentioned this before, but I can play nice.

Jim is off to the side huddled with Felix, chuckling about something. To get everyone chuckling, I suggest we burn one. We'll be more alert. Alert and paranoid. I hand-signal for Oscar to slow the boat. Andy produces a joint and works it back to life. I toss him one of my trusted three BICs. We crouch in the lee of the helm and pass the joint around. And stoned we get. I hope Andy doesn't mistake any seagulls for quail. That could get messy. The thought provokes a smile.

"Felix," Jim says. "I never have complimented you on the quality of the pot. The lids looked small, but it's sure quality over quantity."

Felix looks puzzled.

Oops, I shrug.

"The pot was light and fluffy. I sold Esteban a pound."

Jim looks over at me—I shrug again and add a grin. "Well, you guys never paid for the lids anyway," I use for an excuse.

"Uh-huh, uh-huh, uh-huh," Jim says. "I believe those ten dollars were quashed after we learned you had thousands of dollars in bearer bonds and a pair of murdering mobsters after us."

"Hmm, now that you mention it, Jimbo, I believe you're right. So, technically, the size of the lids no longer mattered since they became more of a perk."

"A perk to get shot at?" Andy snorts.

"Do you have to be so negative, Andy? I haven't got you shot yet. Have you got all the beer packed?" Strategy: if a white lie doesn't work, change the subject. "You know, Andy, that cap covers most of the skunk streak in the back of your head."

"And I still think you're responsible for that too."

Damn, I should pick a change of subject more responsibly. Here's a safe one when you're high. "How about this weather?" Despite themselves, I catch them looking around. The bump in the road is a dot in the rearview mirror. Even though the weed was never a real issue, it was entertaining to pretend it was.

"Well, while you girls—grownups excluded—stare out at nothing, I'll get this ship a-moving again."

I step back before the helm and throttle her up. I turn on the ship-to-shore radio and flip through the channels. Some static and some garbled Spanish is all I'm able to pick up. Fine, I turn it back off. The Gulf is vast and there's absolutely nothing in sight: no ships, no fishing boats and no oil rigs. Not even a single bird can be seen. Off to the northwest, two jet trails diverge at 35,000 feet. Wow, that's deep.

Jim moves next to me.

"According to my calculations, Jimbo, we should make landfall about 50 miles east of Havana and ten miles or so west of Matanzas. Once there, our first course of action will be to comb the shoreline looking for a small runabout with an Evinrude on the back and Florida registration on its bow. It seems like finding a needle in a haystack, but, hey, crazier things have happened."

"And you made them happen, Steve-O."

"Thanks, Jimbo."

"It was a comment—not a compliment."

"You know what they say, Jimbo, 'spare the compliments, spoil the captain.'"

"Steve-O, that doesn't even make sense."

"Can I construe that as a compliment?"

"No."

"Well, you know what Henry Wheeler Shaw said, right?"

"No."

"There's a great power in words if you don't hitch too many of them together." I smile with satisfaction.

"Meaning?" Jim probes.

"I'm a man of few words."

"Well, you're no man of mystery—you're crazy as hell."

"Spoken like a true friend, Jimbo."

"It's rare you perform without an audience. You're in grand form at the moment."

I raise my finger in the air. "Now that, Jimbo, is a compliment. The prosecution rests."

"You ready for another beer, Steve-O?"

"Sure, Jimbo."

Jim returns and hands me an open bottle of Bud. Felix comes to stand on the other side of me. A mile out from our port side there appears to be a shrimp boat heading back to port.

Chapter Twenty-Seven

"Land ahoy!" Felix declares.

Oscar and Andy crowd to the front to see as well. On the horizon, the dim outline of the Cuban shore starts to come into focus. We're also coming into a number of smaller fishing vessels.

"Keep your eyes peeled for naval patrols," I direct.

"Other than us?" Oscar jokes.

I give him a thumbs up. "Good one, Oscar. Put on one of Felix's shirts, or stay mostly out of sight, you know, on the off chance any of these boats have radios."

"Aye, Aye, captain."

I smile. His words make me think of Sandra. I hope she's okay. I back the throttles and bring our speed to 30mph—enough to stay planed, but not enough to draw attention to us. The shape of our boat is ostentatious enough. Not many cigarette boats around, I would imagine. The few boats we come close to are old and rickety. The fishermen aboard are friendly enough and wave a greeting. We all wave back. There are no outboards to be seen. Most appear to be screw drives and leftovers from the '50s.

A hundred yards shy of the beach, I throttle back and bring her below plane so as to allow us to view the boats pulled up on the beach itself. For no particular reason, I turn toward the east and toward Havana.

Jim reads my mind. "I hope they don't make it to Havana if that's where they're headed. That truly would be like finding a needle in a haystack."

"I feel you, Jimbo. Let's hope for the best."

We keep to the shoreline and our eyes peeled. Not many swimmers or sunbathers along this stretch. Since everyone works for the government, I suspect there's not much vacation time allotted. The few swimmers we do see appear to be European. I hear my mother's voice: "Did you remember your sunscreen?" Right, Mom. I push a finger into the exposed part of my chest—so far, I'm fine. Of course, we've been in the sun for less than two hours now. Well, at least Sandra's not here to remind me that I think of everything. A waft of coconut butter hits me. I turn and catch Jim slathering on the lotion. Well, I guess I did think of everything after all: I remembered to bring Jim. I chuckle at my own stupid thought.

"Jimbo, let me use some of that when you get through. We'll use mine if we run low."

Jim eyes me suspiciously but doesn't comment.

I look over at Andy. "Andy, I bet you're too much of a man to use sissy sunblock." I just want to see how long he can hold out, wouldn't you?

Jim hands me the lotion before elbowing me softly in the ribs and pointing to the beach. "Check it out, a taste of Brazil," he says.

Sure enough, there's a lithe, hard-bodied woman strolling up the beach in a fio dental and no top. The sight of her is almost enough to cause me to beach our craft. I cut the engines to idle to prolong the agony of watching her. The incoming waves gently rock our boat and push us nearer.

"Now that's nice, Steve-O," Jim dreamily comments. And nice she is. Her lively step accents the muscles in her calves and rear. She finally feels our eyes and turns to wave and smile. Her teeth are straight and white and her firm breasts turn skyward. Like the males we are, we all gleefully wave back. Unfortunately, our waves are both hello and goodbye. Reluctantly, I tap the throttles forward and propel onward.

"Esta chica es buena, huh, Felix?" I say. The little Spanish I know I consider essential.

"Una buenota, Esteban."

"What's that mean, Felix?" Andy asks.

"That she's a stone fox."

"Amen," I say.

"Amen," the others echo.

It's back to scanning the shoreline. So far, nothing that even resembles the boat we seek. Slowly, the shoreline becomes more congested. Out at sea larger vessels are now visible. Our map calls these waters the Straits of Florida. Havana's skyline is also starting to come into view.

"What do you think, Steve-O?"

"We should turn and head east now. Look toward Matanzas."

"Yeah, that's what I'm thinking. Unless they didn't make it, or pulled the boat out of the water, we're going to find it."

I turn into a wave and hit the throttles. She jumps the wave and the props oscillate a second before biting and shooting us to plane.

I open her up and trim her out. The kid comes out in me—fuck being inconspicuous. We roar down the shoreline. I look back and catch Andy picking himself off of the deck and everyone laughing at him. The rooster tails we're leaving must be 30 feet high and a hundred feet long.

The woman on the beach shades her eyes with one hand and vigorously waves with her other. A thought flashes through my mind: she looks mighty worthy of recruitment. I sigh, I see right through that. "Practice what you preach," I tell myself. "You don't preach abstinence, Son," I hear my dad say. I sigh again, how true. So many women, so little time. For once, I keep it on the straight and narrow and keep us racing eastward. Wow, I really am maturing. "Hand me another beer, Jimbo," I yell over the roar of the engines and wind in my face. Hey, I believe in the reward system and I'm rewarding my maturity.

A few minutes all out and my need for speed is satisfied. I return to my rigorous state of awareness—I keep my eyes peeled.

Andy finally breaks weak and snatches the lotion off the dash. He held out longer than I thought he would. "I didn't see you having any problems with using the lotion, Steve," Andy says.

"That's because my maleness has never been an issue. Need some help with your back?"

"Fuck no!"

I laugh. Fucking Andy—got to love him.

"Good, because I limit myself to working on only one of your phobias per day."

The density of the boats picks up, along with an increase in sizes. Matanzas's skyline is coming into focus. The map indicates it's a port city. We spot it at the same time. There's a small runabout without an engine beached. A number of people surround it.

"Steve-O, that could be it. The one without the engine."

I cut the throttles back even more and turn toward the beach. "I see it, Jimbo. Could be. Could be."

I knock the drives into neutral and raise them. Felix throws the anchor. The small waves turn our boat seaward. I take a moment to roll up my pants the best I can.

"Come on, Felix," I say. "Let's see what we can learn."

I jump from the boat to the shallows and wade the short distance to the shore. Felix follows. A Florida registration adheres to its bow. Bingo.

I look to the eldest of the group. "¿Cómo está?" I ask.

He gestures with his hand. "Así-así." I take it to mean so-so. "¿Qué pasa?"

"¿Hablas English?"

"Sí."

"Where did you get the boat?"

"¿Por qué?"

"I'm asking the questions here." I drop my hand to my holstered pistol. "¿Comprende?"

"Sí, I bought it."

"From?"

"Fisherman."

"Fisherman with two girls?"

He nods. "Sí, dos girls."

"What happened to the motor?"

"Fisherman sells it to someone else. Russian like you—in Jeep."

"Okay, where did the fisherman and the girls go?"

He indicates over his shoulder. "Matanzas maybe—don't know. They took off walking."

He shrugs.

"Felix, can you think of anything else to ask?"

"When, when did they head off walking?"

"Yesterday, early evening."

We wade back to the boat to regroup. The rest of the crew followed the brief conversation.

"Now what, Steve-O?"

"Well, shit. Let's canvas the beach toward Matanzas with the composite and pictures and see if we can pick up their spoor. Felix, you and I can start first. No need for all of us to walk the beach. The rest of y'all can anchor out a ways and we'll stay in radio contact. Directive—"

"Don't drink all the beer," Jim finishes for me.

"Don't drink all the beer." I grab the ship-to-shore and make sure we're on the same channel. "Well, Felix and I vote we drink one for the road. We better take our boots too, so we look official."

"Our AKs too, Esteban?"

"Absolutely, I don't intend on being captured. Jimbo, y'all need to be ready for a quick pick up if need be."

Jim hands me an open beer. "I hear you, Steve-O."

"Fuck it, I want to go too," Andy says pacing the small area available. "In case there's some action."

"Suit yourself. Tape my clips together for me while I finish this beer," I say. "Strange we haven't seen any military yet."

"I find that strange too, Steve-O."

I down my beer, crush it between my hands and toss it overboard. Technically it's not flotsam, for it quickly sinks out of sight. Hey, it will get to the recyclers more quickly this way. You see the big picture by now—I do what I can.

We wade to shore and don our boots. Andy's ensemble includes a big Bowie knife.

"Andy, where did you get the knife?" I ask.

"Bought it at the marina. Check it out. It's got a compass on the end and inside the handle there's a line and a fishing hook and matches. Cool huh?"

"Neat-O," I remark.

Felix chuckles.

The beach is narrow and pristine. The sand white and the water emerald green. Fish of various sizes can be spotted in the waves. Unlike the cluttered beaches of Texas, the beach before us is mostly devoid of inhabitants. Despite this fact, I have the eerie feeling of being observed. The narrow beach gives way to scrub, a smattering of Royal palms and cultivated fields of sugar cane alternating with citrus.

We begin our trek down the beach. We encounter both old and young men and women trying to eke out a living with the fish they catch. Everyone's friendly and eager to help their comrades and we get a couple of hits. Our hits keep us trekking east.

"Don't look now, Steve, but there's a camouflaged bunker about 200 yards inland."

"Shit, I felt like we were being watched. Maybe ripping down the coastline wasn't such a good idea."

"Hell, Esteban, everyone seems to be buying our cover."

We pick up our pace. "That's only because Andy looks like a fucking ruskie, a commie, a Caucasoid."

"Dolichocephalic would be my guess, Esteban."

We laugh at Andy's discomfort. "Ah, fuck you guys. At least I brought the collapsible cooler."

"You got a point there, Andy," I concede. "Stocked with the finest domestic beer: Budweiser. Hell, at least they won't have to torture us to figure out where we're really from."

Andy smirks. "At least that's something."

"True and speaking of which, we seem to be between hidden bunkers, which make this a resplendent place to stop and have a beer."

"Splendorous, I'd say, Esteban."

"Whatever," Andy says as he unslings the cooler from his shoulder and digs us out each a beer.

I roll it across my forehead before pulling the tab. I take a big swallow. "Ah, now that's fucking cold and refreshing." I twirl the can in my hands. "Until Castro is able to sell Bud, this island will never be a utopia."

Felix takes a big pull from his beer. "Amen, Esteban. Amen."

Andy downs his in one continuous swallow—beer splashes the front of his shirt. He audibly belches before crushing the can on the side of his head. Andy, got to love him. I smile.

"What?" he asks.

"Nothing, Andy," I say before crushing my can and digging a hole in the sand to drop it in. If you can't toss it overboard, my policy on foreign soil is to return my cans to the earth. Ever the environmentalist, I am. Please, hold the applause.

The lack of any development seems odd. If Castro would give up on socialism and communism, he'd be sitting on a gold mine. We pass several small drab concrete prefab-looking buildings, which are no doubt a contribution of Castro's benefactor, the Soviet Union. Every now and then we pass a dirt track leading to God knows where. We have yet to see a motorized vehicle of any kind. Other than the cultivated fields, at least this part of Cuba seems unmolested, but so far utopia it's not. I smack a mosquito against my neck—my hand comes away bloody.

Felix interrupts my musing. "Twelve o'clock, Esteban. Chica inbound."

I raise my hand, bringing us to a stop. "I'll handle this. Let me do the talking."

Andy chuckles. "Right, Steve. You forgot you don't speak the language. Don't forget you're supposed to be a commie."

I smile. "That I shan't, Andy, but I do speak the universal language of love." Backed up with a pocket full of greenbacks. Now that, my friends, is a universal language.

We watch as she saunters along closing the distance. She's wearing the skimpiest of bikinis. Her skin is dark and her smile is bright and wide.

"Buenas tardes, camarados," she says.

"Muchas gracias," is what I come up with. Hey, it's a start. A firm foundation to build upon.

She giggles. "¿Eh? ¿Con permiso?"

The whole package comes to mind and I dig deep into my memory banks to retrieve it. "El paquete entero... bien sexy."

She spins once for us and ends with a hand on a seductively cocked hip. Her other hand fingers a simple strand of red and black beads. She eyes Andy as he reddens. "A él le gusta nalgas Cubanas."

Felix and I chuckle at Andy's discomfort.

"She says you like Cuban ass, Andy," Felix says before catching his mistake.

The stunning negrita's smile wanes. She steps forward and rubs Felix's stiff collar between thumb and forefinger.

"Nuevo," she says accusingly. "You're no Cubanos." She points to Andy and me. "And you're American." She takes a couple of steps back and eyes each one of us in turn. "Yes, I speak English quite well."

I beam one of my most endearing smiles. "Guilty as charged." I point at Andy. "It was his idea—he said we could probably pick up chicks this way."

"He's lying," Andy says. "It was all his idea."

Felix and I laugh. The Cuban gal eyes us cautiously.

"What my cowering friend is trying to say is that we're on a humanitarian mission to save a young damsel in distress from the clutches of evil."

"¿Cómo?"

"I'm Steven Paul and saving damsels in distress is what I do—it's who I am." I wait her out—she says nothing. "Perhaps you watch international news," I continue, "and have caught the piece on the demise of Rio's Dom Pedro? For you see, he was holding captive a young American woman by the name of Melissa Wallace, which necessitated her rescue." I grimace. "And the death of Dom."

Incredulousness clouds her pretty face. "I'm supposed to believe that? The news out of Miami says it's the work of the CIA."

I shrug again. "An allegation the Brazilian government would like you to believe, but no, it was moi. Well, and with some help from my crew. That being the case and you being the prettiest Cuban on the beach, we'd like to recruit you to help."

She removes her hand from her hip and it joins the other fiddling with the string of beads around her neck. "You want me to help the CIA? El barbudo"—she frees a hand and gestures a beard—"would shoot me on sight. And I'm the only Cuban on the beach."

"Probably, but we're not the CIA and our attire has you completely fooled. Plus, the position comes with a ticket to ride shotgun on the fastest boat on the water back to Key West." And, of course, there's me as a perk and the right to knead the ache out of my shoulders. I keep that to myself—I don't want to spring everything on her at once—save that fact for my ace in the hole.

"Let's see some identification."

I reach in my pocket and extract quite a fold of U.S. greenbacks in various denominations.

She blinks, swallows and offers a hand.

"What are my options?" she asks as we shake.

"Well, you could run down the beach screaming for help, but the last bunker was a half a mile back." I nod in Andy's direction. "Then, of course, Andy would mow you down before you got far. He's a crack shot, almost bagged a roadrunner, he did.''

I continue to hold her hand, reluctant to let it go. I can feel the sparks that shoot between us.

"The name's Christina. Count me in."

I pull her close, throw an arm across her shoulders and give her a reassuring squeeze. "That's the spirit, girl. Glad to have you aboard." I feel the heat radiating from her. A firm breast being part of the pleasant source. Like hot chocolate, runs through my mind. "By the way, the fellow that blew our cover is Felix."

I snap my finger still holding her close. "Andy, the composite and pictures." I show her the composite first. "Seen this cat?"

"¡Por supuesto!"

"¿Verdad?"

"Sorry, yes really. In fact, they rented a couple of my grandpa's horses and have yet to return them. He's very upset about it."

"And rightfully so. I say we kill all the birds with one stone."

"Okay, but I'm no jinetera. It's just I've never seen so much money before. You know, my reaction just now to all that cash."

"Jockey?" Felix questions.

"Yes, 'jinetera' is what prostitutes are called here in Cuba."

Interesting, not a jinetera. Well, that will save me some money, I muse. I hear my dad's voice. "Son, pussy's never free." I hear you, Dad, I hear you. I release my hold on Christina. Now that's a nice name. I've never been with a Christina before, but it's always only been a matter of time. What are the odds of me not dickin' one down, I ask you? That's how we say it down south: dickin' one down. Kinda grows on you, doesn't it? Has a nice ring to it.

Christina grabs my hand and gives it a tug. "Come on, we're burning daylight. Plus, I want you to meet grandpa."

"You know we should consummate our new relationship, make it official and all," I say.

She smiles at me. "I bet you would like that."

"Well, honestly, yes I would." Honesty is important in our budding relationship. I'm big on honesty.

"I thought when we shook hands that made it official."

"Perhaps to someone untrained in contract law, it would appear so," I say.

"You really killed Dom Pedro?"

"Well, technically, no. But I did blow his foot off and a good chunk out of his shoulder, with my trusted Colt .45, but one of his own men changed teams at the last moment and blew the top of his head off."

"And why would he do that?"

"Well, it's a long story, perhaps better saved as a bedtime story." I smile. "But hey, Dom shot me, that ought to be worth something."

She halts our forward progress. "He shot you, where?" she asks disbelievingly.

I raise my shirt—she eyes the entry and exit holes. "Didn't use much of a bullet, did he?"

I look over the healing wounds. They are kind of embarrassing. "Hell, it's not like I selected the caliber of pistol for him to shoot me with," I say defensively.

She smiles and tugs my hand again. "Come on, killer."

"Well, it did hurt and bleed some." Damn, why couldn't Dom have used a bigger bullet? "When Felix cauterized the wounds with the glowing tip of my knife, now that did fucking hurt," I say.

"I'll vouch for him there," Felix says and smiles. "He sounded something awful before passing out."

"You're not helping here, Felix," I chide. I steal a quick glance at Christina's backside and let her catch me winking at Felix. The action spawns the intended results—her face blossoms into a beautiful self-assured smile. We all laugh.

"His place is right up ahead," she says.

We turn onto a rutted track leading into the foliage.

Chapter Twenty-Eight

Our little quartet breaks into a clearing and we come across a unique sight. Christina beams—we gape. Before us is the first African banyan tree I've ever seen in person and it's huge. Under its branches sets a thatched hut and evenly spaced downward, the trunks of the banyan are used to frame the hut. A lone strand of wire from a nearby pole links it to the island's power grid. Where the light penetrates the dense banyan leaves are strategically placed bougainvillea of every color: snowy reds, purples and oranges. I spot some jasmines and gardenias as well.

"Fucking amazing," I say.

Christina continues to beam.

"These huts are called 'bohios.' The walls are made from the bark of royal palm and its leaves for thatch. He also has some plantain and banana trees that you can't see from here."

A horse whinnies, drawing my attention to a simple corral and lean-to and tack room. Four horses remain and they look fit.

Christina softly says, "Remember guys, you're military."

We nod our assent.

"Grandpa, we have company," she announces as we step forward. A shirtless old man, black as coal, with wrinkles, a full head of hair and a smiling set of teeth steps out. Despite his age, he's lean and taut and has clearly not given up on life at this point. Christina has luckily inherited his smile.

"These nice men have agreed to rent your horses and track the thieves that have failed to return your others."

I raise a finger indicating I need a moment with Christina and pull her aside. "Um, Christina, all I have is U.S. currency."

She smiles. "I know and lots of it. I figure we can afford to rent them. I'll exchange it for him later."

I tap my front tooth as I've recently seen others do. "Gee, you sure we can afford them?" I believe I like this girl.

"Sure, we're rich Americans. Plus, they're fine horses and the only means of transportation available to you."

"You must be an economics student? Or is that an oxymoron in a non-capitalist society?"

"Actually, I'll studying to be a veterinarian and I work part-time in a cabaret some kilometers east of Matanzas."

Hmm, now I know I like this girl. "Cabarets? Castro allows them? Seems like that would be a form of exploitation."

"They are very much a part of our culture. Plus, dancing is enjoyable." She sticks out her hand again, this time for some cash.

"Quick, give me some cash for the horses so we can get going."

I toy with her by handing her a $50, which I know represents about three months of wages in Cuba. She snatches it and then plucks another hundred from my hand.

"We need to rent all four, silly."

What the fuck is up with "silly?" Everywhere I go women are calling me silly lately. Well, that and punching me in the arm. Just another thing to ponder.

We rejoin the others. "Grandpa, they want to rent them all," she says handing grandpa the bills.

"Christina, so much money. We drink, yes?" he proudly says pocketing the money. He quickly steps back into the hut.

"I believe you just made granddaughter of the year," Felix notes.

"Buscar la forma, we Cubans like to say," she says.

Felix translates. "He finds a way."

Grandpa steps out and hands us each a beer. To my surprise, it's cold. The label says "Clara." I pull the tab and take a swallow. I almost gag. It's far worse than even Buckhorn. It's bitter and it's flat. I don't want to be rude, but I'm going to have to find a place to pour the rest out.

Christina takes a brave swallow and doesn't keel over.

"It's government issued. It grows on you," she says masking a smile.

Like black mold, is what I'm thinking.

Grandpa speaks again: "I know it's rotgut." He laughs. He reaches in the doorway and retrieves a bottle of rum. "Now, rum and cigars we know. Take a pull from this, amigos."

I take a pull from the bottle and wipe my mouth with the back of my hand. The rum hits hard, but it is damn good. I nod approval, temporarily unable to speak. I pass the bottle to Felix.

"Well, comrades," Christina says, "I'm going to go change while you boys saddle the horses."

She doesn't know it yet, but with Jim along, we'll be one horse short, which will mean two of us will have to double. With that in mind, it's too bad she's decided to change. For the cause, I intend to share my horse with her. It's all about the cause. You remember I'm big on causes. Well big boy, if you don't take Jim, there will be plenty of horses. I suddenly remember that when my tenets and conscience collide, I forsake my conscience. Well, in situations like this, that is. You know the situation, the for-the-betterment-of-mankind one. It's all about the betterment of mankind.

"Esteban, are you going to stand there or are you going to help us saddle these horses?"

"Oh, right." I must have got stuck there for a second. I resign myself to the fact that sometimes that happens when I'm dwelling on the betterment of mankind and my responsibilities.

I join them in the small corral. I pick me out a stout-looking roan gelding and decide to make him mine. I actually know how to saddle a horse and it's for this reason and this reason only, that I take the time to help Andy with his.

"No, Andy, dammit. You're cinching her too tight." I loosen the girth cinch for him. I would, wouldn't I? I show him the correct way to secure the strap. Grandpa watches but remains mute as he saddles a horse. His eyes smile. I imagine everyone in Cuba knows early on how to saddle a horse. I pat the horse on the rump. "There you go, girl," I tell the big appaloosa mare. All his horses appear well-tended.

Andy starts to mount just like he's seen Chuck Connors in the Rifle Man do a thousand times.

"Hold on there, Hoss," I say. "Let's wait on Christina so we can all mount at the same time. Besides, you're mounting from the wrong side."

"What's the difference?" Andy grumbles.

"It's a right-handed saddle," I say and quickly turn.

"Oh," Andy says.

"Oh, what?" is what I'm thinking. "Here comes Christina anyway."

She's wearing a drab olive-green uniform with red epaulets. Somehow, it's still happening for her. Her belt accentuates her narrow hips and her thick, in a nice way, ass. She's still wearing her beads and leaves enough buttons open on her shirt to flaunt her cleavage. I give her two thumbs up. She rewards me with her dazzling smile. Grandpa hands her the reins to another smaller sorrel with a white blaze on her forehead.

She starts to mount. I hold her back a second with a hand to the shoulder and a wink. "Andy, let me hold the cooler while you mount up."

"Why?" he suspiciously asks.

I secretly wink at him. "I don't want you to shake up the cargo."

He furtively winks back. "Oh yeah. Right." He hands me the cooler and I stand back. This could be interesting.

"Remember how they do it on TV? One big fluid move. Sling that leg over her rump real fast," I encourage.

Andy tentatively puts his foot in the stirrup.

"For Christ sakes, Andy, do you need help mounting?" I berate him as I easily mount mine.

"No," he smugly says. We all hold our breath. Andy slings his leg up, up, up and not over. He fails to clear the rump as the saddle spins from under him and he tumbles to the ground with a thud.

"Ouch," I cringe. "That's got to hurt."

We all laugh. Well, except Andy of course. Grandpa hides his face but bends double.

"Fucker," Andy mumbles.

I innocently shrug. "Hey, I asked if you needed help."

"Fucker," he again mumbles. "You helped me untighten my saddle too and look how that worked out for me."

I consider that for a second. "I almost see your point. But, as always, I see it more as a training lesson…."

"And for my own good," he finishes.

"For your own good. Dust yourself off and tighten your cinch."

I watch for a minute. "Bump her with your knee so she'll let out her breath." I sincerely, yes sincerely, say. Don't want to overload him with too much learning at one spell. I'm considerate in these kinds of ways. To impart knowledge unto others is a noble thing. The Bible may even support my position somehow. Hey, I'm just shooting the possibility out there.

We walk them out of the small corral and I turn mine toward the beach.

"Wrong way," Christina says. "They went this way."

"I know, but we have to pick up a comrade first."

"But we don't have another horse," she begins to protest until she sees my shit-eating grin. "Cozy."

Ain't it the truth? In a way, it kind of supports my Bible theory. Likely, divine intervention made us one horse shy. And the way I rode the mechanical bull last night, there's got to be a God. I radio Jim and tell him to meet us on the beach. That we're about a mile up and on horseback. Moments later on the beach, we can hear the approaching thundering drone of the cigarette's engines. I nonchalantly kick my leg over and drop to the sand.

"Wow," Christina says as the boat nears. "Now that's a boat. It looks like a military boat, but I've never seen one that fast."

I grab the rein of her horse. "Ain't it, though?" I say. "Hop down, we're going to double on my roan."

She hops down like dismounting is second nature to her. We watch Jim wade to shore. He shakes his head when he sees what I have found.

"Fucking, Steve-O," he says. I hand him the mare's reins.

"We're onto their spoor. Mount up. Times a wasting."

Christina mounts our roan and I sling up behind her. The horse whinnies and stomps but settles as I settle. "Settle in tightly," I should say. Instead, I say "Now, girl, don't go and get too friendly with that-there saddle horn." I wrap one arm around her and pacify the other hand on a thick, firm thigh. She wiggles against me in the saddle. The black Cuban vixen.

"And don't you get too comfortable back there, you hear?" she says and giggles. I guess she's watched a lot of TV too. She wiggles again. If slowly growing hard is what she means, I'm getting a might comfortable back here. She seems not to notice as she wiggles again. I repeat my "vixen" thought.

"Okay, Steve-O, who's your latest squeeze?"

"You mean this little filly, Jimbo?" I indicate Christina with a nod. "Her name is Christina. Ain't she something?"

"Well, Christina, nice meeting you and good luck," he says dropping to the sand and pulling on a boot.

"Good luck?" Christina cautiously asks.

"Relax, it's only a figure of speech, woman. It's like saying 'Godspeed.'" I reassuringly pat her thigh while incrementally and innocuously, I might add, encroaching upon her crotch. I can feel the heat broadcasting from thereof and therein. I'm attuned to these kinds of things, you see. It's genetic. A natural receptor to these pulses, these frequencies.

Jim pulls on and ties his second boot. He stands and dusts the sand off before mounting his mare.

"Why are you scowling, Andy?" he asks.

I raise my hand. "I'll field this one, Jimbo. He fell off his horse."

We all laugh, excluding Andy.

"He fucking loosened the saddle," Andy protests.

"You didn't hurt your gun, did you?" Jim asks feigning concern.

"Noooo," Andy says and we all laugh again, including Andy.

"And he didn't damage the beer either," I proudly declare. "I held the cooler for him while he mis-mounted." Yes, I know it's not a word.

"Fucking Esteban," Felix says sparking a new round of laughter.

"You guys were actually able to save someone?" Christina asks.

"As unlikely as that would seem, it's true," Jim says. "Where are we going, Steve-O?"

"Where are we going, Christina?" I forward the question.

She points over her shoulder. "That way. They went that way."

I shrug. "Good enough for me. Oscar!" I holler out. "Anchor out a ways and don't drink all the beer."

He waves his understanding and throttles off. We're momentarily transfixed by the twin rooster tails the cigarette kicks out before she disappears from sight. Man, what a boat.

We head off riding into Cuba's heartland. I unsling the cooler and hand Christina a cold Bud after pressing the cold can to her cheek.

She squeals. "Budweiser! Oh my God, real Budweiser!" She turns her head and gives me a peck on the cheek. "I've wanted to drink one of these forever. I see the commercials all the time. And the Clydesdales! What magnificent horses! You know they're from Scotland?"

"Yep," I say learning something new. If one beer equals first base, well almost first base, four should take daddy home. What a comforting thought. I'll have to dole out the rest carefully.

"Steve-O, what about us?"

Damn, I internally cringe. My new master plan could be in danger. "Surely, you're not thirsty yet, Jimbo?"

"Yep." He smiles. "I think we all are."

Damn the luck. I pull up short in front of Grandpa's. "Christina, see if your grandpa will sell us $20 worth of domestic beer."

"For $20, he'll throw in the Russian fridge to go with it." She laughs as she saunters off and into the hut.

Jim takes it all in. "This is a badass place they have here."

"Yeah, you're in for a real treat, Jimbo, my man."

Felix chuckles but doesn't snitch me straight out. Clara beer: a desperation move if there has ever been. Christina returns with an old galvanized bucket loaded with beer. I pull another Bud out of the cooler to make room for the Clara and conveniently bury the remaining Buds. I slide back on the horse's rump allowing Christina to remount before passing Jim a beer. Felix waves one off. I quickly down a good portion of my Bud and await Jim's reaction. Even Andy gleefully awaits Jim's reaction, having chosen not to rat me out as well. The reaction is less than I imagined, he only manages to spit most of the beer out before almost falling off his horse.

"Time to roll," I announce as I spur our horse a good one and hold on tight. We're out of the gate and galloping, our laughter lost in the exhilaration of the gelding's speed.

I glance back to see Felix gaining on us and Andy stuck in a bone-jarring trot. Jim's still rooted in his spot. I reach around Christina and rein the big horse in. He snorts and stomps, eager to run some more. Felix draws up next to us and we collectively look back. Andy is taking a beating.

"Maybe we should have gotten a mule for sister Sara," I say and we laugh as Andy struggles to stay in the saddle. He doesn't realize that with a little more throttle she'll smooth out, but I'm not going to be the one to break the good news to him.

Christina looks into my eyes. "With those blue eyes...."

"And rugged good looks," I say helping her over the hump.

"You'd make a fine Clint Eastwood, albeit a younger one. How old are you anyway, Steven Paul?"

"Going on 18, ma'am." I'm only about 350-some days shy. "And you, my fair lass?"

"Nineteen," she says as Jim finally catches up.

"Christina, you appear to have crossed over," Jim says in all seriousness. "It may not be too late for you though."

"Thanks, Jimbo, but I think she'll take her chances," I say gallantly sticking up for my future conquest. I down the rest of the beer that didn't foam and slosh out and bounce the can off Andy. "We better hold off on the beer for a while, seeing how it's likely all shook up now."

"Of course, Steve-O."

Christina finishes the last of her beer and hands her can t me so I can bounce it off Andy.

"Hey, fucker!" Andy looks around but has nothing to throw back.

"Hey, Andy, which direction did your knife compass point while you were sprawled on your back?" I gleefully ask. "I bet Christina would like to see your knife."

Andy reddens. "Shouldn't we be going now?" he finally manages.

I shrug. "Sure, just trying to make conversation." I bump the gelding's flanks and we're off again. "So, where does this itinerary take us?"

"There's a small clinic and vet about 15 kilometers from here. A small rural place, but well-stocked. Education and medical is all free here in Cuba. Did you realize we eradicated polio from our county, not to mention all the wonderful cures we've discovered? All vaccinations are free, you know?"

"And mandatory, I would suspect," I say.

"Yes, mandatory. It's for people's own good. You know people from all over the world come here to study medicine. We also have a 97 percent literacy rate. Maybe the best in all the world and by far the best in Latin America."

"Hmm, sounds like you won't be taking a boat ride with us."

She twists so she can see me. "Don't count on me not going, sailor," she says. We maintain eye contact for a long minute. Her eyes are dark and penetrating—the whites bold and clear. I break eye contact to stare at her alluring lips. She's applied a trace of red and the tip of her tongue peeks out. I swallow. She smiles and reaches around to adjust me to a more suitable position. Her grip is firm and promising. We move together with the gentle rhythm of the horse's gait. What a way to bond.

I catch Jim in my peripheral shaking his head and smiling. I turn toward him and mouth, "Daddy's coming home." I feel Christina smile before me. The rate I'm going I may conquer the world, one woman, at a time.

I casually raise my holding-on arm to bump the base of Christina's full breasts. She wiggles again, which I interpret to mean consent. Now that I think of it, I seem to interpret everything that way. Probably a phase, one I hope to never outgrow. I weigh a breast— the glass is definitely over half full. The birds are livelier, the breeze cooler, the clouds fluffier and we're on some kind of mission.

Andy interrupts my reverie with something important. "How much farther?" he asks. Important to him, not me.

"Why, do you need to stop and visit the little girl's room?" I ask.

He remains mute.

"We're about halfway there, Andy," Christina says. "Seven and a half more kilometers, or around four and a quarter more miles."

Our horse stomps, shakes his head and whinnies. He tugs against his reins. "Whoa, boy, gentle," Christina soothingly coos. I wonder if there are any big cats on the island? He whinnies again and the other horses join in. A rider-less dun bursts from the cane and pulls up short before us. His nostrils are flared. He's been dragging his reins and one is missing.

"Coco!" Christina exclaims. She drops from our horse and wraps her arms around the new horse's neck. "This is Coco, grandpa's dun. What happened to you boy?" she asks still comforting the horse. "Where's your brother, boy?" She covers his closest ear, puts a finger and thumb to her mouth and shrills the air with a whistle. Damn impressive.

I hop to the ground as she whistles again. We hear an excited whinny in the distance and soon the crashing sound of cane. Another horse bursts into the clearing—also rider-less.

Christina grabs the latest horse's bridle. "There you are boy," she coos, as she hugs and quiets this horse as well.

"Christina, what do you think this means? Are there bandits or rogues in the area?"

She shakes her head. "No, of course not." We idle in a state of confusion. To fill the downtime, I dig really deep to get us each, yes dammit, a cold Bud. Man, I was sure thinking ahead when I bought the dry ice. We sit there figuratively scratching our heads while Andy literally scratches his nuts. I wonder why he does that when he's thinking. One of life's mysteries, I suppose. Andy thinking, that is.

Chapter Twenty-Nine

I finish my Bud, crush the can and toss it into the cane. The horses now stand quiet and passive. I hear a cicada calling out. I watch Andy crush and toss his can. It stirs some flies into flight. They quickly resettle. Hmm, I think. I go to investigate. Part of the rich, red soil appears to be darker and it doesn't take a rocket scientist to figure out why. Everyone stares as I bend down to probe the earth with a finger. The patch of ground is dry but still smells of copper. The flies are having a field day.

I stand and scan the surrounding area. I spot an area of slightly disturbed earth—I investigate. There's clearly an imprint of a tire turning and a drop of oil—a telltale sign of a leaky motor. The narrow tread appears to be an all-terrain tread. Likely a Jeep.

I straighten and look over at Christina. "Do the military ever pass through here?"

"Sure, but not that often. Mostly horses and horse-drawn carts heading for the free clinic."

I sling my AK around to the front, chamber a round and release the safety. "Christina, you and Felix watch the horses while we look around a minute for clues. Would the military arrest someone and turn these horses loose, Christina?"

"No, of course not. They would know to whom the horses belong. My grandpa has been living here and renting horses for more years than I've been around."

"Okay, spread out, boys," I say as I enter the cane closest to the bloodstain. It doesn't take but seconds to locate more flies and even a bigger feast—a gruesome feast. I swallow back the rising bile—my stomach turns over. "Over here, boys!" I manage to call out. "Christina! Not you, though!" Fuck, not good. The spooked scavengers take to the air. They don't stray far.

"Shit," Jim says peering over my shoulder. "This fucking guy, Gerard, is fucking out of control."

"You think, Jimbo?" I say.

"Fucking A. This is not good, Esteban."

Andy stares while chewing on some beef jerky. We eye him incredulously. He whips his hair out of his eyes. "Riding makes me hungry."

I turn back to the scene before us: two dead soldiers, both dead from gunshot wounds to the back on the head. One of the bodies has been stripped to his soiled briefs. The day's heat has started to turn the bodies putrid. I toe the clothed one's boot. He's stiff as a board.

"Rigor mortis, boys. They've been dead since yesterday. I wonder why they haven't been missed," I think out loud.

"Steve-O, I guess they stole this pair's Jeep. That doesn't bode well for us."

"Nope, and on top of that we don't have the means to bury the two. All we can do is call it in when we're free and clear of the area."

We mope back to the horses and Christina. Christina's face is masked in concern. "What is it, Steven Paul? Tell me. You have to tell me."

I frown before beginning. "It looks like the ones we're chasing killed a couple of your soldiers and stole their Jeep."

"That, comrades, me molestan seriamente, really angers me and this guy is Cuban too. What's wrong with the man?"

"He's got a monkey on his back," I say.

"Heroin?"

"Yeah," I say. "And he had to leave Florida in a hurry. Fucked around and got his woman killed."

"Bastard," Christina fumes. "So that's why he needed to go to this lonely rural clinic—to rob it."

"That's my guess, girl," I say.

"Do you think the two girls are in on all of this?"

"I hope not, but his daughter did pilot the boat as they made their escape and there is evidence at home that the girl we're seeking has gotten involved in heroin use."

"We should turn it over to my government and let them deal with these killers."

I shake my head no. "The jury is still out on the degree of Monique's involvement—that's her name, Monique—and I don't want your judicial system dealing with her unless we determine she's involved."

"Okay, you're right. We have to give her the benefit of the doubt. Let's get moving. I'll ride Coco and lead the other."

"I'm not sure I'll be uncomfortable with that arrangement,"

I sulk.

She smiles. "You'll live to ride again, comrade."

Jim and Felix look at each other and shrug. Andy rips open another pack of jerky with his teeth.

I flip the safety back on and sling the AK to my back while Christina repairs Coco's reins. She'll lead the other by his now singular rein. We all mount up and head off. The reality is that our quarry has likely hit and run by now and also enjoys having a stolen Jeep.

"How long do you think they'll be able to ride around in a stolen Jeep, Christina?"

"Who knows? Everything on the island is in a state of confusion. We have the second-largest military in the Western hemisphere, a thousand tanks, hundreds of fighters and hundreds of short-range missiles. They're Russian Jeeps and they're called Gaz. There is no telling how many thousands of them exist. Half run—half don't. Plus, as you know, we deploy thousands of soldiers to fight in Africa and every male Cuban is required to serve at least three years in the military."

Wayward

"It does sound like a clusterfuck," Felix says.

"Yes, we're very efficient at being inefficient. Planted fields left to rot while families go hungry. We have to rely on ingenuity, hard work and the black market to survive. You know the Soviets give us three billion a year and we in turn buy crappy Soviet products with it and send them all our valuable sugarcane, except what we use to make rum. They get most of our quality tobacco, too."

"And how is it personally for you?" I ask.

"In theory, perfect. Castro declared women and blacks equal to all others and for the most part, we're accepted. I'm allowed to work in the cabaret because I'm not too black. I have a trace of French blood in me." She sighs. "It could be worse."

We mosey along at a leisurely pace. No sense in stressing the horses when our quarry has a one-day head start. The ride is pleasant and I steal glances at Christina every now and then. She looks proud and maintains a good posture. I'm sure she feels my eyes because there's a trace of smugness and self-assurance in her profile.

She pulls her horse in close, removes a strand of her beads and passes them to me. "Here, these are for you. Put them on and they'll protect you."

I loop them over my head and adjust them so they ride within my shirt. "Thanks. How so? How will they protect me?"

"Strings of red and black beads invoke the protection of Eleggua, the Yoruban Orisha, or God of Destiny and the Guardian of the roads in the Santeria religion."

"They didn't protect you from Steve here," Andy comments.

"Perhaps they brought Steven Paul to protect me, Andy," she rebuts. "Steven Paul has a positive aura surrounding him. He'll be protected and he in turn will protect me."

"Works for me, Andy," I say. "Christina, how come we haven't encountered any workers?"

She shrugs. "Who knows? Workers are called macheteros, because most of their work is done with machetes. The field workers are mostly considered quajiros, peasants. Oh, and you Americans are called yanquis."

Andy takes umbrage, imagine that.

"We're not fucking yankees. We all live south of the Mason-Dixon Line."

"What my astute friend is trying to say is, if it was up to him, you'd still be a slave," I say helping Andy express himself.

"Andy!"

Andy reddens. "I wouldn't... I wouldn't say anything like that."

"Only think it," Jim chimes in.

We all laugh at Andy's discomfort.

"We're almost there," Christina announces. "Right around the next bend."

"Just for shits and giggles, Christina, bring up the rear. I'll ride point," I say.

She reins her horse in and drops back while I unsnap the cover to my 9. I remove it and rack a round into its breech. I hold it by my side as I round the bend. To my astonishment, a hundred yards up sits the Jeep in front of a gimcrack plain concrete structure and at this very second, Gerard is climbing in over its tailgate with an AK in one hand and a sack of something in his other hand. Sophia screams "Company!" and all hell breaks loose.

Gerard pivots with a cat's speed and his AK starts spewing flames and leads in our direction. My big horse spooks and rears—I try to regain control but he rears again and this time topples over backward, slamming me to the ground. I grunt from the impact of landing on my own AK.

I roll as the big gelding struggles to regain his footing. The Jeep's wheels begin to spin, nearly dumping Gerard out the back as I helplessly look on. Unwilling to risk hitting Monique, I unload half a clip in vain trying to hit one of the tires. Someone else is firing from behind me as the Jeep rounds the building and disappears from sight.

"Fuckin' shit!" I yell to offset some of the pain coursing through my back. I try to stand only to crumple back to the ground. I can't catch my breath to yell again. I grin and bear it as a bead of sweat rolls down my temple. The firing behind me has stopped, but not the ringing in my ears. I work myself into a sitting position as Christina appears at my side.

"Oh, God! Please say you haven't been hit."

I raise my hand indicating I need a second. I nod my head no, indicating I haven't been hit. Black motes float before my eyes and the edge of my vision darkens before I'm able to gulp air.

Christina plops down on the ground beside me and wraps an arm around me. Felix kneels before me.

"Esteban, are you all right, man?"

"I'll live. I landed on my fucking rifle. I don't know how the fucker missed me. I could hear the whine of bullets. Is everyone okay? The horses... Are they all right?"

Jim steps into view. "Miraculously no one, not even the horses, were hit, Steve-O."

"Hey, where's Andy?" I ask.

"Andy, his saddle and his mare passed me wide open on the way back to the beach," Christina says and we all laugh.

"He won't live this one down, will he, Esteban?"

"Not as long as I'm around."

Christina whistles to call the missing horses back. "They know the way back to grandpa's. Eventually left alone, they'd find their way back." She whistles again.

My gelding whinnies before rounding the corner. He stomps his front hoof.

"Thanks, big guy," I tell him.

Andy's horse trots into view—rider-less.

"Uh-oh," Christina says. "I think she lost her rider." We burst into a fresh round of laughter.

I reach out and drag the cooler to me. Some of the cans didn't survive the fall. I dig down until I find me a Bud. "For the pain," I explain. I tap the top a few times. In theory this will keep the beer from foaming. I pull the tab and for the most part it doesn't spew. I take a long pull as Christina lifts the back of my shirt. She gingerly touches me, causing me to flinch. "Wow it's turning blue," she says before lifting the shirt farther. "Oooh, what happened here?" she asks.

I down the rest of the beer and toss the can to the side.

"Ever heard of self-flagellation?"

"Is it Muslims or is it Hindus that do that?"

"Something like that. Gerard caught me with a baseball bat, in the same swing that killed his woman."

"You're beat up some, but at least my beads protected you from the bullets," she says and grins. "Until now, I didn't know if they worked or not."

"Well, I'm glad I could help you with that." I stick out a hand. "Jimbo, help me up."

He does—he yanks me to my feet. I let the hammer down on my pistol and re-holster it. Christina busies herself dusting the debris from me. She places the cap back on my head as Andy rounds the bend panting.

He mumbles something like, "fucking horse."

I eye him sternly. "Andy, did I order a retreat or did you come to that decision all on your own?"

"It... It... It was the fucking horse!"

"The horse ordered the retreat?" I ask in mock disbelief.

"No... Yes... No, he spooked and just ran away."

"And he decided to return without you?"

"As soon as I got off, the fucker turned and began to trot back."

"Hmm, what do you think of his story, Jimbo?"

"I'd call it a dereliction of duty!"

"Ouch," I say. "That's harsh, Jimbo."

"Well, it's either that or downright desertion."

"Esteban, I'd let him choose between misfeasance, malfeasance, or nonfeasance."

"Andy?"

"Aw, fuck you guys. How about I choose another horse?"

We all laugh. Laughing truly does help the pain. It's a shame Andy is all at whom we can find to laugh, though I'm not complaining.

I turn back serious. "I guess we better check the status of the clinic workers." I lead my horse the remaining distance. That option seems easier then remounting.

"Esteban, I can't believe I didn't hit one of the tires. I didn't want to hit Monique. Hey, you find it strange that she never turned to see who was shooting at them?"

"Yeah, actually I did. I wonder if she was drugged?"

"If she was, she wasn't nodding. To me, she appeared to be looking straight ahead."

I drop my reins as I near the open front door. Out of caution, I announce our presence before crossing the threshold. "Anyone in there? We're here to help, amigos." I shrug and step through. The others crowd in behind me. It takes us seconds to search the small room. We find one dead male and a female who is bound and beaten but still alive. Andy cuts her loose while Felix fetches her some water. From what I can see, the woman's marked up pretty good.

The clinic is trashed—the supply and medicine cabinets clearly raided. Other evidence indicates they took their sweet time here. Dirty dishes and such clutter all the surfaces. There won't be anyone calling for help either. The clinic's sole phone has been smashed to pieces.

I watch and listen as Christina and Felix gather what little information they can from the woman. I can only understand bits and pieces of what's being said, but the redundancy of the questions makes me realize she doesn't know much.

After they've learned what little they can, Christina breaks it down for me.

"She tells me she believes the group is headed to Matanzas or Varadero," Christina explains. "That they had little in the form of narcotics here and that she was beaten because the man believed that she had some money hidden. When I asked her about Monique, she said the girl seemed subdued. That she didn't see her eat or drink anything like the other two. She says those two 'muy loco.'"

"I'll bet."

"She says she see Monique take one narcotic pill."

"You work in Matanzas, so you know it well?

"Yes, I know it well. It's a big old crumbling port city and Varadero is for the foreigners. Only workers are allowed and few of my color," she says and frowns.

I shake my head as I frown. Utopia is not so colorblind after all. Well, neither is the U.S., but it's still the best place in the world, all things considered.

"So, what's the plan now, Steve-O?"

"I guess it's back to the beach and then on to Matanzas. Christina, do you think they'll drive the Jeep all the way there?"

"Possibly. They have rail as an option too. There's a remote station nearby along with the interstate. Either way, they'll be there soon."

"Cuba has a railroad?" Andy asks.

"The only one in the Caribbean. It spans most of our country. Mostly steam engines that date to the early 1900s."

We step back into the waning day. "They manage to keep them running—that is pretty amazing," Jim says.

"Wait till you get to Matanzas. Other than Russian Ladas and Gaz Jeeps, most everything is '50s American. We also have Russian buses and a lot of coaches, or mule taxis. Most people use the free public transit when you can find a spot to stand or hang on."

"Interesting," Jim comments.

I struggle to get back in the saddle. Pain shoots through my lower back. "May have to buy Grandpa's rum too," I say.

"Should have brought some of the valiums, Steve-O."

"Upon Williams's recommendation, I stashed them in the woods."

"How did he know about the valiums?"

"He didn't, Jimbo. He suggested that I hide everything I don't want the Feds to find. He predicts that the Feds will ultimately get a warrant to search Candy's house."

"That makes sense."

I watch Andy settle into his saddle. "Andy, let us know when your horse decides you're ready."

"I couldn't help it that he spooked. Pick on someone else for a while."

"Like Christina because she's black?" I say.

"Andy!" she accuses.

"Hey! I didn't say anything."

We all laugh as Andy reddens once again.

We water our horses and head out. The buzzards must be back at it because only two lazily circle in the distance. Felix has located a tarp to cover the soldiers. That's the best we will be able to do for them until we can notify the authorities of their demise. The ride would be more pleasant if there was something to look at beyond the scrub and the endless row of sugarcane.

A giant rat-like critter scurries across our path.

"Man, that's one giant fucking rat," Andy announces.

"It's actually called a hutia and hutias are related to the rat. They're large arboreal rodents and now a protected species."

"That's stupid," Andy decides. "Why would you want to protect a fucking rat?"

"Andy," Christina says. "They're part of the island's ecosystem and worth protecting. This close to the ocean, we have osprey and inland you'll find red-tailed hawks and nighthawks that find them tasty."

"And the buzzards. Don't forget your buzzards."

"Close," she continues. "Those are actually turkey vultures up ahead. Much of the island's habitat was destroyed years before. Castro wants to make amends to the earth now. A current campaign of reforestation is underway and that's to be the tip of the iceberg."

I hold up my hand. "Okay, professor, that's enough for one day. You're jeopardizing years of my schooling. Do you realize for each fact Andy takes in it pushes one fact out?"

"Really?"

"Cross my heart. Check it out. Isn't that right Andy?"

"Huh?"

"There you go. It's already taking its toll," I say and we all laugh, except you know who.

We make a pit stop to shoo the vultures away and wrap the dead soldiers the best we can. Afterward, Christina says a few words on their behalf and I come to learn that Santeria and the Catholic Church have merged on the island to form a hybrid religion. Christina also reminds me again that the beads protected me from the volley of bullets. Either that or I did a fine job of dodging them while I floundered in the dirt. Or, hold on, perhaps it was divine intervention again, the kind that protected me before the beads? Yet a third possibility, huh? Although that divine intervention allowed several minor injuries and one pansy-ass bullet wound. I'm still pissed about that.

We saddle up and continue our short journey toward the beach. Well, we didn't quite catch them, but we did learn one important thing: they now have two AKs in addition to my pistol. As a consolation prize, Gerard did waste most of one clip shooting at us. You know, sometimes it's the little things like this that matter.

Jim breaks the silence. "Christina, when Steve's quiet like this, it means he's scheming."

"Like how to get into your pants," Andy smirks.

I do a little play on Red Buttons: "Christina, Andy went to a meeting for premature ejaculators and left early."

"Andy!"

"He's lying!"

Jim chimes in. "He decided to address the problem singlehandedly."

We all laugh, except Andy.

"Jim, he doesn't need help or encouragement," Andy says.

"And, Christina, I'm too much of a gentleman to not try to get into your pants," I modestly say.

"Thanks," she says and smiles.

Jim shakes his head. "Christina, that wasn't necessarily a compliment. What's with you women, as shallow as he is, you're still attracted to him?"

"Like moths to a flame, Jimbo, like moths to a flame." I never tire of saying that. I wonder what Stacey Keys is up to? Or Candy? Or Cheryl? Or Sandra?

"He's probably thinking of other women at this very moment," Jim says.

Christina continues to smile. "He'll be thinking about me again when the need arises."

"Hey," I say. "Not bad, Christina. Did you catch the pun there, Jimbo?"

"Unbelievably, yes."

We're still laughing as Grandpa's tree and bohio comes into view. See, I was paying attention earlier. It's all about attentiveness when dealing with the opposite sex. That's your tip for the day. Take it and run with it. I'm big on giving tips, but then again, you get what you pay for.

Grandpa steps from his hut at the sound of our laughter. The sight of the return of his missing horses overwhelms him with joy. He darts back into his hut to retrieve the rum. He excitedly waves his free hand.

"Down! Down! Let us drink. Comrade for you, sí," he says passing me the bottle before I can pain myself to dismount. I take a fortifying slug, pass it to Felix and then ever so slowly slip from the saddle. Grandpa is too animated to notice my discomfort. I wonder if I should look for a different line of work and need only to glance at Christina to decide, nah. Not while there is an unbroken bone left in my body. I bet you're starting to see that my ability to make these do-or-die decisions makes me a natural-born leader.

The bottle makes it back to me. I raise the bottle before taking another drink. "As John Ciardi so wisely put it, 'there's nothing wrong with sobriety done in moderation.'" Yes, a wise man indeed.

Jim shakes his head before joining the others in laughter.

"Where does he store such a treasure trove of wisdom? I must not watch the same TV station."

I sit in the shade and help grandpa polish off the bottle while the others strip the horses of their tack. The rum has a soothing effect and is starting to work wonders on all my aches. I try and buy another bottle, but he refuses the payment. Getting his horses back and all the money he's received for a few rentals has him happier than a punk in a peter patch. I know the thought is somewhat improper, but these things happen when you're 17 and have been weaned on rum, or is that weaned on rum? I get the two confused and perhaps it's a glass of wine at dinner, I mean. Well, with a full bottle of rum, it's probably not important anyway.

It's time to get going again. Yep, another snap decision by the team leader.

I radio Oscar and tell him to meet us at the beach. Christina says she'll be ready in a minute. A U.S.-woman minute, or a Cuban-woman minute? I soon learn that they're one and the same. Christina returns toting one small case and dragging a large one.

She grins. "I packed some of the just-in-case stuff."

I nod my head but smile. "Of course. There's plenty of room on the ship." The gentleman that I am, I offer her my help.

"Andy, Jim—help her with that."

Jim eyes me. I indicate with gestures my numerous injuries. I get a bye. Good thing, because for a minute I thought I was going to have to pull rank.

Christina happily grabs my free hand. "Come on, sailor, the day is waning."

"Let the courting begin," I say. I can't really match her stride, so I rum it the best I can.

Chapter Thirty

Our boat picks us up. Oscar is happy to see us alive and well. I update him on the events of the day and reclaim the helm and power up. He tells me he's been listening to a number of stations out of Florida City and on occasion has picked up Miami stations. Fortunately, heeding my warnings, Oscar didn't drink all the beer. Pretty lucky, huh?

"No boats approached or challenged your authority to be out here, Oscar?" I ask before cutting the throttles and drifting.

"Not a soul. Spotted very few fishing boats too."

"Christina says Matanzas is a big old crumbling port city," I say.

"It is. For some reason, Castro shuns the city. Even so, it's still a major port city. For commercial purposes, it's hurt by the fact that it's so close in proximity to Havana."

Oscar considers that for a moment. "So, what do you think of our boat?" he asks. "Will it fool anybody?"

"It would fool me if I didn't know any better. As long as you don't let anyone aboard, it's perfect. Well, you know, as long as you don't run into any real Soviets."

I take a sip of the rum and pass it to Oscar. "Christina, any thoughts on how we should approach the place?"

"There are a number of small deserted isles in the area, often with coves. I'd drop us off and then hide out in one of them.

"And we dressed as Soviets?" I ask.

"Should be fine, rarely ever see any. Felix's uniform is too new and our soldiers rarely wear a sidearm. At least not at the lower ranks." She self-assuredly smiles. "With me on your side, we'll be fine."

I return her smile. "Well, on top or bottom would be preferable, but I guess you on your side will work as well."

"That's his vote of confidence in you, Christina," Jim says.

She gives me a rum-tasting kiss on the lips. "Ah, that's so sweet of you, Steven Paul."

"Oh boy, another one bites the dust," Jim says.

I lightly pinch Christina's cheek and gently shake. "Ain't she the cat's meow," I say and we all share a laugh. Yes, Sandra was the cat's meow as well. There can be more than one.

I drift and drink some of the remaining beer. I kill the engines and the silence seems unnatural after the throb of the hearty engines. We're alone in the vast sea.

"So, what are we doing, Steve-O?"

Celebrating the fact that I have now officially made it to first base. "Thought we'd drink one or two of the remaining beers and study the situation." I'm big on studying the situation.

"It's one of his trademark moves, Christina—plying them with drink," Jim says.

Damn, Jimbo. Making known one of my well-kept secrets.

I pop the cap off a longneck. "Jimbo, I take umbrage to such an allegation," I say as I pass the beer to Christina. "Don't believe him, Christina. He has no proof to back up such an outrageous allegation. Pass me that rum, Jimbo, would you?"

I take the rum and pass it to Christina. "Here honey, you might want to chase that beer with some of this mild Cuban rum."

"Wow, such a gentleman," she says.

We all laugh a good one again.

"Esteban, we might as well smoke one too."

"Now that's putting on the old thinking cap, Felix," I say. "Andy, twist one up." Stoned, you can see things at so many additional angles. Unfortunately, many of the angles are acute paranoid angles, but sometimes paranoia spawns caution—just not in me.

We crank up the stereo to void the silence. Foreigner's "Dirty White Boy" comes in loud and clear. To my surprise, Christina knows the words to the song and we sing along. It doesn't get much better than Foreigner. I believe the name of the album is Double Vision. Now wouldn't that be appropriate?

The weed is good and the high is intense. Christina giggles as she plops down on my lap and hangs an arm across my shoulder. I hardly notice the large, firm breast poking me in the eye—pun definitely intended. Things are looking up—life is good. I hardly ache at all anymore. I down the rest of the rum and toss the bottle over the side. It should make a good hermit crab shell, one would like to think.

"Steve-O, we ought to at least find one of the coves Christina told us about. Christina, how far are we from these isles?"

"About 30 kilometers."

"Come on, girl, let me up then. The sun will be going down soon and we'll regroup tomorrow."

She giggles and hops from my lap. "Okay, but I want to drive."

"Oh yeah? And what's in it for me?" I say.

She kisses me slower and deeper. "You'll have to wait and see sailor"—she hiccups— "soldier."

"I believe we have a boat to drive then, woman," I gleefully say.

Not much to operating a boat when the chop is nil and we're the lone boat in the sea. She throttles her up and I trim her out for her. Christina is all smiles. Ninety on the water must feel like 150 in a car. I've never been much over 130, which we've done more than once in Jim's big '64 Buick Riviera, with its 430 c.i. H/O power plant.

Christina stands as we roar along. I lean over the captain's seat, wrap my arms around her below her breasts and lay my chin on her shoulder—she leans her head into mine. Daddy's in the car—he's coming hooommmme.

Ten minutes later we come upon an isle. I reclaim the helm and throttle her down. We cross a patch of crystal-clear water and a coral reef. Despite the waning light, the reef is alive with color—so clear and pristine is the water, it appears I can reach down and touch the coral, despite the fact that my depth finder indicates we're in 30 feet of water. Beckoned, everyone leans over the side to take in the coral's beauty. Schools of fish sprint before us in Z-patterns. The reefer-enhanced sight is awe-inspiring.

I circle the small isle and sure enough, it has its own small cove—the inlet mostly concealed in dense mangrove. I idle her through the gap, pop her into neutral, raise the drives and beach her on a wisp of sandy beach. A spooked anhinga takes flight.

"Fucking crane, far out," Andy says.

Close, it's a consummate web-footed diver resembling a crane. A Caribbean coot shrills somewhere on the small isle. I'm puzzled by the fact we have yet to see a boat, or ship for that matter. I surmise we're still some distance from Matanzas, but this little hideout will do for now.

A wise decision, I also decide, as Christina strips down to her bikini. Although I've already seen her in it, I let out a soft whistle of approval—the girl is hot.

She steps into the cabin and soon reappears with a folded beach towel built for two, the tote and a mischievous smile that transforms my own into a wicked grin.

Jim shakes his head. "Of course, she's crossed over."

"Envy rears its ugly head, huh, Jimbo?" I say without malice. "Well, boys, I guess it's time to take official inventory of our essentials." The big cooler contains four lonely longnecks. Not good. The collapsible cooler has four Buds, which in my state of inebriation I mistakenly count as one and eight Claras. Fairness dictates I give them four of the Claras. I'm big on fairness.

I clutch the collapsible in tight—don't want any re-tallying. It's okay to think in double negatives when in a state of inebriation and euphoria and I believe I'm in both. Nevertheless, I spray us both downright proper with OFF! I shake the can. Damn, I hope there's enough for the rest of them. Well, if not, they can always shut themselves up in the cuddy. Having shucked my uniform, I don my beach apparel and I'm ready to make tracks. "Well, boys, you know, when duty calls." I turn the stereo up some more. Credence Clearwater's "As Long as I Can See the Light" pumps through the speakers. I love the song. I joyfully sing one line, "put a candle in the window." Man, that's some badass jam. "And with that," I tip my hat, "I bid you adieu."

I jump from the bow to the beach. Suddenly I feel spry and pain-free. I help Christina, towel and tote to the sand. We scurry off a mere 25 feet in order to stay well within the range of the radio. Christina giggles as she unfolds and spreads the towel.

I plop down and pull her to me.

She digs in the tote. "One second, sailor." She pulls out four bottles of beer and passes them to me. The labels say "Hatuey." I put them into the cooler to chill. Did I mention I love this girl?

I may be in love. As luck, I mean fate, should have it, I've been falling in love about twice a week lately. Trust me, at 17, it happens.

Christina whispers. "Hatuey is good Cuban beer. Look at this," she says pulling just the neck of a bottle of rum from the tote. My heart flutters—she's driven in the nail—fate sealed.

426

She drops it back into the tote and pushes the tote to the side. She eases down on the towel and pulls me to her. My hand finds and cups a full breast as our lips meet.

Christina's kiss is hot and impassioned. She raises long enough to unhook her bikini top and I work the straps from her shoulders and toss it to the side.

I kiss one firm breast then the other. Her breasts are full, her areolae dark and large nipples pert. I'm awed in the way her breasts barely settle when she returns to the towel. Our mouths join once more, our tongues entwine in carnal desire. My hand reaches and settles on her prominent mound. The heat emanating through the sheer material is no longer just my imagination.

Christina takes my hand and slips it under the bikini's band. The hair is coarse and she's wet and receptive. My finger and thumb find her distended swelling button. A moan escapes her as I begin to knead. I grow hard in lustful anticipation—my heart pounds in my ears.

Christina breaks our kiss—her breath is hot and heavy against my ear. "My bikini... Remove my bikini." She directs me—her voice soft but husky.

I raise up and scoot down. In one fluid motion, I pull the bottoms off and toss them to the side. Hastily, I remove my own trunks and toss them to join the other discards.

Christina spreads her legs and beckons me in. In the waning light, I see she is pink and glistening in the center. I need no help in guiding me in.

Her legs enfold me as our mouths join once more. My rhythm is slow but purposeful. Her hips rise to meet each thrust. She seems so exotic beneath me. Almost like a taboo—a forbidden fruit—a black Cuban woman.

The rum and beer have taken some of the edges off our intense coupling. My endurance is enhanced and I revel in our coupling.

No words are needed to tell me when it's time. Christina arcs beneath me. Her legs tighten around me and pull me in even deeper. She holds me in place until her orgasm releases its hold over her.

I take a second to catch my breath. It's my turn to come and I know just how I want it. I raise into a kneeling position and lock Christina's legs up and back with my arms. She eyes me intensely—open and waiting before me.

In the last of the light, I watch myself repeatedly disappearing inside her. The intensity overcomes me. I stare into her eyes as I near the brink. Christina's eyes silently tell me it's okay.

With one final thrust, I release deep inside her. Zapped of the last of my energy, I collapse upon her. She whispers something in my ear that I cannot make out as her fingers comb my damp, blond hair. Life is surely good.

Someone claps and we burst into laughter.

"Fuck 'em," I say.

"Fuck 'em," she echoes.

Conspiratorially, I whisper, "at least they didn't bust us with a Hatuey in hand or hitting from the rum bottle."

"Amen," Christina says sparking another round of laughter.

She's a pretty cool chick. I dig a cold Bud out of the cooler, pull the tab and pass it to her. She ahhhs after taking a refreshing sip.

"Steven Paul, this is good beer."

"Ain't it, though? It's the king of beer." I rest upon an elbow as I watch her sip her beer.

"What happened to your legs?" she asks.

"Bull riding."

"Bull riding, huh? Are you any good?"

"Good, are you kidding? I'm especially known for my unique dismount."

"How so?"

"It is a pike with one-and-a-half twist and backflip."

She laughs. "I don't think so."

I take a swallow of my beer and eye her ardently. "I shit you not. Ask anybody, other than Oscar. He hasn't seen it yet."

"Wow. And you land on your feet every time?"

"Hundred percent of the time so far."

She turns to rest her head on my leg. She circles the entry bullet wound with a finger. "That's neat," Christina says her voice somewhat slurred and her eyes fighting to stay open.

"If we make it, it will be good to see my parents again," she adds and sighs.

I rub her cheek with a thumb as I too lay back. I down my beer and toss it to the side. I take Christina's beer from her slack hand, down it and toss it to the side. My last waking thought is "you're one lucky fucker." Asleep, I hear my dad say, "I see your work, Son." I smile in my sleep.

Sometime during the night, Christina and the chill wake me. The mostly full moon illuminates us.

"Steven Paul, you awake?" Christina whispers.

"Yeah, barely," with a dull rum thump in my head and some serious cotton mouth.

"It's cold. Climb on and warm me up."

No matter how I feel, that's an invitation I can't pass up.

"I have to have something to drink first." I dig in the cooler, retrieve one of the remaining Buds and pull the tab.

"They call it 'hair of the dog' in the states."

I take a swallow and pass her the Bud. She bravely takes a swallow herself and sets the can in the sand. I grab the corner of the towel and drag it across us as I roll on top of her. With a giggle, she guides me in.

"If we were in the States, we could do it in your car. Everyone has cars, don't they?"

I'm content to lie there inside her. "Most everyone. I currently have two." I begin to slowly stroke her as she again runs her fingers through my hair.

"I like your blond hair. I wish I had hair like yours and your blue eyes. What kind of cars do you have?"

"Two Pontiacs, one Bonneville and one Trans Am."

I've never seen a Pontiac. We mostly have '50s Studebakers, Packards, Plymouths and some Cadillacs. Somehow we Cubans find a way to keep them running."

I find it harder to concentrate on her words. Christina catches the pause in the dialogue. "It's okay. Whenever you want. Then we can sleep some more."

Her passiveness beneath doesn't take away from the experience. With a soft grunt, I release deep inside her. Christina cups my face in her hands and kisses me.

"Thank you for warming me up."

"Thank you." The pleasure was all mine. I roll off her and pull her in close. The chill is gone and we both soon drift off.

Chapter Thirty-One

"Wake up children of the corn." I wake to hear Jim yelling. Stole my line, the fucker. Christina rouses, still cuddled next to me. She sheepishly smiles.

"My head hurts some," she informs me." She playfully musses my already mussed hair. "You don't look so good either," she adds.

"And good morning to you too, sweetheart. Or should I say buenas días, comrade?" I yank the towel off and roll away with it, leaving her stranded in the nude on her side of the towel. Her bikini is on my side as well.

"Hey!" she giggles. "You shit."

Someone whistles from the boat as she scrambles over me in an effort to reach her bikini. I snag a foot and she comes up short. I laugh at her predicament and her struggle to free herself. She's feisty and strong and breaks from my grasp. She stands up, does a spin and then bows.

"Happy?" she laughs.

"Yep. And so is my crew, no doubt."

She makes a dive for my trunks but I'm too fast. "Good try, woman."

"I'll get you back, somehow," she says beautiful in the buff. I don my trunks as she steps into her bikini bottoms. She looks beautiful doing so. I eye her approvingly before shaking the sand from the towel and folding it back up.

"Your back looks terrible, but you seem to be moving good this morning."

"Good loving does that for me. About a week's worth should about cure me."

Christina frowns. "Yes, that would be wonderful. I hope things work out."

I remember something about her being happy to see her parents again. "We'll make it, girl." I grab the cooler up and walk the short way to the boat. "We didn't make it far from the boat last night, did we?" I joke.

She laughs. "No, we didn't. I think someone clapped at us last night. We'll blame it on Andy, want to?"

"Absolutely, and I can appreciate a woman with both oars in the water."

"I try," she says and we laugh.

I drop the cooler and towel over the bow and make a step with my hands to assist Christina up. Having done so, I dislodge the boat from the sand and give it a decent push. Jim grabs my hand and yanks me aboard. I forgot how strong Jim really is and that's true even though I have yet to see him work out. I flip on the ignition, turn on the blower and drop the drives into the water. I note our fuel tank is still three-quarters full and decide we're doing okay.

Christina brings me a candy bar that she's foraged from our supplies. "I couldn't find anything to drink. Do you guys even drink anything other than beer?"

"Rum."

"Right. What if you break down in the ocean? You'll die of thirst."

"Nope, that's why we have two engines. And, besides, we plan to live forever." I take a bite of Snickers—pretty damn good, I note. I fire each engine and drop the drives into reverse. We idle back through the mangrove. There's an increased chop today, but nothing this boat can't handle. Some ominous clouds threaten to the east.

"Steve-O, what's your internal dialogue telling you?" I look around at my grinning crew. I zero in on Andy. "Andy, did you sate your voyeuristic tendencies last night?"

"Andy!" Christina scolds.

"Hey! It wasn't me. It was Felix and Oscar!"

I nod my head in mock disgust. "Sure, blame the Mexicans. Why don't you blame Christina for being easy while you're at it?"

"Andy!"

Andy reddens. "Hey! I didn't say anything!"

"Well, you were thinking about it. You owe Christina an apology. Just because she's black doesn't make her easy."

"Andy!"

We all crack up. "Just fucking with you, Andy," I say.

"So, what really is the plan, Steve-O?"

"It's off to Matanzas. Oscar will hide once more within radio range until we need him. Christina will help us exchange some dollars for pesos on the black market, then we'll go to searching. This guy is desperate and getting worse all the time. We'll find him. Ten to one he'll try and use the girls to lure victims. Christina knows the money spots. Let's hope we can catch him before he decides to move on to Varadero. Christina won't be able to help us there."

I drop the drives into forward and bump the throttle, waiting on the engine temperatures to rise.

"I say we shoot the commie on sight," Andy says and then looks uncomfortable having done so. "Not because he's a commie, you know," he adds—his attempt to clean his statement up for Christina's sake.

"Esteban, we should shoot him on sight too. We know he's a killer."

"Jimbo?"

"Shoot the fucker on sight."

"Well, gather around, boys and let's hit the hammer. You too, Christina. You're part of the team." We gather in a tight circle and bump our fists.

Back at the helm, I throttle her up enough to plane out. As we round the isle, ships to the east can now be seen. Some heading to port, the others out to sea. I let her drive herself as I go and put on my Soviet uniform. I add my imitation Ray-Bans.

Back at the helm, Christina joins me. She takes my hand and squeezes it. The sun feels good on my face and arms.

"I'll miss my Grandpa, but I haven't seen my parents in years. They live in Miami. If grandpa would go, I'd ask you to bring him with us, but he'd never leave his home or his horses. He's holding out hope that someday things will change, the embargo will lift and Cubans will be allowed to visit the states and vice-versa."

"I sincerely hope so, if for no other reason than meeting you."

"Thanks."

As we near Matanzas, the density of boat traffic picks up. They're mostly relics spewing blue and black smoke and draped in rust-colored nets. We spot a couple of Russian freighters and pass in the distance what I suspect to be a Cuban gunboat. It either doesn't see us or we don't raise any red flags. The truth, I believe, is that the absurdity of my plan and our disguise likely protect us. "For fools rush in where angels fear to tread," said Pope Alexander. That pretty much covers us. We're doing the work of angels. Hmm, perhaps I'm onto something.

"What are you thinking about, Steven Paul?"

I shake the beads around my neck. "With the addition of these beads, we have our bases covered."

The coastline starts to turn south, an indication we're closing in on Matanzas. The shoreline is dotted with tiny coves interspersed between small stretches of beach. Beyond the beach, it appears to be prairie grass. Out on the sea, a giant supertanker languidly makes for the port. Christina watches me eye the big ship.

"Matanzas is one of the biggest sugar ports in the world. Plus, Matanzas has textile, paper and chemical plants. I've never been by boat, but soon we should start seeing the stacks. Matanzas is also called 'The City of Bridge.' If we head far enough into the bay, we'll see the Rio Yumuri that dumps into the bay from the north. From the south comes another river called 'Rio San Juan.'"

I tweak her cheek. "You're just a bundle of knowledge, ain't you, girl?"

We pass near the edge of a reef and a diver about to flip backward into the sea. In the distance, I now see several belching stacks. The shoreline begins to turn more populous—dotted with bohios and the same drab pre-fab concrete building we saw closer to Grandpa's.

"Did you know we have the world's current heavyweight?"

"Teofilo Stevenson."

"Yeah. And we also have a new socialist constitution."

"And we have a new silver dollar."

"Why?"

"It's our bicentennial, you know, 1976."

"That's right, it is."

"Steve-O, we're passing some decent coves. Maybe we can find one close enough to conceal the boat."

I turn to see Jim standing near. "I don't know, Jimbo. Whatever we do, we need to stay within radio contact range."

"You think we'll need our walkie-talkies?"

I shrug. "Who knows? It might be best if we take them with us, but tape over the 'Tandy' name, though."

Jim chuckles. "Yeah, I didn't think about that. Radio Shack walkie-talkies might give us away."

We start passing shaky docks and shabby piers. Few contain fishing boats and others with boats sunk at their mooring. Despite the evident poverty, those we pass cheerfully wave. Got to appreciate their spirit.

"Christina, I'm thinking about drinking a beer. Would you fetch me the Bud I saved last night?"

"Aye-aye, captain," Christina says conspiratorially, eager to please. Jim eyes me suspiciously.

"Since when have you ever saved your last beer for the next day?"

"Since I started practicing moderation."

"Oh yeah, and exactly when was it this moderation started?"

Christina hands me the open Bud. I take a refreshing swallow.

"Since last night," I say with a smile.

"That's what I thought."

"Ever the skeptic, Jimbo, my man. Ever the skeptic. Andy! Reload my clip."

I cut the throttles even more, right below the boat's plane, making us more consistent with the ever-increasing boat traffic. The boat's still shaped like no other we will come into contact with, but that's beyond my control now. Just as it was beyond my control not to buy this boat. She's a dreamboat. I wonder what I should re-christen her if we make it back to Texas with her. The Stacey Keys? Now that has a nice ring to it. I believe Stacey would be right pleased with that. Perhaps even pleased enough to bump uglies. What a pleasant thought. I don't miss many angles of approach, do I?

"Christina, how much farther inland does this bay go?" I ask.

"Again, I've never been by boat, but I suspect it will continue to turn inward for a while."

"Fair enough. I guess we'll keep going. What is this mill that we're coming up on?"

"Most likely a sugar refinery. Some of the buildings without stacks probably store tobacco. Some of the better leaves are aged for up to four years, before being hand-rolled and boxed."

"Oh yeah? Well, we age some Kentucky bourbon 25 years," I counter.

"Congratulations," Christina says and we both laugh. The vast port city starts to take shape in the distance. We pass the mouth of Rio Yumurí. The city is a beehive of activity, but surprisingly I spot few vehicles. We come to a long pier upon which dozens of fishermen are vying for the best spots. This is close enough for comfort. I cut the engines even further and point us to the shore beyond the pier. I pop her into neutral and run her up on the sand.

"Well, children of the corn, here we are, in the belly of the beast. Christina, let's take your small tote, so we can store our radio and walkie-talkies. Give Oscar the bottle of rum and, Oscar, there's some more beer in the collapsible."

"More beer, huh, Steve-O?"

"The Cuban beer," plus two Buds. I drop my 9's spare clip in my front pocket and sling my AK over my shoulder. I take a look around to see if I overlooked anything that I want to take, but can't think of anything, other than Andy. Just kidding.

Christina appears from the cabin and tosses a set of her civilian clothes into the tote. She digs in her pocket and pulls out a fold of pesos. "Here's what I have until we can get more."

"Beautiful," I say. "I guess we're ready. Oscar, don't drink the whole bottle of rum at once. You have a cooler full of ice water to drink too, so please, please, please, don't leave us stranded here. This is where we'll be picked up if at all possible, but that could always change. Be ready."

"I got your back, Esteban," Oscar says. "Be careful."

I jump to the sand and help Christina down. Andy and Jim jump down to join us. We make for the road, which turns out to be paved in cement. Not a vehicle coming or going in either direction. We start our trek southeast. We pass pedestrians going the other direction. Most nod and smile, others greet us with "buenas días" and I assume the equivalent in Russian, in deference to us "brothers in arms."

Finally, we come upon a coche lumbering along, its oxen looking mightily rejected. For ten pesos, he's willing to reverse course and take us to a section of town where Christina has assured us that we can exchange some dollars, which is officially banned by the government but tolerated to bolster commerce and supplement Cuba's meager wages.

Soon the road turns to cobblers and into an area where government-sanctioned businesses and abodes vie for space behind faded facades. Represented, is a mix of architectures, some dating back hundreds of years. Many are neocolonial, recognizable by their faded blue walls and two-story arcades. This we learn from Christina. She tells us wealthy planters built them in the 1830s and '40s.

It's truly amazing. A '50s Chevy rumbles by with its massive chrome grille. To look around is to stumble into a time warp. Christina explains the importance of religion and the city's architecture. Some churches and convents span four city blocks. Then there's Cuban baroque, neo-gothic and even some modernism. The amount of labor that must have gone into many of the city's buildings is incomprehensible, the decor beyond ornate.

The ride is actually quite enjoyable. Not only does the cart provide us with transportation, but it also protects us from the ever-rising sun. Christina explains that this is the time of year when Canadians and Europeans tend to avoid Cuba because of the intense heat and high humidity. That may very well play to our advantage because there will be fewer tourists for Gerard to fleece or set up to rob.

We arrive at a lovely square named Plaza de la Vigla, which seems almost suspended between the Calico Garcia Bridge, dating 1849 and the Concordia Bridge. This, Christina tells us, is the original site of the city.

"The square is also home to a statue of the Unknown Soldier, erected in homage to the victims of the war for independence, which ended on April 25th, 1879."

I hold out my hand. "Christina, pesos, por favor," I say stepping from the cart. Christina steps off behind me and pulls me to the side. She hands me a variety of denominations and I in turn hand her a crisp $100 bill and five $20s. "Wait for me at the De Las Vigla and Calle over there. They have good food. Plus, it's a bar."

I wink and turn back to the cart and pass the old Cuban 30 pesos of paper, or little over a dollar. I point to the ground and tell him to wait. "Espera, ¿sí?"

He smiles a toothless smile that divides his face. "Sí, señor."

We converge on the establishment. Andy's picked up a spoor—he smells food. With its ornate interior, the place has an ambiance reminiscent of a Vienna coffeehouse. Throughout are stained glass and old photos and drawings of Matanzas in its heyday and glory. The city is clearly rich in history and reminds me in ways of Rio and in other ways like the French Quarter in New Orleans.

I note we're the only ones with weapons as we find a suitable table. A male waiter with a pencil mustache and perfect posture approaches our table.

"Cinco Hatuey, por favor," I say smugly. The waiter steps back, turns and leaves to fetch our beer while everyone at our table stares. I shrug. "I figured you guys would like a beer."

"I want some food to wash it down with," Andy says.

I dribble my hand. "Shhh, keep it down, comrade. Let me, Felix and Christina do the talking."

Jim whispers. "Um, Steve-O, you don't quite know the language either."

"Discrete. Here he comes with the cerveza."

Jim smiles. "That's what I thought, Steve-O."

"Un filete, Felix," I tell Felix knowing he knows how everyone other than Christina likes their steaks. I kick back and take a pull from my beer as Felix orders God knows what to go with our steaks, besides the "ensalada" that I picked up on. I look at some of the other diners and I note none of their plates contain much in the way of food. They probably need less, not being in the position to waste 40 percent of their food as we Americans do. It only reinforces the fact I'm proud to be American.

"Felix, make some rounds and see if anyone has seen them," I say.

"Sure, might as well."

Christina spots us and heads over. She takes a seat next to me and pushes her beer toward me.

"No hair of the dog for me." She smiles. "Yes, I listen and learn. Did you guys order something to eat?"

"Yeah."

"Me too?"

"Of course, honey."

"I wonder how many in the states you call 'honey?'"

"All he can," Jim says matter-of-factly. The hater.

"Only because practice makes perfect," I'm quick to assure her.

Felix returns without results. He shrugs. "Well, it was worth the try, Esteban. What's our plan for after we eat?"

"Look for the same thing he'll be searching for: heroin. Then this evening, check out the places he's likely to search for victims."

Our food arrives and you couldn't peel the disappointment from Andy's face. They're not the steaks we're accustomed to. The rest of the meal is nothing to write home about either. Even the salads look a day old. The saving grace at the table is the ice-cold Hatueys. Not Budweiser, but not bad. We keep our conversation to the minimum since some of us don't speak Spanish. You would think they'd take the opportunity to learn, correcto? Well, as they say, you can lead a horse to water, but you can't necessarily make him drink. Then again, we don't want Andy to drown.

Christina pays our tab and leaves what she says is a generous tip. Our meals, beer and tip cost the equivalent of less than five U.S. dollars—amazing. By my calculations, that makes us like zillionaires here in Cuba. I doubt it would change my modest behavior much if I were to live here.

We step back into the square. Our mule taxi is still idling at the curb.

"Christina, perhaps we should try and hire a gypsy taxi or something with a tad more zip."

"Most cars are illegally available for hire," she says confirming my suspicions.

"Well, then, how about that big old Buick Roadmaster over there?"

"I'll go ask."

I peel off a ten note and pass it to our old mule taxi driver. "Gracious. No mas. Adios, amigo," I tell him.

He grins again as he accepts the bill. "Gracias, gracias, señor."

Christina whistles and waves us over. I guess we're fixing to ride in style.

"This one is perfect," she excitedly tells us. "He doesn't speak a lick of English, so for all he knows we're speaking in Russian."

I nod to the smiling mulatto and point to his car with approval. "Christina and I will ride shotgun," I announce before opening the door for her and following her in. The interior is big and roomy, but our air conditioner is the rolled down windows and a small fan screwed to the dash.

Our driver points to the gas hand and oil pressure gauge.

"Petrol, ¿sí? Lubricar, ¿sí?"

I nod my head "Sí. Christina, tell him that we want to hire him for the entire day."

She smiles. "I already have."

What a gal—I told you she was the cat's meow.

"I told him we'd pay him extra for his absolute discretion."

446

"In that case," I say before leaning over and kissing her and settling my hand between her legs. "I plan to get my money's worth."

Christina laughs before slapping at my hand. "Not that type of discretion, sailor." Sailors and discretion. Hmm, now that's an oxymoron.

Chapter Thirty-Two

Lead foot our driver is not. We make our best time going downhill, him being just as timid with his brake pedal as with the gas. I believe he'll milk a few more hundred thousand miles out of the Big Buick with his strategy. We stop and fill up with gas and oil. When we started, the fuel hand was below empty. He now eyes his gauges proudly—sitting straight and tall in his seat.

"Yes, Cuban men want to be macho," Christina comments.

"Not sweet and endearing like me?" I tease.

"No, nothing like you," she teases back.

"Hopefully, they broke the mold after him, Christina," Jim cracks from the back seat.

"Christina's maturity makes her immune to your snide remarks, Jimbo, my man. Ain't that right, honey?"

"Sticks and stones, Jimbo," she says and giggles at the frivolity of it all. Her giggles spark our own laughter. Even our driver smiles.

Christina and Felix get into a running dialogue with our driver, of which I understand only bits and pieces. I get the gist of it though—where can one buy some heroin? He turns us north toward the bay and port. Here again, the most logical place to search is where the stuff comes in—on the boats. I'm no expert but imagine it's mostly Mexican black tar and Cancun is only a short hop from the east coast. I imagine most finds its way through Havana or the south coast, but we have to go with what we know or think we know and that is they've headed this way. The enormity of the city and bay has me feeling like we're seeking a needle in a haystack when it comes to finding the trio, but I keep these thoughts to myself.

A military jeep passes us going the opposite direction—it pays us no mind. The second-largest military in the western hemisphere and this is the first military presence we've seen since yesterday.

"Steve-O, our fucking disguises are really working."

"Brilliant, Esteban."

I modestly shrug. "Quit, you're embarrassing me, but I do what I can."

We all share the laugh as we come upon the bay and what appears to be a hardworking section and lair to some tough-looking seafarers. Boats of all shapes in and out of the water are represented.

Most are beyond salvage and are currently being used for shade where some of the non-working drink beer and pass around bottles of rum. Our driver comes to a stop. All eyes are on us.

I look over my shoulder. "Andy, go see what you can find out."

"Fuck that!" he says sparking a fresh round of laughter.

"Okay, boys and girls. We need to look tough and intimidating to pull this off. You know, like I look in the ring," I say.

Christina's mouth drops. "You're a boxer too?"

"And TV repairmen and future car salesman," Jim says. "Christina, he's not a boxer."

I raise my finger. "But, Christina, that's not the point. The point is I could be if I wanted. In elementary school, they told me I could be president someday."

"Steve, they told us all that," Andy smirks.

"The difference is you believed them, Andy."

"Huh?"

"Never mind," I say pushing open the door. "Come on, let's find these fuckers so we can get the fuck out of here."

There are several whistles as Christina alights from the Buick. I unsnap the cover to my holster. The movement brings the whistles to an end but instills no fear in their eyes. Well, they'll just have to see things my way. I put my hand on a fold of pesos. Yep, my ace in the hole. I step forward and relieve the first one of his bottles of rum, turn it up, down it and toss it to the ground. For dramatic effect, I wipe my mouth with the back of my hand and drop a couple 20 notes on the ground beside him.

"Gracias, comrade."

One of the bigger, nastier ones scrambles to his drunken feet.

"¿Qué es tu problema?" he spits out.

What's my problem, huh? I'm not keen on the way he's looking at me, but I don't know how to say that. I do know how to say what the fuck you looking at and settle with that: "¿Qué coño estás mirando?"

Felix steps between us for the good cop/bad cop bit even though we're supposed to be military. Lucky for the drunken sailor, for I would have hated to demonstrate my superior speed to him. Just kidding. I would never forsake the woman and children in my care. Covet the neighbor's wife, perhaps—forsake my friends, never.

"Esteban, give the fucker 20 pesos and he'll tell us what he knows."

I pass the note over.

"Esteban, huh? Why he speak English too?" he says with a sneer. I notice for the first time the stench that is his breath.

"Well? I'm waiting, what do you know?"

He spits on the ground. "Nothing, fucking gringo."

Wrong answer. I step forward and knee him in the nuts, doubling him before me. I pluck the bill from his hand and knee him in the nose for good measure. With a grunt, he topples to the dirt. I raise the bill before the stunned eyes. "Anyone else know nothing? There's no takers for the bill?"

We move on.

"Great technique, Steve-O. Smother them with charm," Jim says and snickers.

"Jimbo, you can coddle and hold the next one's hand. See whose method produces the best results."

"Maybe, y'all should let me try the next group," says Christina.

Got her saying "y'all" now. "Go for it, big girl," I say stepping before the next group.

Christina takes the photos and composites from Felix and shows them in front of the faces of the group sitting and drinking in the shade of a derelict boat up on blocks. I wait as she goes through her spiel. She passes a ten-dollar note to an outstretched hand before turning with a smile.

"They haven't seen any of the trio, but he tells me where many of the locals go for their heroin."

"Well?" we collectively ask.

"A quarter-mile up there's a clean Boston Whaler with Twin 200 Mercs, whatever that means, at the docks. He says we can't miss it, but he warns the guy is 'muy loco,' and has 'machos malos hombres' working for him. He says he doesn't know how the guy will react to us being military."

"Maybe we should let Felix talk to the guy. Tell him we're not there to fuck with him if he tells us what we want to know."

"These people actually believe we're military. Pretty amazing," Jim says.

"Well you know, Jimbo, Andy's very convincing, being from the motherland and all," I say.

"Whatever."

We load up in the big Buick for the short drive down the potholed street. The Boston Whaler is easy to spot. It stands out like a sore thumb—a bright white tooth in a decaying mouth. Several men stand at discreet distances from the boat. A Russian Lada with four passengers pulls away without looking back.

"Well, Felix, let's see you work your magic. Christina, you stay in the car this time. Jim... Andy, spread out some. I'll walk out to the boat with Felix."

We all pile out as nervous eyes bore through us. I watch one place a hand behind his back. I nod in his direction letting him know I'm on to him.

We walk down the short dock. The Boston Whaler is like no other I've ever seen. It has a small cuddy cabin and the sound of an air conditioner can be heard as we near. I wonder why he didn't just buy a SeaRay or something?

A brute of a man steps from the stern onto the dock. He looks past Felix to me. He puffs out his barrel chest and addresses me in Russian—of course. I remain passive and nod at Felix.

He shrugs and switches to Spanish. A fucking Russian. Who would have thought? This guy's not selling Mexican tar, the roots of his heroin trace to Afghanistan, no doubt. He looks at the composite Felix shows him and to my utter surprise, he nods an affirmation. The dialogue continues. The bodyguard points toward the west and then shakes Felix's hand.

"Bingo," Felix says as we walk down the short dock. The stationed men's postures deflate in relief as we reenter the big Buick.

"They were here all right," Felix continues. "Last night. Spent their last $20. He's surprised they haven't been back today. He said they were still driving the Gaz and that we can find it three blocks up on the left. He said it likely broke down or ran out of gas. He said as of this morning it was still there. He was surprised it hasn't been cannibalized for parts yet."

I point ahead to get our driver moving again. "Good work, Felix. Let's check on the Jeep," I say. "Maybe someone around there has some information. Felix, he didn't say anything about me not answering him?"

"Nope, not a thing, Esteban."

Sure enough, the Gaz is right where it was said to be. We all pile out to look it over. It still looks intact. The vehicle, like most military vehicles, is keyless. I turn the ignition on—the battery's needle jumps to positive, the gas needle stays below E. I'm surprised it still has its battery. Despite being out of gas, it could still be broken down and is only empty because someone siphoned out all the gas.

"Felix, ask around, see if we can find out where they went. Let's see if we can make these wheels ours. Christina, have our driver take you for gas."

I unstrap the five-gallon can on the back of the Gaz and place it on the floorboard of the Buick.

"Andy, you ride with them. And no fondling Christina."

"Andy! You better not fondle me."

Andy reddens. "I wouldn't... I mean, I won't."

We all laugh at his discomfort. Jim shakes his head. "Let's see what we can come up with." We watch as the Buick pulls away and disappears around a corner.

"She's all right, Steve-O. How was she by the way?"

"Now, Jimbo, you know my policy about kissing and telling."

"Yeah, yeah. That's why I'm asking."

"Like a caged animal trying to get free," I say with male pride.

"Esteban, I've got to give it to you, she's hot."

We laugh for a long second, rooted in place before canvassing the area. Several acknowledge seeing the trio, but no one has a clue as to where they were headed beyond heading south. Them being out of wheels again is a big break for us. We'll find them, I reassure myself.

"Do you think we're okay to drive the Jeep around?" Jim asks.

"We're military—we can do what we want."

The Buick returns with the gas. Andy pours it into the tank and primes the carburetor with a good shot. I turn on the ignition and hit the starter button. With a bang and a puff of blue smoke, it tries to crank. I fan the gas pedal to keep it running. Finally, the engine catches and settles into a rough idle. I give it half throttle until the blue smoke clears and it begins to hit on all four cylinders. I pull $50 from my wad and hand it to Christina. "Pay our driver and tell him he can have the rest of the day off."

"Steven Paul, this is three months wages."

"I know."

She shrugs. "Okay."

I squeeze between the two buckets to the back. "Felix, you can drive and Andy, Jim, you can arm wrestle over who gets shotgun."

"Jim can have it. I don't feel like arm wrestling."

"Suit yourself, but, Christina, if I didn't know better, I'd say Andy is sweet on you and wants to sit near you."

"Andy!"

We all laugh at Andy's discomfort. I do my part to protect her. I nestle my hand in the warmth of her crotch.

"Where to, Esteban?"

"Christina, any suggestions?"

"Not until this evening. Then I'd say the Tropicana where I work. Any men with money to spend will be there tonight."

"What time?" I ask.

She looks at the sky. "If it doesn't rain, it's open from ten tonight until two in the morning.

"That's a lot of hours to kill, Steve-O."

"Any suggestions?"

"Esteban, because of the gulf stream, the fishing is supposed to be excellent off the north coast."

"You're suggesting we go fishing?"

"Why not? I'm sure we can buy some reels and bait around here somewhere."

"We'll need a camera too, Steve-O. Take pictures of our catch."

"Fuck it, why not? We need to load up on beer too and we better get some more sunblock. I think mine fell overboard."

"Right, Steve-O."

We spend the next hour buying supplies. Including us, we have the Jeep loaded to capacity. Now I truly hope we don't run into any military because we literally stick out now in the form of long, heavy-duty sea fishing rods. The good news is we've made contact with Oscar. The ability to do so when needed has been nagging me at the back of my mind. We also acquire a large tarp and some rope to cover our Gaz. 'Tis a day for fishing, it is.

We rendezvous with Oscar and our boat and manage to pay a local fisherman to keep an eye on our Gaz. He doesn't seem to be the least suspicious about our plans to fish. He must think we're on leave or something. Or perhaps Cubans are not suspicious by nature?

The sun, the wind, the cold beer and the camaraderie are refreshing.

"Felix, what kind of fish do you think are out here?" I ask.

"I'm no expert, but in deep water, there will be Bluefin tuna, swordfish, albacore, sailfish, mako sharks, dorado, blue marlin and several additional varieties of shark."

I laugh, "Good thing you're not an expert."

Our bucket of live bait is frozen, but in the warm sun, it should thaw rapidly. I run our boat to the northwest and away from Matanzas traffic and beyond the barrier reefs.

We're in open sea and not another soul in sight. The water is deep and beyond our depth finder's ability to measure. We all pick a spot to fish. I pick the captain's seat because it swivels. Unfortunately, our boat is not designed for deep-sea fishing. The closest thing there are to rod holders is cup holders. I forget to share this concern as I jerry-rig my rod with extra rope and buckle myself in. I mean, what could possibly go wrong?

"I got a bite! I got a bite!" Andy screams.

I struggle to free myself. Andy's rod is bowed and the fish is taking line.

"Let him run with it, Andy!" I yell, excited about the prospect of landing some big fish. "That's it, let him run with it!" I yell again. It seems like the right thing to do.

I mean, that's what they yell at the guys on TV. You know the ones—the ones strapped into their special fishing chairs.

The reel whines as the fish takes line and fights against the drag. Hmm, the reel's almost out of line. What could that possibly mean? I cringe in suspense. I look over at Felix and we both shrug.

"Hold on real tight now, Andy!" I warn, or perhaps I inform? I often get the two confused.

The line pulls tight! Up, up, up and over the rail Andy goes and with a big splash, he hits the water and is off. Wow! His head parts the sea and leaves a wake. He reminds me of a water skier who's failed to get up but refuses to let go of the rope. "Hold on Andy! You got him right where you want him!" I manage before crumbling to the deck, my laughter sucking the air from my lungs. "Man overboard!" I squeak, convulsing—too much to do any better. Now this is fishing. Andy will have to relive over and over the one that got away. I'm duty bound to see to it.

Laughing, Jim offers me a hand and pulls me to my feet. I wipe the tears from my eyes. Andy has lost his rod and is swimming back toward the boat.

"Dammit, Andy! You're scaring all the fish away!" I yell.

"You can swim after we're done fishing," Jim yells.

This is too good. "Someone hand me the gaff so I can help him aboard," I manage to say.

"I say let's chum the water instead, Esteban."

"Well, I don't know about you guys," Christina says, "but I intend to give him a hand." And she does—she starts us all clapping.

I forget all about Andy as I hear the whine of my own reel. I scramble to buckle myself in. Safely ensconced in my seat, I stick the long handle of my rod under the base of my chair. Felix excitedly joins me.

"Stiffen the drag, Felix, he's taking the line much too fast."

Felix does—the line slows as the rod bows even more. I forget all my pains and, feet planted on the rail, lean back against the pull. A hundred yards out a sailfish breaks the surface, fighting against the resistance before crashing back into the sea.

"Go, Steven Paul! Go!" Christina yells in my ear.

"Fucking A, Esteban!"

Jim has the camera out and is going to try and snap a picture if the big fish breaches again. Felix increases the drag some more for me. My arms strain against the pull. I've never caught a fish like this one. He breaks the surface again and I hear the click of the camera. I feel the fish's airborne thrashing through my arms down to the base of my spine before he crashes back to the sea. Even my legs feel the strain.

"Beer!" I yell.

Christina wipes my face with a shirt and puts a beer to my lips, I take a big swallow—Jim catches it on film. The fish's awesome power pulls the boat in the direction it tries to flee. Christina drops the beer as her own rod begins to bow. She scrambles after it, only to watch it disappear over the side.

"Shit!" she yells.

"You're on your own, Esteban," Felix yells as he darts to his own rod and readies himself for a bite. Jim follows suit. I turn and spot Andy sitting on the engine's cowling. He seems to be talking to himself but watching me. He's impressed in the manner with which I'm handling my hooked fish.

I start the arduous task of landing the fish. Strain after strain allows me to make incremental progress and slowly, I start to win the battle. The fish no longer breaks the surface—it's slowly tiring, as am I. Christina keeps the sweat from my eyes and I'm breathing hard and sweating profusely. My recent injuries have interfered with my routine workouts and it's starting to affect my strength. The hundred-plus yards of line seems like a mile as the minutes tick by.

"Got one!" Felix yells. At the same time, Jim's rod is yanked from his hands and disappears over the side. I manage to laugh as Christina massages the muscles in my shoulders. We make a good team.

Felix's fish briefly breaks the surface. "What is it, Felix?" I yell.

"Bluefin tuna, I think and he's a big one."

"You know, Felix," Jim says, "the Japs pay top dollar for tunas. They actually bid on individual fish."

I'm starting to win the battle and have regained the ability to laugh. "Jimbo, why aren't you and Andy fishing?"

"The same reason Christina isn't fishing, Steve-O."

"She doesn't need to fish, Jimbo, she's already on the winning team. Ain't that right, honey?"

She nods, puts a fresh beer to my lips and wipes the sweat from my brow. And a fine team we make.

Oscar uses the gaff and yanks Felix's tuna into the boat. It's a beautiful fish. I intend to catch and release my fish after a photo, so we'll have to get it into the boat somehow without a gaff. I get a glimpse of him every now and then as he nears the surface and boat.

"Oscar, Jim: help me get him in the boat without a gaff. I'm going to turn him loose." I've reeled him in as far as I can. Jim holds Oscar by the back of his pants, as Oscar leans out over the water. He grabs the fish by his dorsal and long snout.

"On the count of three," he says. "One... Two... Three." I heave on the rod, as Jim yanks on Oscar and Oscar on the fish. Up and over the fish comes and, with one strong flip of the tail, Oscar crashes to the deck tripping Jim and taking Jim with him. We get a good laugh as Oscar and Jim try to get clear of the thrashing fish. They sure don't do it like this on TV.

I move over and step on its head so I can unhook him without doing any damage. He's a beauty—I've never caught anything like him before. I never cease to amaze myself. A natural-born sportsman. Is there anything I'm not good at? Unlikely.

Jim lifts himself from the deck and tries to wipe the fish slime from a trouser leg. Not happening.

"Jimbo, if you're through floundering on the deck, do you think you can manage to snap a photo? Christina, grab its tail."

Together we hoist the fish from the deck and grin from ear to ear as Jim snaps a couple of photos.

"Let's let him go now, Christina."

Together we drop the fish over the side. He floats in place for a second and then with a swift whip of his tail he disappears into the deep. Too cool.

I lean over and rinse my hands in the choppy surf and let out a sigh of relief. Despite all my returning aches, I feel wonderful.

I take my aches, a fresh beer and Christina to sit in the shade. I drift off, lost in thought and relaxed by the gentle rock of our boat.

Chapter Thirty-Three

I awake stiff and sore. Christina's sleeping head rests on my shoulder. Everyone's asleep in various positions. Cottonmouth nearly chokes me. The beer can that still remains, half full and hours old, I toss it to the sea. Christina stirs, mumbles and drifts back off. The sun is nearing the sea to the west. Our boat smells like fish.

Misery loves company. I kiss Christina on her temple, waking her. She groggily smiles up at me. I plant another kiss on her forehead. She hugs my arm. Silently, I wish her the best.

Christina pats me on the leg. "How about some beef jerky and another cold beer?"

I think I'm in love—what a woman. "You'd do that for me?" I meekly ask.

She giggles. "You're silly. I'll be right back."

I admire her rear as she stands and stretches. She's packing back there, I'm here to tell you. Packing in a very nice way.

She sits back beside me and hands me a cold beer and a pack of jerky. "The beer smells like fish because there's a headless tuna in the cooler now."

"We'll live," I proclaim as we chew in silence and enjoy each other's presence. Somewhere along, we both drift back off again.

465

I dream I'm on my new Yamaha YZ-250 and Christina's clinging to me as I toy with the cops that chase us. I'm always amazed at the frivolity of their never-ending pursuit. We slide to a stop where the dirt road tees into Scenic Drive. To my horror, in the cove, Tony C bubbles to the surface. Not good. Andy must not have buckled him in. Uh-oh, Vinnie pops to the surface, a giant fishhook protruding from his mouth. I hear the sirens in the distance. Shit!

"What? What?" Someone's kicking me in the foot. I gingerly open my eyes to find Jim smiling down at me. I let my breath out realizing it was only a dream. "What?"

"Get up, the sun's almost set. Maybe we should head back before it's completely dark."

I stick out my hand for an answer. Jim pulls me to my feet. I feel as stiff as my fishing rod. I pull the yawning Christina to her feet.

"Time we got a move on it, sleeping beauty." I twist at the waist a few times to gain some semblance of mobility. I feel like I've been run through the wringer. I chuckle at my own condition when I remember what Will Rogers once said. "Everything is funny as long as it's happening to someone else."

"What's so funny, Steven Paul?"

"Thinking about Andy falling overboard," I say as I hit the ignition and flip on the blower. I allow 30 seconds to elapse and fire the engines. I note we're still sitting pretty as far as fuel's concerned. I engage the drives and throttle her up. She shoots to a plane. I turn us to the northwest and let her run all out for a little while. She's one sweet boat, I think for the hundredth time. Hope we make it back and get to keep her.

The sun drops into the sea, but there's enough ambient light to see. As we near Matanzas, I back the throttles to bring us down to a respectable speed.

We hit the coast again and follow the curve into the bay. Not many of the piers and docks are lit. The ones that are, appear to be so by a single bulb. The City of Matanzas emits a soft glow. The near-full moon disappears behind a dense gray cloud.

Christina tracks my eyes. "June is the beginning of our hurricane season," she comments.

"Comforting," I say. "Keep an eye out for the right pier."

"It's hard to see, but I think it's further up ahead."

"It's the next one down," Oscar says from behind. "Since it's getting dark, what do you think about me hanging right here until you radio and tell me to do otherwise? If you radio, that is."

"I don't see a problem with it, but you'll have to stay alert—be ready to haul ass at a moment's notice."

Oscar nods his assent. "No problemo."

I kill the engines as I run her onto the beach. "Oscar, anchor her out 30 feet or so—make it a little harder for anyone to sneak up on you."

I ease to the sand and assist Christina in getting down. I'm sure she's quite capable of getting down on her own, but my old gentlemen's habits are hard to break. Our Jeep is where we left it along with our grinning fisherman. I peel him off $20, American. He's puzzled but manages to grin even wider. I have Christina instruct him to keep a watch out and to yell at the boat if anyone other than us shows up.

We load up and with some effort our Gaz cranks. "Direct me to the Plaza, Christina. We might as well get us something to eat. Do they have anything worth consuming other than the beer?"

"Rum. Oh, and they do have some good cigars for sale. You can't buy good ones everywhere. Lots of counterfeits sold."

Maybe I should get Wallace a box. Though it would be hard to deny that we've been to Cuba if we get caught with them.

The ride to the plaza is uneventful, as is the food we end up consuming. I have to say, as friendly as the people are, the food sucks.

I buy two boxes of El Mapa Mundis and we each fire up one, including Christina. Not bad if you like blowing smoke rings, I think, deciding I'll stick to Mary Jane from here on out.

It's going on ten, so we wrap things up. Christina assures me our uniforms and weapons are acceptable and we'll be mingling with the Valdero crowd that comes there. The more I think about it, the more I like our odds of catching Gerard and gang at the Tropicana Matanzas.

The Tropicana is eight kilometers east of Matanzas and a crowd is gathering to await the 10:00 opening. It's next door to Hotel Canimao and some of tonight's patrons are filing from its doors. More cars are arriving than we've seen in total up to this point. Rentals from Valdero, Christina informs me. She also points out two unarmed police near the entrance but assures me some of their police carry weapons. We find a spot to park the Gaz and unload. No need to guard the Gaz, Christina also assures me, because "nobody's stupid enough to steal a government Jeep." If there's a message there, I'm not sure what it is. Ignorance is bliss. I look at the scowl on Andy's face and decide not always. He's still pissed about the dinner, but in all honesty, he's far from being ignorant. Perhaps underachiever is a kinder word. I said it before and I'll say it again: "He may not win many races, but he's still my dog."

There's an air of excitement as we join the crowd. A large cover charge by Cuban standards buys our entrance. Right off, I like the place's open-air ambiance and festive aura.

A gaudy, but scantily dressed waitress rushes to Christina's side and they embrace. The waitress openly eyes us before making a judgment. I help with the process by blessing her with a wink.

She in turn wags a finger before beaming again and resuming her hundred-mile-an-hour, one-sided conversation. I like her immediately and am tempted to pluck one of the feathers that adorn her. Christina's friend rushes off.

"She's going to get us some drinks with Havana Club, which is really Bacardi rum. The Bacardi Family made Cuban rum famous."

Interesting. One's never too young to learn.

The stage comes alive in lights and sounds. A string of dancers garnished in multi-colored feathers and not much else brings the crowd to their feet. Now, one unaccompanied could have some serious fun here.

Christina's friend returns with our drinks and they have some kick to them. The stage keeps drawing my attention, but I'm aware of the fact Christina is showing her friend the pictures and composite. She nods her head before darting off. Christina protectively entwines our arms and is content to take delicate sips of her drink. I'm shocked to notice mine nearly gone. Too much.

"Spread out and keep your eyes peeled. Andy, pass out the walkie-talkies. This time we're going to get the fucker and save the girl," I say.

I clip my radio to my side, insert my earbud and turn it on. Christina and I position ourselves so we can keep an eye on the entrance. Christina tells me the only other entrance is in the back and is mostly used by employees, V.I.P.s and those the staff routinely let in without paying. I fleetingly wonder why I don't fall under the V.I.P. category? Too rich? Too handsome? Yep, I'm still easily amused.

"Are you even paying attention, Steven Paul?"

"Yes, lovely dancers."

"Not that! The door! Sophia just walked in the door!"

I struggle to spot her. "You're shitting?"

"No, I'm not. Look 25 meters to your right."

I spot her—the girl looks radiant, sophisticated beyond her years. I shake my head. Fucking Gerard is the worst kind of sleazeball—he's replaced his dead woman with his daughter. The question remains, where's Monique?

I put the radio to my lips and key the mike. "Boys and girls, we have a visual. Sophia's entered the Tropicana. Regroup."

Christina's excited friend hustles to her side. ¡Mira! ¡Mira!" she points. "¡A la derecha!"

"Sí, gracias," I say.

She frowns and hugs Christina again before pointing to my necklace of beads. She smiles and, after another quick hug, rushes off. Maybe she was trying to tell me to travel safely? Or perhaps to protect Christina? Both of which are on my to-do list.

I send the boys out to post up a block east, a block west and one to cover the rear exit. I let them decide among them but remind them to be careful because Gerard will no doubt be near.

Christina and I shadow Sophia as she slithers through the crowd in search of prey. The way she's being hungrily eyed, she'll end up having her choice. I toy with the idea of flashing some serious cash before her eyes. I sadly recall how it worked out for me last time and I'm not dressed for the occasion—my big guns being a sure turn-off this time.

I sigh at the thought of such a waste. Christina stomps my foot reminding me not to physically sigh. I believe she's afraid it might blow our cover.

We watch as Sophia selects her prey. A softie with not a real-world chance of picking up such a girl. He's quick to buy her a drink. Watching the scene makes me realize it's a cruel, cruel world. Why couldn't everyone be beautiful and handsome like Christina and me? That and world peace. I almost sigh again, but I'm a quick study.

The slight breeze is tugging at the guy's combover. A tic in his left eye betrays his nervousness. I amuse myself with another thought—why can't they all be suave like me?

Sophia closes the gap and is hanging onto the poor sap's every word. The art of seduction. I give her a nine on a scale of ten. Me being a ten. Ain't I having fun?

Christina stomps my foot again. "Hey, I didn't say anything, I didn't even sigh."

She smiles. "That one was for general purposes."

"Covering your bases, are you?"

"Yep. To blend in, you better order us another drink."

"Sure. Hold my machinegun, would you?" We both get a chuckle out of that, but I do manage to get a waitress's attention and order us a couple of the Hatuey that I'm starting to like.

One by one my crew radios that they're in position. I acknowledge them by keying my mike a couple of times. We sip and watch. The poor sap doesn't stand a chance.

Sophia hooks the guy's arm and, after whispering something, starts to nudge him toward the exit. We give them some lead as I radio the crew to report Sophia and victim are on the move— heading toward the front entrance. I determine Andy is covering the rear. I instruct him to stay in place, so he'll be in a position to parallel them a block over no matter which direction they head.

"Got her," Jim radios. "She's heading east away from the hotel."

"Roger that, Jim," Felix radios. "Andy, head east."

"East?"

"The same direction we were going to get here," Felix radios.

"Ten-four."

We step out into the night. People are still arriving from both directions. I sling my AK to my back, obscuring it from view, but unsnap my pistol's cover. We lean into each other and drunkenly follow at a discrete distance.

We watch as Sophia tugs the guy in the direction of an unlit alley they've come upon. The guy's hesitance is overcome by Sophia's insistent tugs. They disappear from sight.

I key my mike. "Andy! They're heading your way! The alley, it's their trap!"

Gunfire erupts.

Of course.

"Stay! Christina," I yell as I pull my pistol, cock the hammer and run toward the alley. Halfway there, the sap stumbles from the alley and crumples to the street. To my surprise, Sophia, with a pistol in hand, steps out as well. She yanks at the guy's wallet undeterred by the continued gunfire somewhere behind her in the alley.

I draw a bead on her. "Freeze, Sophia!"

She spins and rises—she manages to squeeze off several shots.

My own pistol booms and kicks, spinning Sophia. Incredibly, she dives back into the alley. Felix appears around the corner from the east. The patter of running feet registers: I turn at the sound of

Jim's approach. There's pandemonium at the entrance of the Tropicana—the two police are dragging a wounded one to safety. One of Sophia's bullets claimed another victim.

I wave both Felix and Jim to a stop, duck down and with extended pistol peer around the corner and down the alley where I find Gerard exchanging gunfire with Andy from his concealment in a recessed doorway. Haloed and backlit by the emanating light from the other end of the alley is a staggering Sophia inanely trying to reach her father.

I watch as the pistol falls from her hand.

"Gerard!" I yell, mindful not to hit Andy with a stray bullet or ricochet. The tip of Gerard's AK whips around in my direction and in a burst of flames and echoing booms, Gerard's AK answers my call. Sophia's shape dissolves and becomes one with that of the trash-strewn alley.

The lull in the gunfire is deafening. Gerard steps from his relative safety. "No!" he screams and runs toward me.

I drop him with one bullet to the head.

I've actually killed someone. It's not a pleasant feeling. I scramble to Sophia's side to see if she's alive. She's riddled with bullets, but her eyes are open and she's conscious.

"Daddy?" she chokes.

I hold her down. "No, Sophia. Where's your friend Monique?"

Sophia's eyes close. I shake her. "Your friend Monique, where is she?" Her head falls to the side in reply. "Shit."

"Over here, Steve!" Andy yells.

We all rush to where Andy stands in front of the recessed doorway. There, cowering in the corner is a frightened Monique.

I move slowly to her—crouching as I do. I remember doing the same with Candy's frightened dog, Bonnie. Monique withdraws even more. In the background sirens wail. "Shit," I say again. "Monique, we're here to take you home, back to Austin and your parents. I promised your mother, Marie Anne, that I'd bring you home.

With the sound of her mother's name, something unsnaps and she raises her hand to me. I take it, pull her up and draw her near. "It's over now," I coo as I stroke her hair.

"Steve-O, we've got to get the fuck out of here."

Felix tugs at my shirt. "Esteban, we have to get the fuck out of here, like right fucking now!"

I release my hold on her but firmly clutch her hand.

"Christina, grab her other hand. We've got to go the back way to get to our Jeep. Let's move!"

We scramble down the alley back the way Andy came—Christina and I mostly forcing Monique to keep pace. We round the corner—the sirens near. Around the next block is our Gaz. The others beat us to it and Jim has it fired and in gear. Felix pulls Monique into the Jeep and I push Christina to hurry her along. I clear the tailgate as Jim drops the clutch.

We round the next turn and Jim points us west. Our overladen pile of junk struggles to gain speed. Two Gazzes and a siren-equipped Lada streak by. To my dismay, brake lights flare on one of the Gazzes and the Lada. Shit, they're turning around.

"We're going to have company, Jimbo," I yell over the wind and the whine of the small engine.

"This is all the fucking thing will do," Jim hollers back.

There's no question they're going to catch us—we're miles from the pier and our boat. We blast past facades.

"Christina! You and Monique up front right now! Andy! Felix! Back here with me! Christina, keep your heads down!"

They exchange places as the Lada and Gaz close the gap.

"Andy, give Christina the radio. Christina, raise Oscar, tell him to have the engines fired and ready." She nods her understanding.

Other headlights appear in the distance before us. Not good.

I pull the bolt back on my AK and chamber a round. Felix and Andy follow suit. Christina strips Jim of his AK and chambers a round herself. She's made a decision—she's chosen a chance at freedom.

Jim slams on the brakes and makes a quick right, nearly slinging me from the back. He follows it with a left and another right, avoiding the vehicles we encounter. The new ones join the pursuers.

"Try and avoid shooting anyone," I yell.

The faster Lada in the lead rams us, jarring our ride.

"I don't believe they plan to shoot at us," Andy yells.

The passenger in the Lada offers a second opinion—he sticks a revolver out his window, but we round a curve and he can't get a shot off. I decide on a preemptive strike—as we enter the next straight, I squeeze off enough rounds to take out both front tires. The Lada spins out of control. The Gaz behind it clips it as it barrels past, causing the Lada to flip and crash into a storefront. I take out the Gaz's tires as well and cringe as I watch it spin and eject its passengers. We're in some serious fucking trouble. Andy and Felix get off some rounds as well. The chasers are not quite so eager to close the gap now.

"It's trying to run hot," Jim yells.

Of course. Not much I can do about that. I make the sign of the cross and rub my beads for good measure. Not that I believe, mind you—it's for Christina's sake, seeing how she's eyeing me with concern. I wink and she wanly smiles before returning her attention to the front.

Monique is again lost in her own world—staring but not seeing what lies before her. She may be traumatized for a long time. I'm not a believer in lifelong traumatism, but what Monique's recently experienced may call for a lengthy condition.

The valves are starting to clatter, but we're still holding our pursuers at bay.

"I've made contact," Christina yells over her shoulder as we come out on the stretch that harbors our boat. Deep down our Gaz begins to knock and we lose speed. We're not going to make it!

"Give me the radio, Christina." I take it and key the mike. "Oscar, we're coming up short. We'll have to make a stand—we're under fire. We're maybe a half-mile shy."

"I hear you. I'll find you, Esteban," Oscar radios back.

"Prepare to abandon ship, boys and girls. Christina, you and Jim are in charge of Monique's safety. Make for the water. We'll hold them off."

With a last clank, the motor gives. We drift to the side of the road. I jump to the ground and lead the way. Andy and Felix join me as Jim cuts the Gaz's wheels and ekes the last of the Gaz's momentum toward the water and a short, darkened pier.

Collectively, we squeeze off enough rounds to bring our pursuers to a halt. No one's that eager to save the day. Bullets zing over our flattened bodies. A siren eerily shrills from the north, effectively catching us in the middle. I sigh in earnest as the roar of our boat's engines become discernible among the now chorus of sirens. I flip my clip over and work the bolt once more. I'm down to 30 rounds and almost two full clips for my pistol. I fire on the approaching Ladas from the north. They take evasive action and peel from the road. I watch them as they unload and scatter in different directions. I scan over my shoulder to the north. They're doing the same, advancing in bits and spurts. Andy and Jim are hindering any significant advance.

On the pier, I can barely make out the three figures as they disappear from view.

The ship-to-shore squawks. "Got them! Hurry!"

"Ready boys? On the count of three. One... Two... Three!"

We rise and sprint the short distance to the pier, each of us squeezing off shots as we go. We make the pier and our feet thunder across the old wooden planks. Bullets whiz and whine by. The end of the pier is rapidly approaching. I take a leap of faith and take to the air—the warm seawater engulfs me. Maintaining the grip on my rifle, I kick to the surface. Felix and Andy's heads pop to the surface. We're within feet of our boat. Eager hands scramble to help us aboard. I roll to my back to catch my breath as our engines roar to life. In a sweeping arc, our bow is pointed toward the sea. The thump of the surf against the hull—music to the ears.

In hysterics, Christina piles on top of me. She smothers my face with kisses. I join her in the laughter, as does everyone but Monique. I can't believe we survived the ordeal.

"Whoa! That was a rush," I manage.

"Fucking A, Esteban," Felix hollers. Bruemmer

I spot Monique clutching herself. The sight brings an abrupt halt to my celebration. "Christina, would you go and try and comfort her."

"Sure."

I manage to stand and realize I'm still clutching my AK. I lay it flat to the deck and join Oscar at the helm. Jim hands me a needed beer. We bump bottles before taking needed gulps.

"Unfuckingbelievable, Steve-O"

I push my wet hair from my forehead. "Ain't that the truth? Don't hit any islands, Oscar," I joke.

Our tach reads 4000rpm and we're screaming along at 85mph. I bump the trim. The needle jumps to 87. That's all there is folks.

A tap on the shoulder gets my attention. "Um, Esteban, what do you think those lights are?"

"Shit. Choppers." Of course.

"That's my guess, Esteban."

I flip the switch, killing our running lights. Andy douses the cabin lights. With the cabin light extinguished, we roar along in near darkness. Out of the bay, Oscar puts us on a northwestern course. More lights in the sky appear out of the west. Havana must be responding. We're far from being out of the woods.

"Oscar, find our island and cove and hurry."

To my dismay, they're not just choppers—they're choppers with powerful searchlights.

"They'll still spot us, Steve-O."

"We're going to run her into some mangroves and hope for the best. Andy, reload our clips. If they back us into a corner, we're going to come out swinging."

Hey, it's a plan.

Chapter Thirty-Four

An outline of an island appears on our starboard and Oscar steers us toward it. "I doubt it's the same island, Esteban, but it may be our one and only option."

I nod my assent. The choppers in the distance have begun a systematic crisscross search pattern—slow, but thorough.

"Wish we wouldn't have left our tarp behind," I think out loud.

"We didn't," Oscar says. "The fisherman brought it down to me. He was curious about our boat. It's folded and in the seat compartment."

Well, that's a break. The tarp is a bluish-green, not unlike the color of the shallows. It will conceal a good portion of our boat.

We slow for the island. We're in luck—at least this side is dense in the mangrove. We duck as Oscar plows into it. Branches snap and crack but go a long way toward our effort of concealment. The numerous branches make a chore out of utilizing the tarp, but there are enough hands pulling and tugging to get the job done.

Other than the lap of the surf against our boat, the throbbing of the ever-nearing choppers drowns everything else out.

I grab a couple of beers from the cooler and duck into the cabin to join Christina and Monique. I hand Christina a beer and sit on the other side of Monique. "You okay, Monique? Would you like a beer?" I wait her out—she remains silent. "A shot of Rum?"

She looks at me with her big dark eyes.

"We're not going to make it, are we?" she says framed by the light of a flashlight.

I drape my arm across her shoulders. "Of course, we're going to make it. Rescuing people is what my friends and I do—we always make it." I give her a small shake and squeeze.

The sound of the choppers is piercing. The boat beyond the cabin is momentarily illuminated. The others are hunkered down, rifles in their laps. The chopper passes overhead throwing them back into the dark.

The chop of the rotors lessens as they continue their search beyond our temporary haven. The relief is tangible.

"See, Monique, they're gone," I say with assurance.

"Who are you?"

"Beyond the expletives, some call me Steven Paul."

"Steven Paul," she echoes. "And my parents sent you?"

"Them and Detective Williams, who by the way said, 'if you don't bring her back safe and sound, I'll arrest you the next time I see you.'"

"My parent's friend wouldn't say that."

"You're right, he also said, 'unmolested by you,' while poking me in the chest with a finger."

She attempts a weak smile as she reaches for my beer. Maybe I've broken through a little. Now to get her thousands of miles home.

Monique takes a sip of the beer and places it back in my hands, "How come your beer smells like fish?"

"We went fishing."

"On the way to rescuing me?" she asks sounding incredulous.

I point to Christina. "It was her idea."

Christina reaches across Monique to take a swipe at me. "No, it wasn't. It was Felix or somebodys."

I smile. "Hear her tell it, she only went along for the ride."

A genuine smile transforms Monique's face—she's stunning in the dim light. "You two some kind of couple?"

"Sadly, no," Christina says. "Like the cliché, 'we're only two ships passing in the night.' In a way, Steven Paul's rescuing me as well. Taking me to the U.S. so I can be reunited with my parents."

"Reunited? How long has it been?"

"So long I can't remember their faces without the help of old photos. They've been living in exile since I was a little girl."

"I'll never take my parents for granted again," Monique says with conviction.

I take a swallow of my beer and pass it back. "That's a good plan because I have a strict policy of one rescue per household."

Someone turns on and tunes in a rock station. AC/DC's "Highway to Hell" pipes through the speakers to console us. I close my eyes and lean back against the bulkhead. Man, I'm tired. This damsel in distress business is quite taxing. "You get shot at quite a lot too, Son." Thanks, Dad, I'll dwell on that for a while.

Exhaustion overtakes me and my chin drops to my chest for a restless sleep. Numerous times the sound of choppers brings me to the surface only for me to drift back off.

The rock of the boat wakes me. I'm instantly alert. It was a large wake that rocked our boat. Large wakes are made by large boats. Monique's head rests on my shoulder, the flashlight in her lap down to a trickle of light. The girls slept right through it.

Jim steps through the cabin door at a crouch. "Steve-O, you awake?"

"Yeah. I felt it."

"They're still looking. The wake was caused by a good-sized gunboat about 200 yards out. If we're still here when the sun rises, they won't miss us next time."

"I feel you, Jimbo. How much time do we have?"

"An hour at the most."

I ease from under Monique and tilt her against Christina. Neither stirs. I join my crew under the tarp where only the dash lights illuminate us.

"Well, boys and girls, no time like the present. Which way was the boat headed, Jimbo?"

"North."

"Of course." I ponder the situation. "Well, as much as I hate it, we'll have to backtrack a mile or so, keep the island between us. Then cut across ten or 15 miles and head due north. We make a run for Key West then, boys."

"I think you're right, Steve-O. They won't be able to pick us up on their sonar until we're out of range."

"It's been hours since I've heard a chopper," Felix says. "I think we might make it."

I nervously laugh. "I'll construe that as a vote of confidence. Let's do it."

The tarp's easier taking down than putting up. I crank up Lynyrd Skynyrd's "Tuesday's Gone With The Wind" and chime in where I can. "Train roll on...."

I forego the blower and hit the starters. The powerful engines rumble to life. I put the drives in reverse and power out of mangroves. Despite ducking, it's hard to avoid all the branches. One scrapes me along the neck and draws blood. I look to the sky as we pull free. "Can we have one bloodless stage in this operation?" Of course, I'm being facetious. The Big Man upstairs wouldn't have invented first aid kits if he wanted it any other way.

The gunboat's no longer in sight, but the path it churned is still visible. "That must have been one hell of a gunboat, Jimbo," I say as I drop the drives into forward halting our rearward motion.

"Well, I didn't want to scare the girls by calling it a ship if they were awake."

"What's this about a ship, Jimbo?" Christina asks from the opening to the cabin.

I wink in case Monique can hear. "Nothing to worry about, honey," I say as I hit the throttles and our boat shoots to a plane. I round a quarter of the island and peg the gyrocompass on due south. We run all out as the sun in the east threatens to rise. I look to the sky again and wonder where the cloud cover is when you need it?

A minute out, I change course to due west and plan to run 15 minutes before pointing us toward home. I'm giving the big ship plenty of berth. It makes sense, doesn't it?

The cool wind feels good on my face. It would be easy to forget we're still in peril. Not really. I dismiss the errant thought as, well, errant. I lay into the change of course. I like the feel and power of our boat as it cuts into the chop. A crosswind buries my cap at sea. I strip the buttons of my shirt, peel it from my sore body, wad it and toss it into the wind. The boots are next to go, followed by the pants. I toe the socks off, leaving me and my boxers. It feels liberating—do or die. The charade, for me at least, is over.

My crew follows suit and to the sea, their stuff goes—their change of clothes as well. Jim tosses my extras for me.

Everyone becomes more jubilant as the miles and minutes tick by. I stand to catch more of the wind. Christina, having caught some of our mania, is down to her bikini. She takes my hand and beams.

"Six o'clock, Esteban! Gunships!" Felix yells.

I do a double-take over my shoulder. "Oh fucking no. SHIT! Battle Stations! Christina, to the cabin."

She defies me and grabs my AK off the deck where Andy left it after reloading the clips. She stares at the approaching choppers.

I get on our boat's radio. "Mayday, repeat mayday. This is a mayday."

"Go ahead. I'm Captain Oliver of the U.S. Coastguard. What's the nature of your emergency?"

"We're 40 miles due west of Key West and are coming under fire from Cuban gunships."

"Your boat, please, and nature of your craft?"

"The Stacey Keys. We're a recreational fishing vessel."

"Roger that. We'll do what we can."

"The Stacey Keys? And we're under fire, Steve-O?"

I shrug. "I thought it sounded plausible. And besides, we'll likely be under fire any minute now."

"They're gaining on us. Can't be much more than ten or 15 miles an hour faster than us," Oscar yells.

"I don't think they'll fire on us in international waters," Andy announces.

One of the gunships demurs. Twin trails interspersed with tracers of heavy machine fire pelt the water, narrowly missing us.

Andy takes potshots at one of the choppers with his AK. We can't outrun them and we might not escape the next set of rounds. All I can do is make a tougher target and perhaps take some of the fight to them. I lean into a turn, pull my pistol and cock the hammer. I unload half a clip as we pass under them.

I cut her back the other way. Several rounds pock our bow before we cross back under them. We're all shooting now. I unload the second half of my 9's clip.

One of the choppers goes into an awkward spin before falling into the sea. Two U.S. fighters streak by overhead. The second gunship turns to hightail it back to Cuba.

We scream with relief and jubilation. Our radio squawks. I cut it off.

"Andy, remove the hammer and sickles." I pop open the dash and pass the Florida registration sticker to Jim. "If you would, Jimbo, my man, reregister our boat please."

Christina hugs me tight and plants a hard kiss on me. "I told you the beads would protect you."

"That they did. Oscar, take over. Let's check on Monique."

We duck to enter the cabin. "Monique, both your hands please," I say. We tug her to her feet and pull her out to meet the early morning sun. "We're 20 minutes from Key West. We're home free now." At least I think we are. We downed a Cuban gunship, but only in support of our embargo. I smile at the absurdity of my thought. "Well, ladies and gentlemen, we have mere minutes to drink all the remaining evidence and police the brass."

Felix passes out the Cuban beer while Carlos produces the bottle of rum entrusted to him. We all gather around in a tight circle and raise our bottle. Even Monique partakes. We clink our bottles together in celebration. Andy downs his beer in one long draw and tosses it to the sea. I take a pull from the rum and chase it with my beer. I pass the rum to Oscar to finish off.

"Let me have the bottle back when you're done, Oscar. Christina, fetch the remaining pesos."

She does and I stuff the remaining bills into the empty bottle, cork it and toss it into our wake. I watch as it surfaces and bobs in the chop. No telling where it will turn up. The two fighters streak by overhead back en route to their naval base. Boats appear in the distance. We're clearly in U.S. waters again.

"Andy, put all our weapons in one duffle bag except my old .45. I'm going to drop everyone on the beach. Make for the Bonneville. We don't know what kind of reception to expect. I'm going to dock in the slip next to Paul's and make for the Top to fetch Sandra. If I'm not at the car in 20 minutes, leave without me."

"Our luggage is in your suite," Andy says.

"Fuck our luggage, Andy," Jim says. "We can buy more."

I quickly don my beach attire as everyone dresses in the clothes they wore when we boarded the boat. I place my .45 in the dash and pat my rear pocket to reassure myself that my cash and the boat's folded title are within.

"Here, captain," Christina says, "this is the last beer. I thought it appropriate that you drink it. I want one last kiss too since you're going to 'fetch Sandra.' I assume she's one of your many girlfriends?"

I ignore her question and give her a strong hug and a deep kiss.

"Thanks," she says. "Besides me, there's no other evidence of Cuba on board. The cigars we lost along with the composite and pictures."

"If I don't make it back, have Jim write down my address and phone number." I smile. "You never know—it's a small world." I pull out my fold of cash and peel off ten, crisp $100 bills and try to hand them to her. "Here, take it. It's some start-fresh cash."

"I can't take it, Steven Paul. My parents will help me."

"This is payment for being part of the team. I mean, you did down a chopper," I say and smile.

"I seriously doubt that."

"Well, I suppose I can pay Andy with it instead."

She snatches it from my hand. "I seriously doubt that."

We get a good laugh out of that.

"Tell everyone to prepare to abandon ship."

On tiptoes, she gives me another quick kiss. "Prepare to abandon ship!" she yells. She snatches up her satchel with all her worldly goods and prepares to disembark.

I cut the throttles as we near the beach. "Everyone be casual. Look back and wave—shit like that. Felix, don't forget your tuna."

"Um, I'm going to leave it with you, Esteban."

One by one, I watch them jump to the shallow water and make their way the few short steps to the beach. I throw her in reverse, kicking up a cloud of sand and idle her back into the surf. They all turn back to wave. I detect a sadness in Christina, but she's too far away to be sure. I salute the bunch and I drop the drives in gear and hammer the throttles. I roar down the coastline, before reversing course for the old harbor.

"I hope we get to keep you, girl," I tell the boat. She's some fine boat.

I throttle her back for the no-wake zone. Nothing appears out of synch, but I'm picking up a vibe, nevertheless. I idle her down alongside the pier containing Paul's slip and turn into his neighbor's. Clapping draws my attention to a smiling Paul, who's once again drinking beer in the lee of his flybridge despite the early hour and relative coolness.

"Steven Paul, I see you made it back in one piece. I hope you didn't lose any of your friends?"

"Nope, Paul, sure didn't. I dropped them at the beach."

"Lots of radio traffic this morning...."

The sound of my bilge pump kicking in halts Paul in mid-sentence. We both look to the aft of my boat where a steady stream of water pumps from my boat. It clicks off and the stream dies.

"Taking on water somewhere, Steven Paul."

He gets up and we both look over at the bow of my boat to find two ragged holes at the waterline.

"Uh-oh," I say.

"You can explain now or later, but if you want to explain it later, you might want to get going. There will be a mess of them sniffing around here any time now."

"Anything stand out?"

"It seems the U.S. Coastguard plucked two Cuban chopper pilots out of the water. They were responding to a distress call."

"The pilots' or mine?"

He laughs. "I knew you were involved from the get-go, but I'd say they were responding to both of yours." He laughs and shakes his head as he points to a missed shell lodged against the engine shroud.

I pluck it from the deck and toss it into the water.

"There's a big fresh tuna in the cooler, help yourself."

"You went fishing too? Didn't even have a pole when you guys left."

"Something like that." I peel off five, crisp hundred-dollar bills and pass them over to him. "Tell them you were paid to watch my boat and you expect me back any day."

I jump to the pier and we shake. "Plug the holes while you're at it too," I joke.

"I will. And I'll give them the bum steer too."

"That's why you make the big bucks. Later."

I hurry my way to the Top. Not many people out at this time of the morning, albeit some obvious tourists. No one seems to pay me much mind. I find a familiar face at the reception desk. I plan to surprise Sandra.

"The keys to my suite, please."

"That's not possible, sir."

"Not possible?" I frown.

"You checked out."

"Oh." Hell, that sure takes the wind out of my sails. The thought of "gone with your money," hits me like a ton of bricks. I feel a bead of sweat form on my temple and threaten to make an appearance. "I see," I croak.

"But she left you something, sir. Actually, two things. One second, please."

The second seems like two days. Not fucking again. I must have "fuck me" stamped on my forehead.

"Here we go, sir. Your bank bag from our safe and this thick letter the young lady wished for us to give you."

I accept both with shaking hands.

"You okay, sir?"

"Marvelous... Um, thank you." I turn to leave.

"Your luggage, sir. We have the luggage from your suite too."

"Oh. Okay, I'll be back for it in a little bit."

"Right you are, sir."

Right you are, sir. I don't even know what that's supposed to mean. I turn my back to the clerk and hold my breath as I unzip the bank bag. I sigh with relief at the sight of the cash, but I feel like an ass for doubting Sandra. Despite the past, the sight of the cash restores my faith in humanity.

Now for the letter. With all the letters I've received lately, I should hire a personal secretary. I'd probably only end up sleeping with her and end up getting a letter from her as well. The thought provokes a wan smile. I eye the envelope. Hmm?

I tear off the end and shake off the contents. A small bundle of cash surrounded by a lone sheet of paper drops into my hand. Without counting, I know it's most of the $4,000 I left her.

"Dear Steven Paul,

> "I hope this letter finds you and your boys safely returned. This is a hard letter for me to write. I found and read Candy's to you and I hope this one doesn't hurt as much as hers did. Despite it, you carried on much like Candy wanted you to. I'd like to believe I made a difference. I know how much I've come to care about you and I can honestly say I've never met anyone like you. The experience will stay with me forever. The feelings are mutual.

> "Hell, enough rambling, I guess I should get to the heart of this letter. What it comes down to is that Candy tracked you down here to the Keys and we had a long heart-to-heart. Simply put, she's ready to come home. She says she misses you and Bonnie so much it hurts. For this reason, I have to step aside. She said I'm welcome to stay but I

could never be content. To see you and know you're Candy's would hurt too much. I hope you understand.

"Anyway, you'll find most of your cash. I paid for the last night of the suite and kept a little for myself. I knew you wouldn't mind. You're not the most frugal person (smile). I truly can't thank you enough. You brought me home and I'll be forever grateful.

"Guess what? I took a job at Cowboy Bill's and will be rooming with Tracy and will be working with her and Brenda. You remember Brenda, I suspect. (laugh) Hell, Tracy too. I notice you notice girls like us. Not the easy ones, but the pretty ones. Well, maybe the easy ones too. That almost sounds like something you would say, doesn't it?

"So, that's what's happening with me. Don't worry, I'll be fine. We plan on getting us a phone. I'll call when we get one. Sorry, but I have to go and cry for a while.

"Love you, Sandra."

I don't know how long I stand there. The clerk brings me back.

"Sir, you sure you're all right?"

I smile. "Yep. Hey, can you spare a hotel envelope, a page of stationery and a pen?"

"Yes, sir," he says producing the items.

I jot a simple letter letting Sandra know how much I care for her and will miss her. I stuff the bills into it and seal it. I write for Sandra on the envelope. I hand the pen back as I take my leave.

As I step out there feels to be more of a bustle, an air of excitement.

I cross the street to Cowboy Bill's and pull on the door. Locked. Of course it is, stupid. They probably don't open until around 11:00. I try and peer through the tinted glass of a window and lamely knock. I try and stuff the envelope under the door—no go.

I catch the reflection of a couple MP's and a policeman in the window. They appear to be searching for something. "Or someone, Son." Not now, Dad.

I'll nonchalantly walk away. I tuck the bank bag and envelope under my arm and begin my leisurely stroll to where my Bonneville is parked. Whoo, I don't think they noticed me. What a break, big boy, I tell myself.

"Oh, sir! Sir!"

I cringe.

"Hold up a minute!"

Chapter Thirty-Five

I stop dead in my tracks. Maybe if I don't turn around, they'll disappear. "And, when was the last time that worked for you, Son?" Dad!

There's a tug at my shirt. "Sir." I slowly turn. It's a cop. "You dropped this envelope... Are you all right, sir?"

"Oh, yeah. Thanks."

"Have you noticed anyone unusual this morning?"

"No, sir," I tell the policeman. "I just came from my suite at the Top."

"Nice place. Expensive, but nice. Have a nice day."

I stroll off whistling an upbeat tune. You know the one. Smooth, big boy, real smooth. No cracking your thick veneer. I chuckle as I pick up my pace. Around the corner sits my big ride. I break into a grin and near run. Christina opens the door and lets me in. We're packed in like sardines, as Jim puts my ride in reverse. Or more accurately, packed in like four whites, two Mexicans and one Black. Oh, and one big blue cooler, aptly named, you'll remember, "Big Blue." We're one big happy melting pot.

"Where's Sandra, Steve-O?"

"Funny you should ask, Jimbo, my man. It's a long story. Where should I start?"

"Start like, where is she?"

"Rooming with Tracy."

"Oh. Hey, a couple of MP vehicles passed on their way to the harbor. Probably found our boat by now."

"Yeah, Steve. Like what are we going to do about our $35,000 boat?"

"Drop you off and let you claim it, Andy."

"I don't think so." We all laugh, including Andy.

"I'm working on a plan as we speak. Hey, Jimbo, we better stop and get some ice and beer. It's a long drive."

"Plus, it might be one of the only times Andy has anything meaningful sitting in his lap," Jim adds.

"Pretty good, Jimbo. It's nice to know my influence is not for naught," I say pleased with both of us.

Jim chuckles. "I thought you would appreciate that. I've been working on my Andyisms."

"That's not even a word, Jim," Andy sneers.

"But you don't know that, Andy," Jim retorts.

"Oh," Andy says.

Life sure is good. I'm starting to believe all my plans are bulletproof. Well, maybe that's not the word I'm looking for. How about 'foolproof'? Wait, that can't be it either. "For mama didn't raise no fool," I tell myself. You get the picture.

We stop at the store and load up on goodies. I buy the Mexicans a jar of jalapeños to go with their jerky. I'm just naturally thoughtful like that. I'm sure I'm not telling you anything new. I'm quite sure you've picked up on that by now. I wish you could have friends so thoughtful, huh?

At the store, Christina places a collect call and she's overwhelmed with joy and apprehension. I'm truly happy for her. We're to meet her parents at a Texaco truck stop in Homestead. She feels good sitting in my lap—I hate to give her up. I glance at Monique and even makeup-free she's stunning. She's not talking, but maybe after we drop Christina off, I can draw her out of her shell. I feel almost duty-bound to do so. I would, wouldn't I? Ah, to be young and vulnerable. I hope I never grow out of it. Yes, it's a recurring thought and, no, mediation likely wouldn't help.

The reunion is a mixture of joy and sadness. Joy for the reunion and sadness that our short relationship is likely at an end. The trip back to Austin is a long and draining one, but we decide to drive straight through. Jim and I take turns driving while Monique and the rest of them nod in and out. Oh, and we piss on a lot of bridges along the way.

It takes 26 hours to complete our trip. We merely watch from the car as Monique dashes up the stairs and is reunited with her parents. I simply wave as they hug and kiss before dragging her through the door. This is definitely one of the upsides of my career choice. Of course, legally I'm not old enough to make such a choice, if it was contractual by nature, that is. But I don't make the laws, I only break them.

Since we're on the east side, we drop Felix and Oscar off in their neighborhood. I give them ten grand out of the bank bag to split. Not much considering the number of bullets directed at us, but it's still a nice chunk of change. Besides, this was more of a pro bono kind of job. I have Felix stash our weapons since there's a good chance there's still some Feds in my near future.

I take the wheel, drop off Jim next and go the fatal route Tony C and Vinnie took—to Scenic Drive and the back entrance to the acreage abutting Andy's back yard. I let Andy off at the bottom of the track that leads to his house and pass on through to the park. If the Feds are waiting for me, they won't expect me to approach from back here. To hedge my bet, I park in the concealment of the park and decide to sneak the rest of the way.

I wave at the west Austin Tarrytown mothers watching over their rug rats. They wave back, impressed by my deep Florida tan. Hey, I can't help it if I tan easily. Up and over the backyard cedar fence I go. So far, so good. I sneak across the yard and crack the gate to the front. I spot no cops but parked across the street is the Channel 7 News van and sitting in the passenger seat is my one true love, Stacey Keys.

I wave my hand through the crack—she stares straight ahead. I open the gate and jump up and down—she stares straight ahead. I pick up a rock and take out her window—oops—I get her attention.

Her mouth drops open as she does a double-take. Though no one other than her driver can hear, she mouths "Steven Paul?"

I nod my head in affirmation. I put a finger to my lips in hope I relay discretion.

She nods and pushes her door open. The remaining glass falls to the street. She looks up and down the road. Does some twists, some bends, some stretches. I'm tempted to throw another rock.

I throw my hands to my hips in mock frustration. She grits her teeth and mumbles "Okay, okay. Geez, I'm coming."

She puts her fingers in the pockets and casually and conspicuously ambles over. At the gate, I grab and pull her through, slamming the gate behind her.

"Steven Paul! The Stacey Keys?! You had to name your boat 'The Stacey Keys,' did you?"

"You make it sound like a bad thing put like that."

"Well... Well... Well..."

"Spit it out, woman."

"Well it is," she spits out in frustration.

"Will it help if I say I'm sorry?"

"Of course, they found your boat. It is your boat, isn't it?"

"Mayyyybbbbeee."

"Of course it is. It's been in the news the last 24 hours. There's no way they'll not tie it to you."

"So where are my friends, the Feds?"

"Oh, they're around, waiting for your return."

"You sure fill out them jeans, Mrs. Stacey."

"What?"

"The jeans look right nice on you."

"Ugh. You're going to cause me to pull my hair out," she says pacing back and forth. "You know, everyone at the office now thinks we have something going."

"Don't we?" I innocently ask.

"No. Hell, maybe? Hell, I don't know."

Maybe registers loud and clear. Hope in a hand basket, I'll take it and run with it. "Stacey, I believe you're smitten."

"No."

"Said with not enough conviction, Stacey."

"You're a one-man wrecking ball."

I crowd her toward the fence—our mouths only inches apart. I feel her hot breath on my face. If I'm not mistaken there's a perceptible rise and fall to her breasts.

"Oh, the hell with it," she says as she pulls my face to hers and our lips lock....

Chapter Thirty-Six

What a kiss I'm here to tell you. Of course, you know my policy about kissing and telling but it was a long time ago and if there isn't a statute of limitations when it comes to kissing and telling, there shouldn't be.

I tell you what, that summer of '76 was far from over so come back and visit and get me mentally out of my cell for a while and I'll share some more with you. Sadly, some of you missed out on my recounting of the previous week and a half of our adventure leading up to our mission to save Monique, but do not despair, for I took it upon myself to chronicle the previous days as Hindsight and Vertigo.

I would, wouldn't I?

Check it out. I think you'll find this period of time entertaining and in all fairness, you really do need to see the entire picture before making a sound diagnosis.

Well, ladies and gentlemen, boys and girls, until next time. I'll keep the cell lights on. Oh, and ladies, I'm still graciously accepting scantily clad photos and letters via snail mail here at the big Wynne Unit. My prisoner number is #1638937. I shit you not.

Later, Steven Paul

PS: Go out and adopt a hard-to-adopt animal today.

About the Author

Steven Paul Wilson is the author of six novels in the Steven Paul Series and two in The Eddie Winston Series. He was raised in Austin, Texas and considers it and Lexington, Texas home. He currently writes from his prison cell in the Texas Department of Criminal Justice where he's currently working on his ninth novel. He's an avid reader and animal rights advocate who hopes to someday be freed and to convert the family ranch into an animal sanctuary. He also hopes his colorful life translates into good reading. To learn more about the author, visit him at stevenpaulwilson.com.

Steven Paul Wilson

Donations: Please scan this QR Code to donate to this Indie author. Thank you for your generosity!

www.ingramcontent.com/pod-product-compliance
Lightning Source LLC
Chambersburg PA
CBHW051935020726
47501CB00001B/129